WITCHBLADE®

·VOLUME 8·

written by:
Ron Marz

Witchblade created by:
Marc Silvestri, David Wohl,
Brian Haberlin and Michael Turner

published by
Top Cow Productions, Inc.
Los Angeles

WITCHBLADE

written by: **Ron Marz**
art by: **Stjepan Sejic**
letters by: **Troy Peteri**

For Top Cow Productions, Inc.:
Marc Silvestri - Chief Executive Officer
Matt Hawkins - President and Chief Operating Officer
Filip Sablik - Publisher
Phil Smith - Managing Editor
Bryan Rountree - Assistant to the Publisher
Christine Dinh - Marketing Assistant
Mark Haynes - Webmaster
Ryan Anderson, Anthony McAfee and **Ernesto Gomez** - Interns

for *image* comics
publisher:
Eric Stephenson

888-COMIC-BOOK

to find the comic shop
nearest you call:
1-888-COMICBOOK

Want more info? check out:
www.topcow.com and ***www.thetopcowstore.com***
for news and exclusive Top Cow merchandise!

For this edition
Cover Art by:
Stjepan Sejic

For this edition
Book Design and Layout by:
Phil Smith

New Witchblade logo
Design by:
Todd Klein

Witchblade volume 8 Trade Paperback
July 2010. FIRST PRINTING. ISBN: 978-1-60706-102-1
Published by Image Comics Inc. Office of Publication: 2134 Allston Way, 2nd Floor Berkeley, CA 94704. $14.99 U.S.D.
Originally published in single magazine form as WITCHBLADE 125-130. Witchblade © 2010 Top Cow Productions, Inc.
All rights reserved. "Witchblade," the Witchblade logos, and the likeness of all characters (human or otherwise) featured
herein are registered trademarks of Top Cow Productions, Inc. Image Comics and the Image Comics logo are trademarks
of Image Comics, Inc. The characters, events, and stories in this publication are entirely fictional. Any resemblance to
actual persons (living or dead), events, institutions, or locales, without satiric intent, is coincidental. No portion of this
publication may be reproduced or transmitted, in any form or by any means, without the express written permission of Top
Cow Productions, Inc.
PRINTED IN CHINA.

TABLE OF CONTENTS

Ages ago Bernie Wrightson used to live nearby and had a huge Halloween party each year. I met Ron Marz at one of these get-togethers. He was a college student then, working part time at a local newspaper. One of his assignments had been to interview Bernie and the two of them had become friends.

Ron immediately struck me as someone who had his head screwed on straight, which is an uncommon experience when you're dealing with people in or interested in the comic book field. As a group, we tend to be socially awkward if not totally bat-shit crazy. As time went on, Ron became a racquetball opponent at least a couple times a week and a very close friend.

The only conflict we ever had was when Ron inexplicably decided to give me this hideous painted bust of Elvis Presley as a birthday present. I appreciated the thought so much that a week later I took it down to his office at the newspaper and chained it to his desk in plain sight for all to see.

A couple of weeks later Elvis returned. While I was out, Ron had broken into my house, slipped the King beneath the sheets of my bed and decorated the room with empty liquor and pill bottles. This exchange went on between Ron and I and a few other folks until Elvis just disappeared one day, never to be seen again.

Ron later connected up with me during one of my frequent sojourns to southern Mexico, back in the eighties, and clearly showed he had huevos, by accompanying Jim Sherman, Les Anderson and myself on one of our ill-planned and, quite frankly insane spelunking expeditions. Our supplies on these adventures usually consisted of a few flashlights, some rope and beer. As I recall, he followed us into a hole somewhere around San Cristobal de Casa that took us about three and a half miles in and a mile below the surface. Not many in or out of the comic book business would have jumped at such a not-so-golden opportunity.

I firmly believe that a bit of lunacy is required in any creative endeavor. Mr. Marz has proven both in life and in his considerable body of work that he has a very quiet and controlled streak of madness constantly working its way through his system.

He doesn't try to bury you with an avalanche of text. Ron knows that words are tools, not riches to be displayed for the purpose of bedazzlement. He always picks the right tools and uses them judiciously. He knows far better than most when to let the visual tell the story.

What you now have in hand is a prime example of this skill. Read and enjoy and beware of young writers bearing busts of Elvis.

Jim Starlin
April 2010, New York

Detroit-born writer-artist Jim Starlin broke into comics at Marvel in 1972, and has been working on and off in the industry ever since. Highlights of his long list of credits include: Amazing Spider-man, Batman, 'Breed, Captain Marvel, Cosmic Odyssey, Daredevil/ Black Widow: Abattoir, Doctor Strange, Dreadstar, Gilgamesh II, Hardcore Station, Infinity Gauntlet, Iron Man, Master of Kung Fu, Silver Surfer, Thanos Quest, Warlock and the Infinity Watch, Warlock , Wyrd: The Reluctant Warrior , Thanos, Mystery in Space, Death of the New Gods, and Kid Kosmos: Kidnapped. Starlin is currently writing and drawing the final 'Breed miniseries.

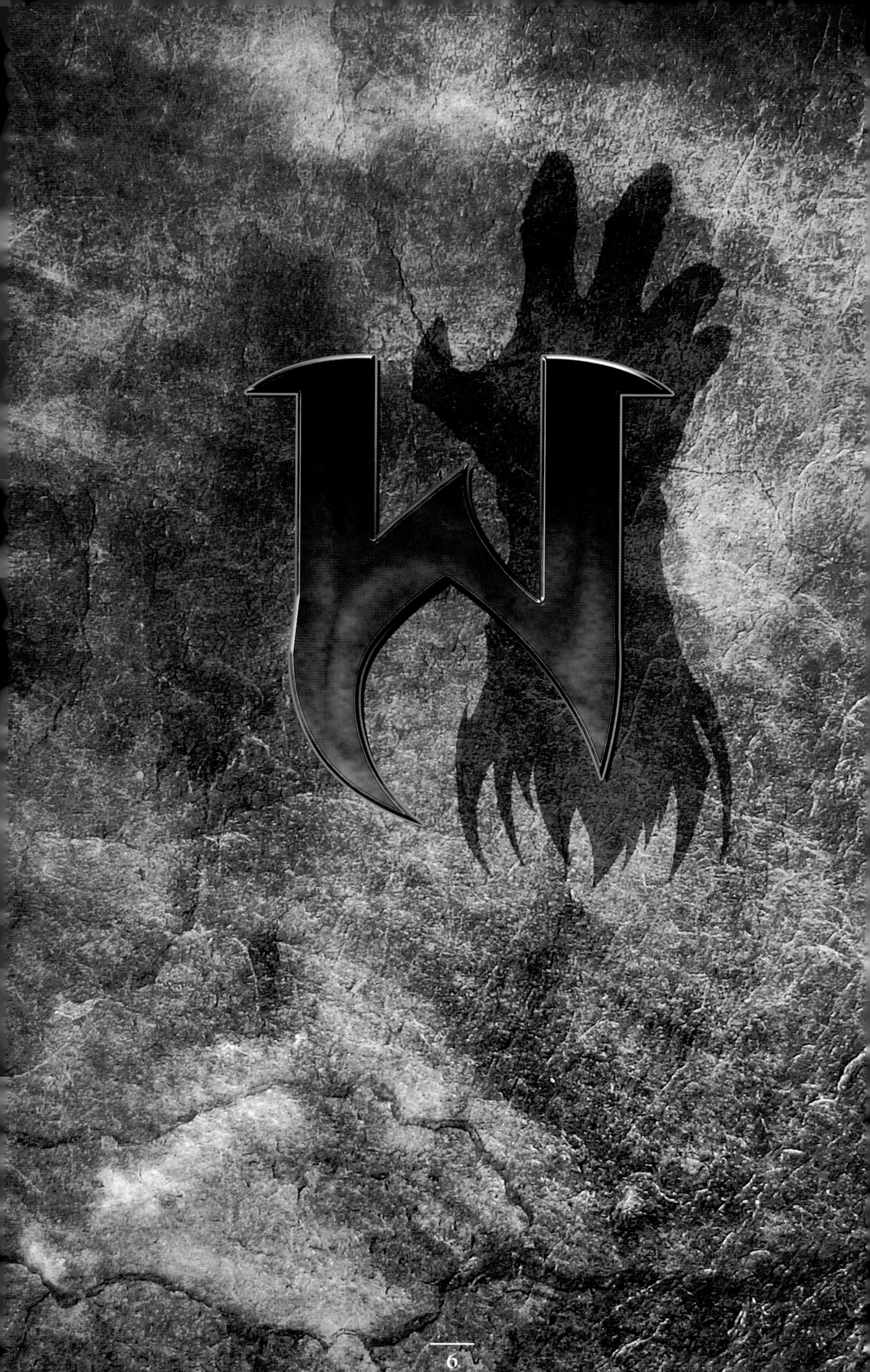

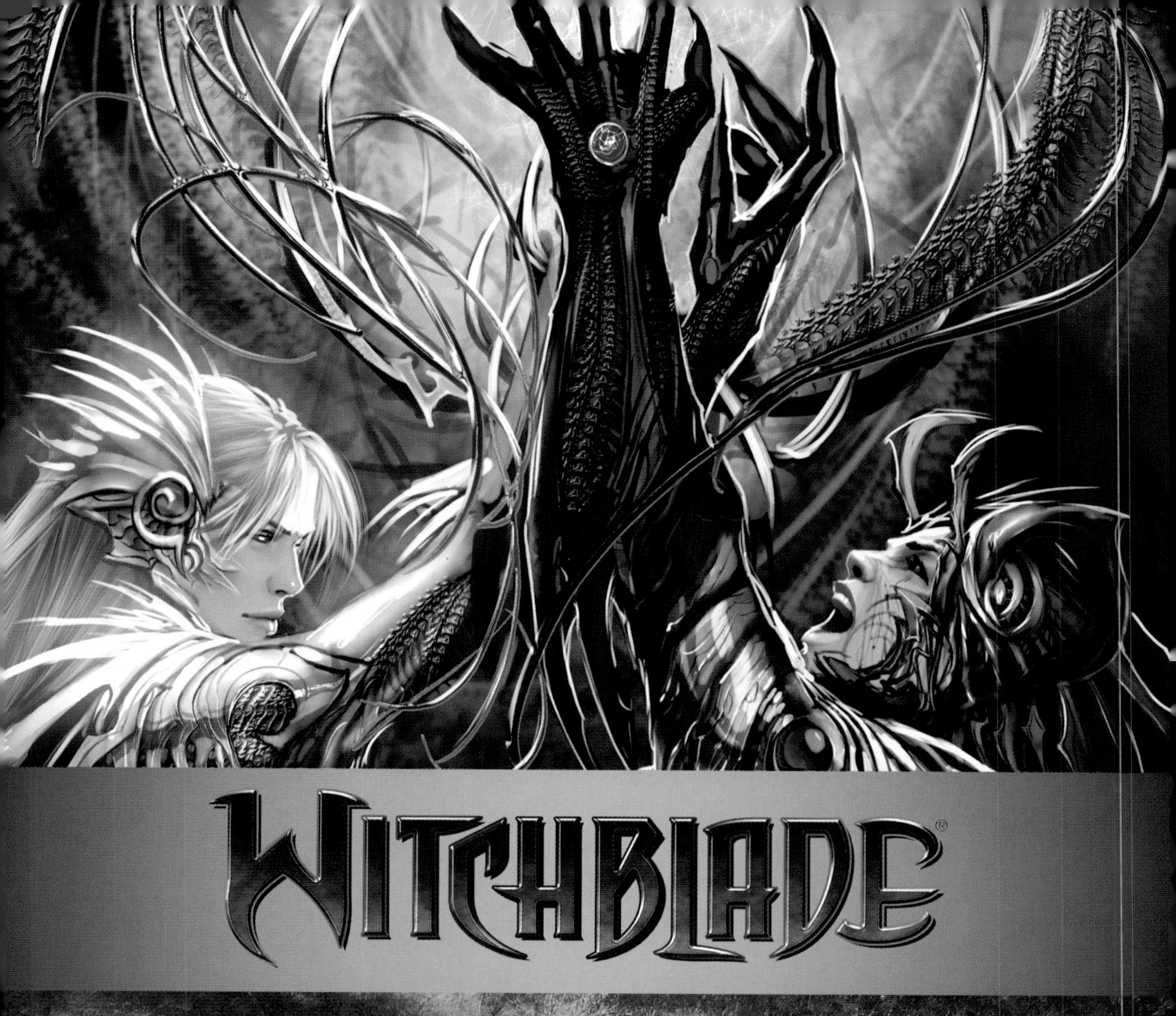

Witchblade®

War of the Witchblades

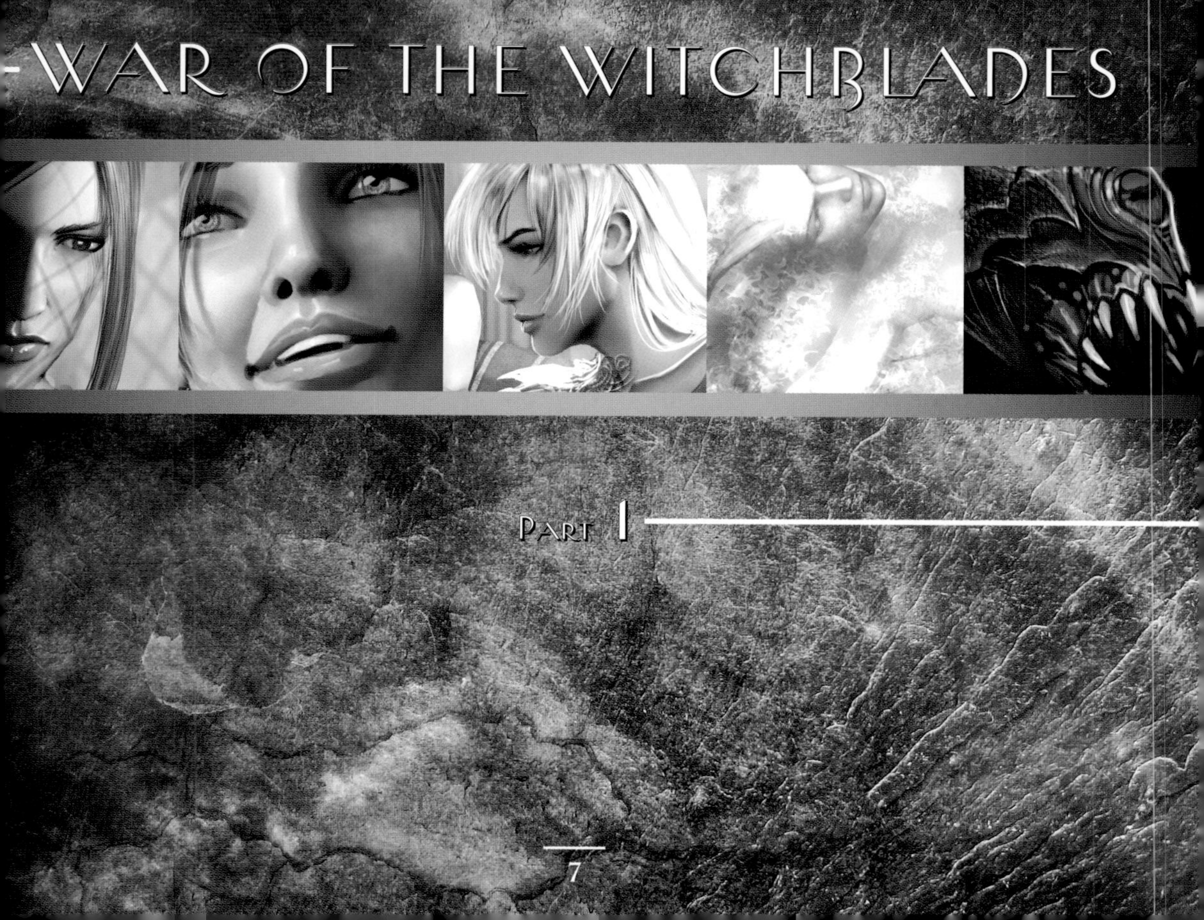

Part 1

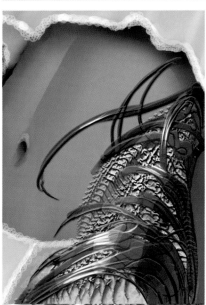

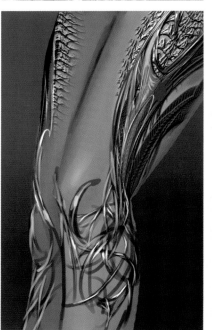
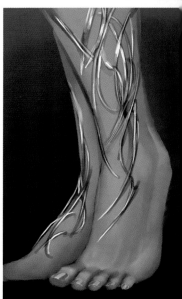

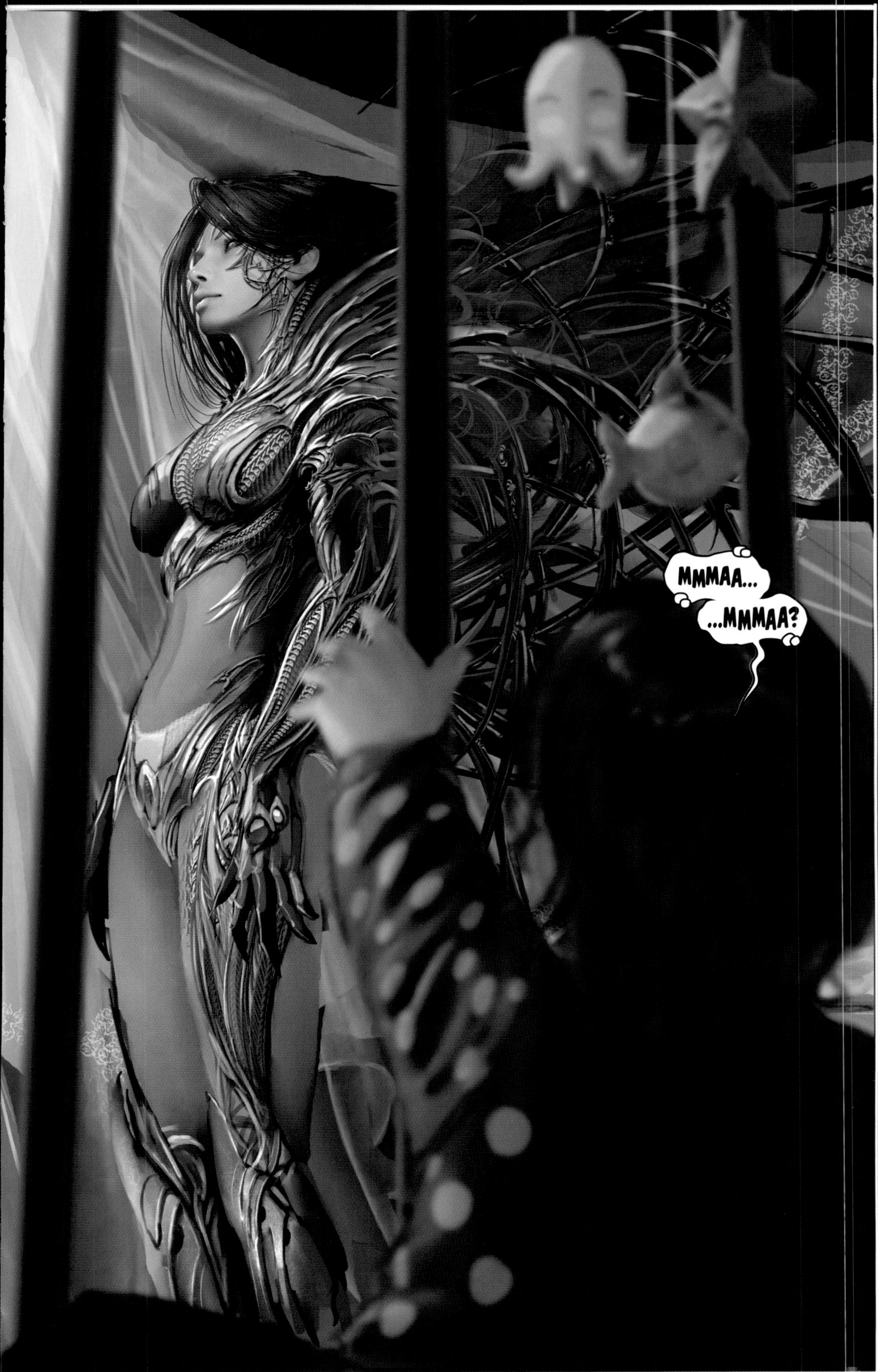
MMMAA...
...MMMAA?

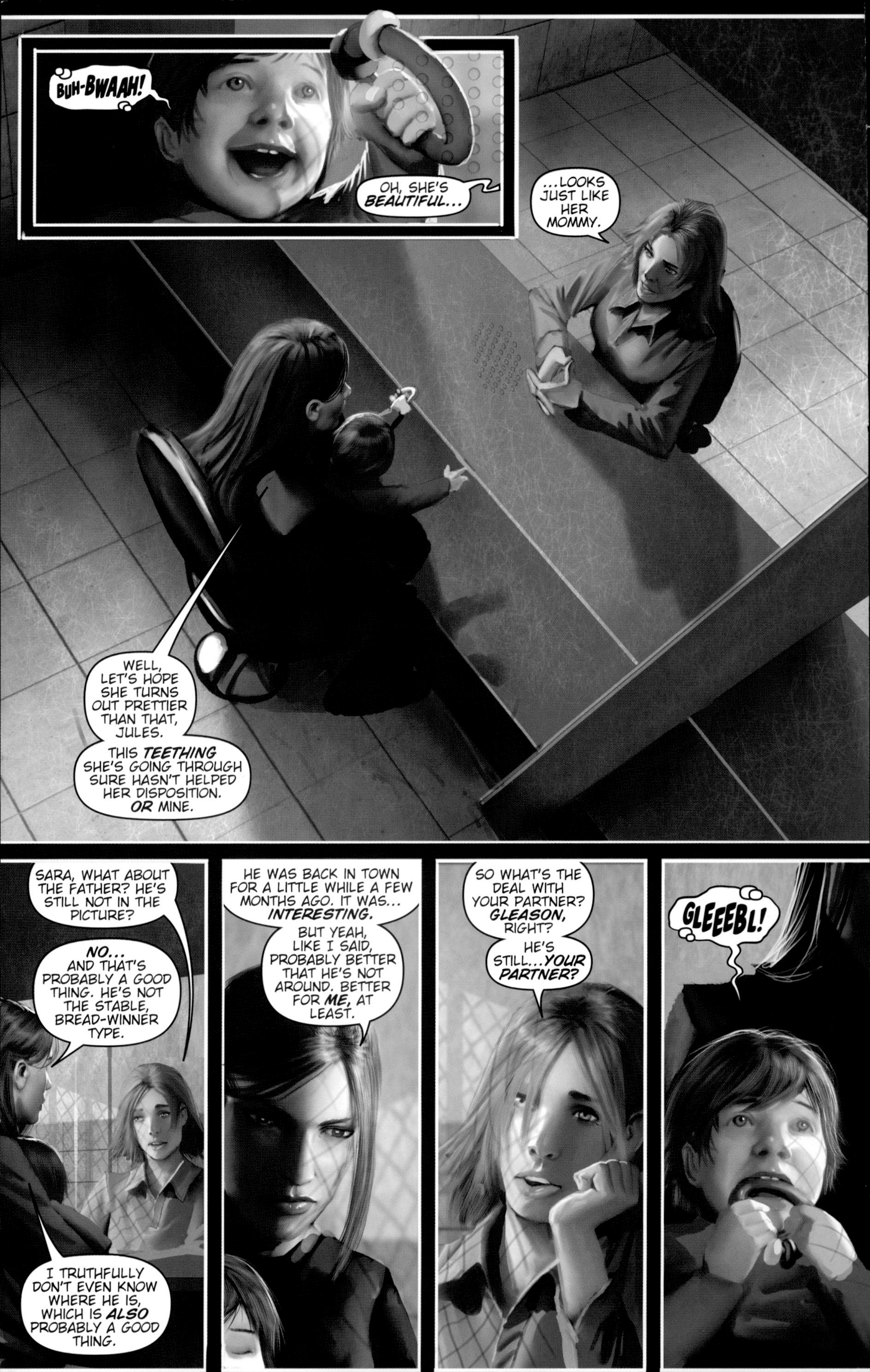
BUH-BWAAH!
OH, SHE'S BEAUTIFUL...
...LOOKS JUST LIKE HER MOMMY.
WELL, LET'S HOPE SHE TURNS OUT PRETTIER THAN THAT, JULES.
THIS TEETHING SHE'S GOING THROUGH SURE HASN'T HELPED HER DISPOSITION. OR MINE.
SARA, WHAT ABOUT THE FATHER? HE'S STILL NOT IN THE PICTURE?
NO... AND THAT'S PROBABLY A GOOD THING. HE'S NOT THE STABLE, BREAD-WINNER TYPE.
I TRUTHFULLY DON'T EVEN KNOW WHERE HE IS, WHICH IS ALSO PROBABLY A GOOD THING.
HE WAS BACK IN TOWN FOR A LITTLE WHILE A FEW MONTHS AGO. IT WAS... INTERESTING.
BUT YEAH, LIKE I SAID, PROBABLY BETTER THAT HE'S NOT AROUND. BETTER FOR ME, AT LEAST.
SO WHAT'S THE DEAL WITH YOUR PARTNER? GLEASON, RIGHT?
HE'S STILL... YOUR PARTNER?
GLEEEBL!

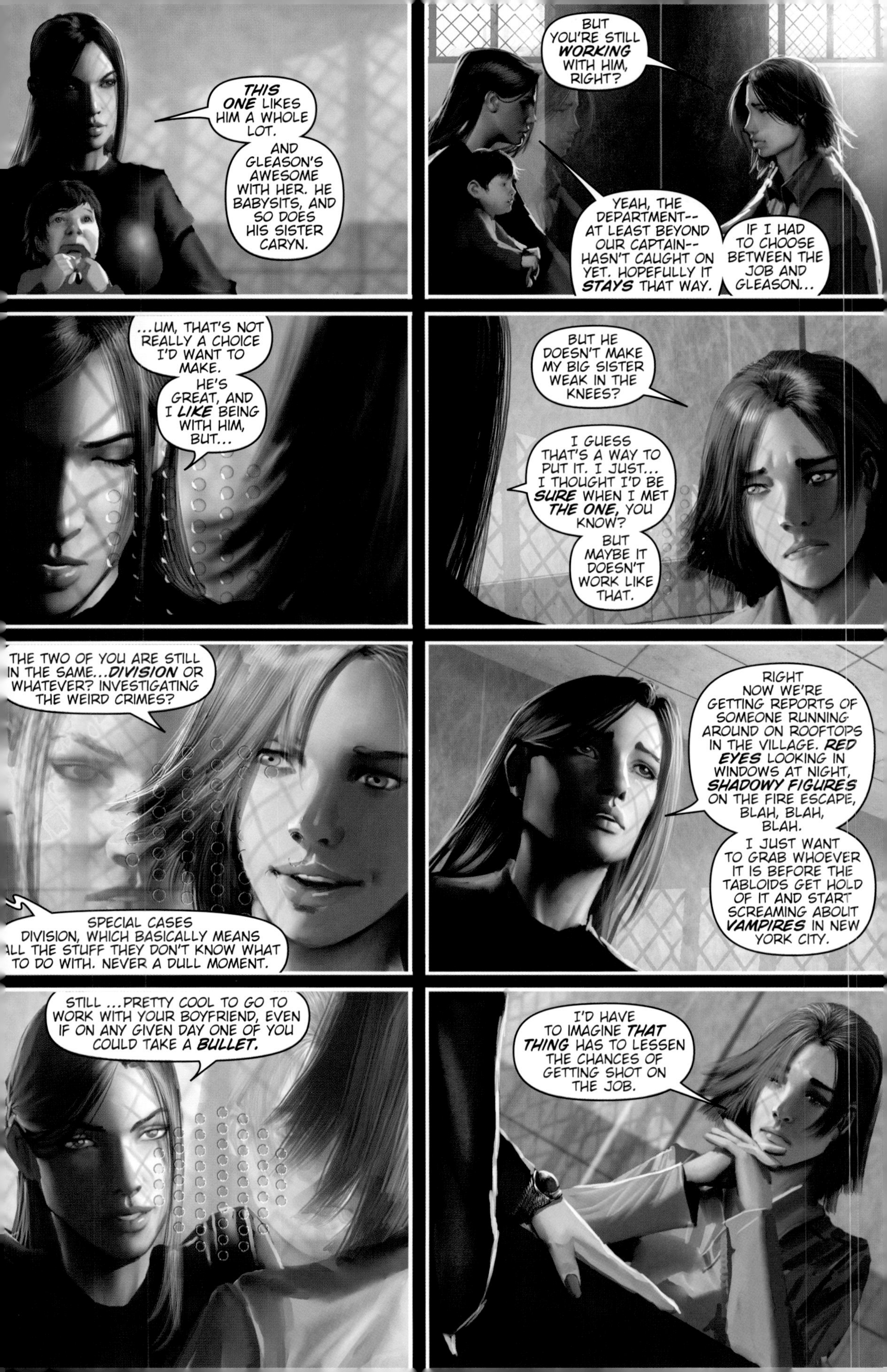
THIS ONE LIKES HIM A WHOLE LOT.
AND GLEASON'S AWESOME WITH HER. HE BABYSITS, AND SO DOES HIS SISTER CARYN.
BUT YOU'RE STILL WORKING WITH HIM, RIGHT?
YEAH, THE DEPARTMENT-- AT LEAST BEYOND OUR CAPTAIN-- HASN'T CAUGHT ON YET. HOPEFULLY IT STAYS THAT WAY.
IF I HAD TO CHOOSE BETWEEN THE JOB AND GLEASON...
...UM, THAT'S NOT REALLY A CHOICE I'D WANT TO MAKE.
HE'S GREAT, AND I LIKE BEING WITH HIM, BUT...
BUT HE DOESN'T MAKE MY BIG SISTER WEAK IN THE KNEES?
I GUESS THAT'S A WAY TO PUT IT. I JUST... I THOUGHT I'D BE SURE WHEN I MET THE ONE, YOU KNOW?
BUT MAYBE IT DOESN'T WORK LIKE THAT.
THE TWO OF YOU ARE STILL IN THE SAME...DIVISION OR WHATEVER? INVESTIGATING THE WEIRD CRIMES?
SPECIAL CASES DIVISION, WHICH BASICALLY MEANS ALL THE STUFF THEY DON'T KNOW WHAT TO DO WITH. NEVER A DULL MOMENT.
RIGHT NOW WE'RE GETTING REPORTS OF SOMEONE RUNNING AROUND ON ROOFTOPS IN THE VILLAGE. RED EYES LOOKING IN WINDOWS AT NIGHT, SHADOWY FIGURES ON THE FIRE ESCAPE, BLAH, BLAH, BLAH.
I JUST WANT TO GRAB WHOEVER IT IS BEFORE THE TABLOIDS GET HOLD OF IT AND START SCREAMING ABOUT VAMPIRES IN NEW YORK CITY.
STILL ...PRETTY COOL TO GO TO WORK WITH YOUR BOYFRIEND, EVEN IF ON ANY GIVEN DAY ONE OF YOU COULD TAKE A BULLET.
I'D HAVE TO IMAGINE THAT THING HAS TO LESSEN THE CHANCES OF GETTING SHOT ON THE JOB.

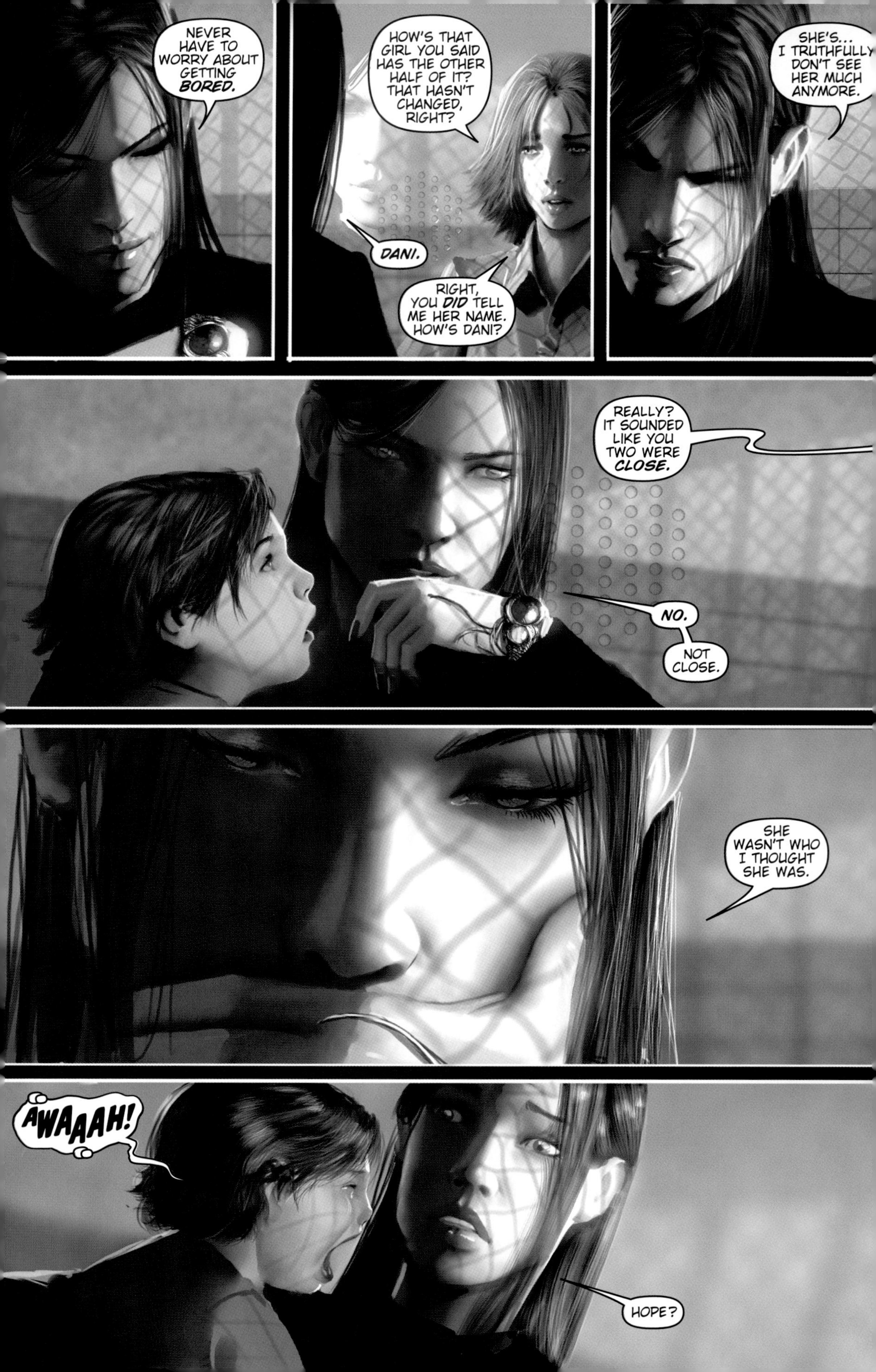
NEVER HAVE TO WORRY ABOUT GETTING BORED.
HOW'S THAT GIRL YOU SAID HAS THE OTHER HALF OF IT? THAT HASN'T CHANGED, RIGHT?
DANI.
RIGHT, YOU DID TELL ME HER NAME. HOW'S DANI?
SHE'S... I TRUTHFULLY DON'T SEE HER MUCH ANYMORE.
REALLY? IT SOUNDED LIKE YOU TWO WERE CLOSE.
NO.
NOT CLOSE.
SHE WASN'T WHO I THOUGHT SHE WAS.
AWAAAH!
HOPE?

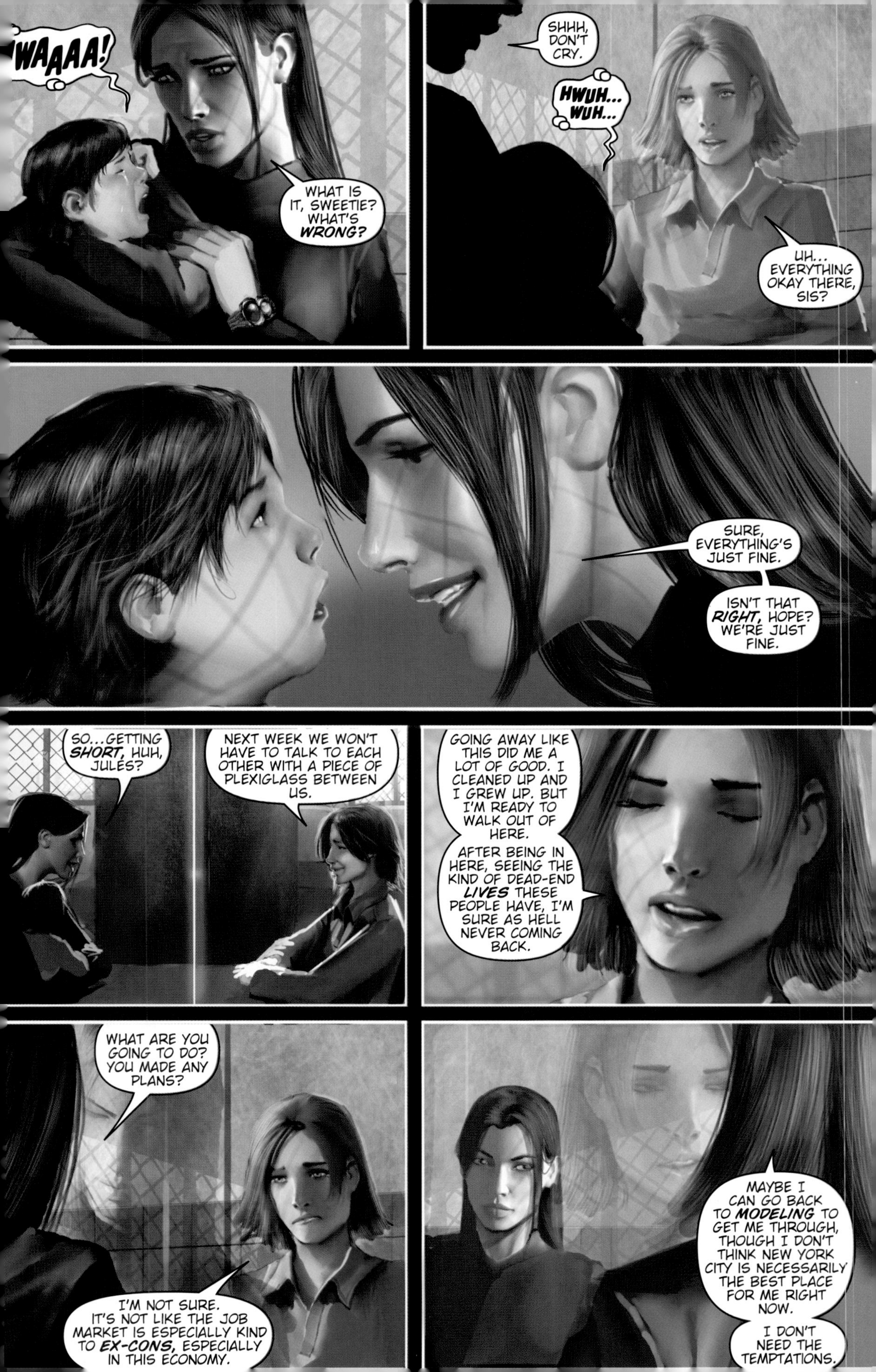
WAAAA!
WHAT IS IT, SWEETIE? WHAT'S WRONG?
SHHH, DON'T CRY.
HWUH... WUH...
UH... EVERYTHING OKAY THERE, SIS?
SURE, EVERYTHING'S JUST FINE.
ISN'T THAT RIGHT, HOPE? WE'RE JUST FINE.
SO...GETTING SHORT, HUH, JULES?
NEXT WEEK WE WON'T HAVE TO TALK TO EACH OTHER WITH A PIECE OF PLEXIGLASS BETWEEN US.
GOING AWAY LIKE THIS DID ME A LOT OF GOOD. I CLEANED UP AND I GREW UP. BUT I'M READY TO WALK OUT OF HERE.
AFTER BEING IN HERE, SEEING THE KIND OF DEAD-END LIVES THESE PEOPLE HAVE, I'M SURE AS HELL NEVER COMING BACK.
WHAT ARE YOU GOING TO DO? YOU MADE ANY PLANS?
I'M NOT SURE. IT'S NOT LIKE THE JOB MARKET IS ESPECIALLY KIND TO EX-CONS, ESPECIALLY IN THIS ECONOMY.
MAYBE I CAN GO BACK TO MODELING TO GET ME THROUGH, THOUGH I DON'T THINK NEW YORK CITY IS NECESSARILY THE BEST PLACE FOR ME RIGHT NOW.
I DON'T NEED THE TEMPTATIONS.

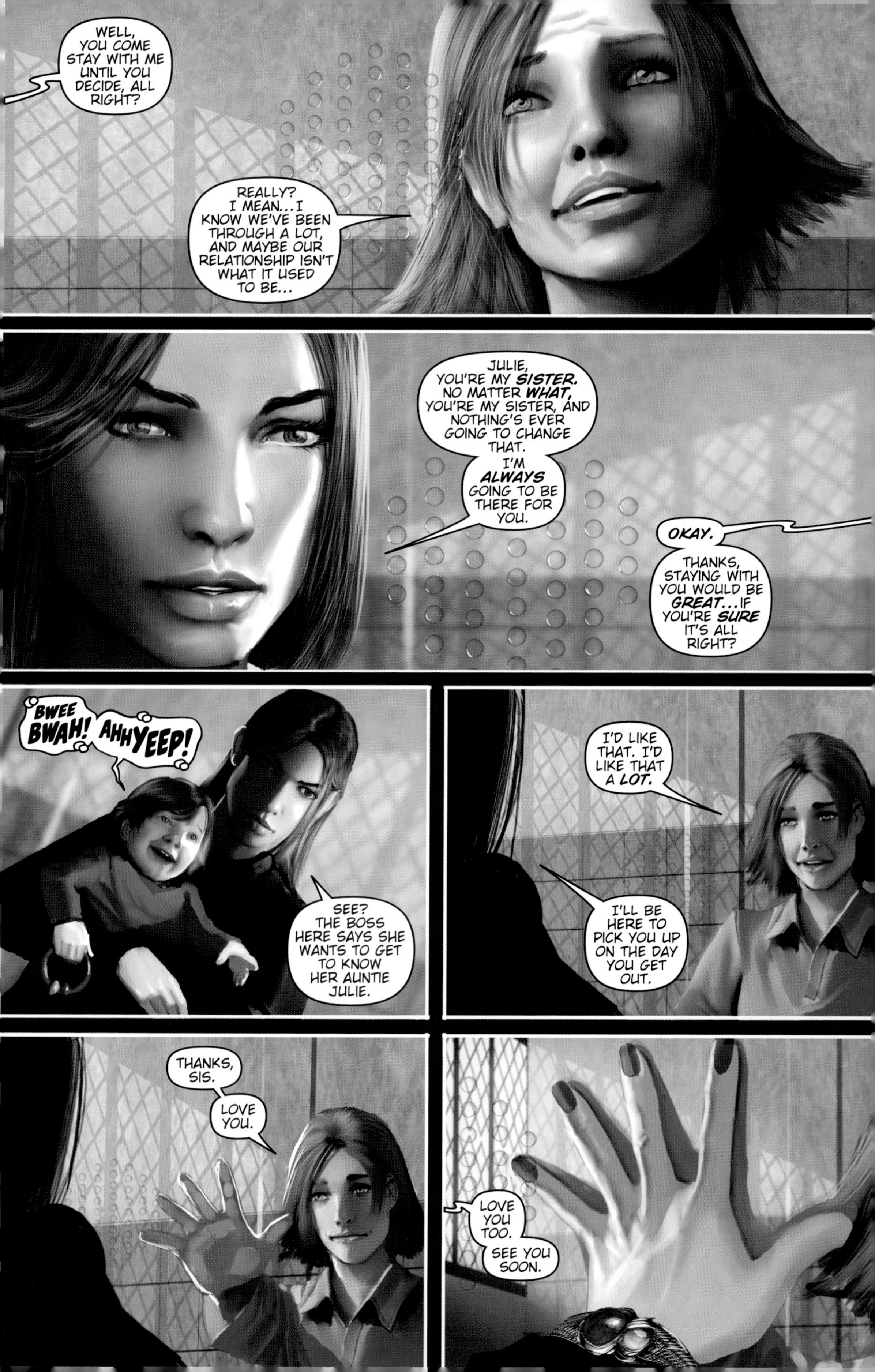
WELL, YOU COME STAY WITH ME UNTIL YOU DECIDE, ALL RIGHT?
REALLY? I MEAN...I KNOW WE'VE BEEN THROUGH A LOT, AND MAYBE OUR RELATIONSHIP ISN'T WHAT IT USED TO BE...
JULIE, YOU'RE MY SISTER. NO MATTER WHAT, YOU'RE MY SISTER, AND NOTHING'S EVER GOING TO CHANGE THAT.
I'M ALWAYS GOING TO BE THERE FOR YOU.
OKAY.
THANKS, STAYING WITH YOU WOULD BE GREAT...IF YOU'RE SURE IT'S ALL RIGHT?
BWEE BWAH! AHHYEEP!
SEE? THE BOSS HERE SAYS SHE WANTS TO GET TO KNOW HER AUNTIE JULIE.
I'D LIKE THAT. I'D LIKE THAT A LOT.
I'LL BE HERE TO PICK YOU UP ON THE DAY YOU GET OUT.
THANKS, SIS.
LOVE YOU.
LOVE YOU TOO.
SEE YOU SOON.

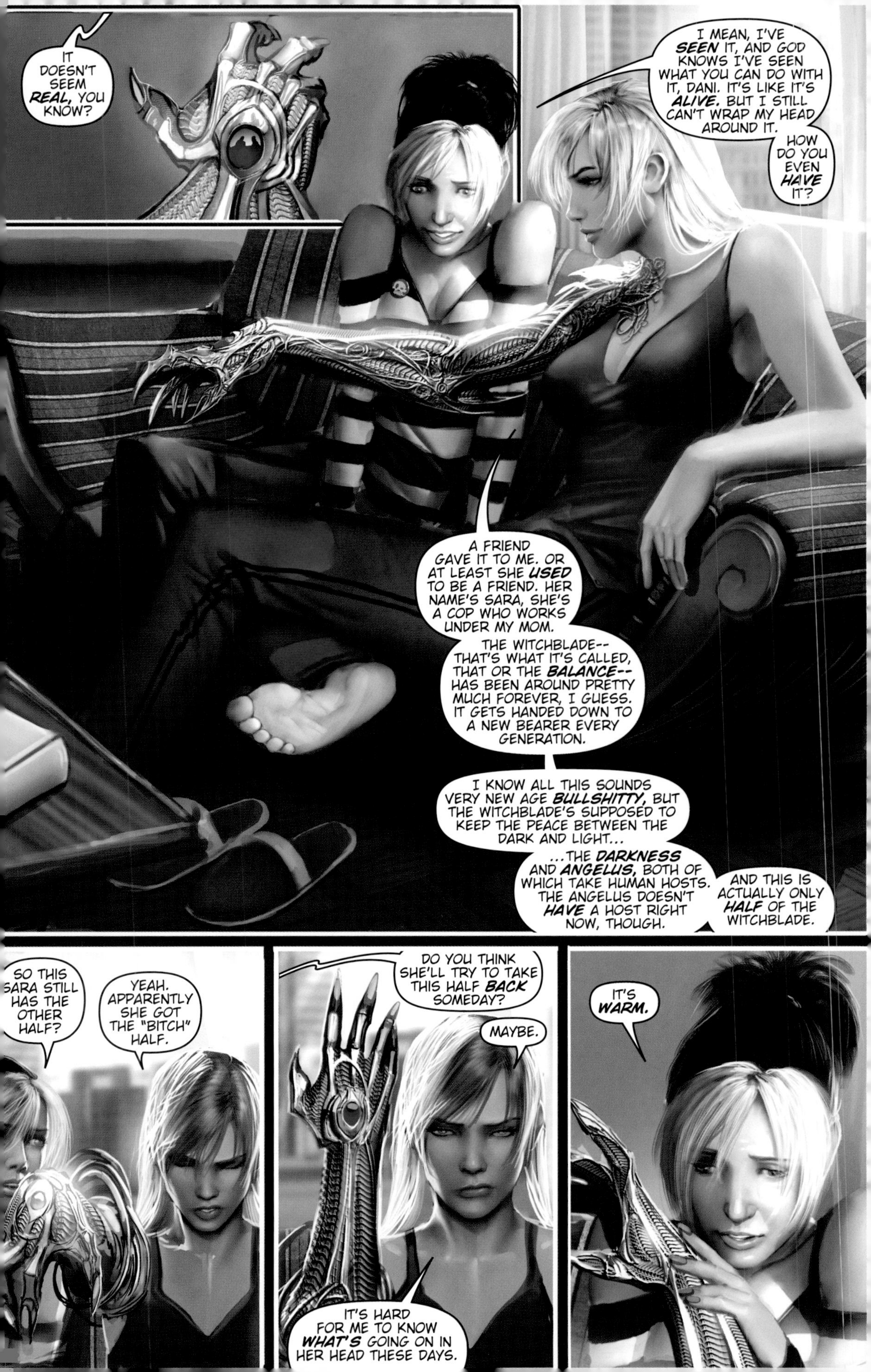

IT DOESN'T SEEM REAL, YOU KNOW?
I MEAN, I'VE SEEN IT, AND GOD KNOWS I'VE SEEN WHAT YOU CAN DO WITH IT, DANI. IT'S LIKE IT'S ALIVE. BUT I STILL CAN'T WRAP MY HEAD AROUND IT.
HOW DO YOU EVEN HAVE IT?
A FRIEND GAVE IT TO ME. OR AT LEAST SHE USED TO BE A FRIEND. HER NAME'S SARA, SHE'S A COP WHO WORKS UNDER MY MOM.
THE WITCHBLADE-- THAT'S WHAT IT'S CALLED, THAT OR THE BALANCE-- HAS BEEN AROUND PRETTY MUCH FOREVER, I GUESS. IT GETS HANDED DOWN TO A NEW BEARER EVERY GENERATION.
I KNOW ALL THIS SOUNDS VERY NEW AGE BULLSHITTY, BUT THE WITCHBLADE'S SUPPOSED TO KEEP THE PEACE BETWEEN THE DARK AND LIGHT...
...THE DARKNESS AND ANGELUS, BOTH OF WHICH TAKE HUMAN HOSTS. THE ANGELUS DOESN'T HAVE A HOST RIGHT NOW, THOUGH.
AND THIS IS ACTUALLY ONLY HALF OF THE WITCHBLADE.
SO THIS SARA STILL HAS THE OTHER HALF?
YEAH. APPARENTLY SHE GOT THE "BITCH" HALF.
DO YOU THINK SHE'LL TRY TO TAKE THIS HALF BACK SOMEDAY?
MAYBE.
IT'S HARD FOR ME TO KNOW WHAT'S GOING ON IN HER HEAD THESE DAYS.
IT'S WARM.

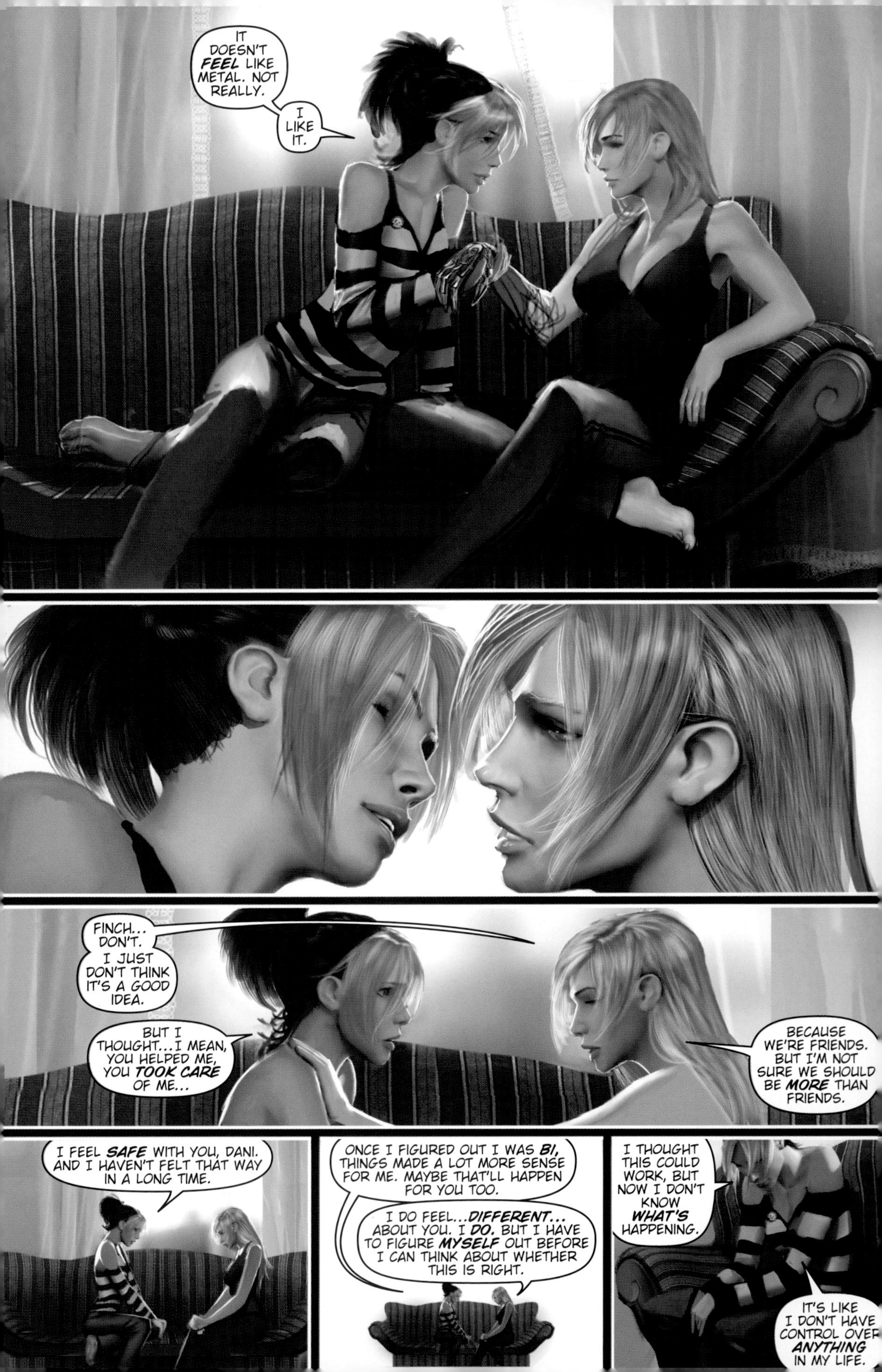
IT DOESN'T FEEL LIKE METAL. NOT REALLY.
I LIKE IT.
FINCH... DON'T. I JUST DON'T THINK IT'S A GOOD IDEA.
BUT I THOUGHT... I MEAN, YOU HELPED ME, YOU TOOK CARE OF ME...
BECAUSE WE'RE FRIENDS. BUT I'M NOT SURE WE SHOULD BE MORE THAN FRIENDS.
I FEEL SAFE WITH YOU, DANI. AND I HAVEN'T FELT THAT WAY IN A LONG TIME.
ONCE I FIGURED OUT I WAS BI, THINGS MADE A LOT MORE SENSE FOR ME. MAYBE THAT'LL HAPPEN FOR YOU TOO.
I DO FEEL...DIFFERENT... ABOUT YOU. I DO. BUT I HAVE TO FIGURE MYSELF OUT BEFORE I CAN THINK ABOUT WHETHER THIS IS RIGHT.
I THOUGHT THIS COULD WORK, BUT NOW I DON'T KNOW WHAT'S HAPPENING.
IT'S LIKE I DON'T HAVE CONTROL OVER ANYTHING IN MY LIFE.

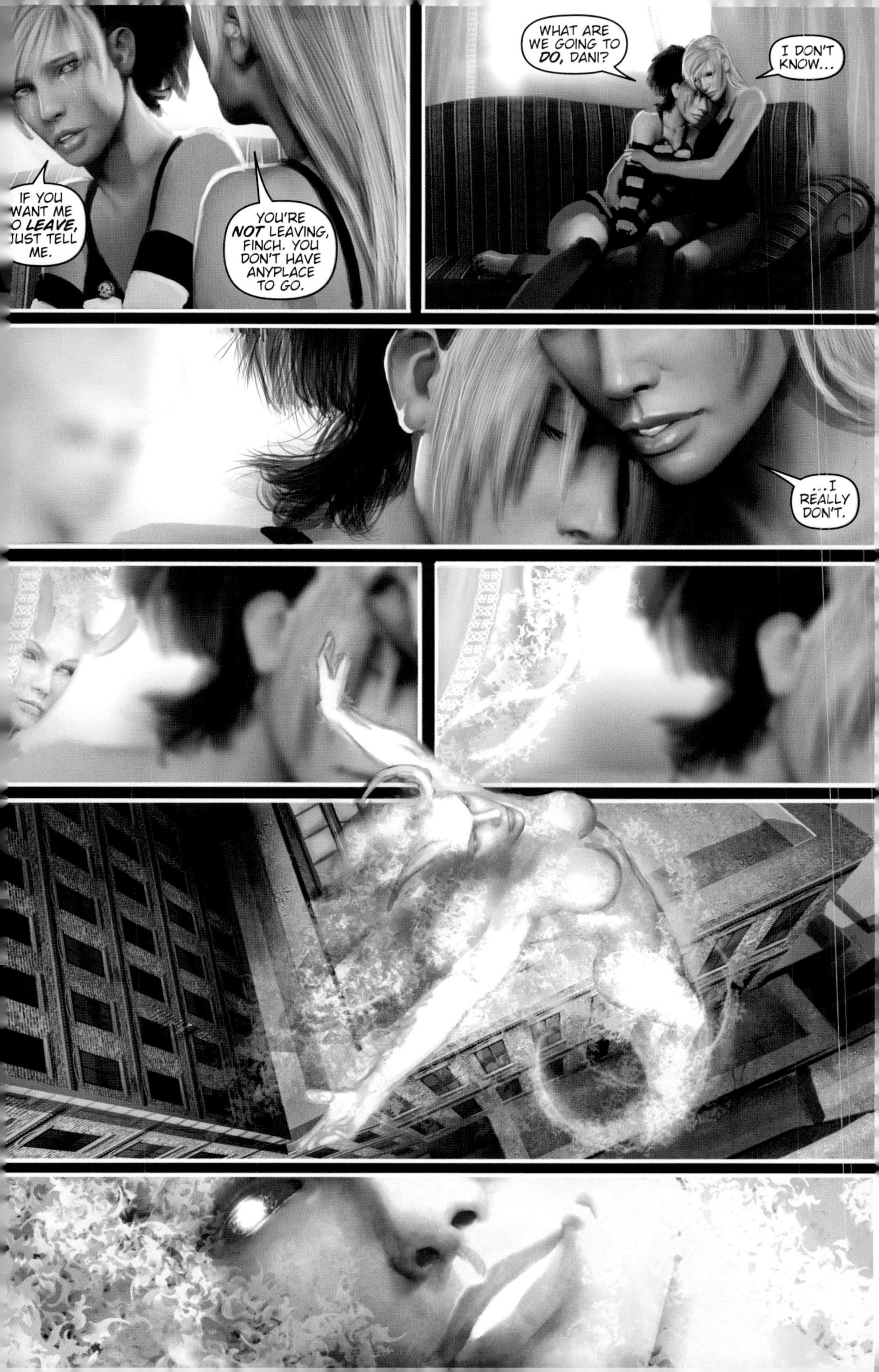
IF YOU WANT ME TO LEAVE, JUST TELL ME.
YOU'RE NOT LEAVING, FINCH. YOU DON'T HAVE ANYPLACE TO GO.
WHAT ARE WE GOING TO DO, DANI?
I DON'T KNOW...
...I REALLY DON'T.

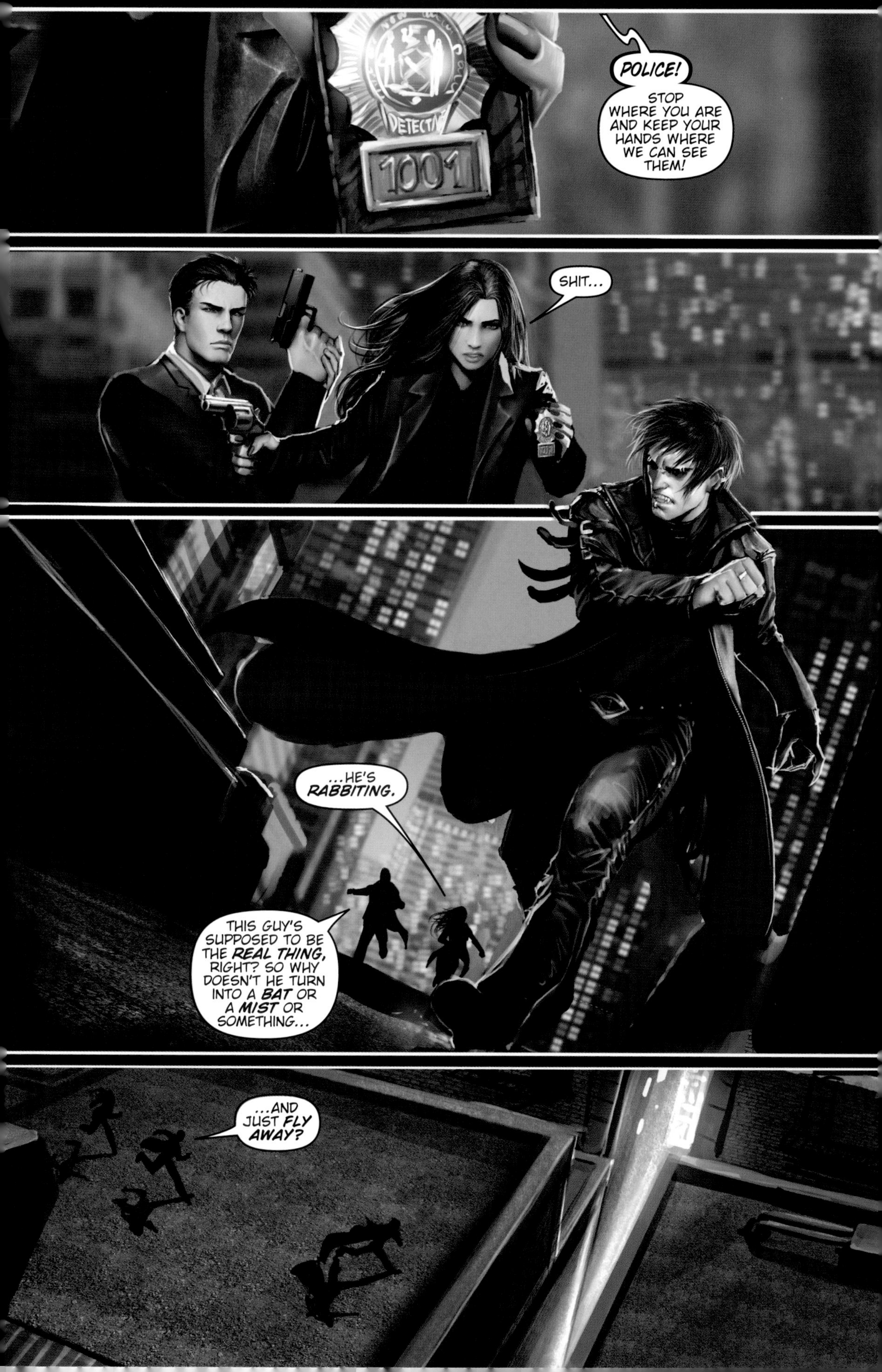
POLICE!
STOP WHERE YOU ARE AND KEEP YOUR HANDS WHERE WE CAN SEE THEM!
1001
SHIT...
...HE'S RABBITING.
THIS GUY'S SUPPOSED TO BE THE REAL THING, RIGHT? SO WHY DOESN'T HE TURN INTO A BAT OR A MIST OR SOMETHING...
...AND JUST FLY AWAY?

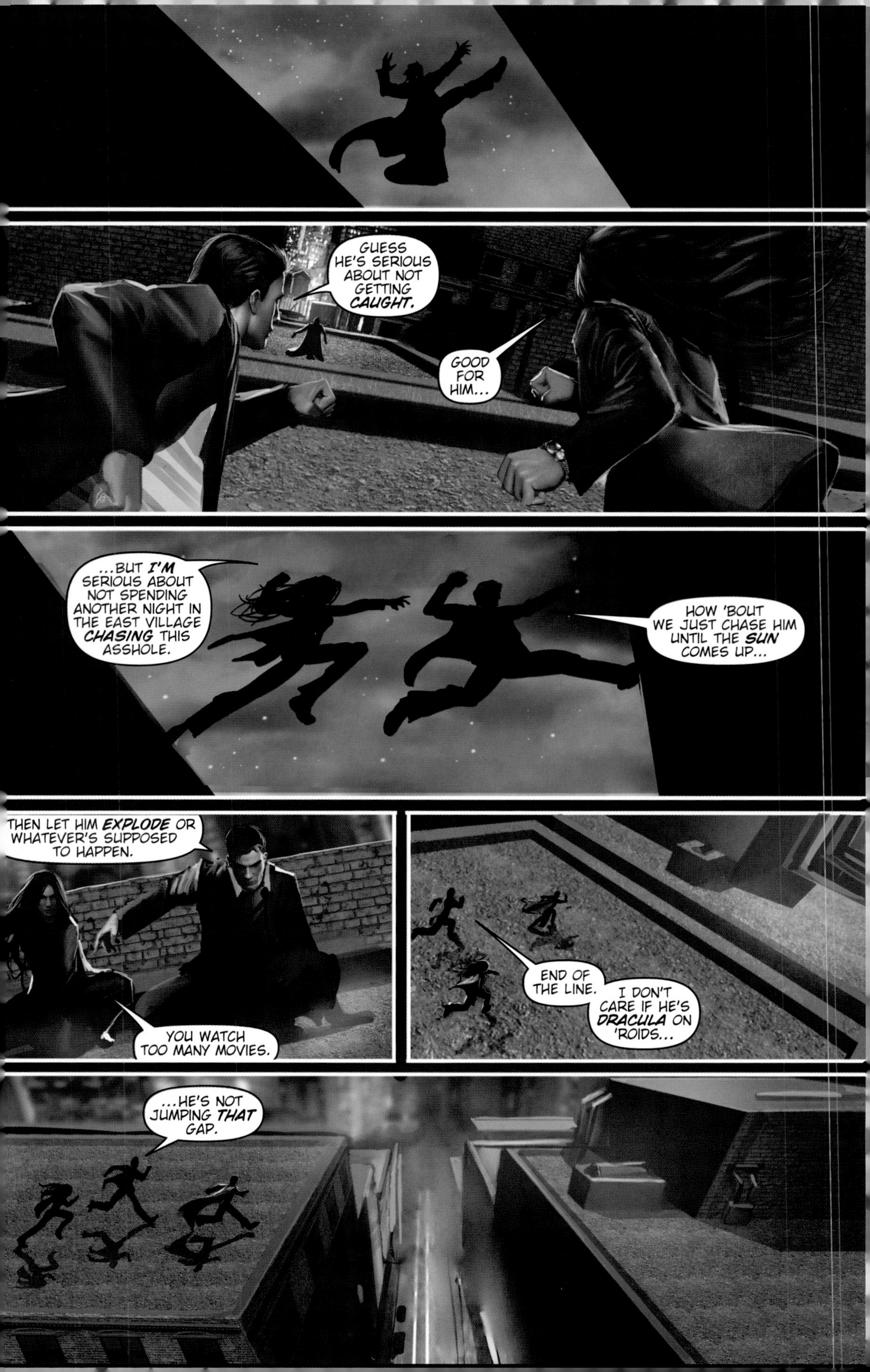
GUESS HE'S SERIOUS ABOUT NOT GETTING CAUGHT.
GOOD FOR HIM...
...BUT I'M SERIOUS ABOUT NOT SPENDING ANOTHER NIGHT IN THE EAST VILLAGE CHASING THIS ASSHOLE.
HOW 'BOUT WE JUST CHASE HIM UNTIL THE SUN COMES UP...
THEN LET HIM EXPLODE OR WHATEVER'S SUPPOSED TO HAPPEN.
YOU WATCH TOO MANY MOVIES.
END OF THE LINE.
I DON'T CARE IF HE'S DRACULA ON 'ROIDS...
...HE'S NOT JUMPING THAT GAP.

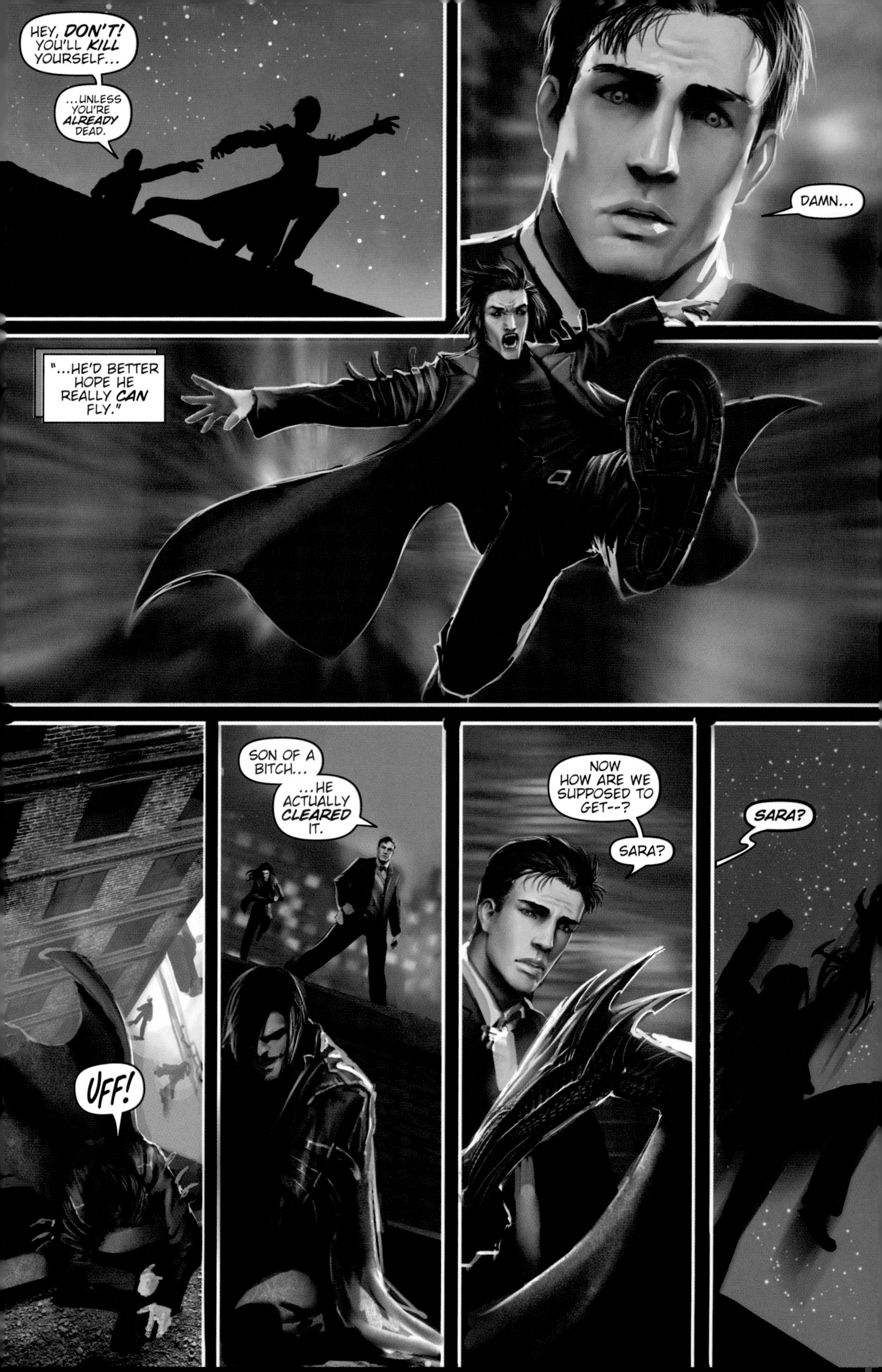
HEY, DON'T! YOU'LL KILL YOURSELF...
...UNLESS YOU'RE ALREADY DEAD.
DAMN...
"...HE'D BETTER HOPE HE REALLY CAN FLY."
UFF!
SON OF A BITCH...
...HE ACTUALLY CLEARED IT.
NOW HOW ARE WE SUPPOSED TO GET--?
SARA?
SARA?

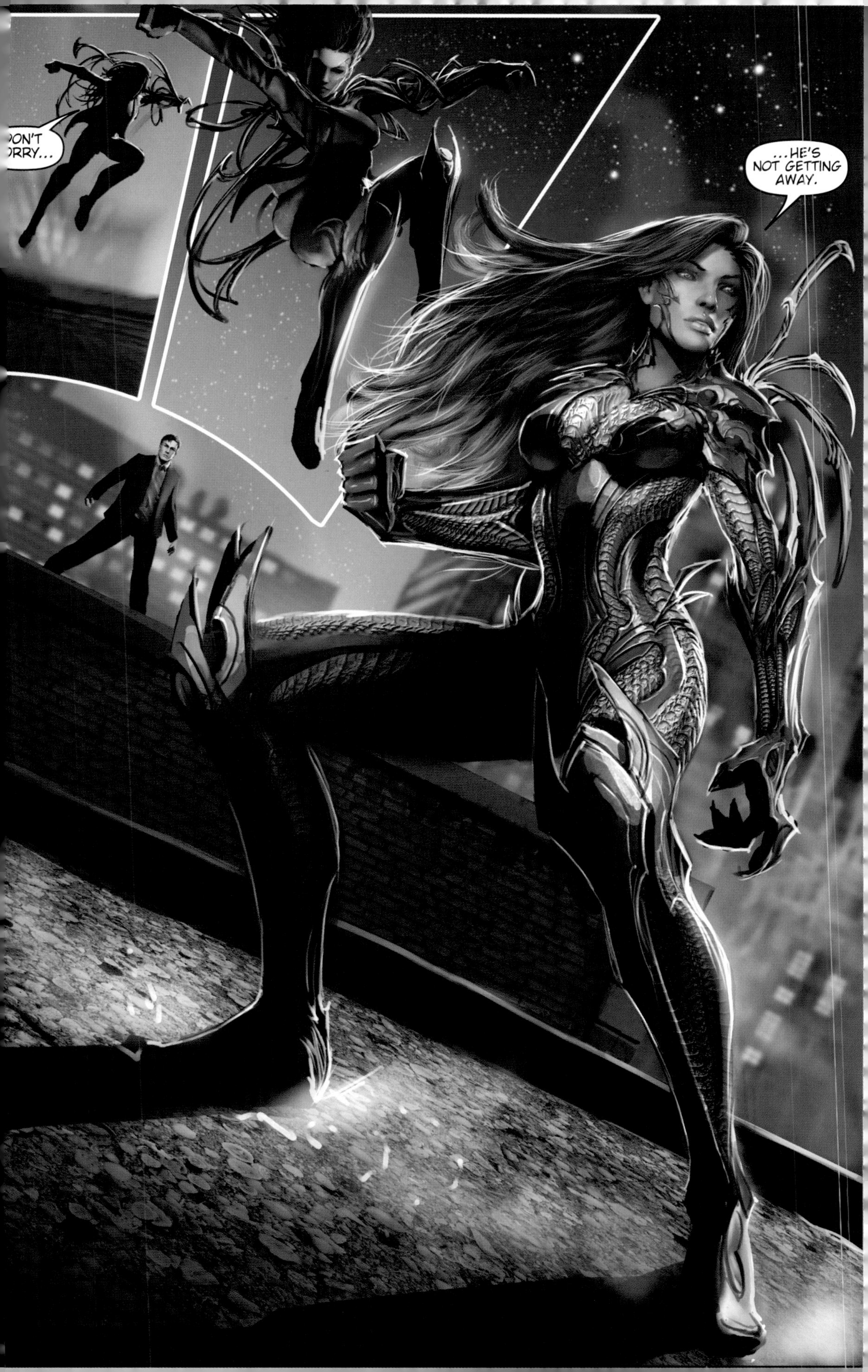

DON'T
ORRY...
...HE'S
NOT GETTING
AWAY.

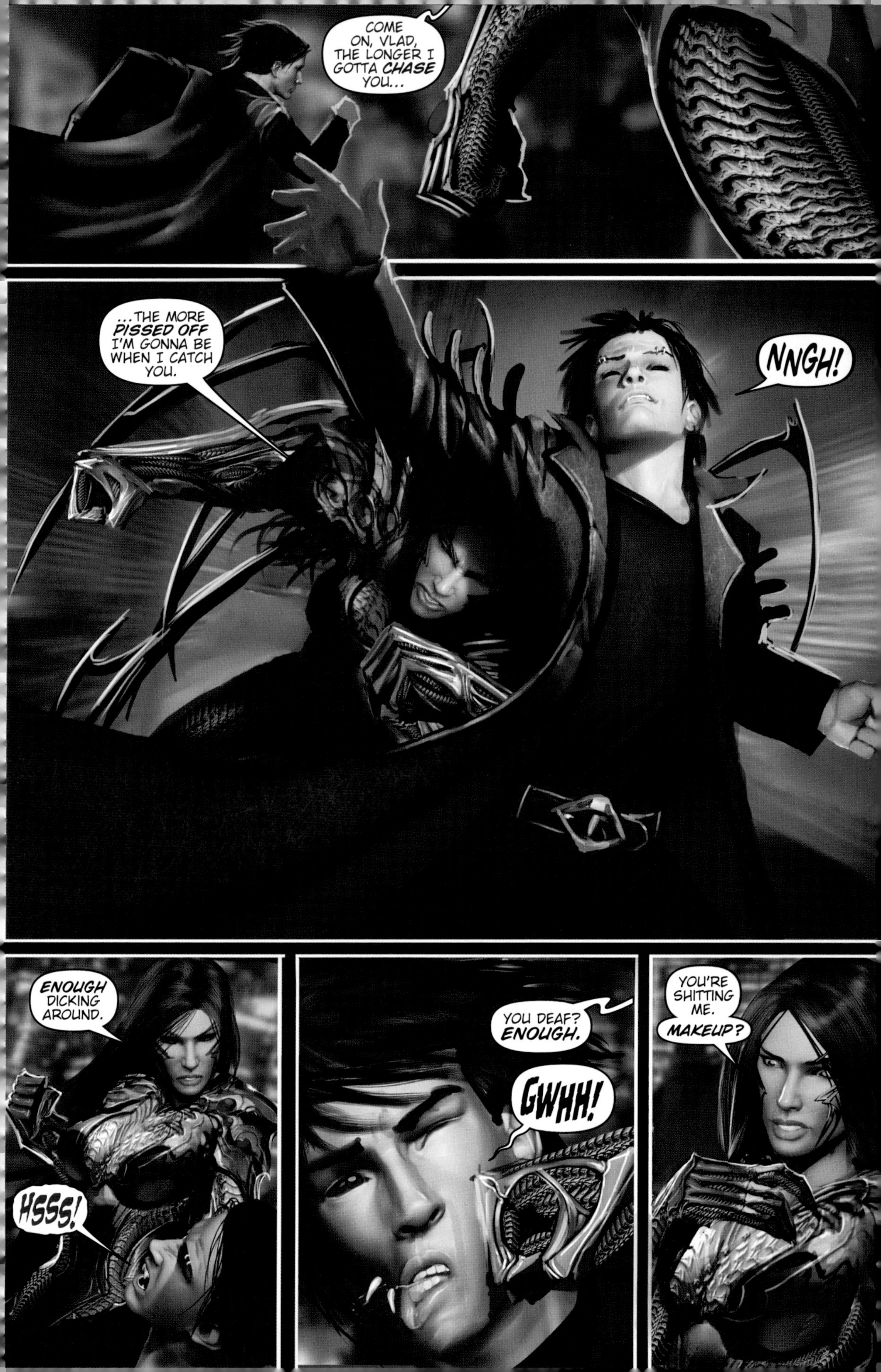
COME ON, VLAD, THE LONGER I GOTTA CHASE YOU...
...THE MORE PISSED OFF I'M GONNA BE WHEN I CATCH YOU.
NNGH!
ENOUGH DICKING AROUND.
HSSS!
YOU DEAF? ENOUGH.
GWHH!
YOU'RE SHITTING ME. MAKEUP?

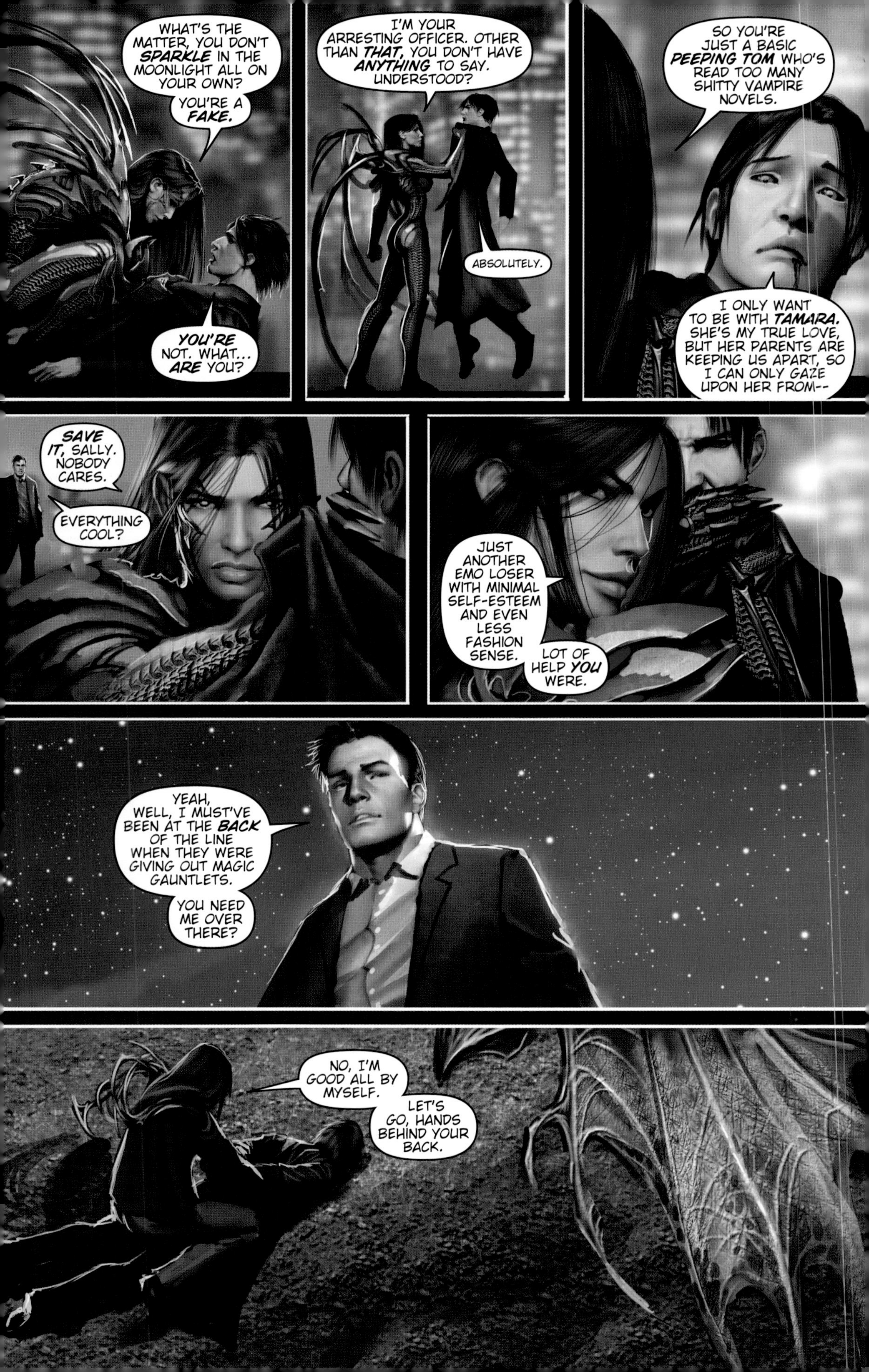
WHAT'S THE MATTER, YOU DON'T SPARKLE IN THE MOONLIGHT ALL ON YOUR OWN?
YOU'RE A FAKE.
YOU'RE NOT. WHAT... ARE YOU?
I'M YOUR ARRESTING OFFICER. OTHER THAN THAT, YOU DON'T HAVE ANYTHING TO SAY. UNDERSTOOD?
ABSOLUTELY.
SO YOU'RE JUST A BASIC PEEPING TOM WHO'S READ TOO MANY SHITTY VAMPIRE NOVELS.
I ONLY WANT TO BE WITH TAMARA. SHE'S MY TRUE LOVE, BUT HER PARENTS ARE KEEPING US APART, SO I CAN ONLY GAZE UPON HER FROM--
SAVE IT, SALLY. NOBODY CARES.
EVERYTHING COOL?
JUST ANOTHER EMO LOSER WITH MINIMAL SELF-ESTEEM AND EVEN LESS FASHION SENSE.
LOT OF HELP YOU WERE.
YEAH, WELL, I MUST'VE BEEN AT THE BACK OF THE LINE WHEN THEY WERE GIVING OUT MAGIC GAUNTLETS.
YOU NEED ME OVER THERE?
NO, I'M GOOD ALL BY MYSELF.
LET'S GO, HANDS BEHIND YOUR BACK.

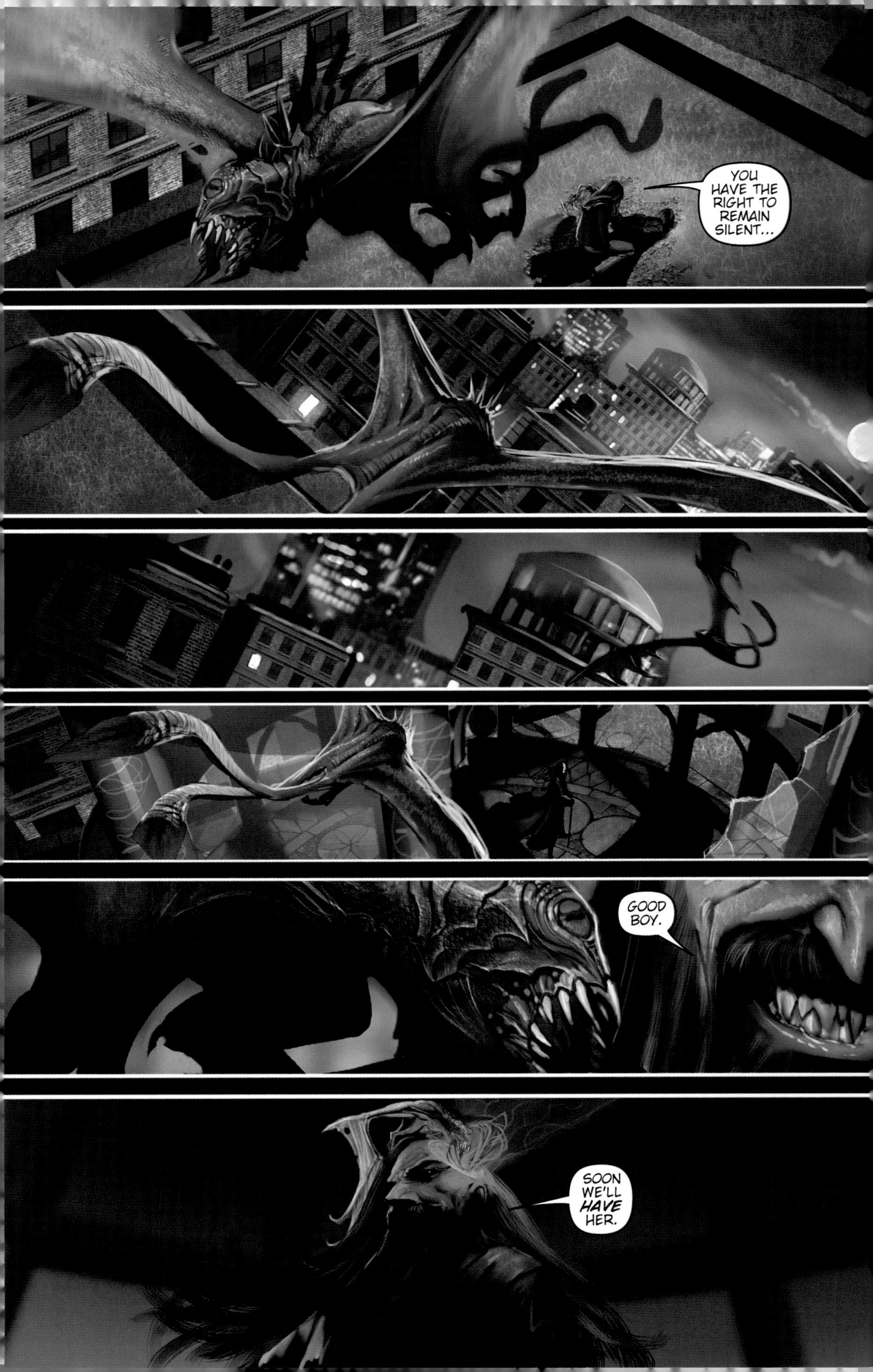
YOU HAVE THE RIGHT TO REMAIN SILENT...
GOOD BOY.
SOON WE'LL *HAVE* HER.

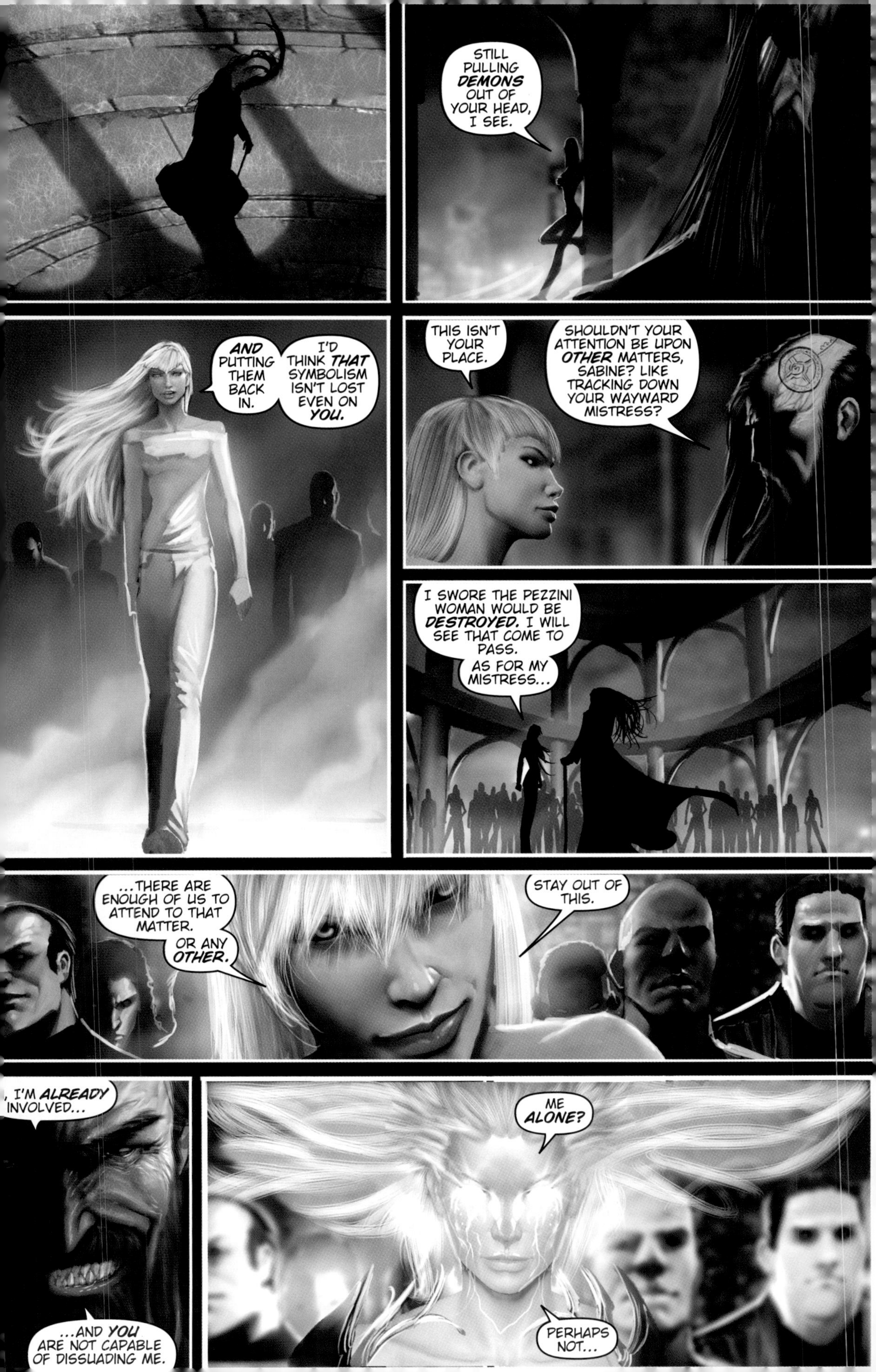
STILL PULLING DEMONS OUT OF YOUR HEAD, I SEE.
AND PUTTING THEM BACK IN.
I'D THINK THAT SYMBOLISM ISN'T LOST EVEN ON YOU.
THIS ISN'T YOUR PLACE.
SHOULDN'T YOUR ATTENTION BE UPON OTHER MATTERS, SABINE? LIKE TRACKING DOWN YOUR WAYWARD MISTRESS?
I SWORE THE PEZZINI WOMAN WOULD BE DESTROYED. I WILL SEE THAT COME TO PASS.
AS FOR MY MISTRESS...
...THERE ARE ENOUGH OF US TO ATTEND TO THAT MATTER.
OR ANY OTHER.
STAY OUT OF THIS.
, I'M ALREADY INVOLVED...
...AND YOU ARE NOT CAPABLE OF DISSUADING ME.
ME ALONE?
PERHAPS NOT...

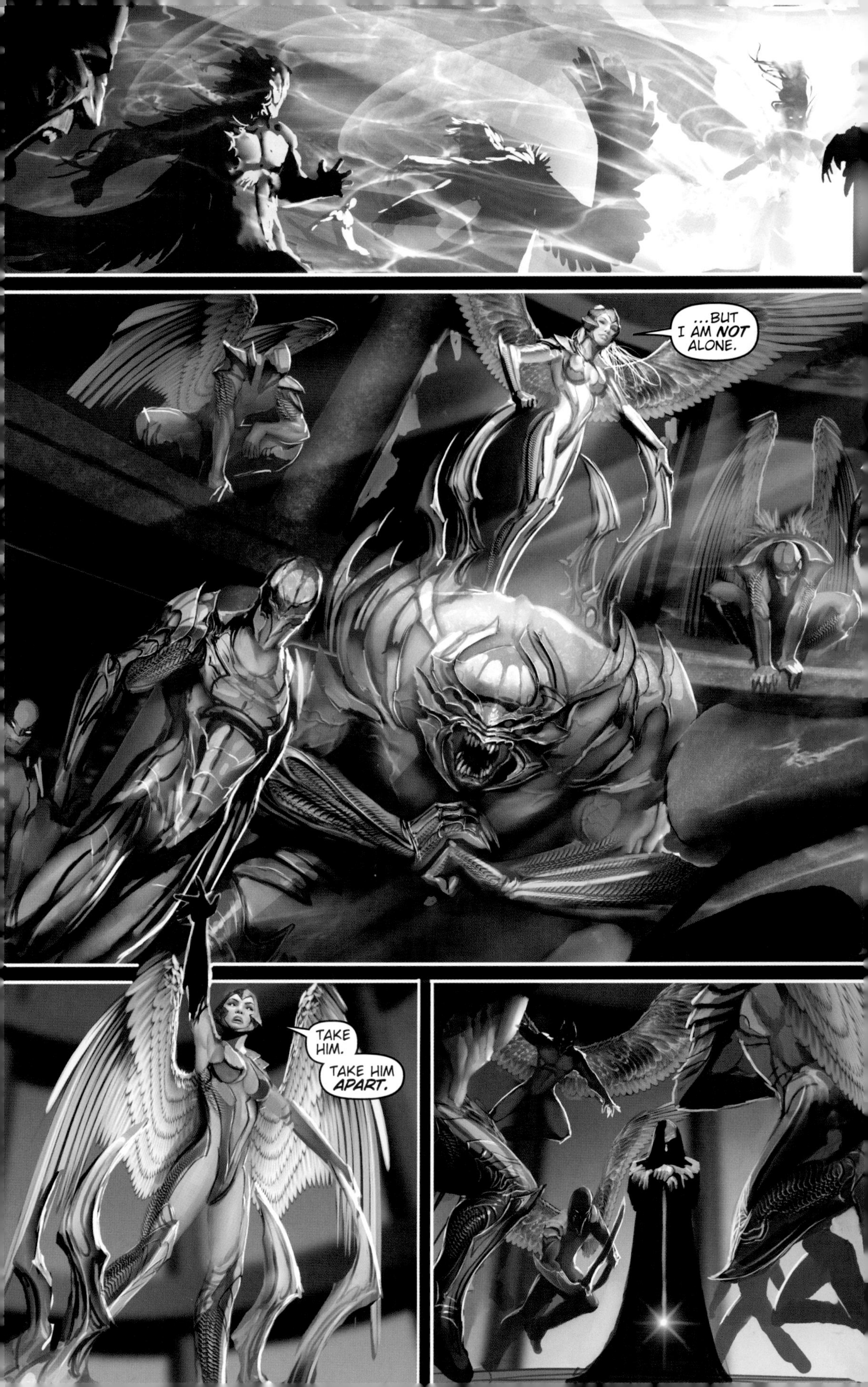
...BUT I AM NOT ALONE.
TAKE HIM.
TAKE HIM APART.

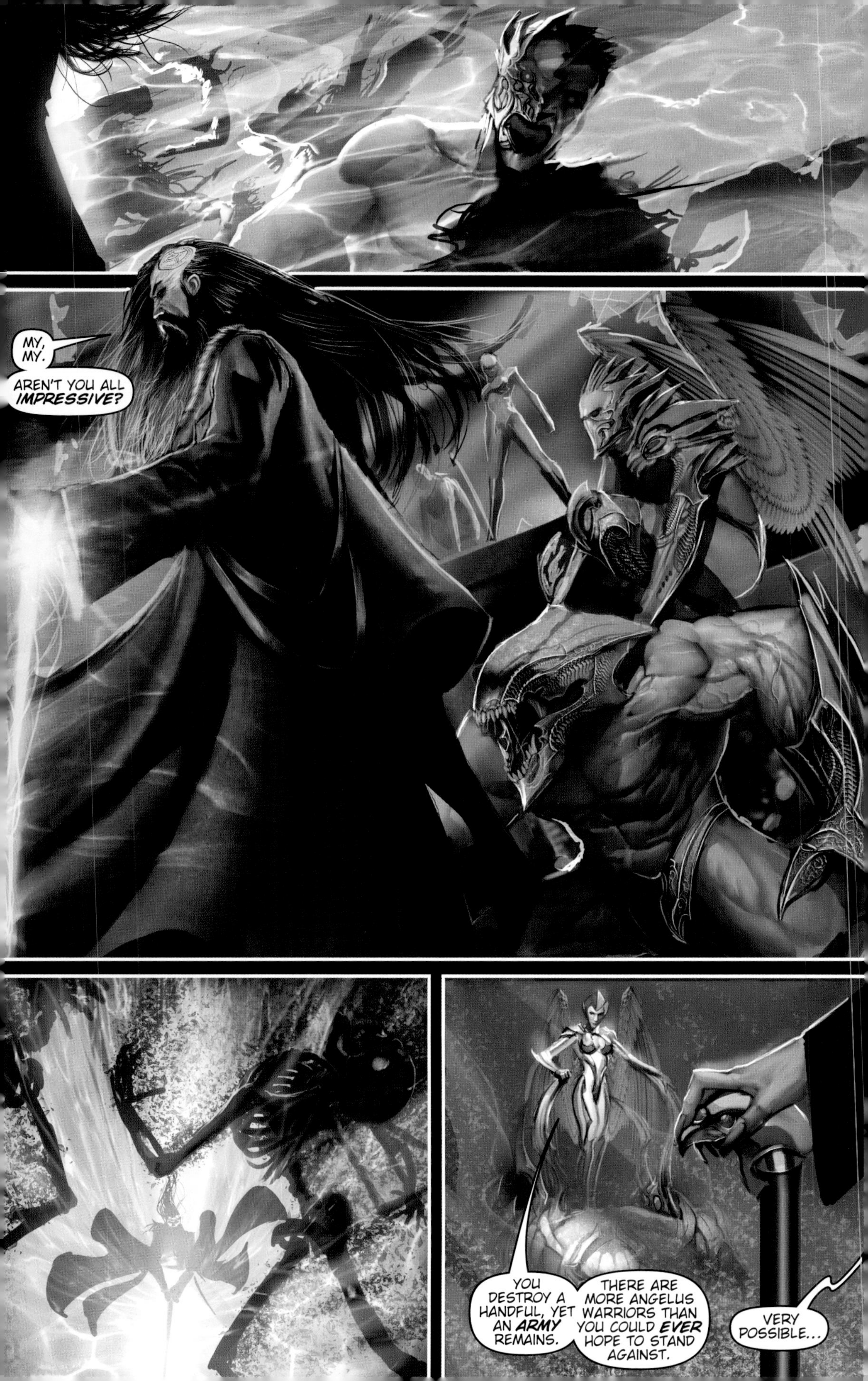
MY, MY.
AREN'T YOU ALL IMPRESSIVE?
YOU DESTROY A HANDFUL, YET AN ARMY REMAINS.
THERE ARE MORE ANGELUS WARRIORS THAN YOU COULD EVER HOPE TO STAND AGAINST.
VERY POSSIBLE...

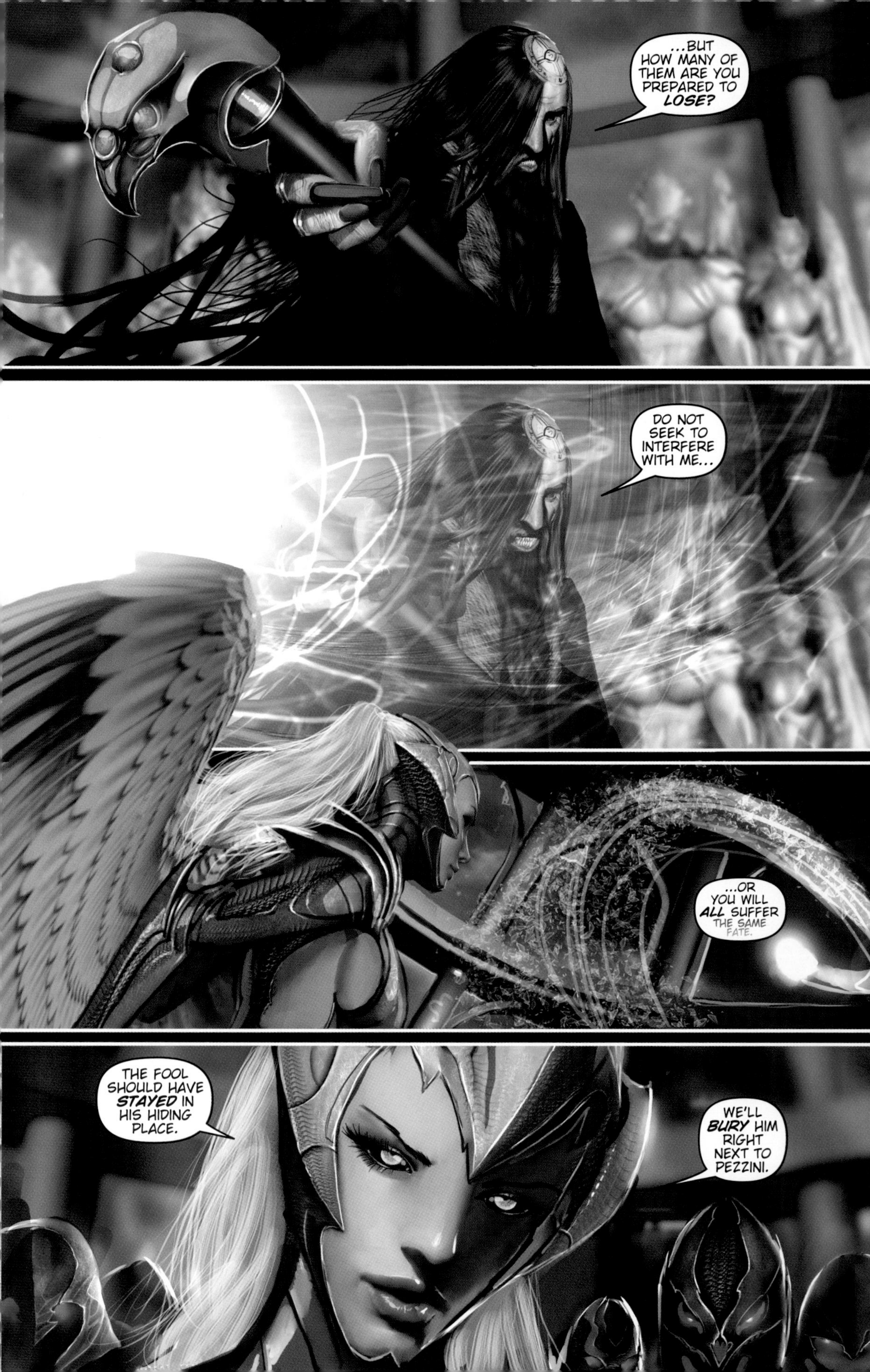
...BUT HOW MANY OF THEM ARE YOU PREPARED TO LOSE?
DO NOT SEEK TO INTERFERE WITH ME...
...OR YOU WILL ALL SUFFER THE SAME FATE.
THE FOOL SHOULD HAVE STAYED IN HIS HIDING PLACE.
WE'LL BURY HIM RIGHT NEXT TO PEZZINI.

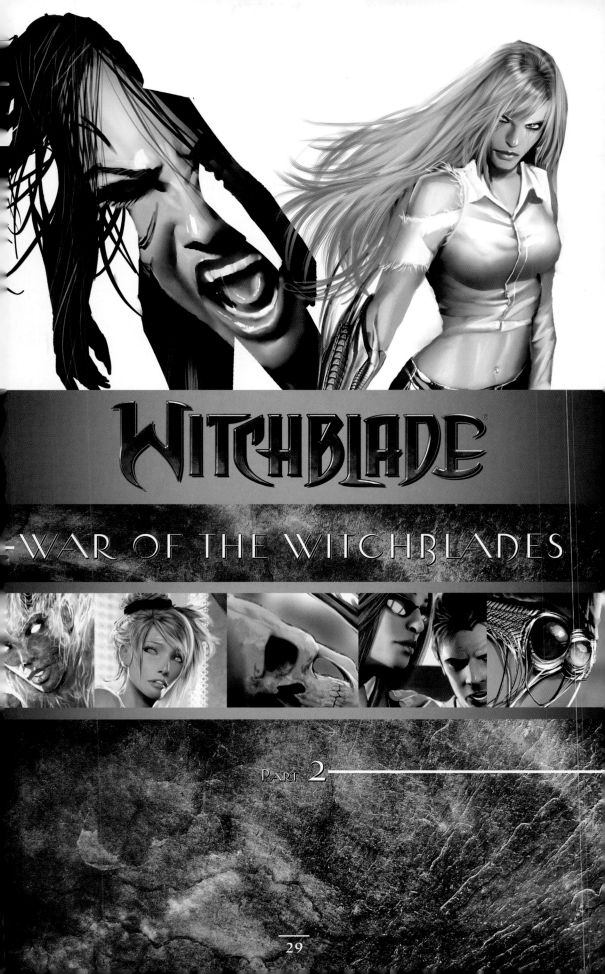

WITCHBLADE

-WAR OF THE WITCHBLADES

PART 2

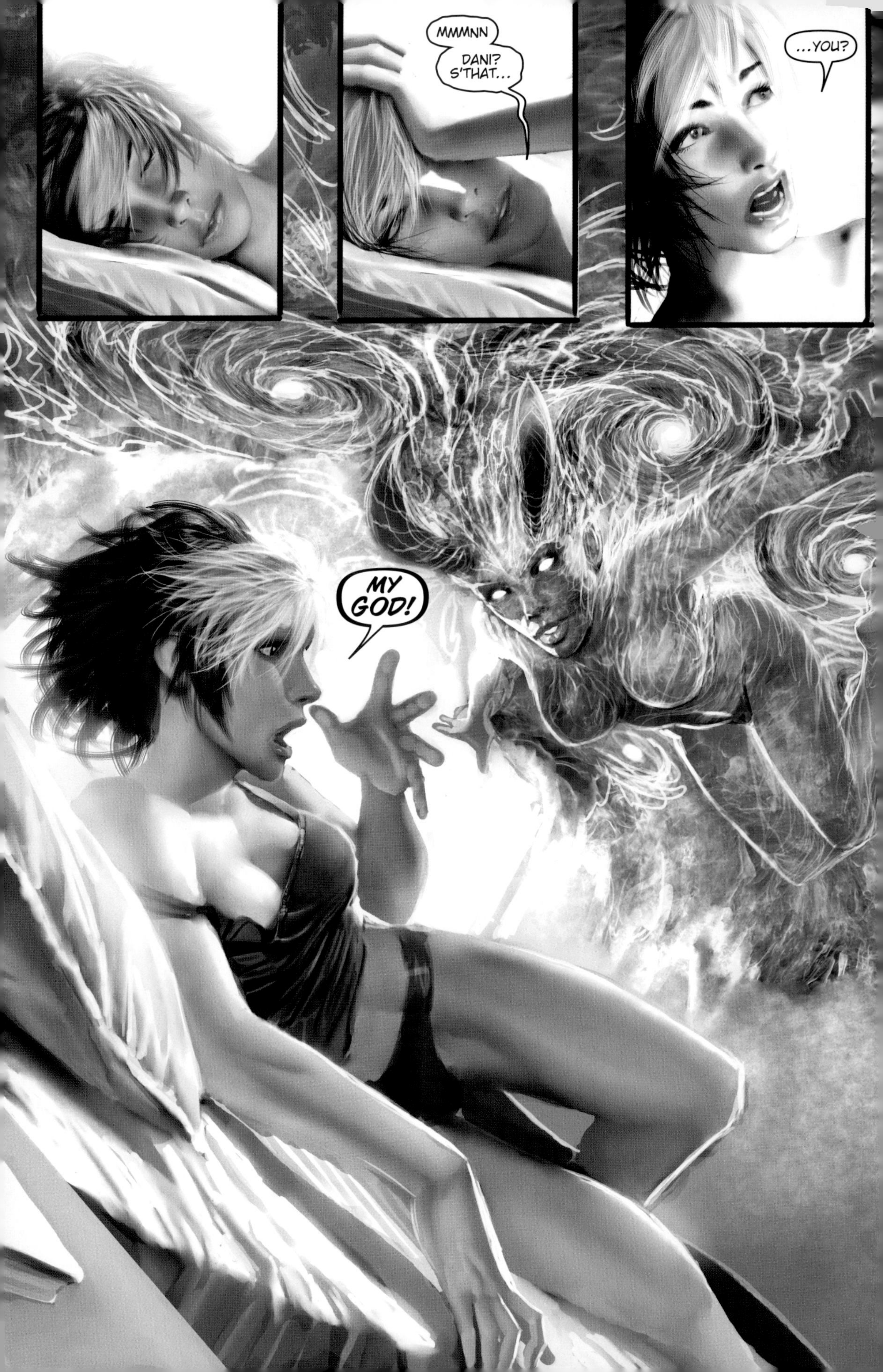
MMMNN
DANI? S'THAT...
...YOU?
MY GOD!

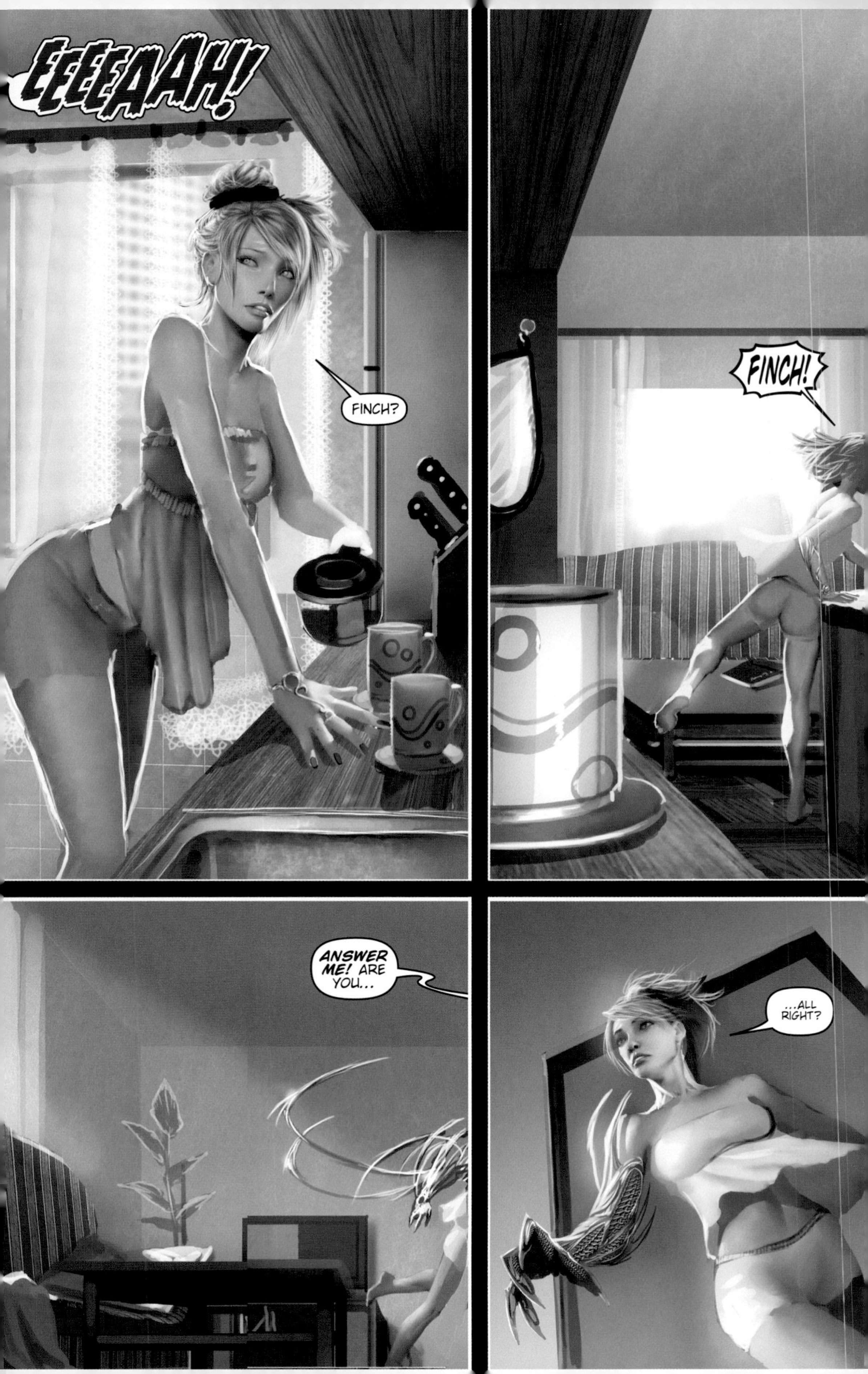
EEEEAAH!
FINCH?
FINCH!
ANSWER ME! ARE YOU...
...ALL RIGHT?

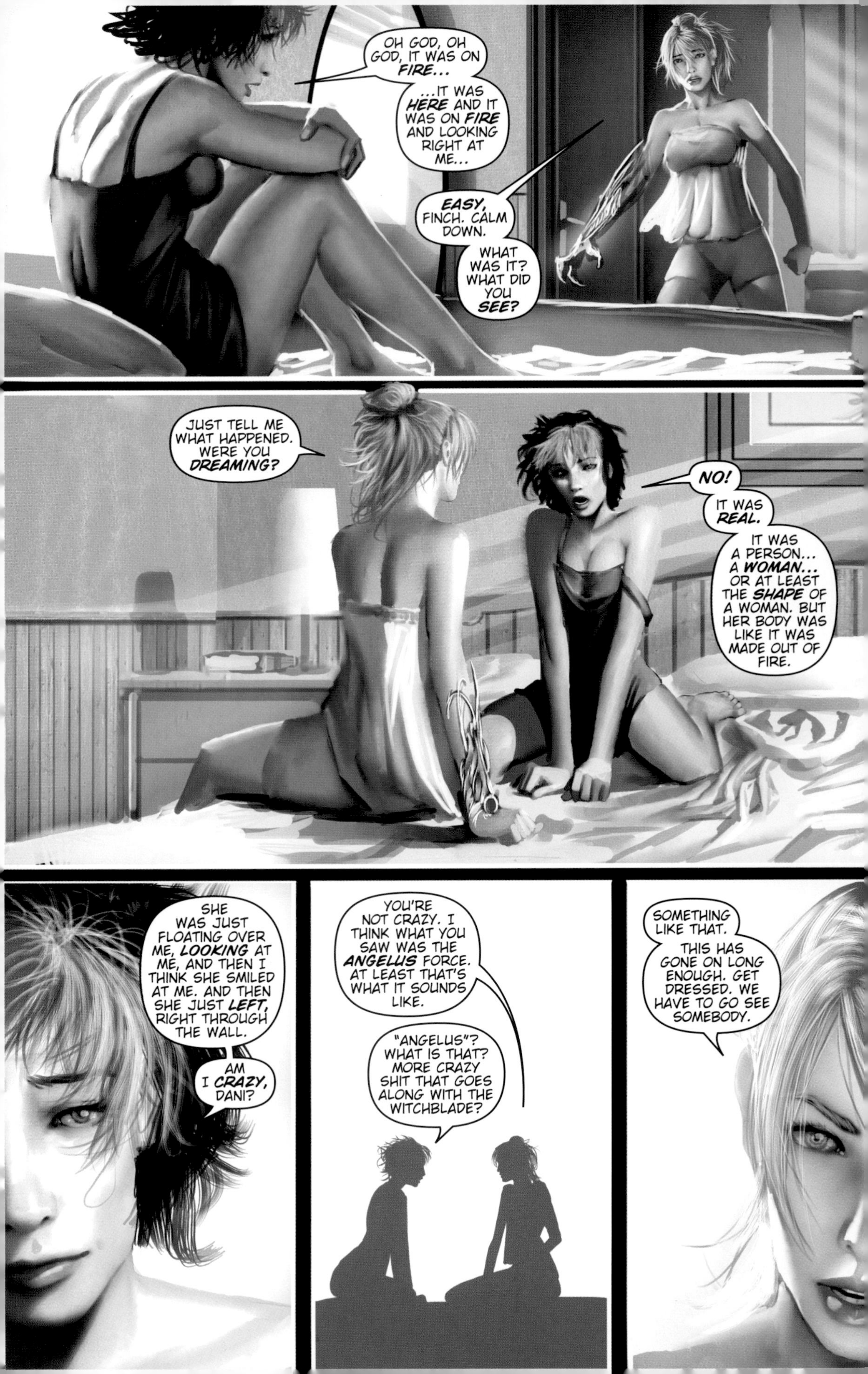
OH GOD, OH GOD, IT WAS ON FIRE...
...IT WAS HERE AND IT WAS ON FIRE AND LOOKING RIGHT AT ME...
EASY, FINCH. CALM DOWN.
WHAT WAS IT? WHAT DID YOU SEE?
JUST TELL ME WHAT HAPPENED. WERE YOU DREAMING?
NO!
IT WAS REAL.
IT WAS A PERSON... A WOMAN... OR AT LEAST THE SHAPE OF A WOMAN. BUT HER BODY WAS LIKE IT WAS MADE OUT OF FIRE.
SHE WAS JUST FLOATING OVER ME, LOOKING AT ME, AND THEN I THINK SHE SMILED AT ME. AND THEN SHE JUST LEFT, RIGHT THROUGH THE WALL.
AM I CRAZY, DANI?
YOU'RE NOT CRAZY. I THINK WHAT YOU SAW WAS THE ANGELUS FORCE. AT LEAST THAT'S WHAT IT SOUNDS LIKE.
"ANGELUS"? WHAT IS THAT? MORE CRAZY SHIT THAT GOES ALONG WITH THE WITCHBLADE?
SOMETHING LIKE THAT.
THIS HAS GONE ON LONG ENOUGH. GET DRESSED. WE HAVE TO GO SEE SOMEBODY.

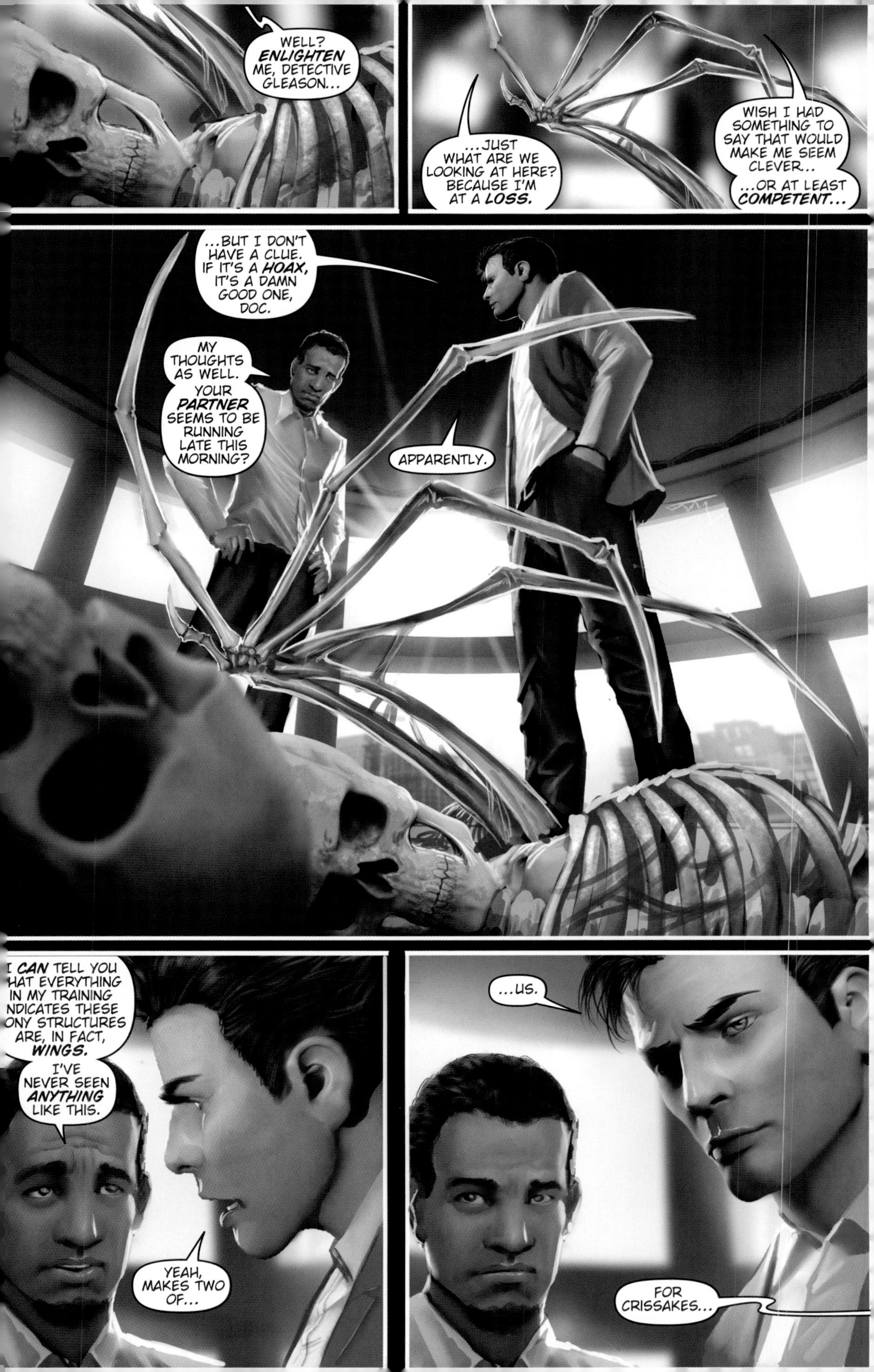
WELL? ENLIGHTEN ME, DETECTIVE GLEASON...
...JUST WHAT ARE WE LOOKING AT HERE? BECAUSE I'M AT A LOSS.
WISH I HAD SOMETHING TO SAY THAT WOULD MAKE ME SEEM CLEVER...
...OR AT LEAST COMPETENT...
...BUT I DON'T HAVE A CLUE. IF IT'S A HOAX, IT'S A DAMN GOOD ONE, DOC.
MY THOUGHTS AS WELL. YOUR PARTNER SEEMS TO BE RUNNING LATE THIS MORNING?
APPARENTLY.
I CAN TELL YOU HAT EVERYTHING IN MY TRAINING NDICATES THESE ONY STRUCTURES ARE, IN FACT, WINGS.
I'VE NEVER SEEN ANYTHING LIKE THIS.
YEAH, MAKES TWO OF...
...US.
FOR CRISSAKES...

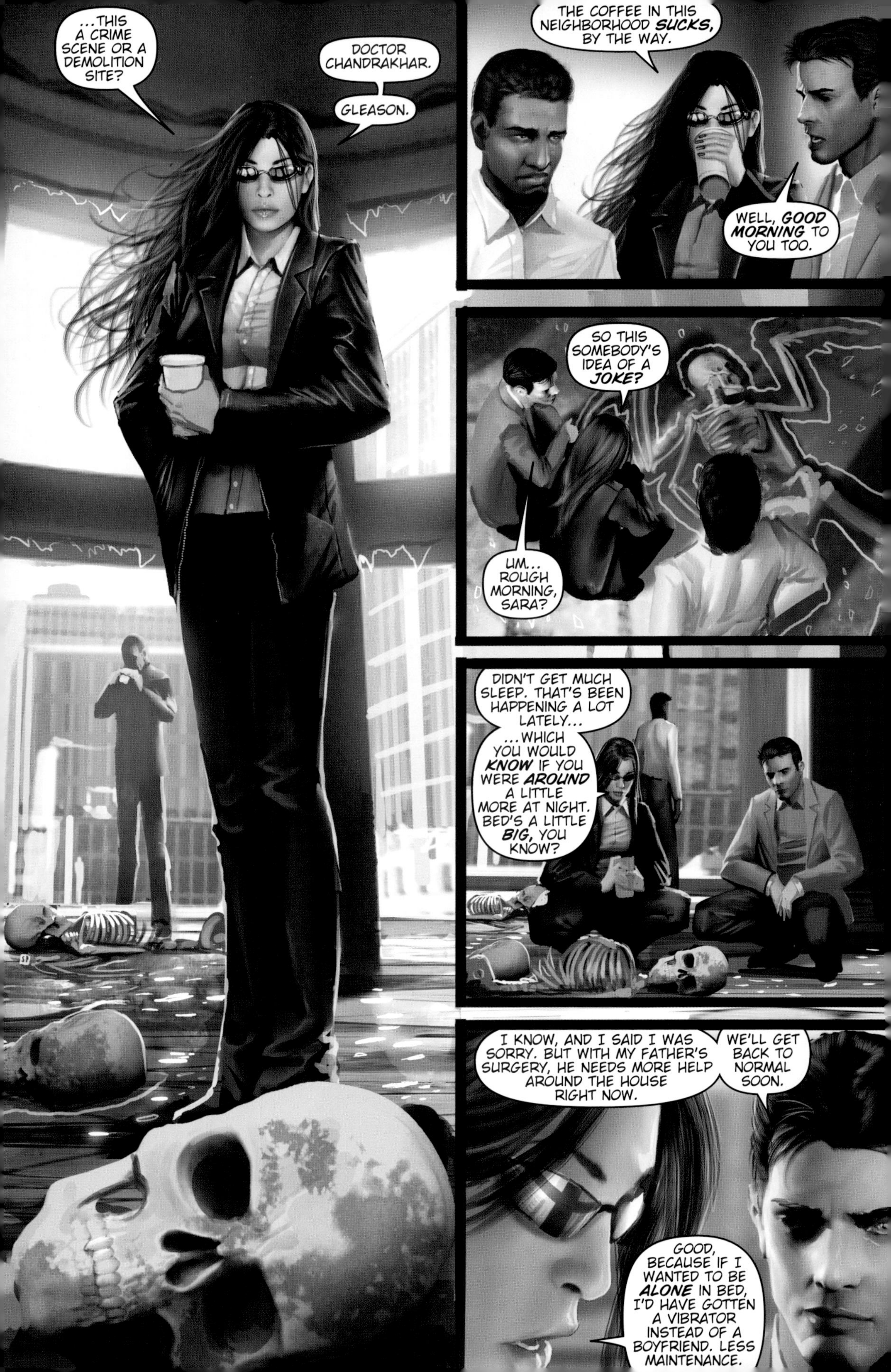
...THIS A CRIME SCENE OR A DEMOLITION SITE?
DOCTOR CHANDRAKHAR.
GLEASON.
THE COFFEE IN THIS NEIGHBORHOOD SUCKS, BY THE WAY.
WELL, GOOD MORNING TO YOU TOO.
SO THIS SOMEBODY'S IDEA OF A JOKE?
UM... ROUGH MORNING, SARA?
DIDN'T GET MUCH SLEEP. THAT'S BEEN HAPPENING A LOT LATELY...
...WHICH YOU WOULD KNOW IF YOU WERE AROUND A LITTLE MORE AT NIGHT. BED'S A LITTLE BIG, YOU KNOW?
I KNOW, AND I SAID I WAS SORRY. BUT WITH MY FATHER'S SURGERY, HE NEEDS MORE HELP AROUND THE HOUSE RIGHT NOW.
WE'LL GET BACK TO NORMAL SOON.
GOOD, BECAUSE IF I WANTED TO BE ALONE IN BED, I'D HAVE GOTTEN A VIBRATOR INSTEAD OF A BOYFRIEND. LESS MAINTENANCE.

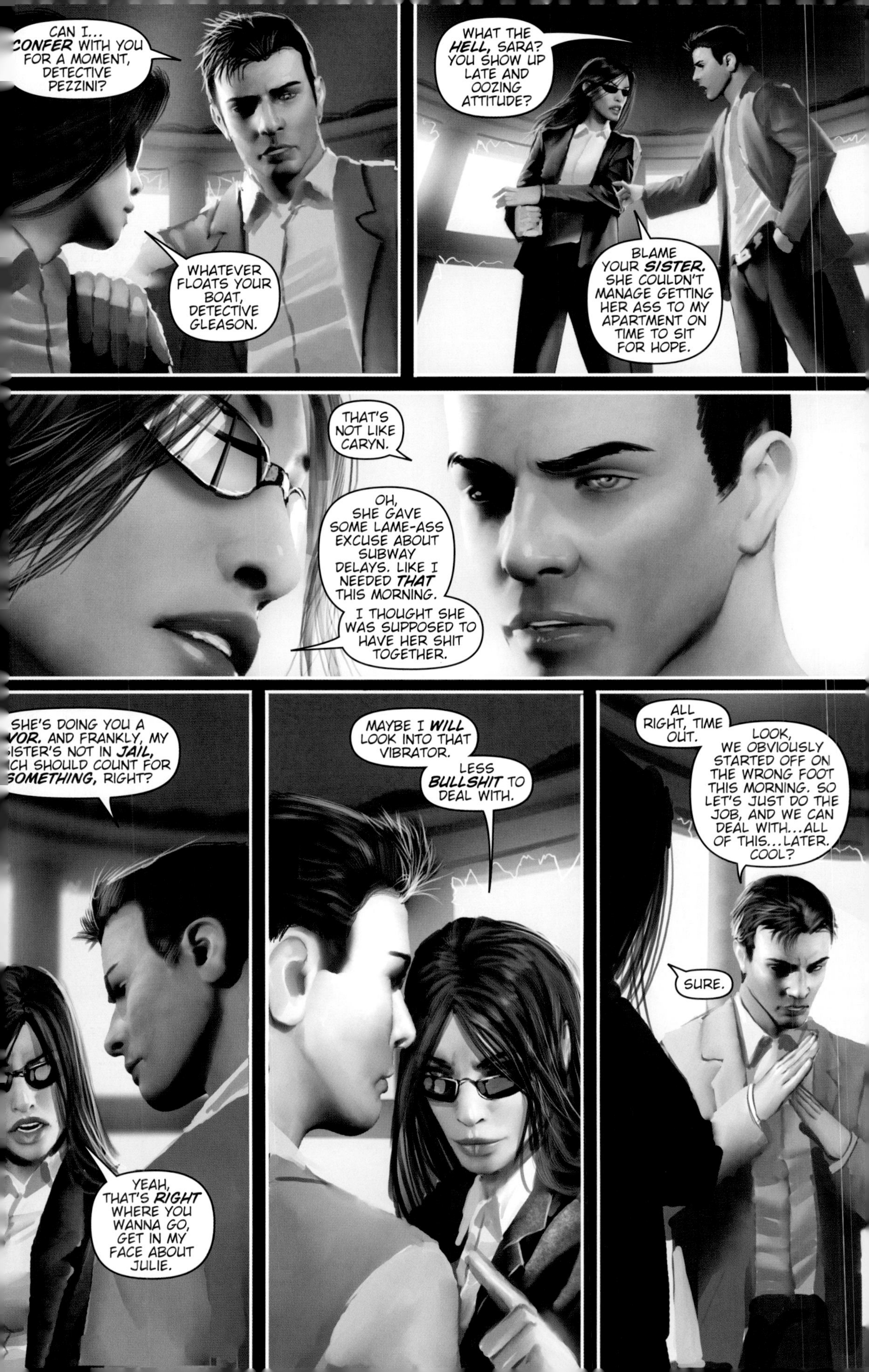
CAN I... CONFER WITH YOU FOR A MOMENT, DETECTIVE PEZZINI?
WHATEVER FLOATS YOUR BOAT, DETECTIVE GLEASON.
WHAT THE HELL, SARA? YOU SHOW UP LATE AND OOZING ATTITUDE?
BLAME YOUR SISTER. SHE COULDN'T MANAGE GETTING HER ASS TO MY APARTMENT ON TIME TO SIT FOR HOPE.
THAT'S NOT LIKE CARYN.
OH, SHE GAVE SOME LAME-ASS EXCUSE ABOUT SUBWAY DELAYS. LIKE I NEEDED THAT THIS MORNING.
I THOUGHT SHE WAS SUPPOSED TO HAVE HER SHIT TOGETHER.
SHE'S DOING YOU A VOR. AND FRANKLY, MY SISTER'S NOT IN JAIL, ICH SHOULD COUNT FOR SOMETHING, RIGHT?
YEAH, THAT'S RIGHT WHERE YOU WANNA GO, GET IN MY FACE ABOUT JULIE.
MAYBE I WILL LOOK INTO THAT VIBRATOR.
LESS BULLSHIT TO DEAL WITH.
ALL RIGHT, TIME OUT.
LOOK, WE OBVIOUSLY STARTED OFF ON THE WRONG FOOT THIS MORNING. SO LET'S JUST DO THE JOB, AND WE CAN DEAL WITH...ALL OF THIS...LATER. COOL?
SURE.

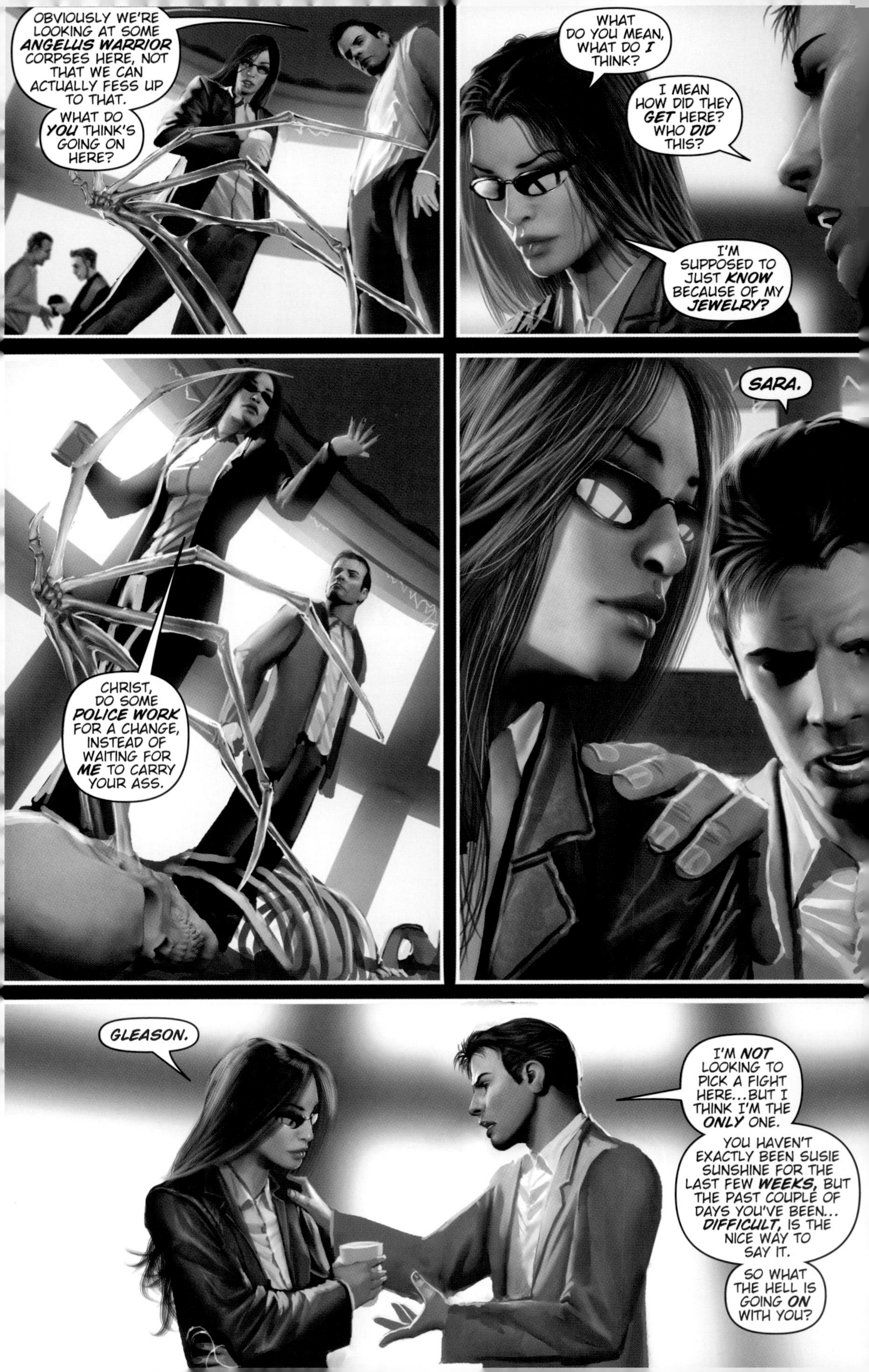

OBVIOUSLY WE'RE LOOKING AT SOME **ANGELUS WARRIOR** CORPSES HERE, NOT THAT WE CAN ACTUALLY FESS UP TO THAT.
WHAT DO **YOU** THINK'S GOING ON HERE?
WHAT DO YOU MEAN, WHAT DO **I** THINK?
I MEAN HOW DID THEY **GET** HERE? WHO **DID** THIS?
I'M SUPPOSED TO JUST **KNOW** BECAUSE OF MY **JEWELRY?**
CHRIST, DO SOME **POLICE WORK** FOR A CHANGE, INSTEAD OF WAITING FOR **ME** TO CARRY YOUR ASS.
SARA.
GLEASON.
I'M **NOT** LOOKING TO PICK A FIGHT HERE...BUT I THINK I'M THE **ONLY** ONE.
YOU HAVEN'T EXACTLY BEEN SUSIE SUNSHINE FOR THE LAST FEW **WEEKS,** BUT THE PAST COUPLE OF DAYS YOU'VE BEEN... **DIFFICULT,** IS THE NICE WAY TO SAY IT.
SO WHAT THE HELL IS GOING **ON** WITH YOU?

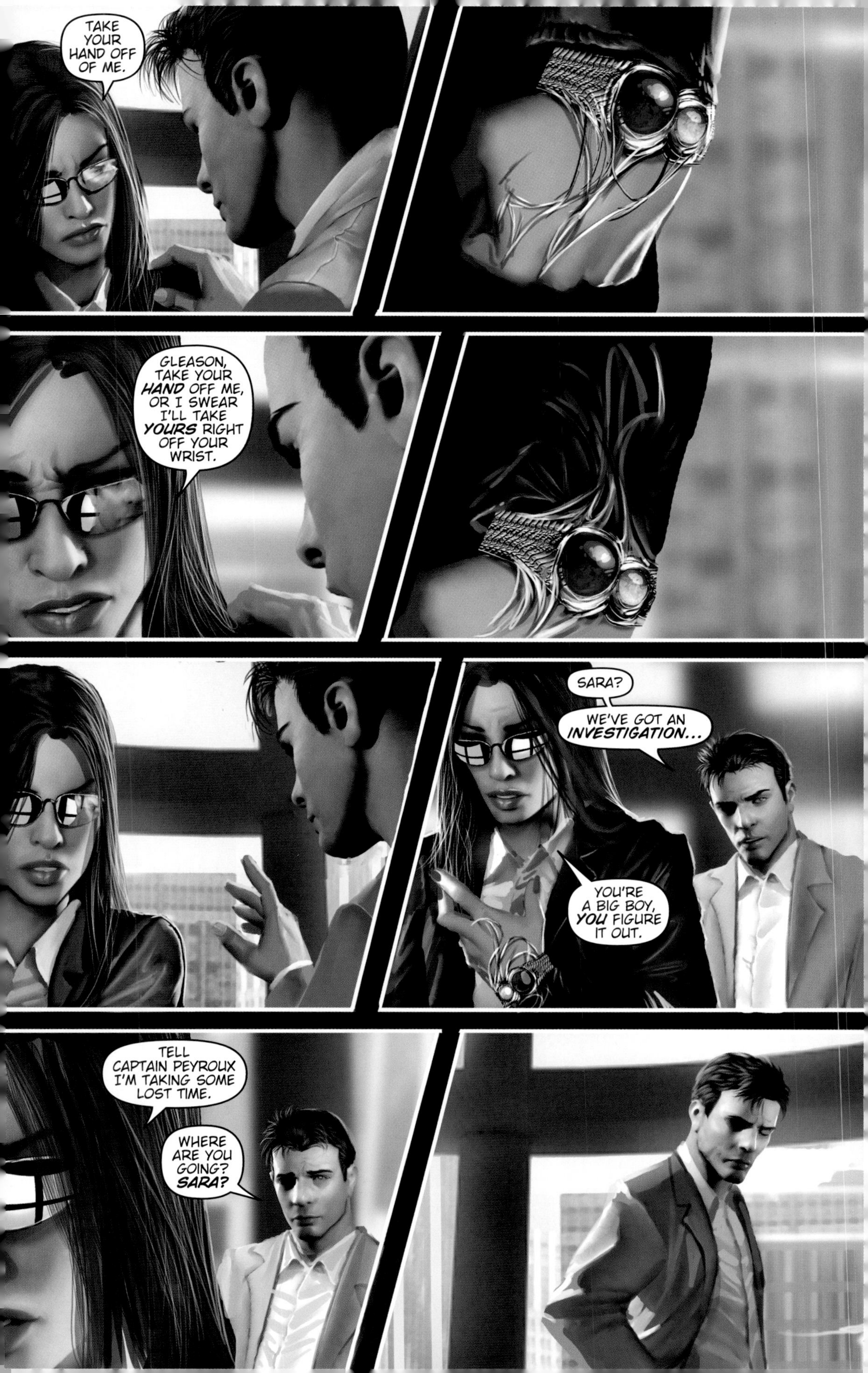
TAKE YOUR HAND OFF OF ME.
GLEASON, TAKE YOUR *HAND* OFF ME, OR I SWEAR I'LL TAKE *YOURS* RIGHT OFF YOUR WRIST.
SARA?
WE'VE GOT AN *INVESTIGATION...*
YOU'RE A BIG BOY, *YOU* FIGURE IT OUT.
TELL CAPTAIN PEYROUX I'M TAKING SOME LOST TIME.
WHERE ARE YOU GOING? *SARA?*

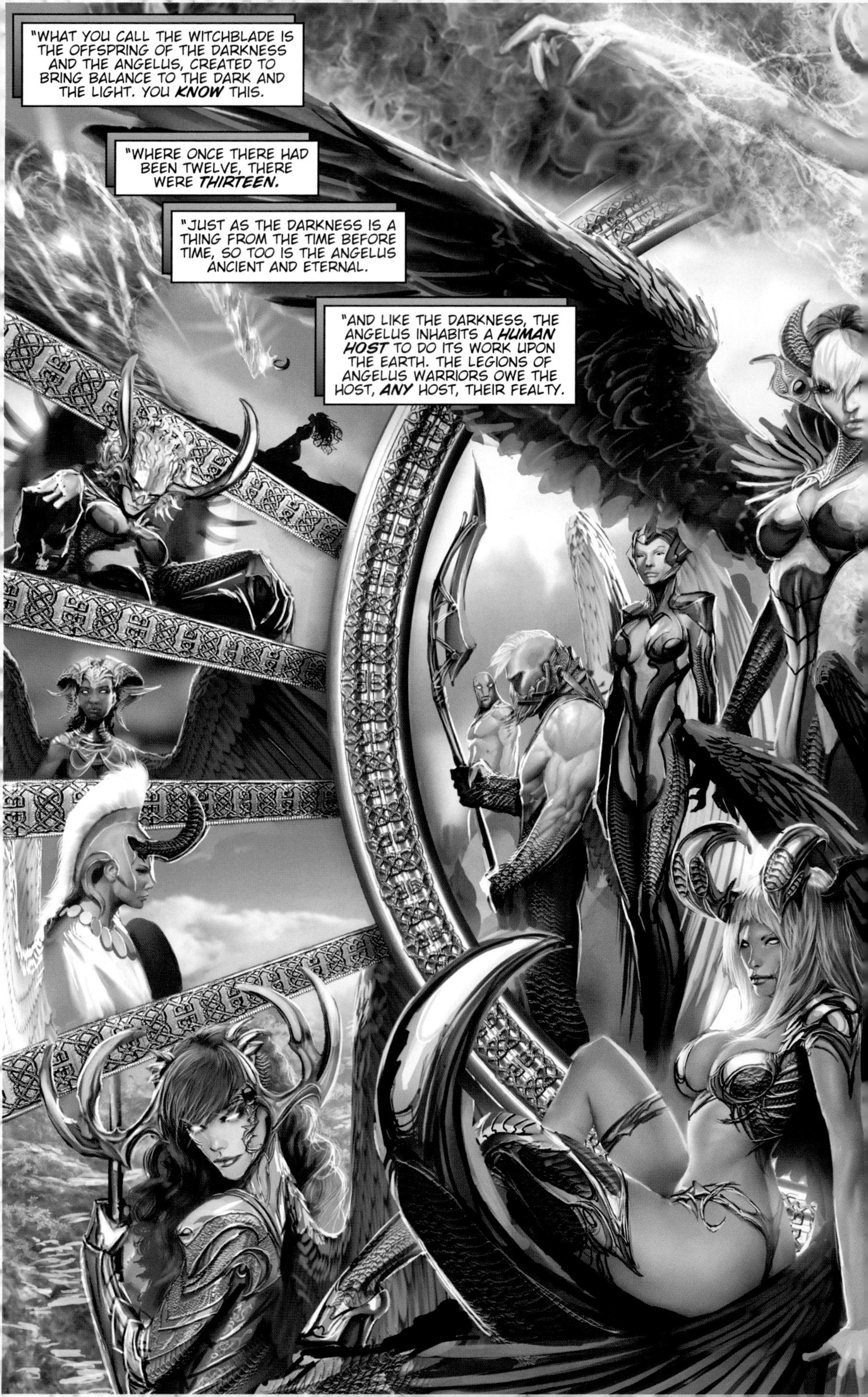
"WHAT YOU CALL THE WITCHBLADE IS THE OFFSPRING OF THE DARKNESS AND THE ANGELUS, CREATED TO BRING BALANCE TO THE DARK AND THE LIGHT. YOU KNOW THIS.
"WHERE ONCE THERE HAD BEEN TWELVE, THERE WERE THIRTEEN.
"JUST AS THE DARKNESS IS A THING FROM THE TIME BEFORE TIME, SO TOO IS THE ANGELUS ANCIENT AND ETERNAL.
"AND LIKE THE DARKNESS, THE ANGELUS INHABITS A HUMAN HOST TO DO ITS WORK UPON THE EARTH. THE LEGIONS OF ANGELUS WARRIORS OWE THE HOST, ANY HOST, THEIR FEALTY.

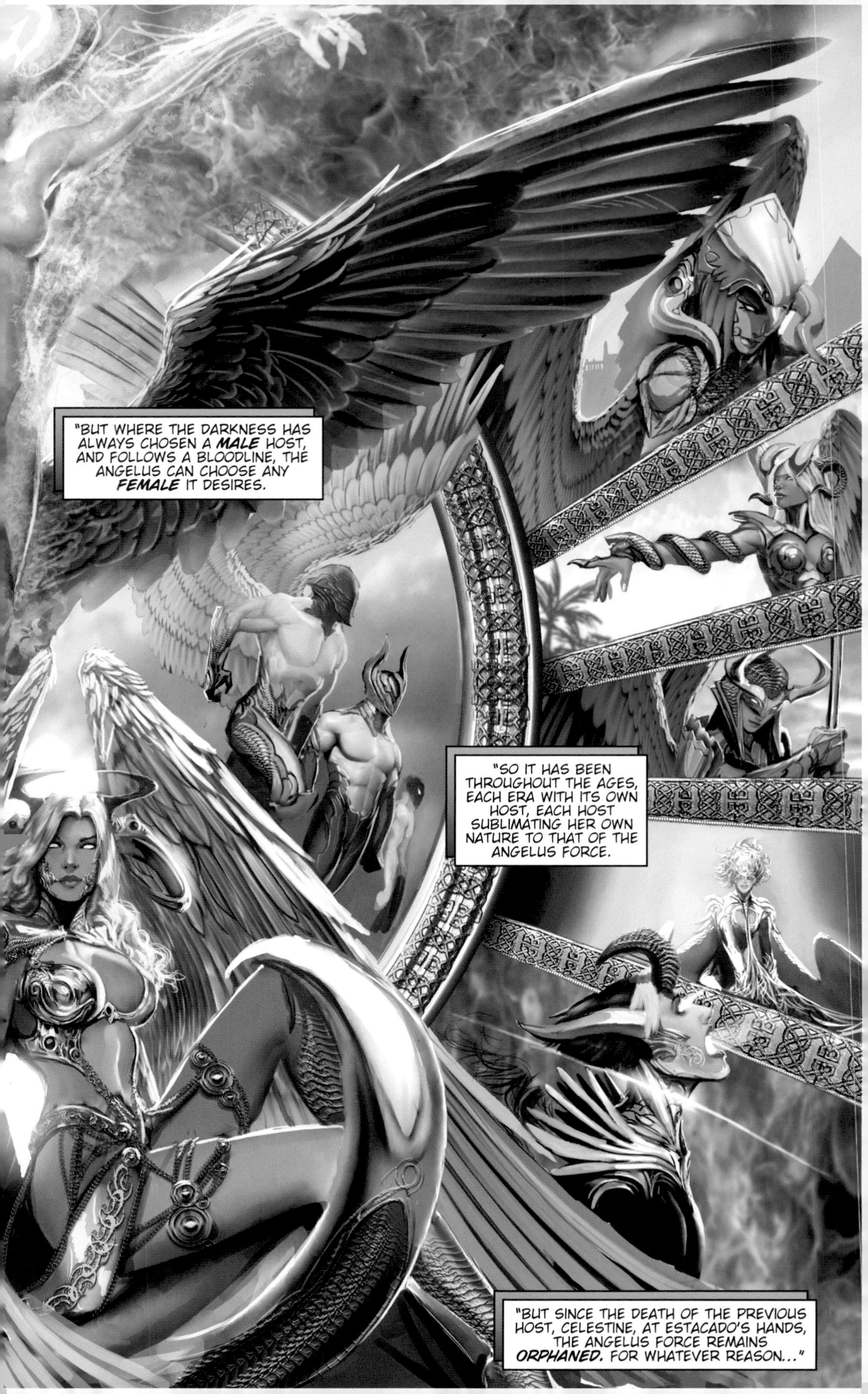
"BUT WHERE THE DARKNESS HAS ALWAYS CHOSEN A **MALE** HOST, AND FOLLOWS A BLOODLINE, THE ANGELUS CAN CHOOSE ANY **FEMALE** IT DESIRES.
"SO IT HAS BEEN THROUGHOUT THE AGES, EACH ERA WITH ITS OWN HOST, EACH HOST SUBLIMATING HER OWN NATURE TO THAT OF THE ANGELUS FORCE.
"BUT SINCE THE DEATH OF THE PREVIOUS HOST, CELESTINE, AT ESTACADO'S HANDS, THE ANGELUS FORCE REMAINS **ORPHANED**. FOR WHATEVER REASON..."

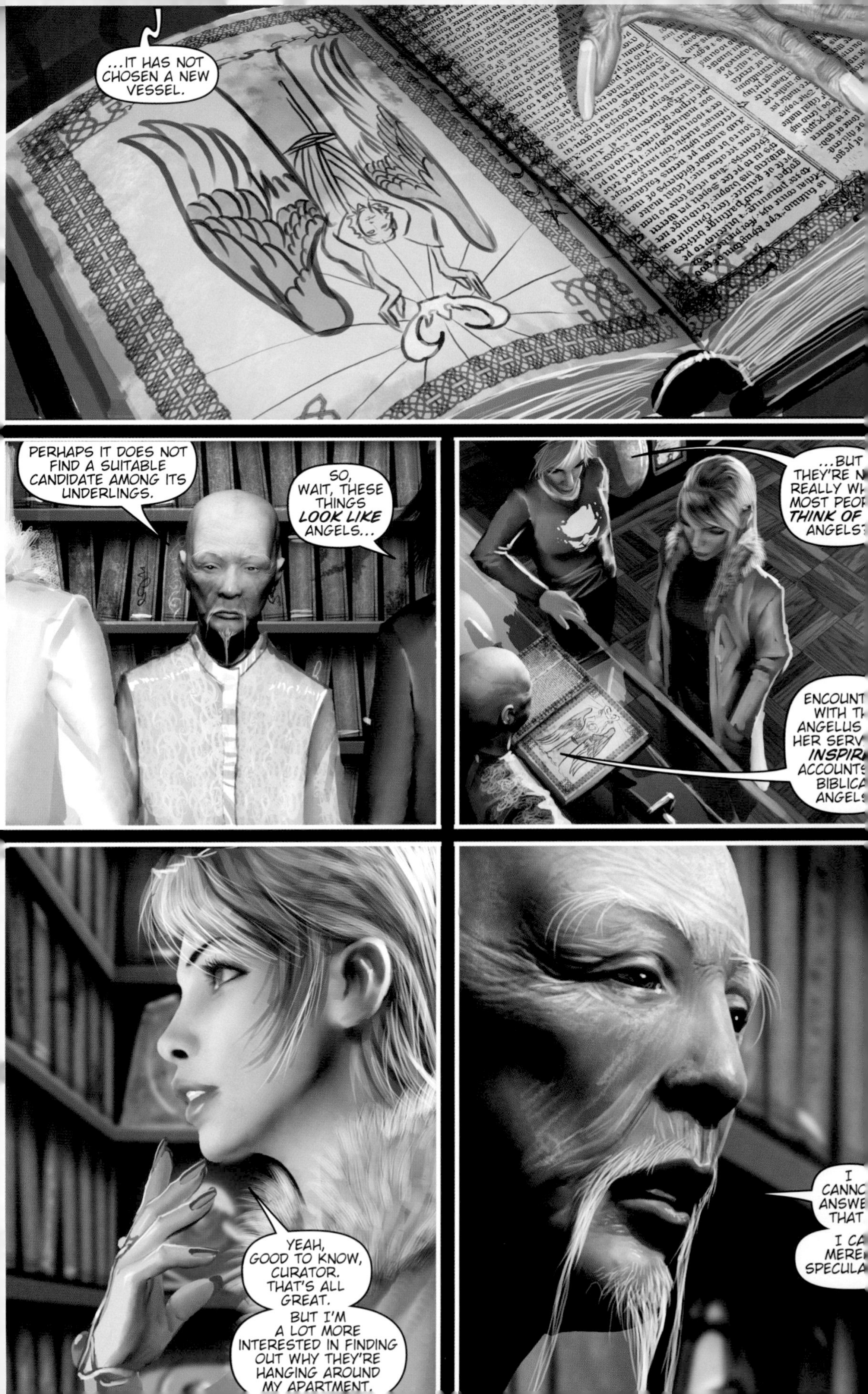

...IT HAS NOT CHOSEN A NEW VESSEL.
PERHAPS IT DOES NOT FIND A SUITABLE CANDIDATE AMONG ITS UNDERLINGS.
SO, WAIT, THESE THINGS *LOOK LIKE* ANGELS...
...BUT THEY'RE N REALLY WH MOST PEOP *THINK OF* ANGELS
ENCOUNT WITH TH ANGELUS HER SERV *INSPIR* ACCOUNTS BIBLICA ANGELS
YEAH, GOOD TO KNOW, CURATOR. THAT'S ALL GREAT.
BUT I'M A LOT MORE INTERESTED IN FINDING OUT WHY THEY'RE HANGING AROUND MY APARTMENT.
I CANNO ANSWE THAT
I CA MERE SPECULA

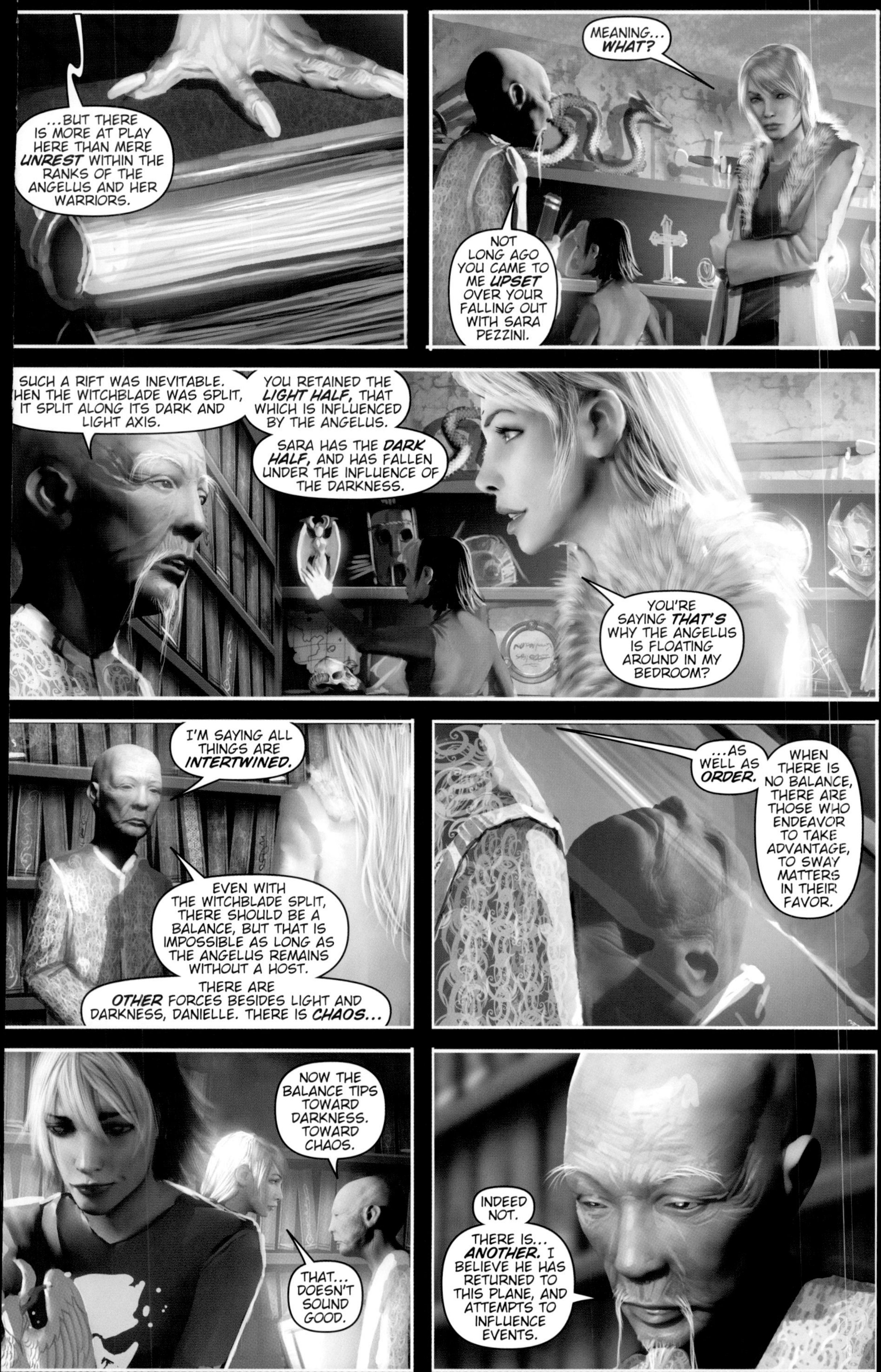
...BUT THERE IS MORE AT PLAY HERE THAN MERE UNREST WITHIN THE RANKS OF THE ANGELUS AND HER WARRIORS.
MEANING... WHAT?
NOT LONG AGO YOU CAME TO ME UPSET OVER YOUR FALLING OUT WITH SARA PEZZINI.
SUCH A RIFT WAS INEVITABLE. HEN THE WITCHBLADE WAS SPLIT, IT SPLIT ALONG ITS DARK AND LIGHT AXIS.
YOU RETAINED THE LIGHT HALF, THAT WHICH IS INFLUENCED BY THE ANGELUS.
SARA HAS THE DARK HALF, AND HAS FALLEN UNDER THE INFLUENCE OF THE DARKNESS.
YOU'RE SAYING THAT'S WHY THE ANGELUS IS FLOATING AROUND IN MY BEDROOM?
I'M SAYING ALL THINGS ARE INTERTWINED.
EVEN WITH THE WITCHBLADE SPLIT, THERE SHOULD BE A BALANCE, BUT THAT IS IMPOSSIBLE AS LONG AS THE ANGELUS REMAINS WITHOUT A HOST.
THERE ARE OTHER FORCES BESIDES LIGHT AND DARKNESS, DANIELLE. THERE IS CHAOS...
...AS WELL AS ORDER.
WHEN THERE IS NO BALANCE, THERE ARE THOSE WHO ENDEAVOR TO TAKE ADVANTAGE, TO SWAY MATTERS IN THEIR FAVOR.
NOW THE BALANCE TIPS TOWARD DARKNESS. TOWARD CHAOS.
THAT... DOESN'T SOUND GOOD.
INDEED NOT.
THERE IS... ANOTHER. I BELIEVE HE HAS RETURNED TO THIS PLANE, AND ATTEMPTS TO INFLUENCE EVENTS.

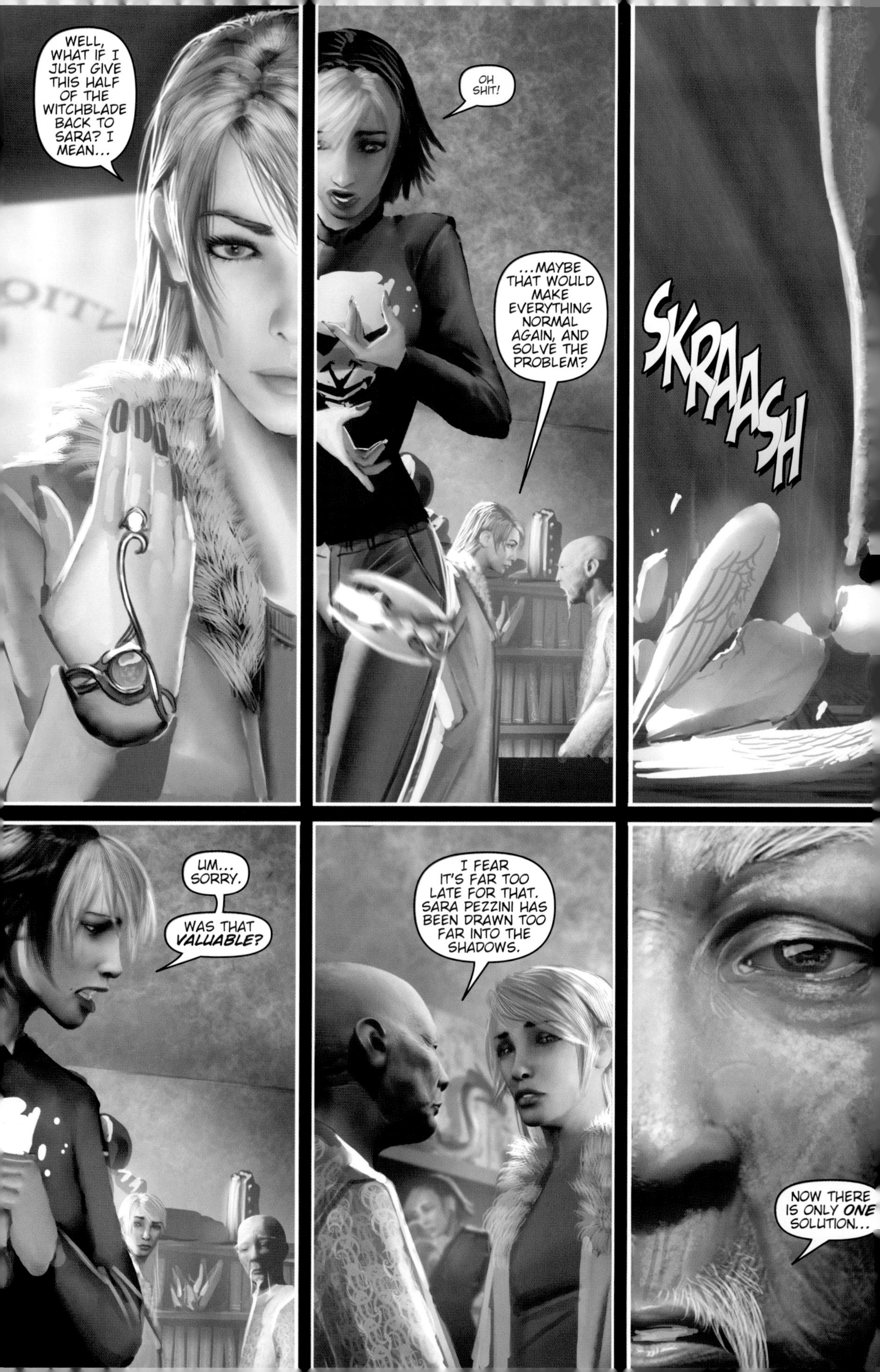
WELL, WHAT IF I JUST GIVE THIS HALF OF THE WITCHBLADE BACK TO SARA? I MEAN...
OH SHIT!
...MAYBE THAT WOULD MAKE EVERYTHING NORMAL AGAIN, AND SOLVE THE PROBLEM?
SKRAASH
UM... SORRY.
WAS THAT *VALUABLE?*
I FEAR IT'S FAR TOO LATE FOR THAT. SARA PEZZINI HAS BEEN DRAWN TOO FAR INTO THE SHADOWS.
NOW THERE IS ONLY *ONE* SOLUTION...

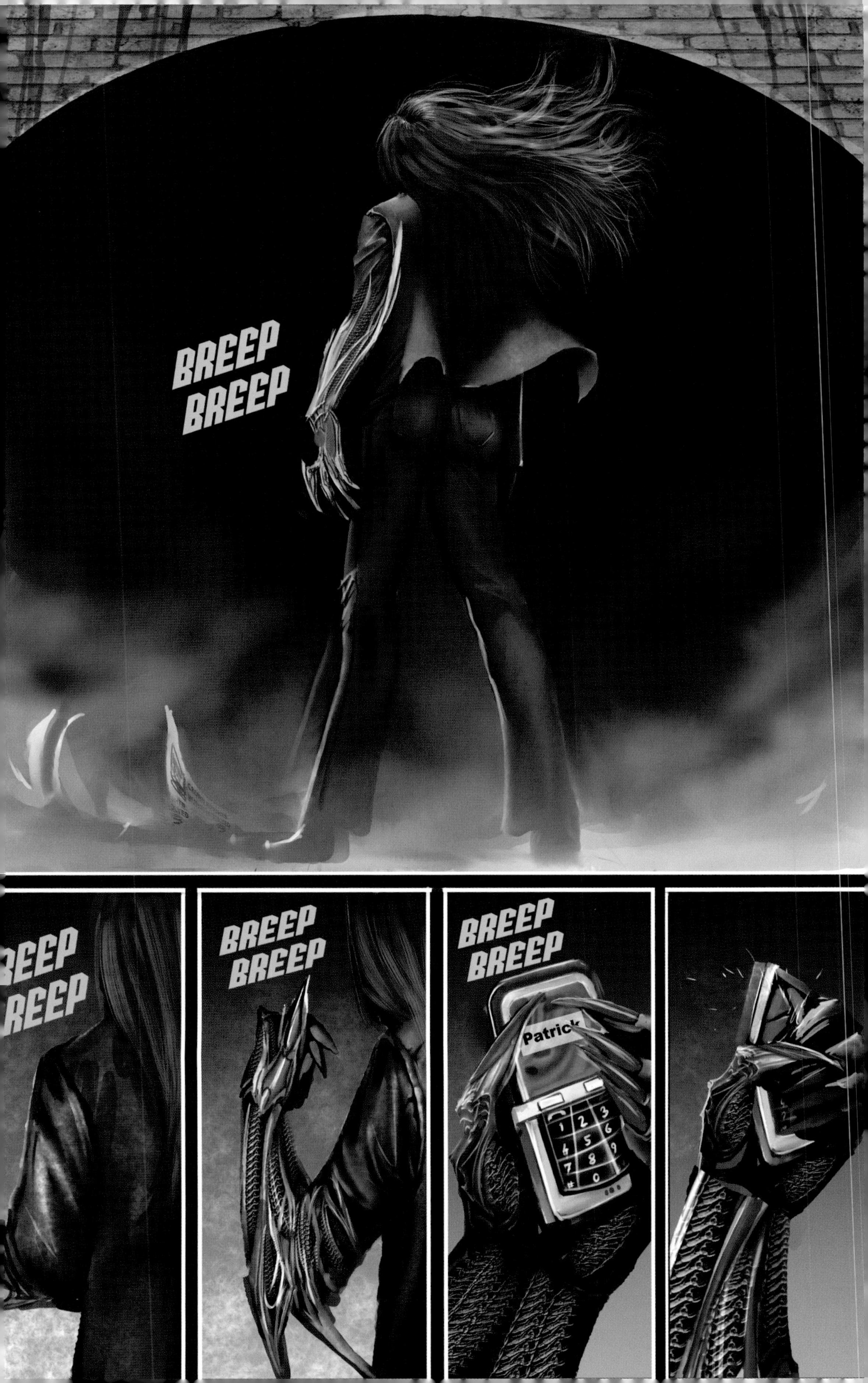
BREEP
BREEP
BREEP
BREEP
BREEP
BREEP
Patrick

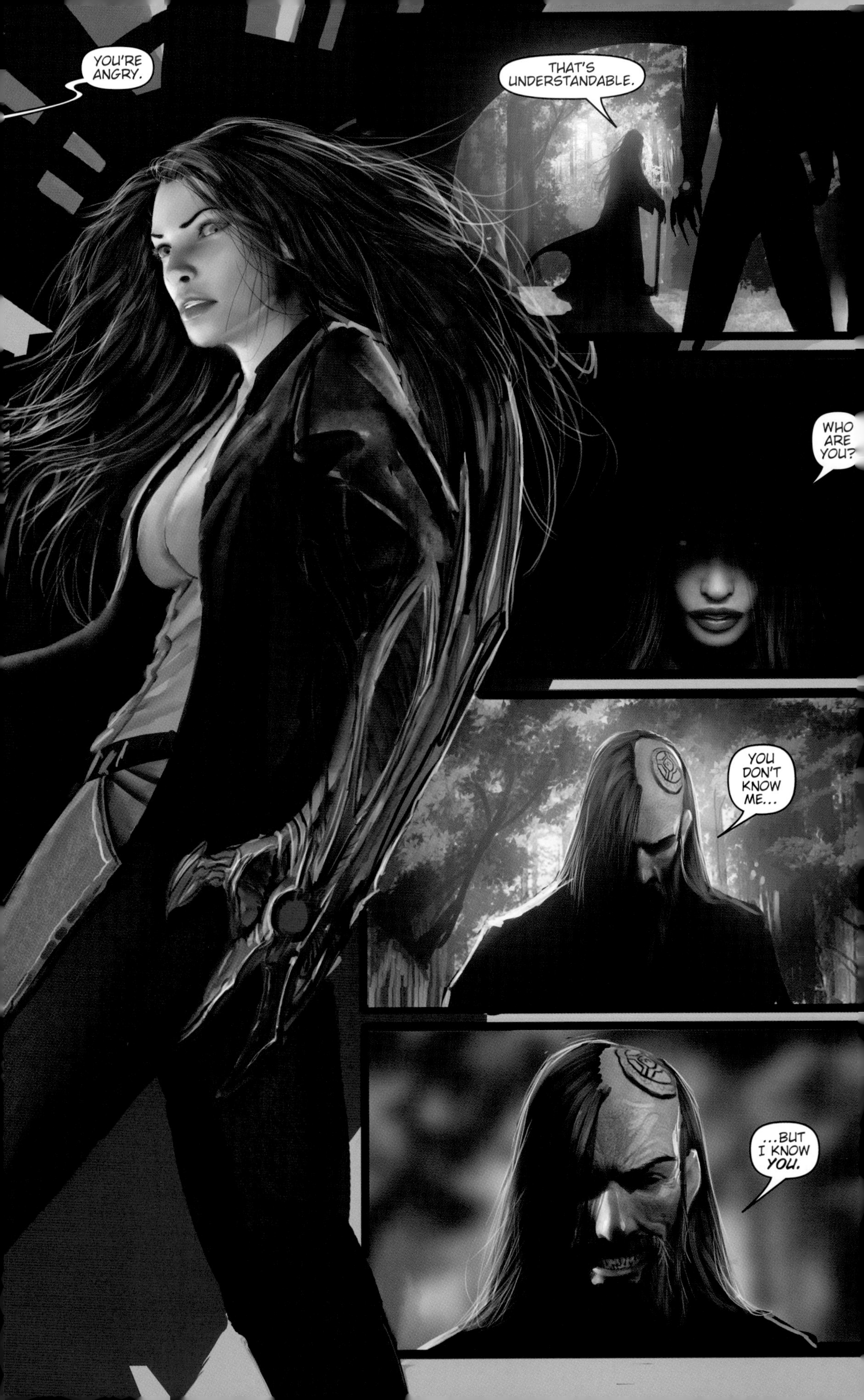
YOU'RE ANGRY.
THAT'S UNDERSTANDABLE.
WHO ARE YOU?
YOU DON'T KNOW ME...
...BUT I KNOW *YOU.*

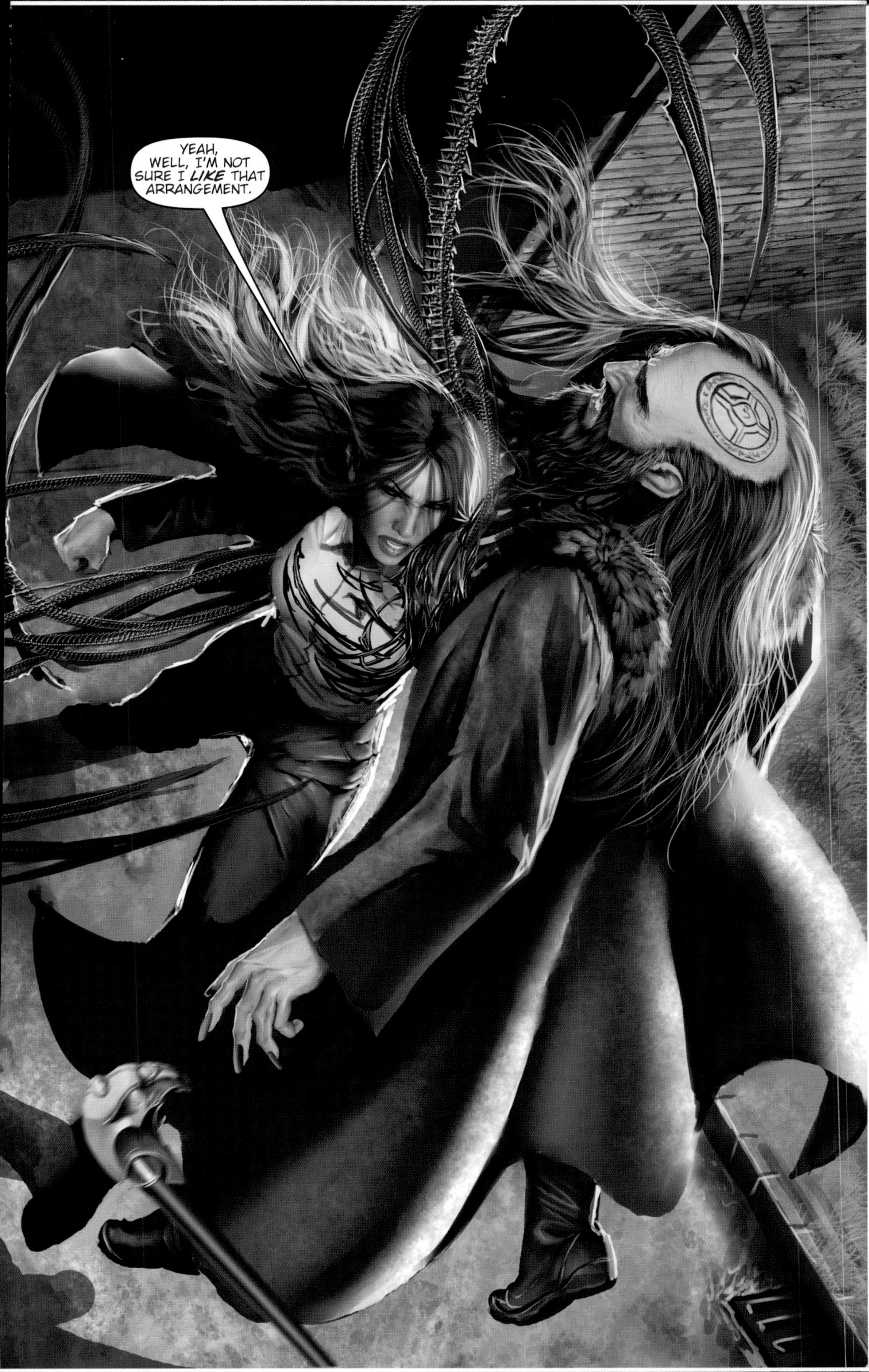
YEAH, WELL, I'M NOT SURE I LIKE THAT ARRANGEMENT.

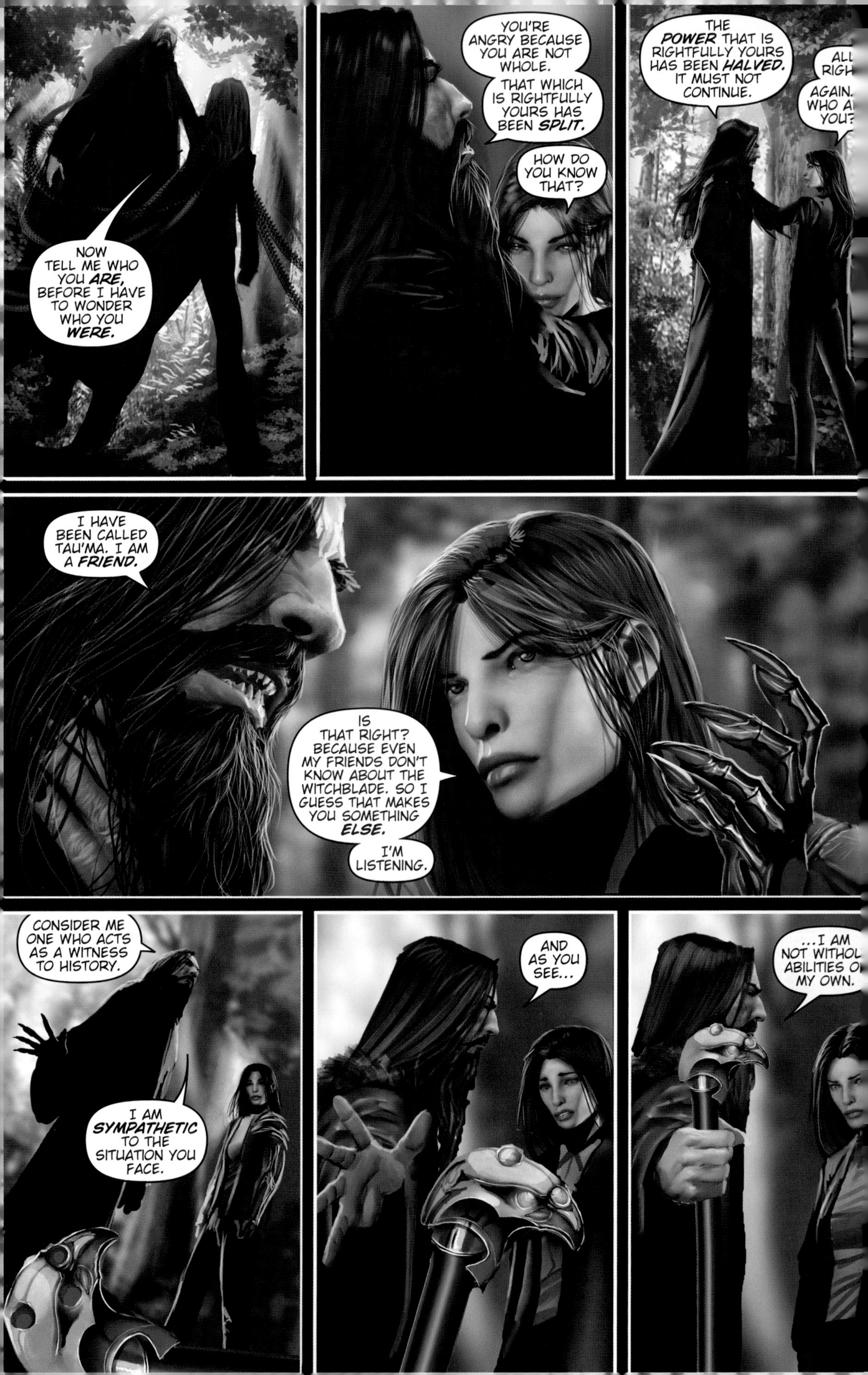
NOW TELL ME WHO YOU ARE, BEFORE I HAVE TO WONDER WHO YOU WERE.
YOU'RE ANGRY BECAUSE YOU ARE NOT WHOLE.
THAT WHICH IS RIGHTFULLY YOURS HAS BEEN SPLIT.
HOW DO YOU KNOW THAT?
THE POWER THAT IS RIGHTFULLY YOURS HAS BEEN HALVED. IT MUST NOT CONTINUE.
ALL RIGH
AGAIN. WHO A YOU?
I HAVE BEEN CALLED TAU'MA. I AM A FRIEND.
IS THAT RIGHT? BECAUSE EVEN MY FRIENDS DON'T KNOW ABOUT THE WITCHBLADE. SO I GUESS THAT MAKES YOU SOMETHING ELSE.
I'M LISTENING.
CONSIDER ME ONE WHO ACTS AS A WITNESS TO HISTORY.
I AM SYMPATHETIC TO THE SITUATION YOU FACE.
AND AS YOU SEE...
...I AM NOT WITHOU ABILITIES O MY OWN.

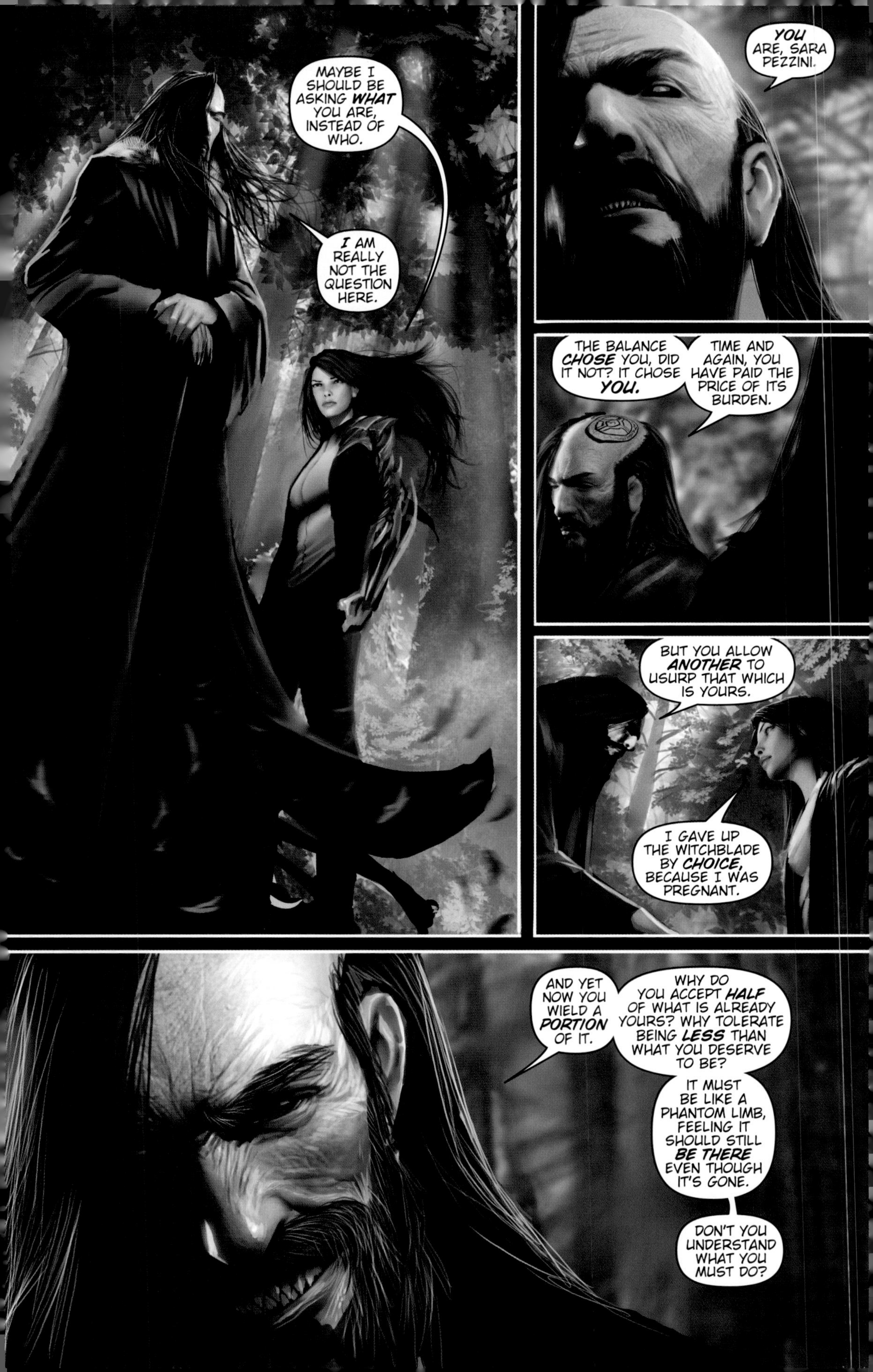
MAYBE I SHOULD BE ASKING WHAT YOU ARE, INSTEAD OF WHO.
I AM REALLY NOT THE QUESTION HERE.
YOU ARE, SARA PEZZINI.
THE BALANCE CHOSE YOU, DID IT NOT? IT CHOSE YOU.
TIME AND AGAIN, YOU HAVE PAID THE PRICE OF ITS BURDEN.
BUT YOU ALLOW ANOTHER TO USURP THAT WHICH IS YOURS.
I GAVE UP THE WITCHBLADE BY CHOICE, BECAUSE I WAS PREGNANT.
AND YET NOW YOU WIELD A PORTION OF IT.
WHY DO YOU ACCEPT HALF OF WHAT IS ALREADY YOURS? WHY TOLERATE BEING LESS THAN WHAT YOU DESERVE TO BE?
IT MUST BE LIKE A PHANTOM LIMB, FEELING IT SHOULD STILL BE THERE EVEN THOUGH IT'S GONE.
DON'T YOU UNDERSTAND WHAT YOU MUST DO?

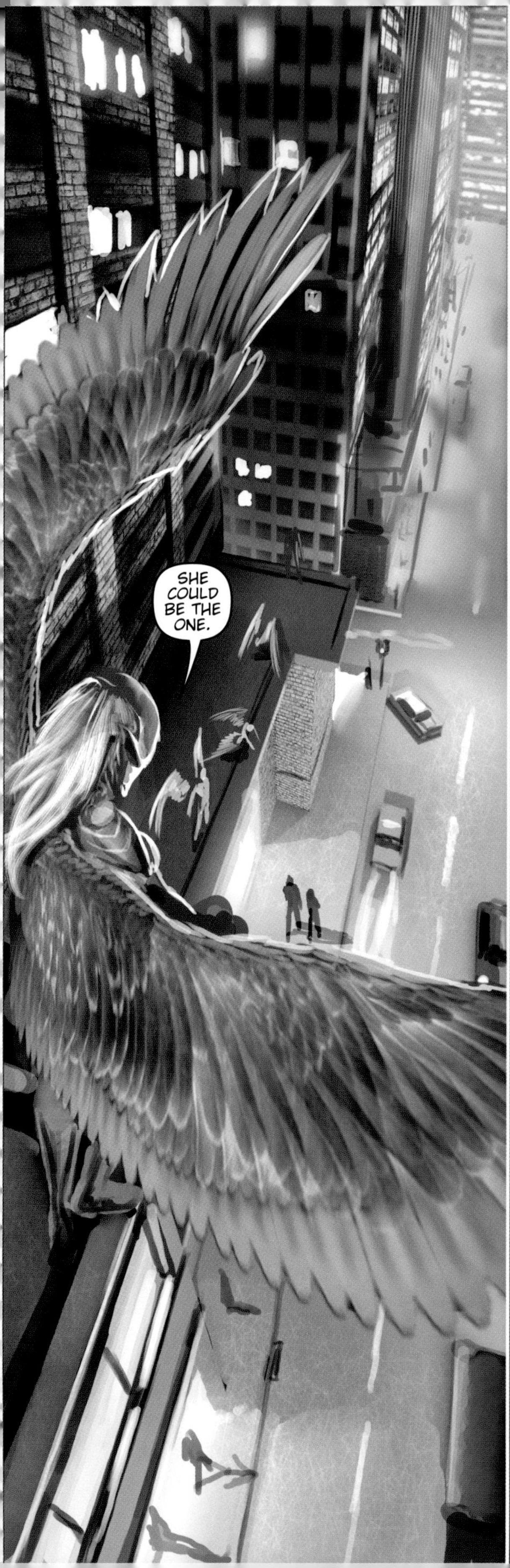
SHE COULD BE THE ONE.

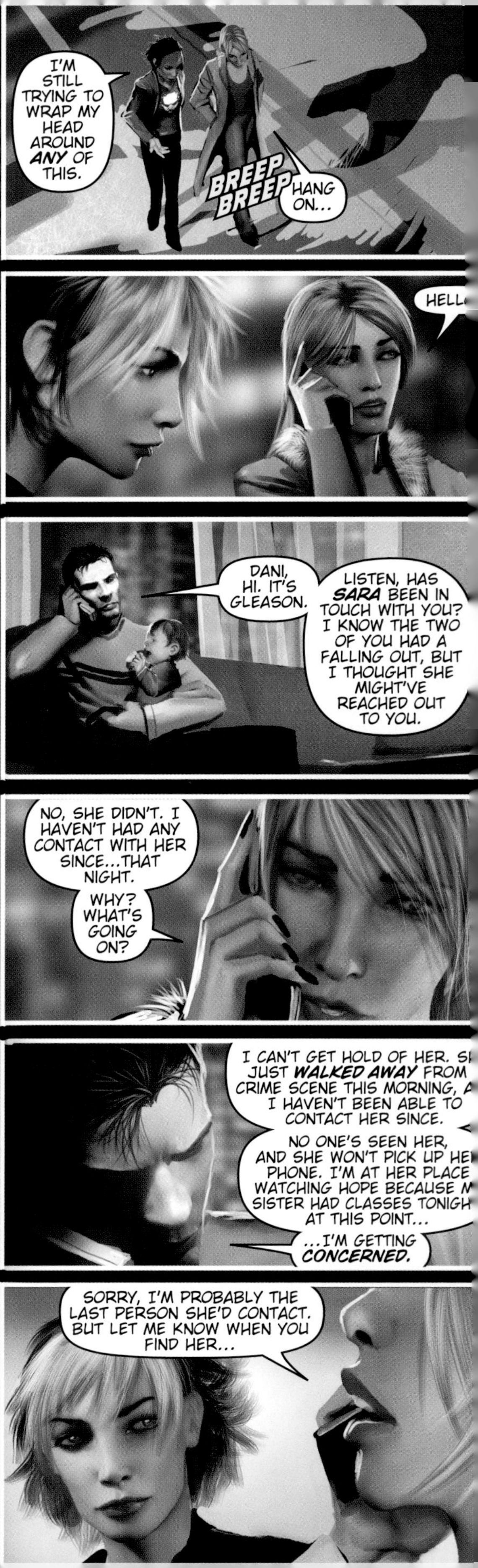
I'M STILL TRYING TO WRAP MY HEAD AROUND ANY OF THIS.
BREEP BREEP
HANG ON...
HELL
DANI, HI. IT'S GLEASON.
LISTEN, HAS SARA BEEN IN TOUCH WITH YOU? I KNOW THE TWO OF YOU HAD A FALLING OUT, BUT I THOUGHT SHE MIGHT'VE REACHED OUT TO YOU.
NO, SHE DIDN'T. I HAVEN'T HAD ANY CONTACT WITH HER SINCE...THAT NIGHT.
WHY? WHAT'S GOING ON?
I CAN'T GET HOLD OF HER. SH JUST WALKED AWAY FROM CRIME SCENE THIS MORNING, A I HAVEN'T BEEN ABLE TO CONTACT HER SINCE.
NO ONE'S SEEN HER, AND SHE WON'T PICK UP HE PHONE. I'M AT HER PLACE WATCHING HOPE BECAUSE M SISTER HAD CLASSES TONIGH AT THIS POINT...
...I'M GETTING CONCERNED.
SORRY, I'M PROBABLY THE LAST PERSON SHE'D CONTACT. BUT LET ME KNOW WHEN YOU FIND HER...

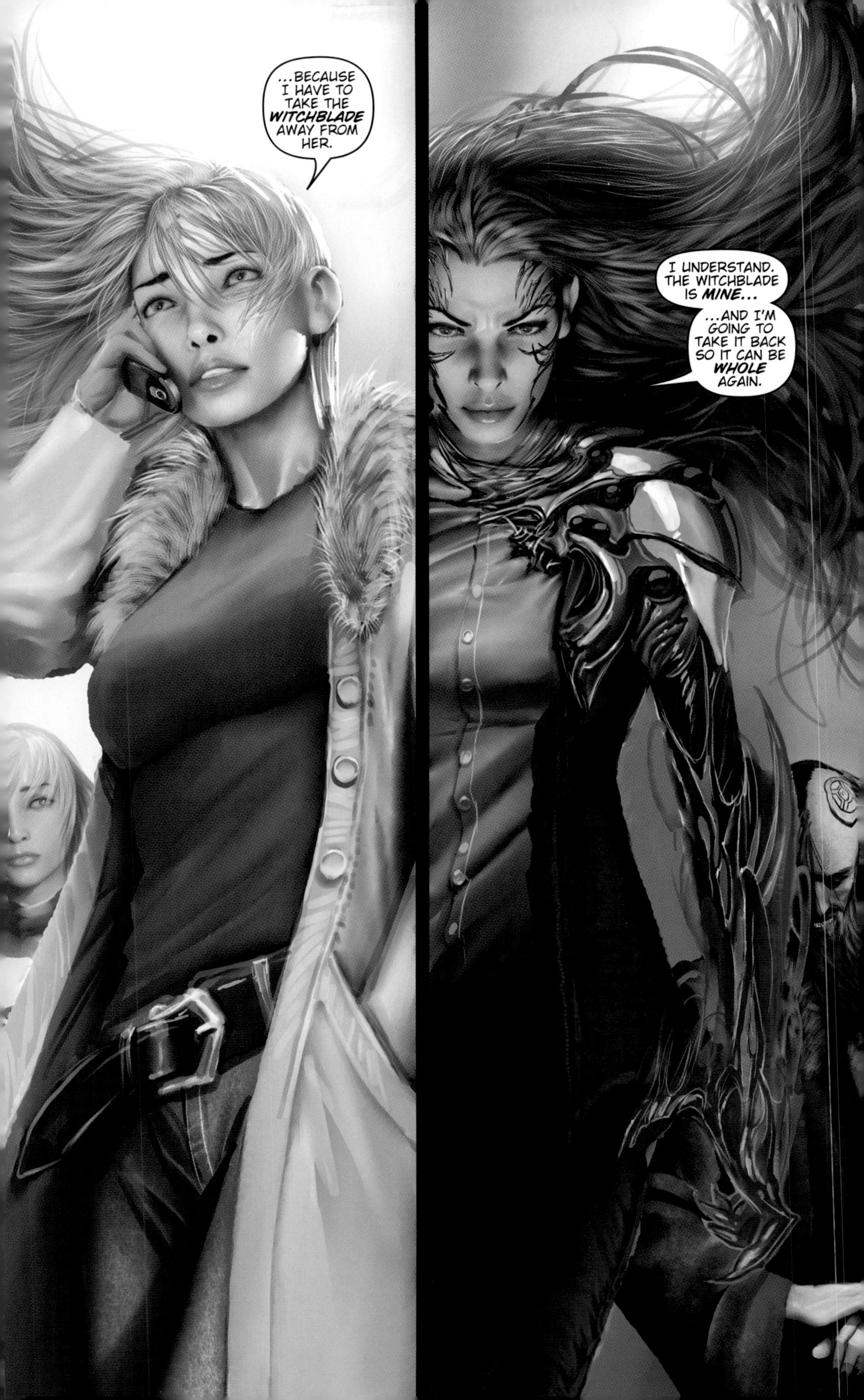

...BECAUSE I HAVE TO TAKE THE **WITCHBLADE** AWAY FROM HER.
I UNDERSTAND. THE WITCHBLADE IS **MINE...**
...AND I'M GOING TO TAKE IT BACK SO IT CAN BE **WHOLE** AGAIN.

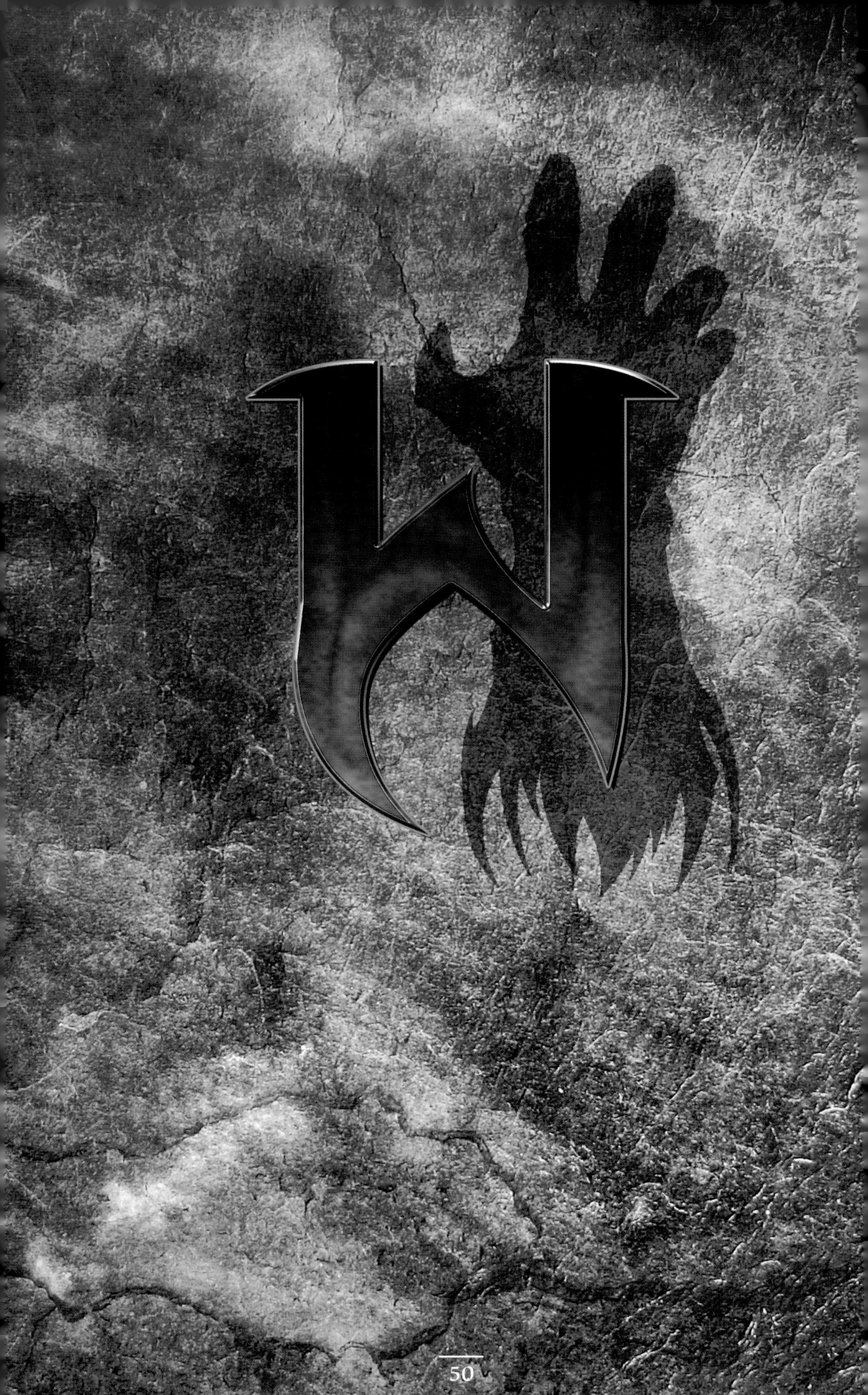

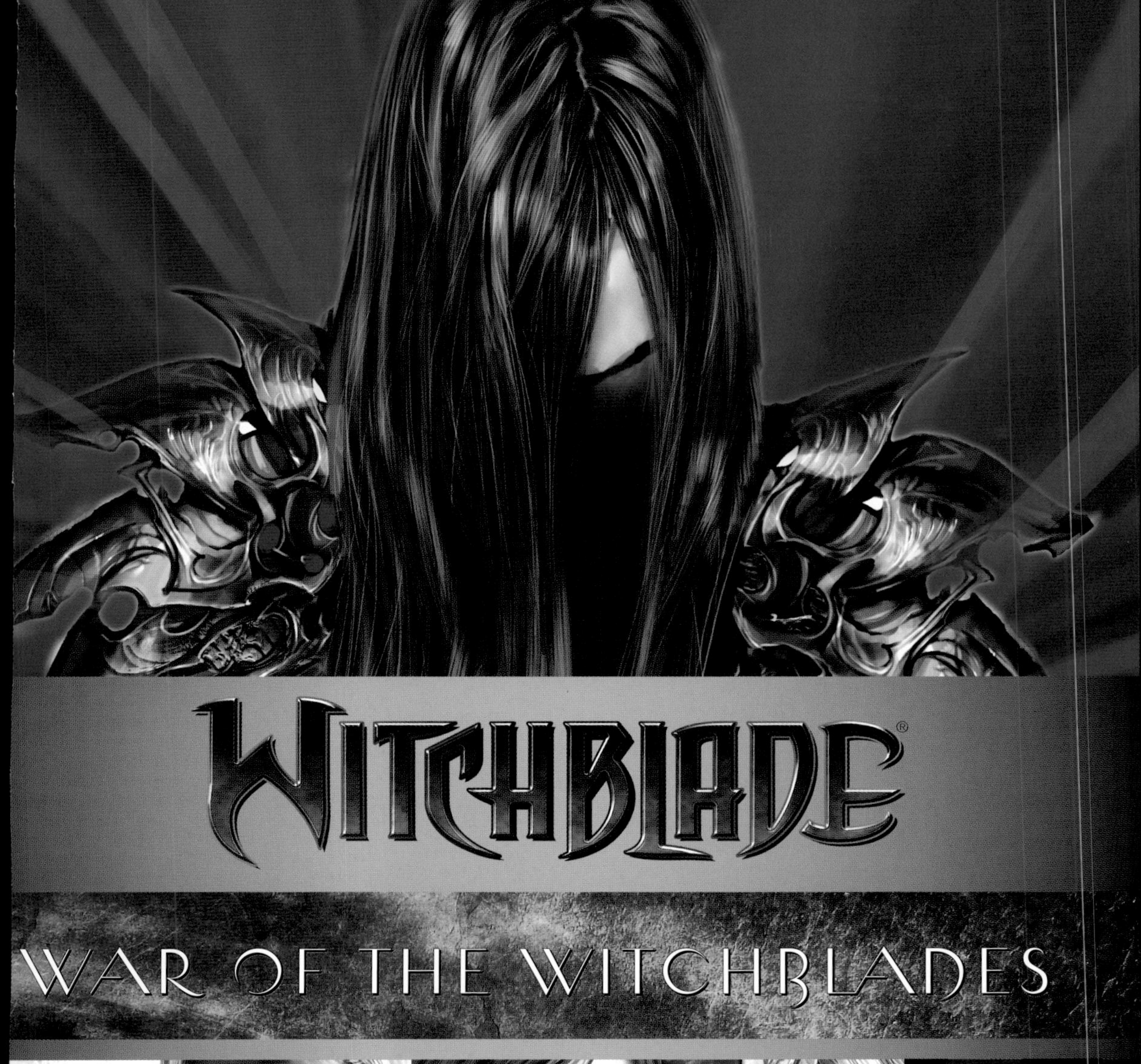

WITCHBLADE®

WAR OF THE WITCHBLADES

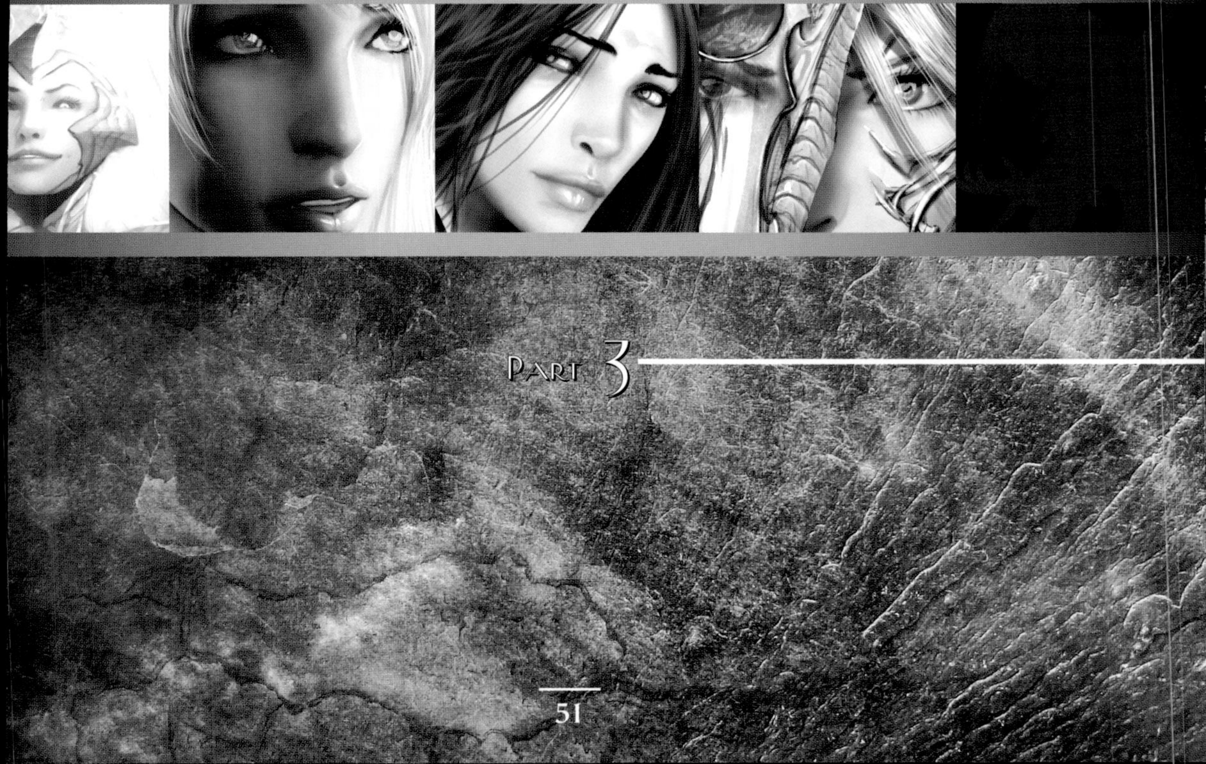

PART 3

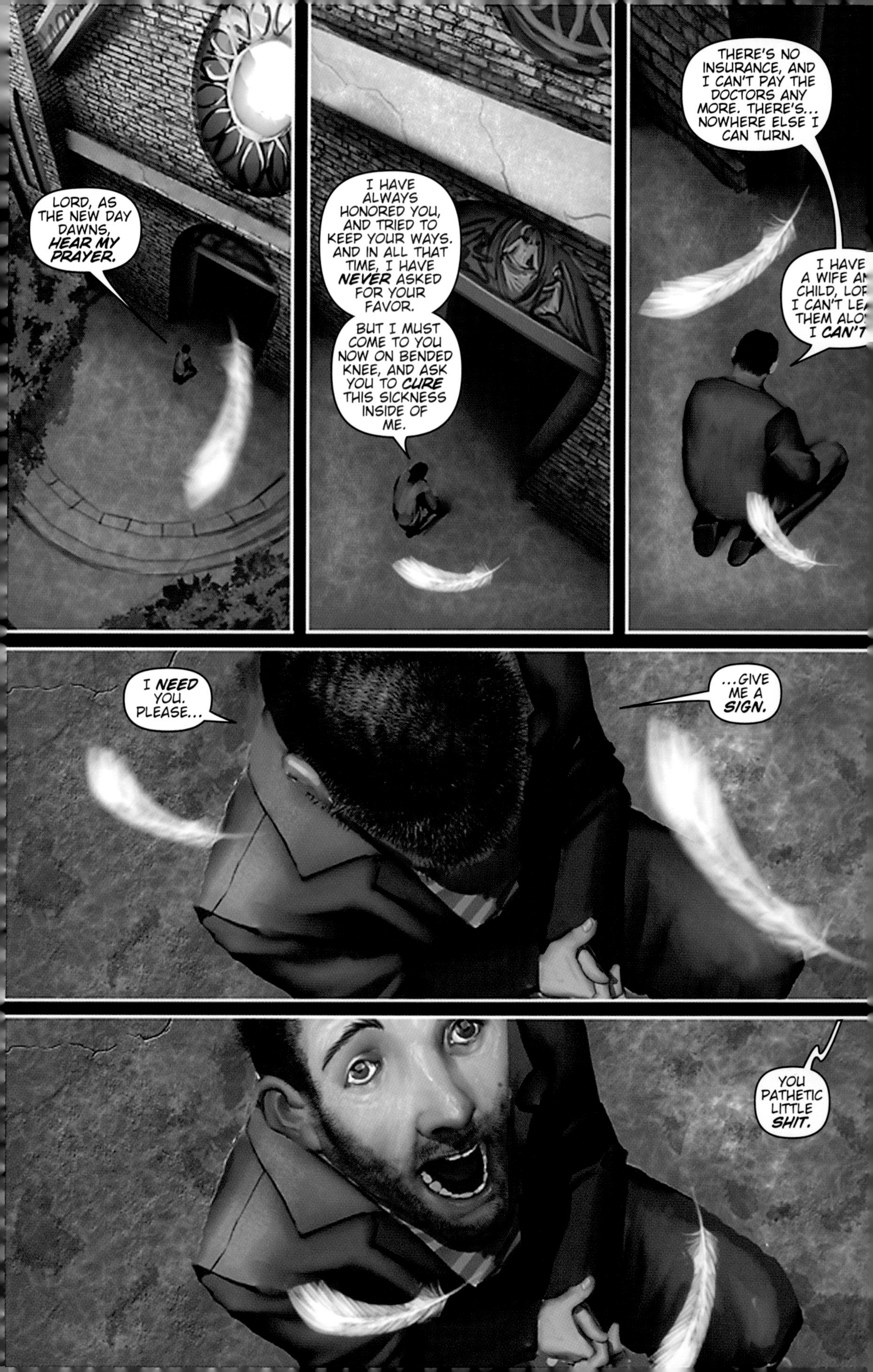
LORD, AS THE NEW DAY DAWNS, HEAR MY PRAYER.
I HAVE ALWAYS HONORED YOU, AND TRIED TO KEEP YOUR WAYS. AND IN ALL THAT TIME, I HAVE NEVER ASKED FOR YOUR FAVOR.
BUT I MUST COME TO YOU NOW ON BENDED KNEE, AND ASK YOU TO CURE THIS SICKNESS INSIDE OF ME.
THERE'S NO INSURANCE, AND I CAN'T PAY THE DOCTORS ANY MORE. THERE'S... NOWHERE ELSE I CAN TURN.
I NEED YOU. PLEASE...
...GIVE ME A SIGN.
YOU PATHETIC LITTLE SHIT.

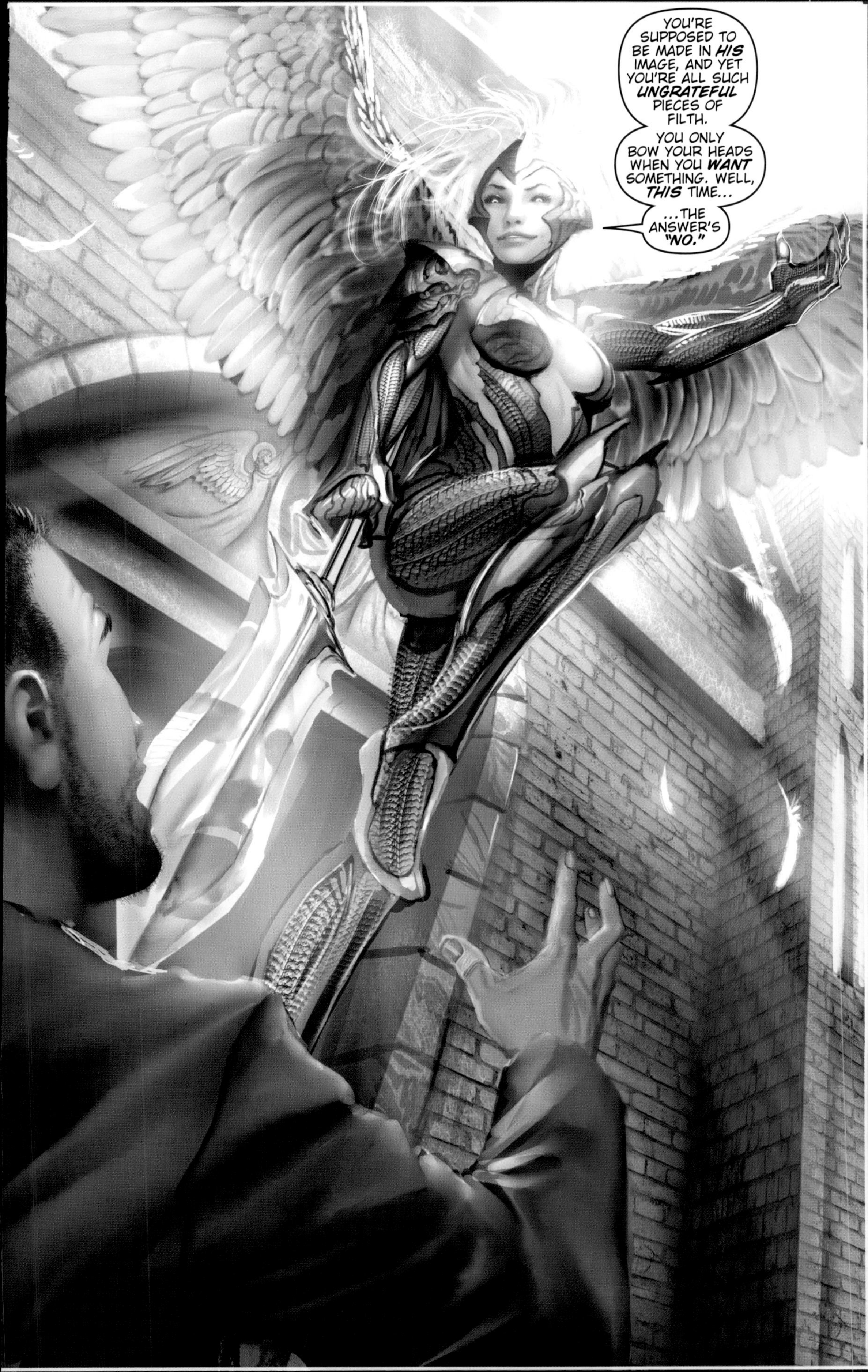
YOU'RE SUPPOSED TO BE MADE IN HIS IMAGE, AND YET YOU'RE ALL SUCH UNGRATEFUL PIECES OF FILTH.
YOU ONLY BOW YOUR HEADS WHEN YOU WANT SOMETHING. WELL, THIS TIME...
...THE ANSWER'S "NO."

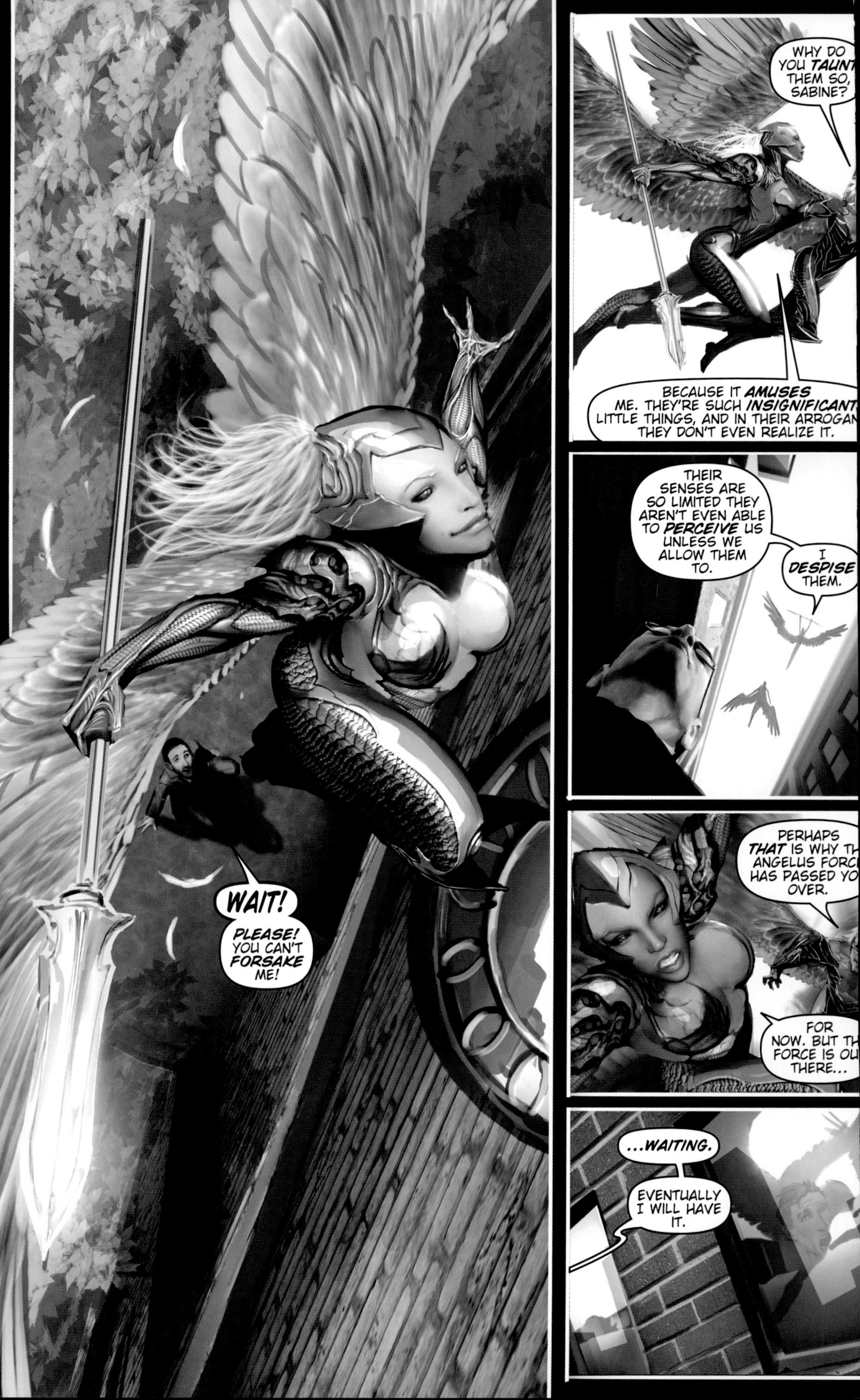
WAIT!
PLEASE! YOU CAN'T FORSAKE ME!
WHY DO YOU TAUNT THEM SO, SABINE?
BECAUSE IT AMUSES ME. THEY'RE SUCH INSIGNIFICANT LITTLE THINGS, AND IN THEIR ARROGAN THEY DON'T EVEN REALIZE IT.
THEIR SENSES ARE SO LIMITED THEY AREN'T EVEN ABLE TO PERCEIVE US UNLESS WE ALLOW THEM TO.
I DESPISE THEM.
PERHAPS THAT IS WHY TH ANGELUS FORC HAS PASSED YO OVER.
FOR NOW. BUT TH FORCE IS OU THERE...
...WAITING.
EVENTUALLY I WILL HAVE IT.

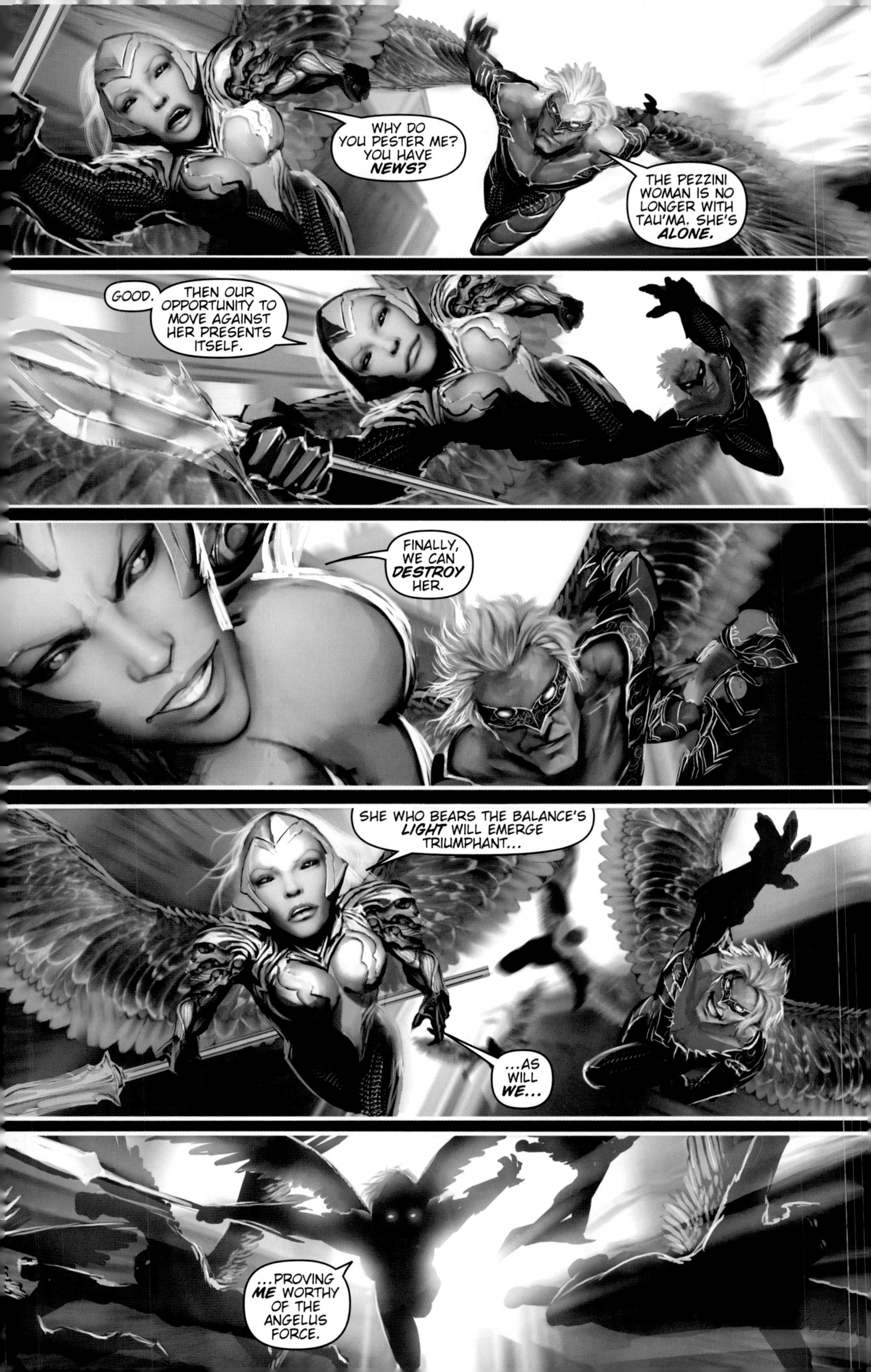
WHY DO YOU PESTER ME? YOU HAVE NEWS?
THE PEZZINI WOMAN IS NO LONGER WITH TAU'MA. SHE'S ALONE.
GOOD.
THEN OUR OPPORTUNITY TO MOVE AGAINST HER PRESENTS ITSELF.
FINALLY, WE CAN DESTROY HER.
SHE WHO BEARS THE BALANCE'S LIGHT WILL EMERGE TRIUMPHANT...
...AS WILL WE...
...PROVING ME WORTHY OF THE ANGELUS FORCE.

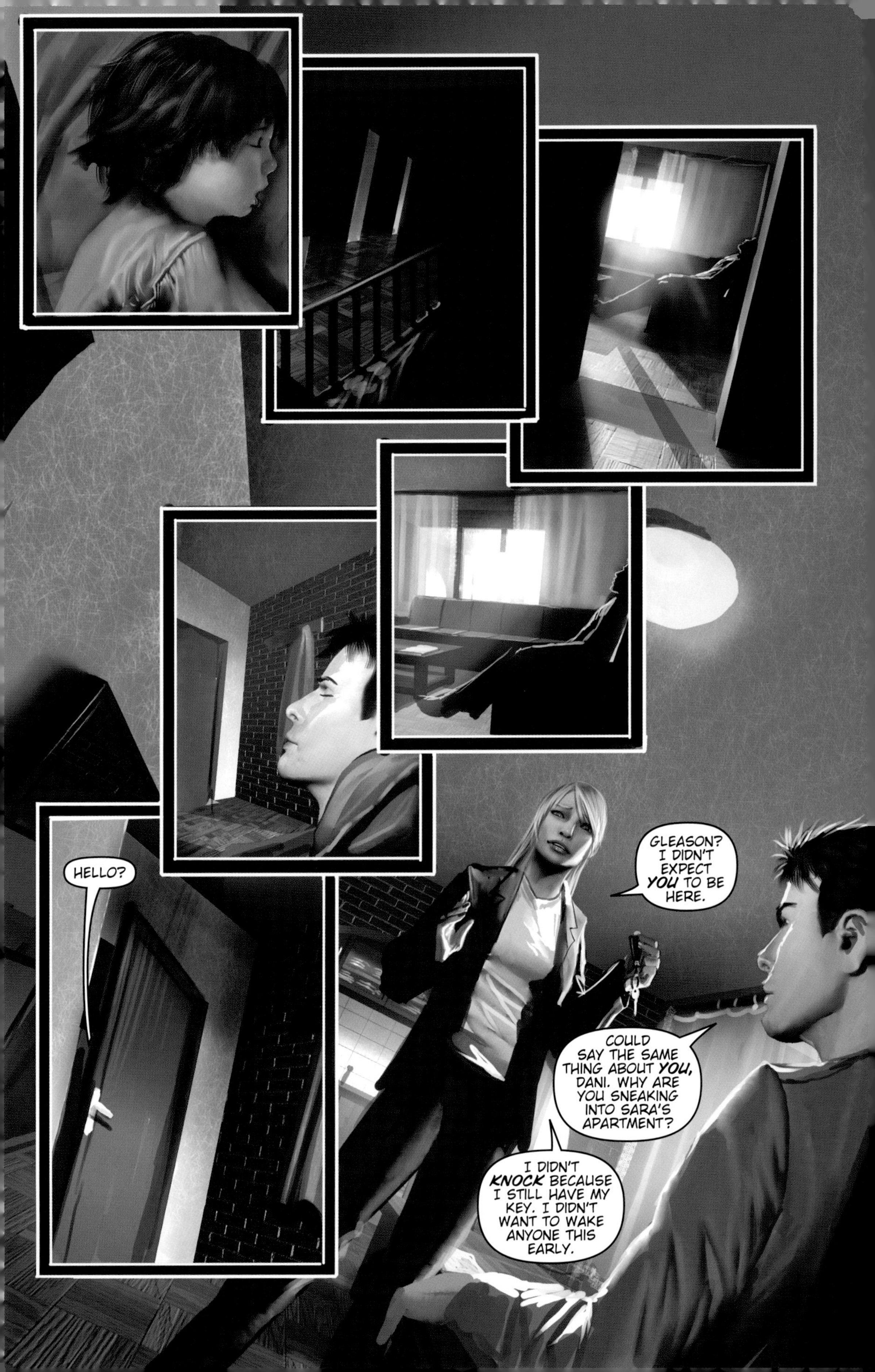
HELLO?
GLEASON? I DIDN'T EXPECT YOU TO BE HERE.
COULD SAY THE SAME THING ABOUT YOU, DANI. WHY ARE YOU SNEAKING INTO SARA'S APARTMENT?
I DIDN'T KNOCK BECAUSE I STILL HAVE MY KEY. I DIDN'T WANT TO WAKE ANYONE THIS EARLY.

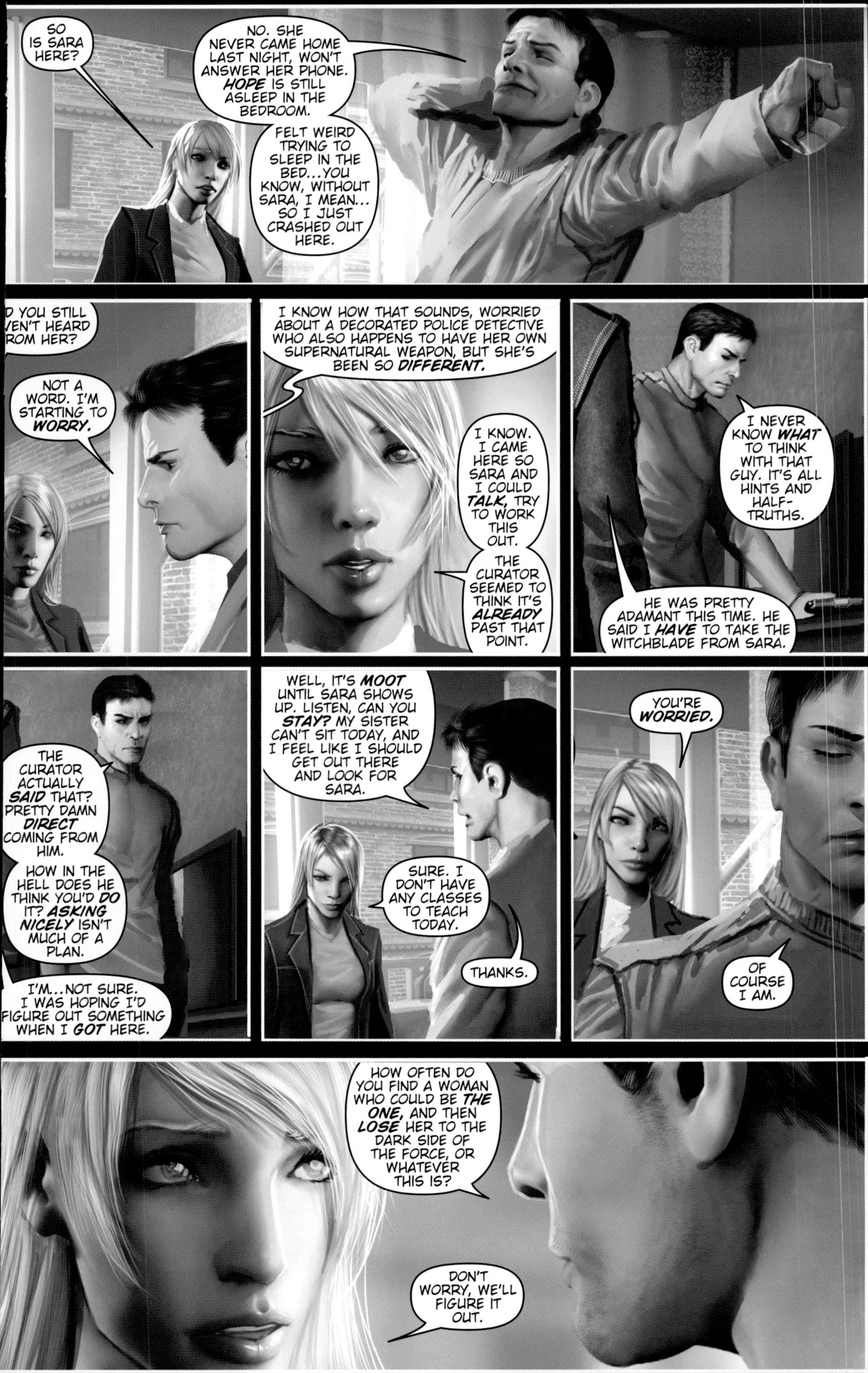
SO IS SARA HERE?
NO. SHE NEVER CAME HOME LAST NIGHT, WON'T ANSWER HER PHONE. HOPE IS STILL ASLEEP IN THE BEDROOM.
FELT WEIRD TRYING TO SLEEP IN THE BED...YOU KNOW, WITHOUT SARA, I MEAN... SO I JUST CRASHED OUT HERE.
D YOU STILL VEN'T HEARD ROM HER?
NOT A WORD. I'M STARTING TO WORRY.
I KNOW HOW THAT SOUNDS, WORRIED ABOUT A DECORATED POLICE DETECTIVE WHO ALSO HAPPENS TO HAVE HER OWN SUPERNATURAL WEAPON, BUT SHE'S BEEN SO DIFFERENT.
I KNOW. I CAME HERE SO SARA AND I COULD TALK, TRY TO WORK THIS OUT.
THE CURATOR SEEMED TO THINK IT'S ALREADY PAST THAT POINT.
I NEVER KNOW WHAT TO THINK WITH THAT GUY. IT'S ALL HINTS AND HALF-TRUTHS.
HE WAS PRETTY ADAMANT THIS TIME. HE SAID I HAVE TO TAKE THE WITCHBLADE FROM SARA.
THE CURATOR ACTUALLY SAID THAT? PRETTY DAMN DIRECT COMING FROM HIM.
HOW IN THE HELL DOES HE THINK YOU'D DO IT? ASKING NICELY ISN'T MUCH OF A PLAN.
I'M...NOT SURE. I WAS HOPING I'D FIGURE OUT SOMETHING WHEN I GOT HERE.
WELL, IT'S MOOT UNTIL SARA SHOWS UP. LISTEN, CAN YOU STAY? MY SISTER CAN'T SIT TODAY, AND I FEEL LIKE I SHOULD GET OUT THERE AND LOOK FOR SARA.
SURE. I DON'T HAVE ANY CLASSES TO TEACH TODAY.
THANKS.
YOU'RE WORRIED.
OF COURSE I AM.
HOW OFTEN DO YOU FIND A WOMAN WHO COULD BE THE ONE, AND THEN LOSE HER TO THE DARK SIDE OF THE FORCE, OR WHATEVER THIS IS?
DON'T WORRY, WE'LL FIGURE IT OUT.

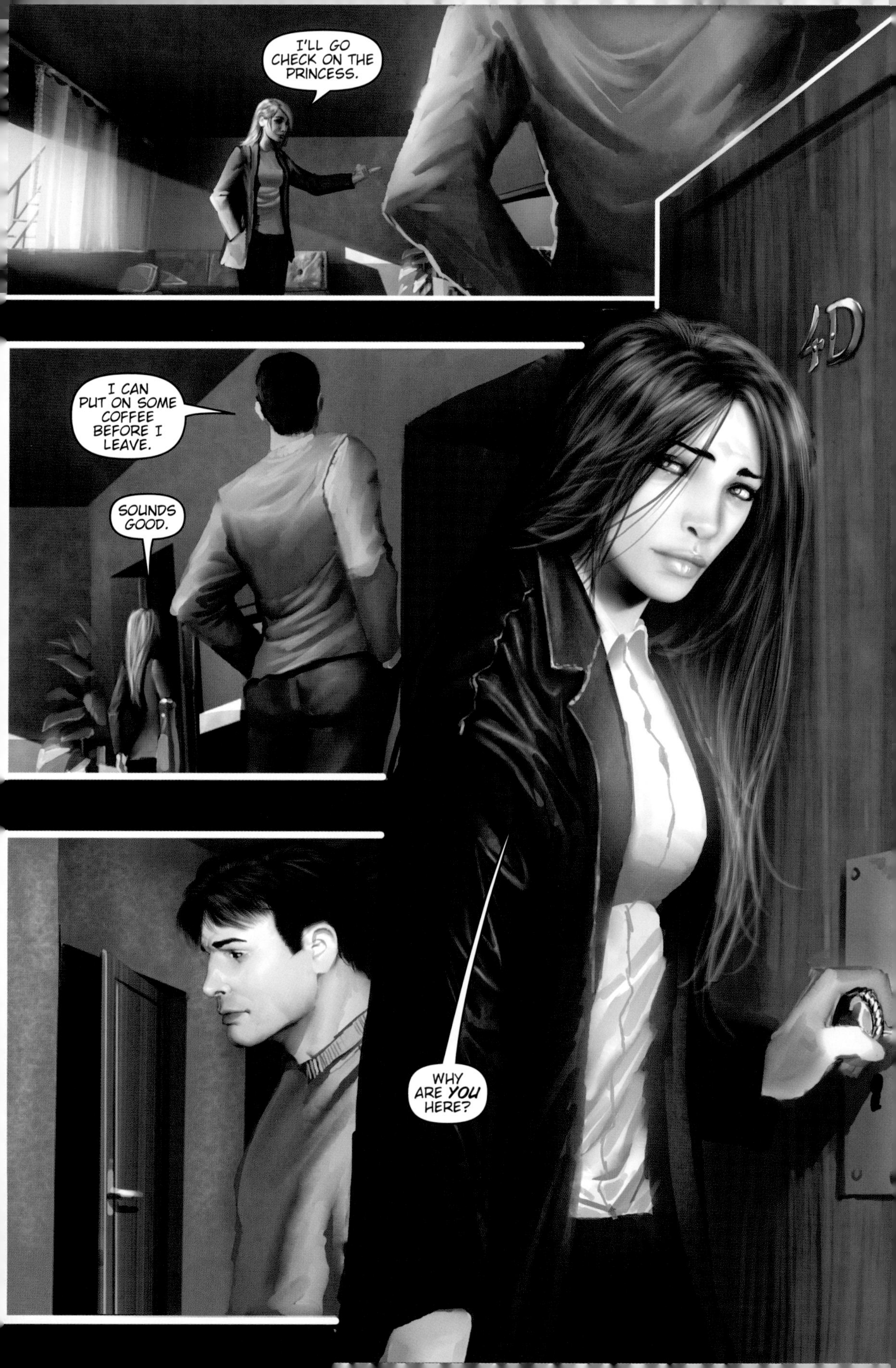
I'LL GO CHECK ON THE PRINCESS.
I CAN PUT ON SOME COFFEE BEFORE I LEAVE.
SOUNDS GOOD.
4D
WHY ARE *YOU* HERE?

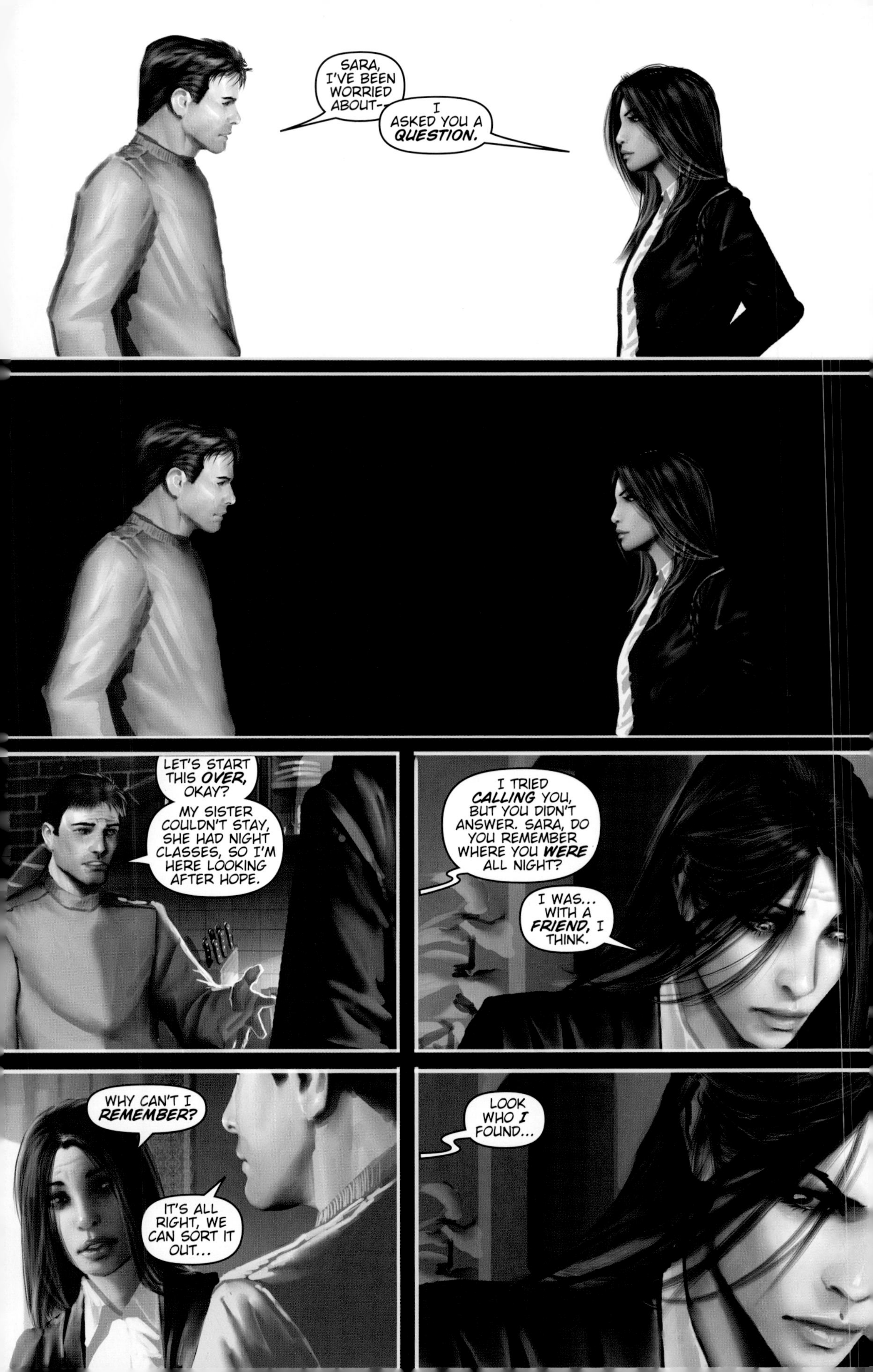
SARA, I'VE BEEN WORRIED ABOUT--
I ASKED YOU A **QUESTION.**
LET'S START THIS **OVER,** OKAY?
MY SISTER COULDN'T STAY, SHE HAD NIGHT CLASSES, SO I'M HERE LOOKING AFTER HOPE.
I TRIED **CALLING** YOU, BUT YOU DIDN'T ANSWER. SARA, DO YOU REMEMBER WHERE YOU **WERE** ALL NIGHT?
I WAS... WITH A **FRIEND,** I THINK.
WHY CAN'T I **REMEMBER?**
IT'S ALL RIGHT, WE CAN SORT IT OUT...
LOOK WHO **I** FOUND...

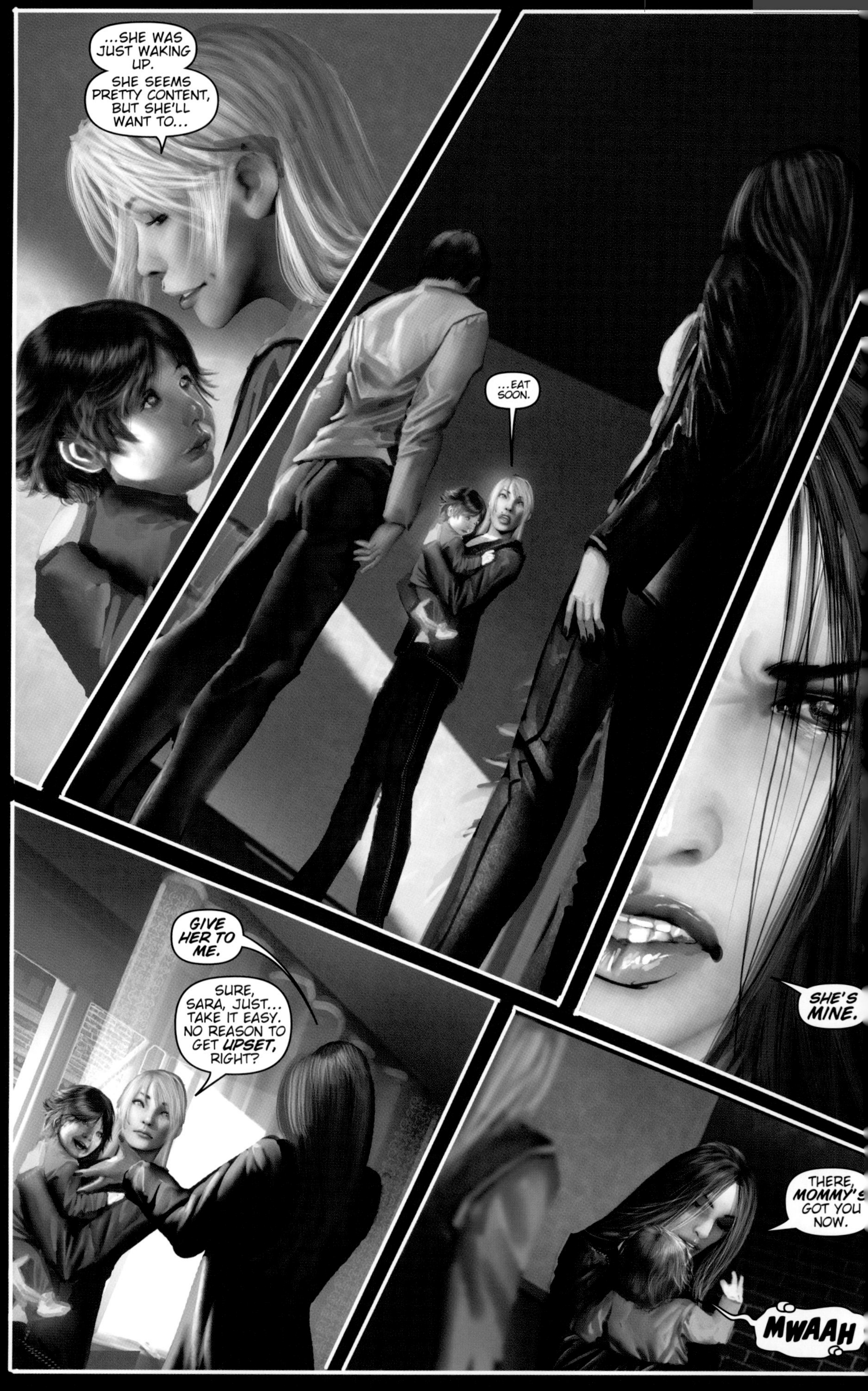
...SHE WAS JUST WAKING UP.
SHE SEEMS PRETTY CONTENT, BUT SHE'LL WANT TO...
...EAT SOON.
SHE'S MINE.
GIVE HER TO ME.
SURE, SARA, JUST... TAKE IT EASY. NO REASON TO GET UPSET, RIGHT?
THERE, MOMMY's GOT YOU NOW.
MWAAH

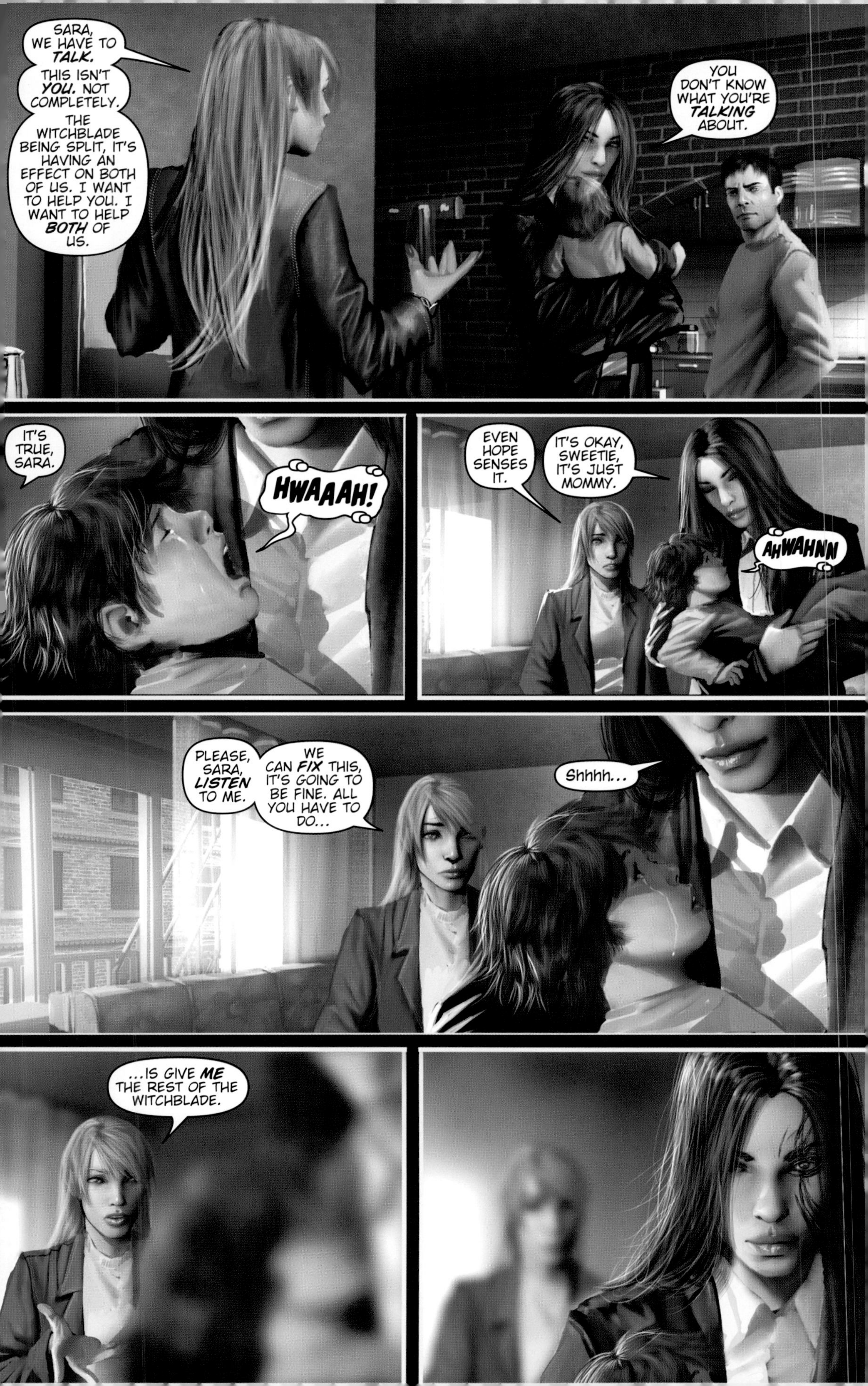
SARA, WE HAVE TO TALK.
THIS ISN'T YOU. NOT COMPLETELY.
THE WITCHBLADE BEING SPLIT, IT'S HAVING AN EFFECT ON BOTH OF US. I WANT TO HELP YOU. I WANT TO HELP BOTH OF US.
YOU DON'T KNOW WHAT YOU'RE TALKING ABOUT.
IT'S TRUE, SARA.
HWAAAH!
EVEN HOPE SENSES IT.
IT'S OKAY, SWEETIE, IT'S JUST MOMMY.
AHWAHNN
PLEASE, SARA, LISTEN TO ME.
WE CAN FIX THIS, IT'S GOING TO BE FINE. ALL YOU HAVE TO DO...
Shhhh...
...IS GIVE ME THE REST OF THE WITCHBLADE.

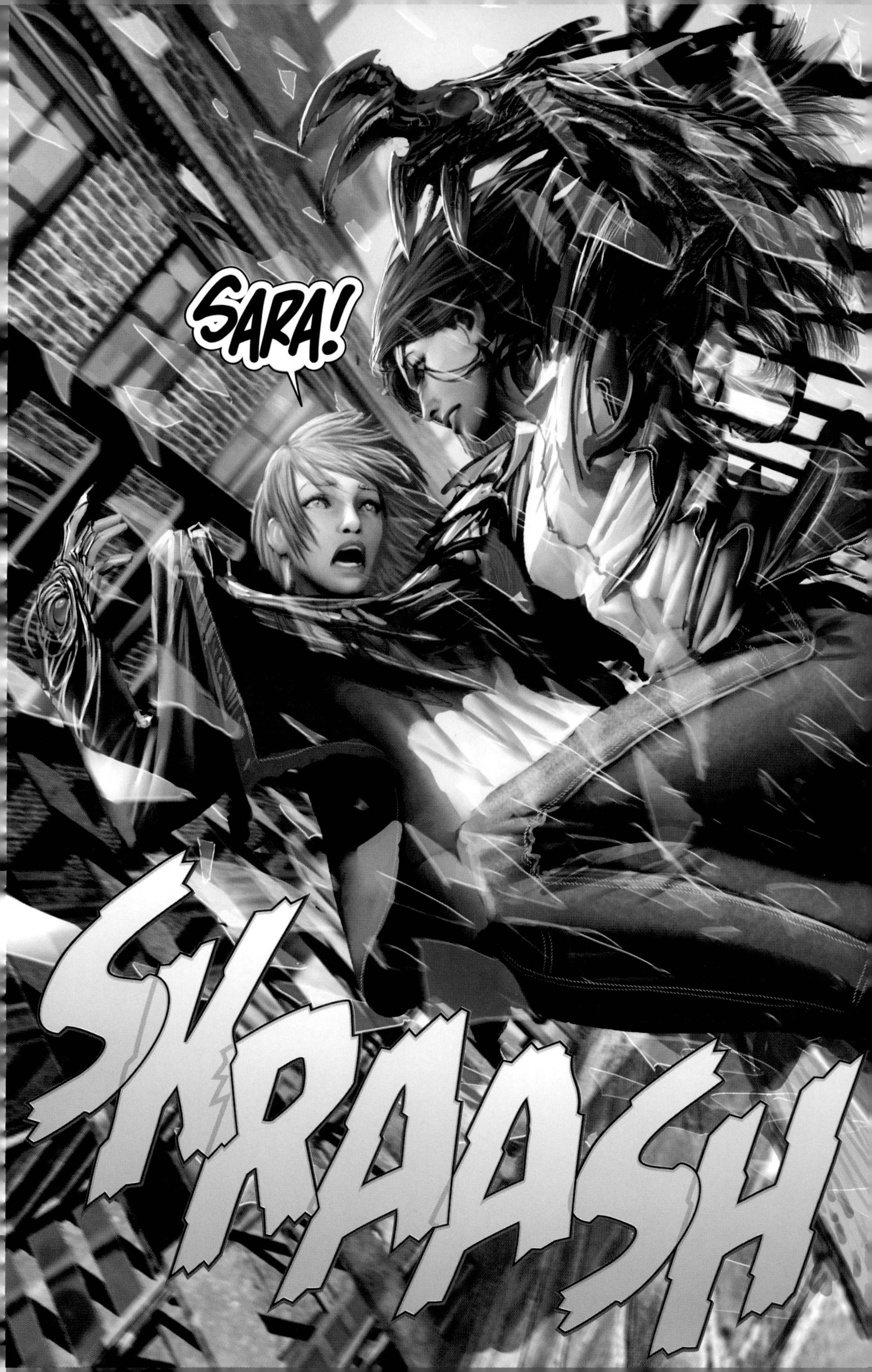
SARA!
SKRAASH

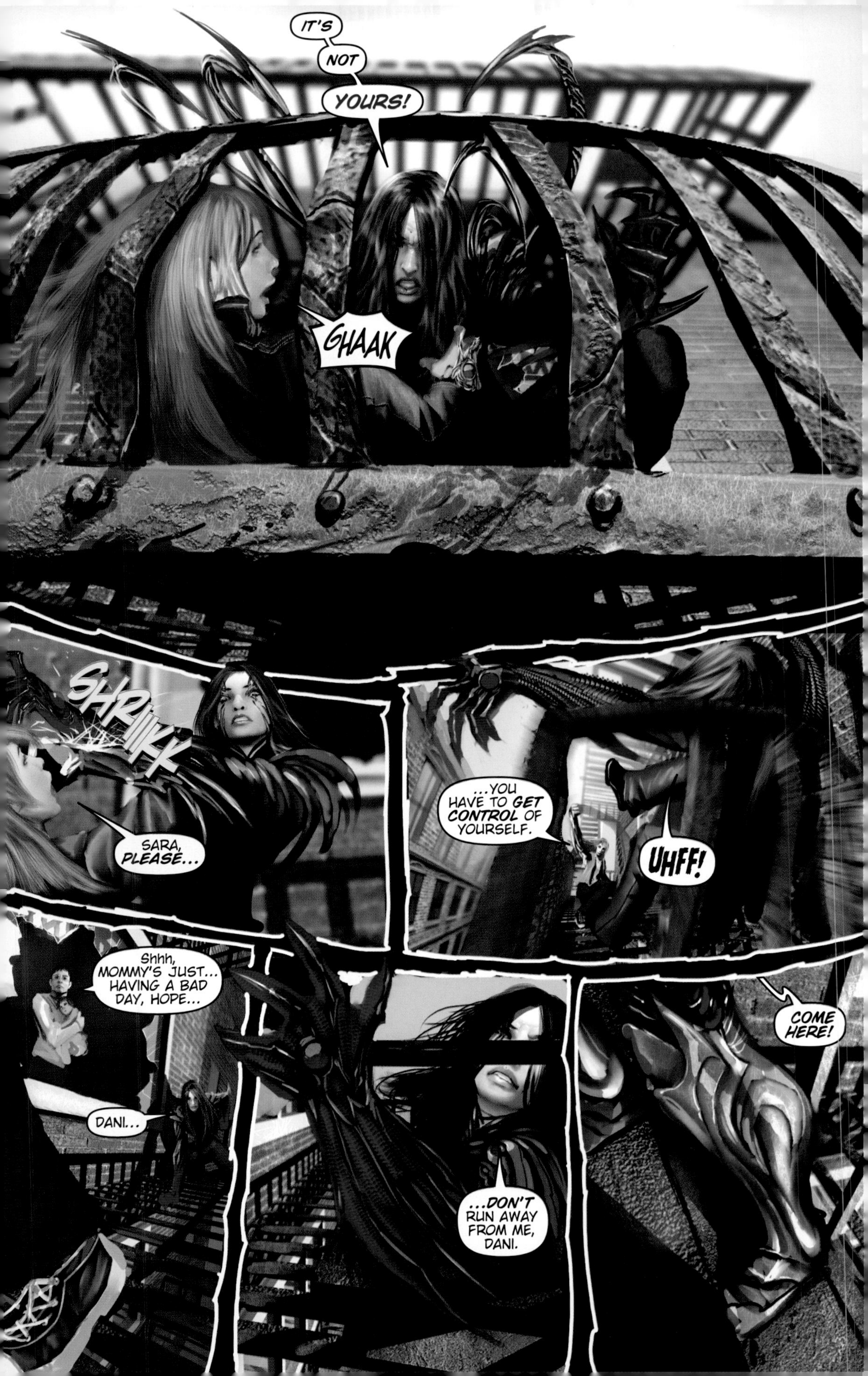
IT'S
NOT
YOURS!
GHAAK
SHRIIIKK
SARA, PLEASE...
...YOU HAVE TO GET CONTROL OF YOURSELF.
UHFF!
Shhh, MOMMY'S JUST... HAVING A BAD DAY, HOPE...
DANI...
...DON'T RUN AWAY FROM ME, DANI.
COME HERE!

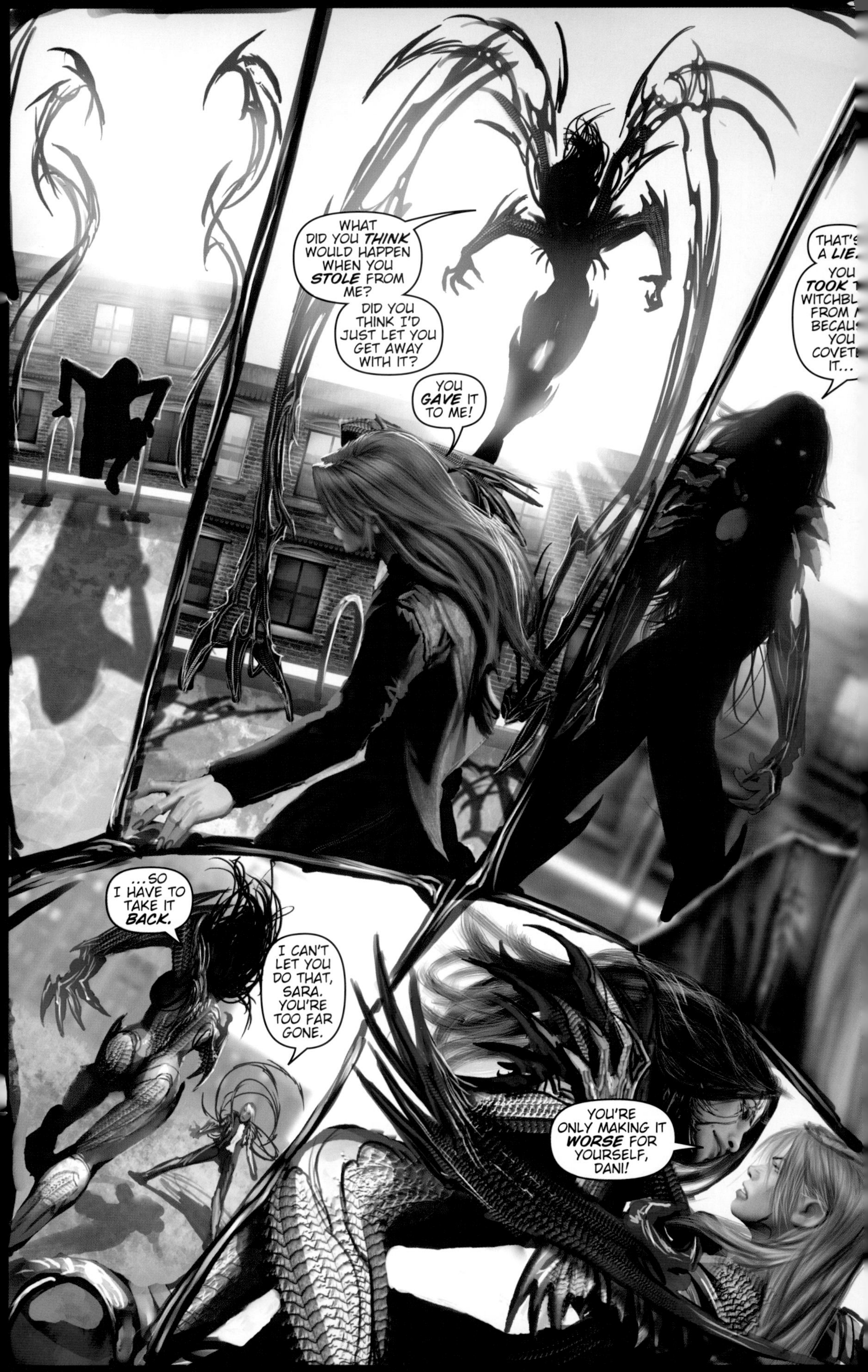

WHAT DID YOU THINK WOULD HAPPEN WHEN YOU STOLE FROM ME?
DID YOU THINK I'D JUST LET YOU GET AWAY WITH IT?
YOU GAVE IT TO ME!
THAT'S A LIE. YOU TOOK T WITCHBL FROM BECAUS YOU COVETE IT...
...SO I HAVE TO TAKE IT BACK.
I CAN'T LET YOU DO THAT, SARA. YOU'RE TOO FAR GONE.
YOU'RE ONLY MAKING IT WORSE FOR YOURSELF, DANI!

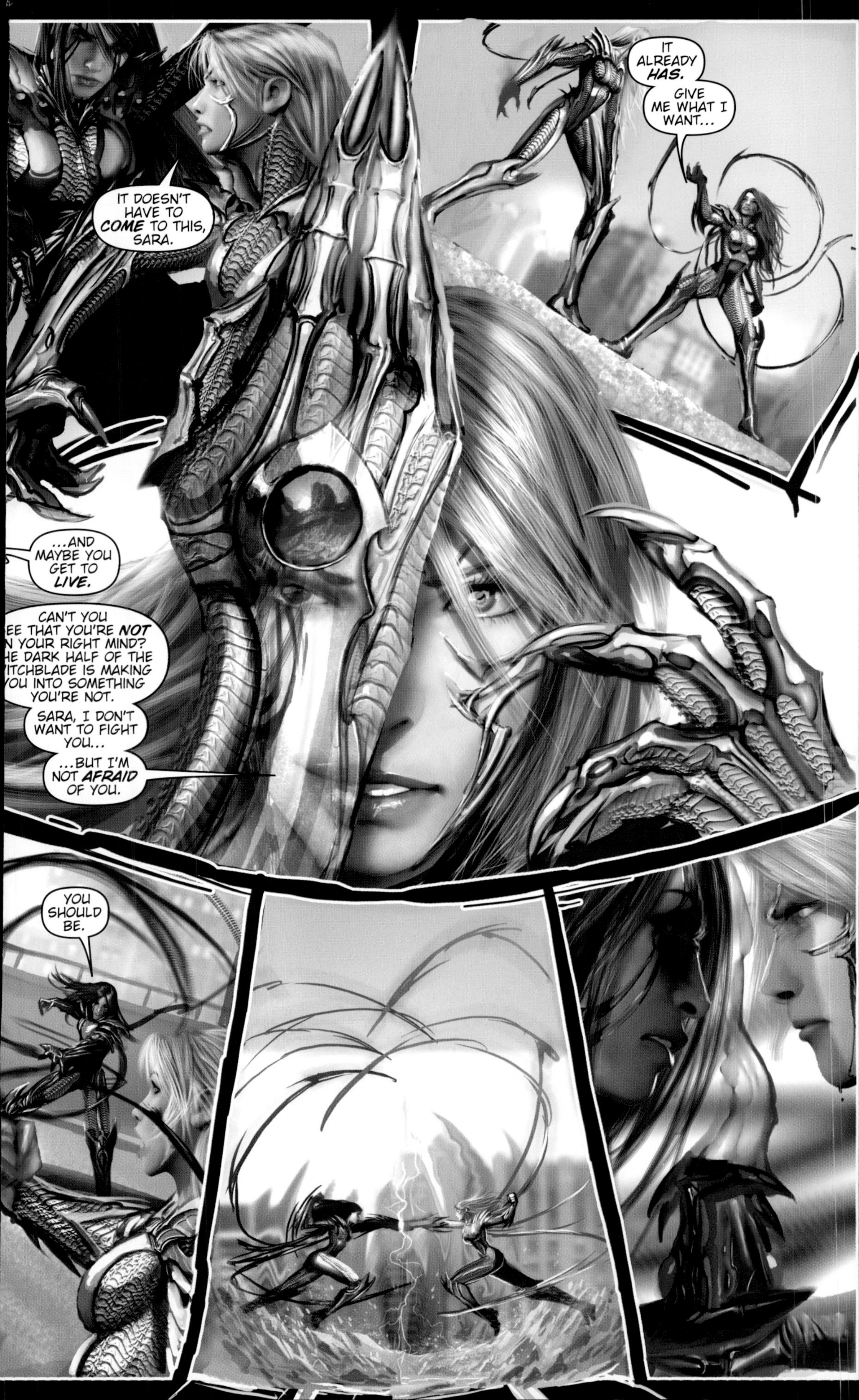
IT DOESN'T HAVE TO COME TO THIS, SARA.
IT ALREADY HAS.
GIVE ME WHAT I WANT...
...AND MAYBE YOU GET TO LIVE.
CAN'T YOU SEE THAT YOU'RE NOT IN YOUR RIGHT MIND? THE DARK HALF OF THE WITCHBLADE IS MAKING YOU INTO SOMETHING YOU'RE NOT.
SARA, I DON'T WANT TO FIGHT YOU...
...BUT I'M NOT AFRAID OF YOU.
YOU SHOULD BE.

NO.

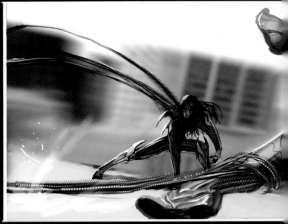

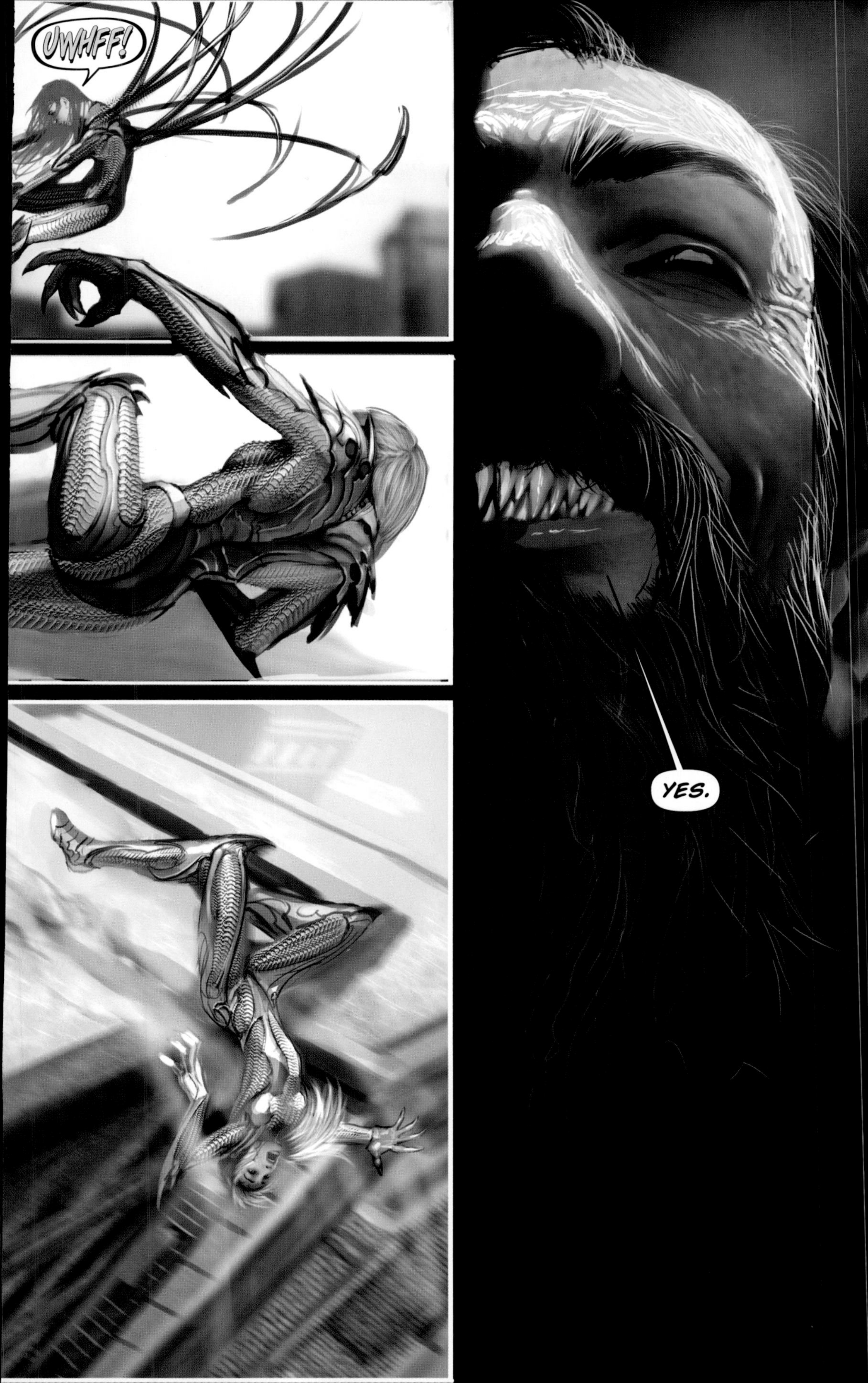
UWHFF!
YES.

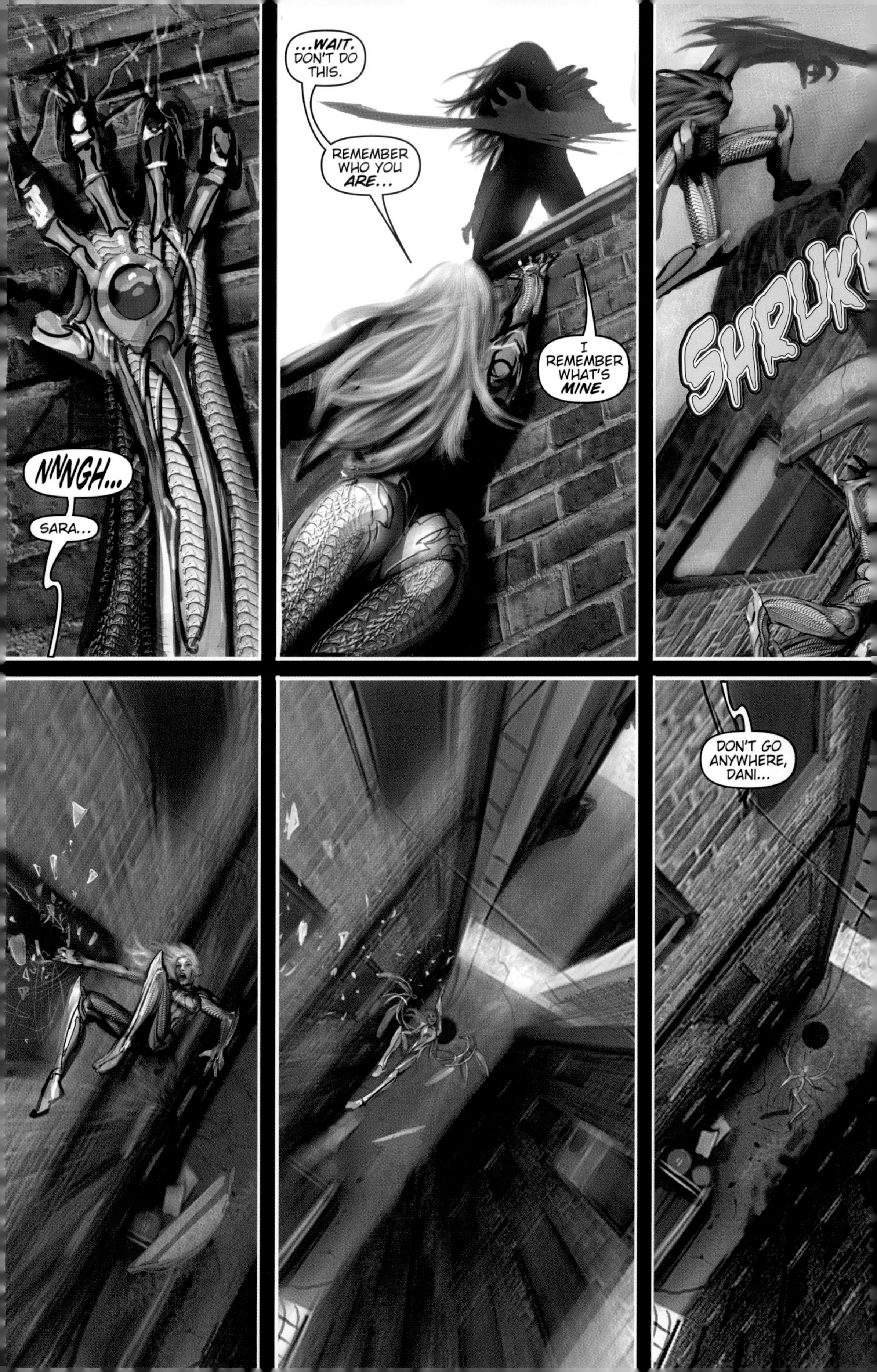
NNNGH...
SARA...
...WAIT. DON'T DO THIS.
REMEMBER WHO YOU ARE...
I REMEMBER WHAT'S MINE.
SHRUK
DON'T GO ANYWHERE, DANI...

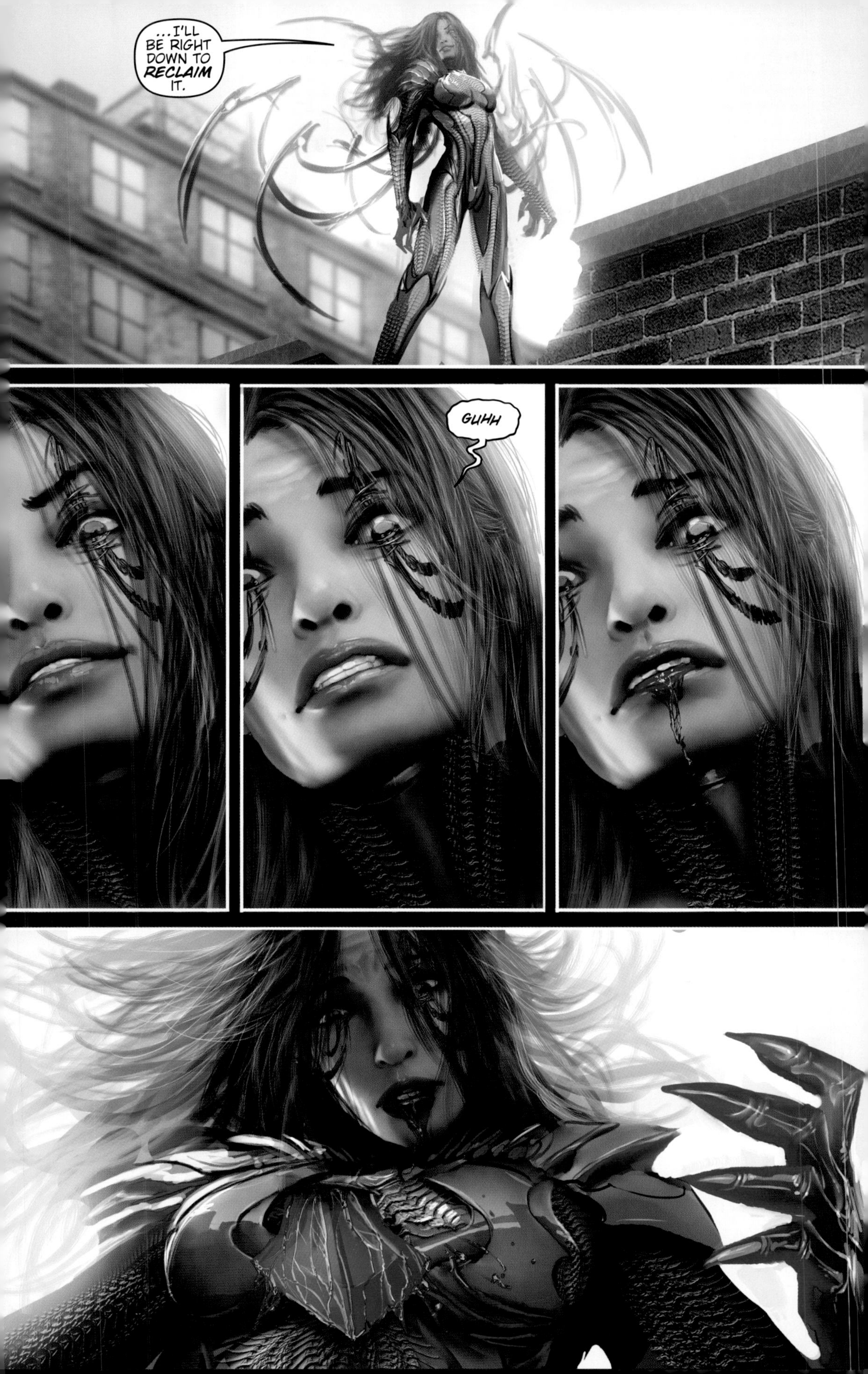
...I'LL BE RIGHT DOWN TO RECLAIM IT.
GUHH

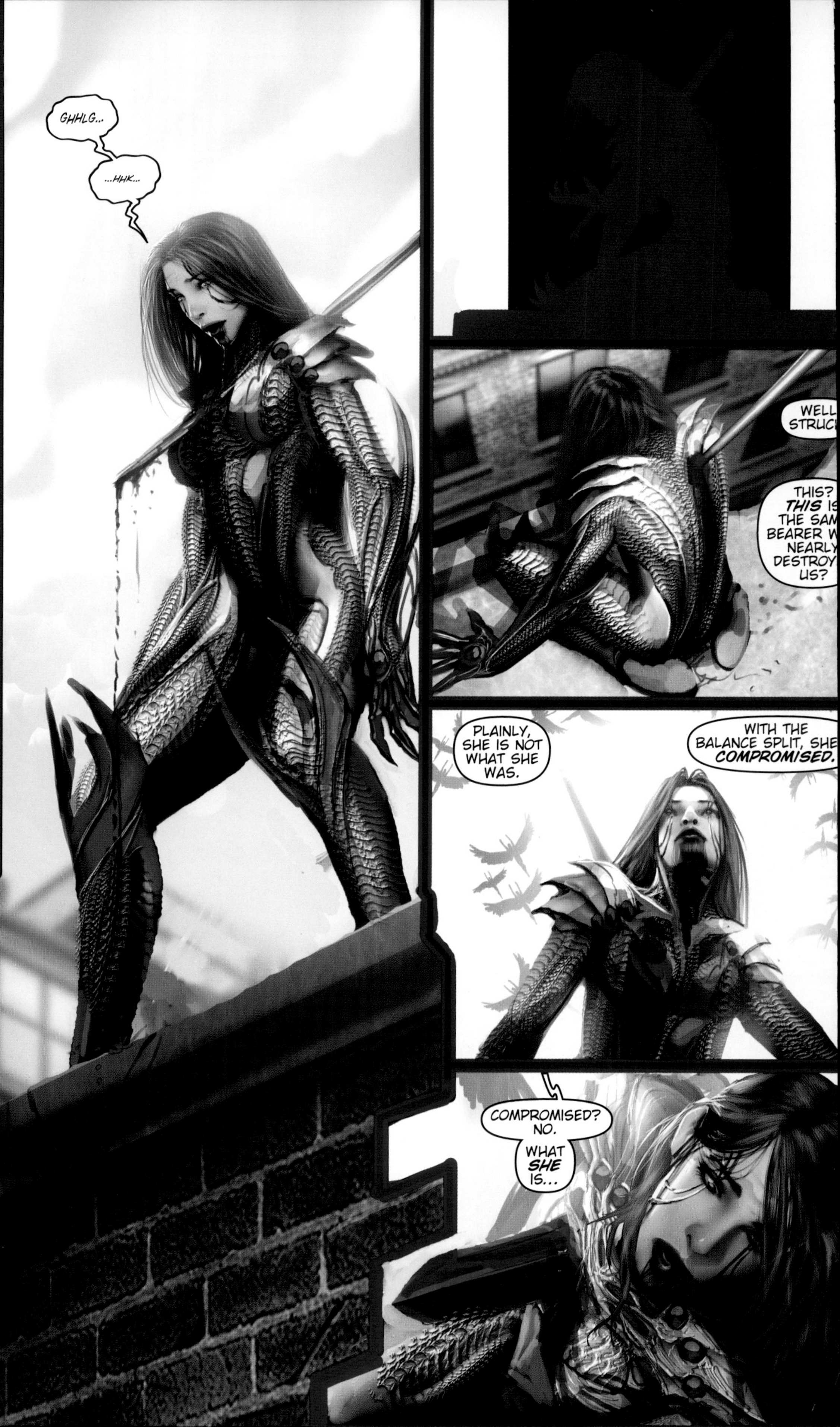
GHHLG...
...HHK...
WELL STRUC
THIS? THIS IS THE SAM BEARER W NEARLY DESTROY US?
PLAINLY, SHE IS NOT WHAT SHE WAS.
WITH THE BALANCE SPLIT, SHE COMPROMISED.
COMPROMISED? NO.
WHAT SHE IS...

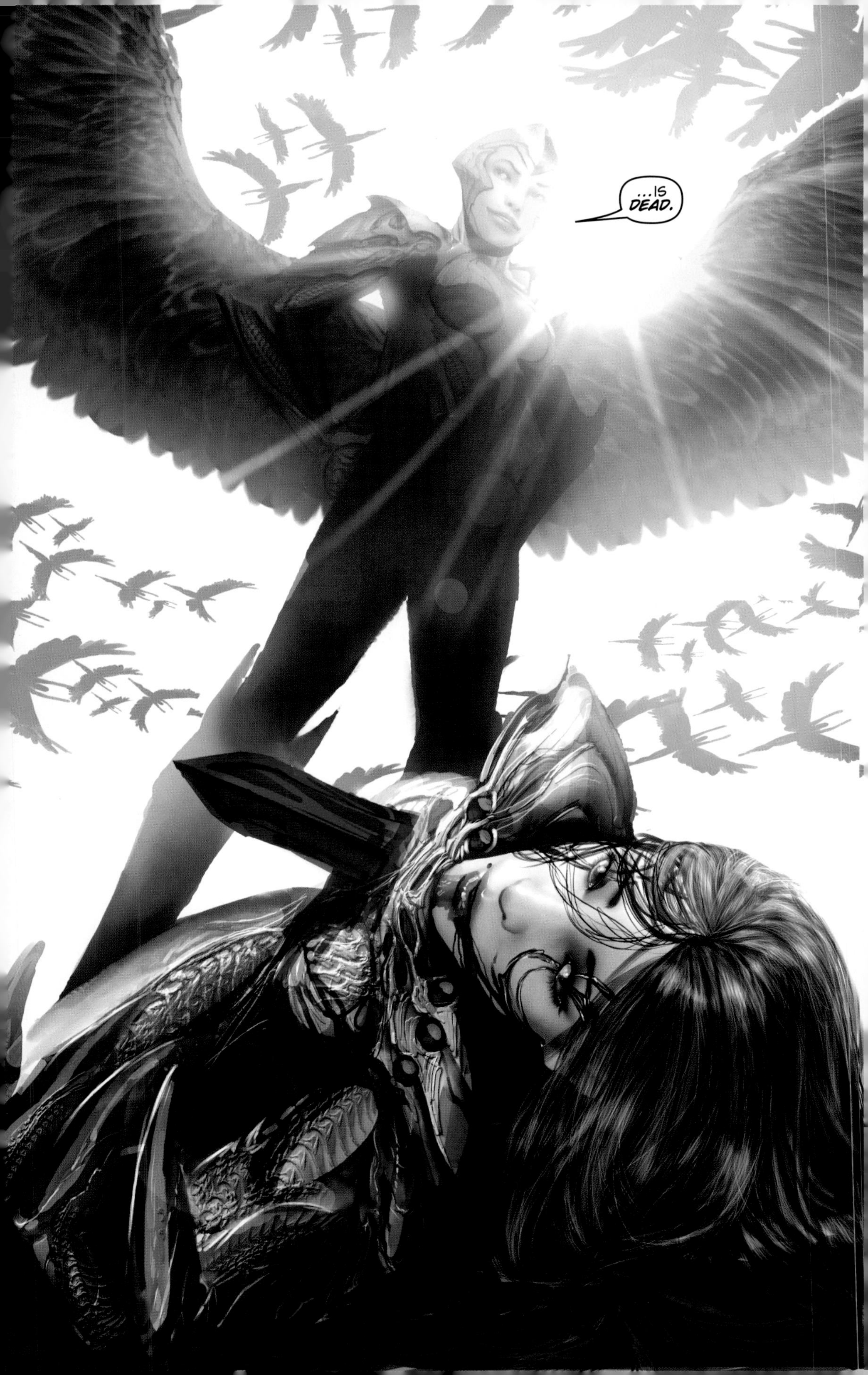
...IS DEAD.

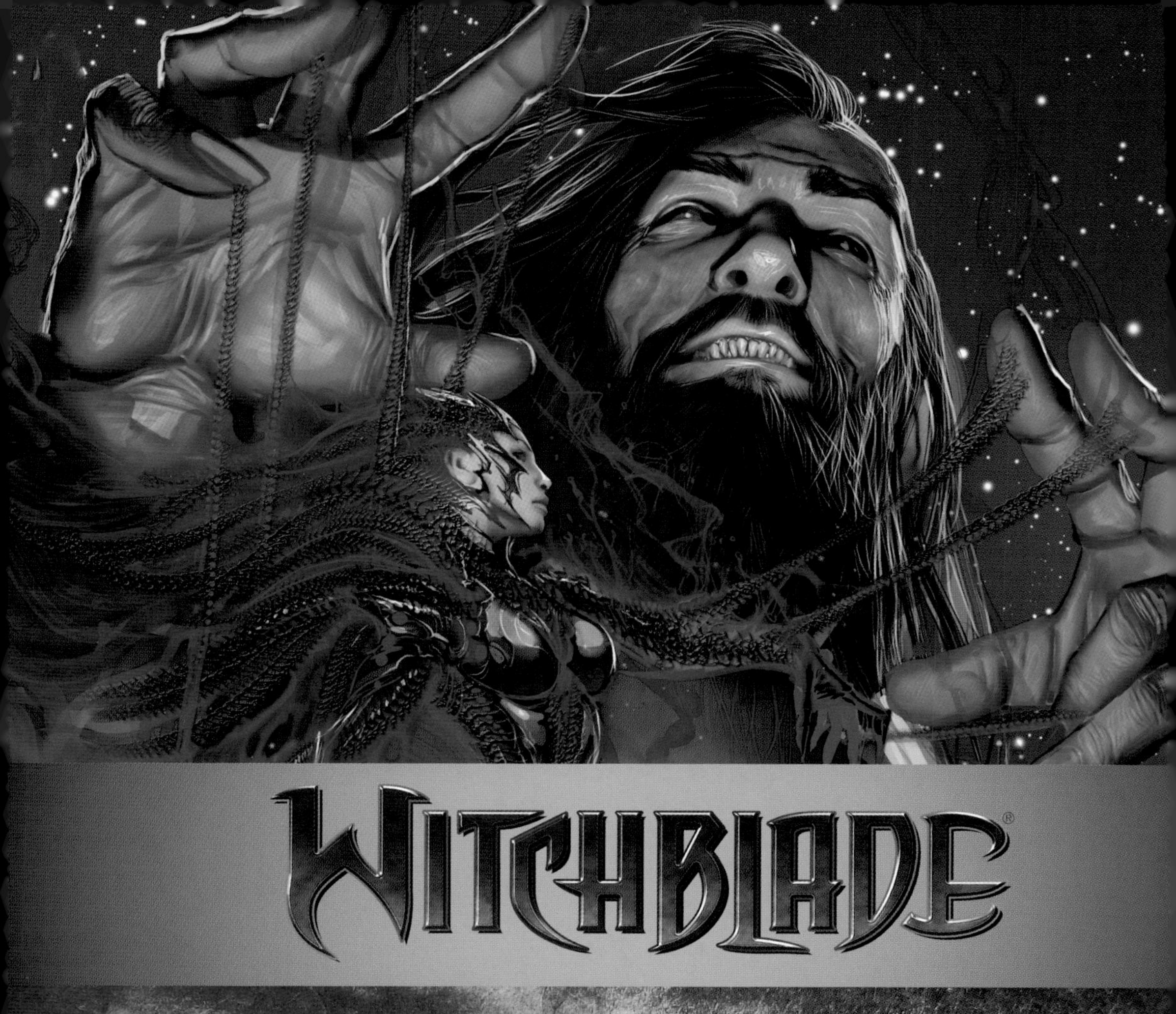

WITCHBLADE®

WAR OF THE WITCHBLADES

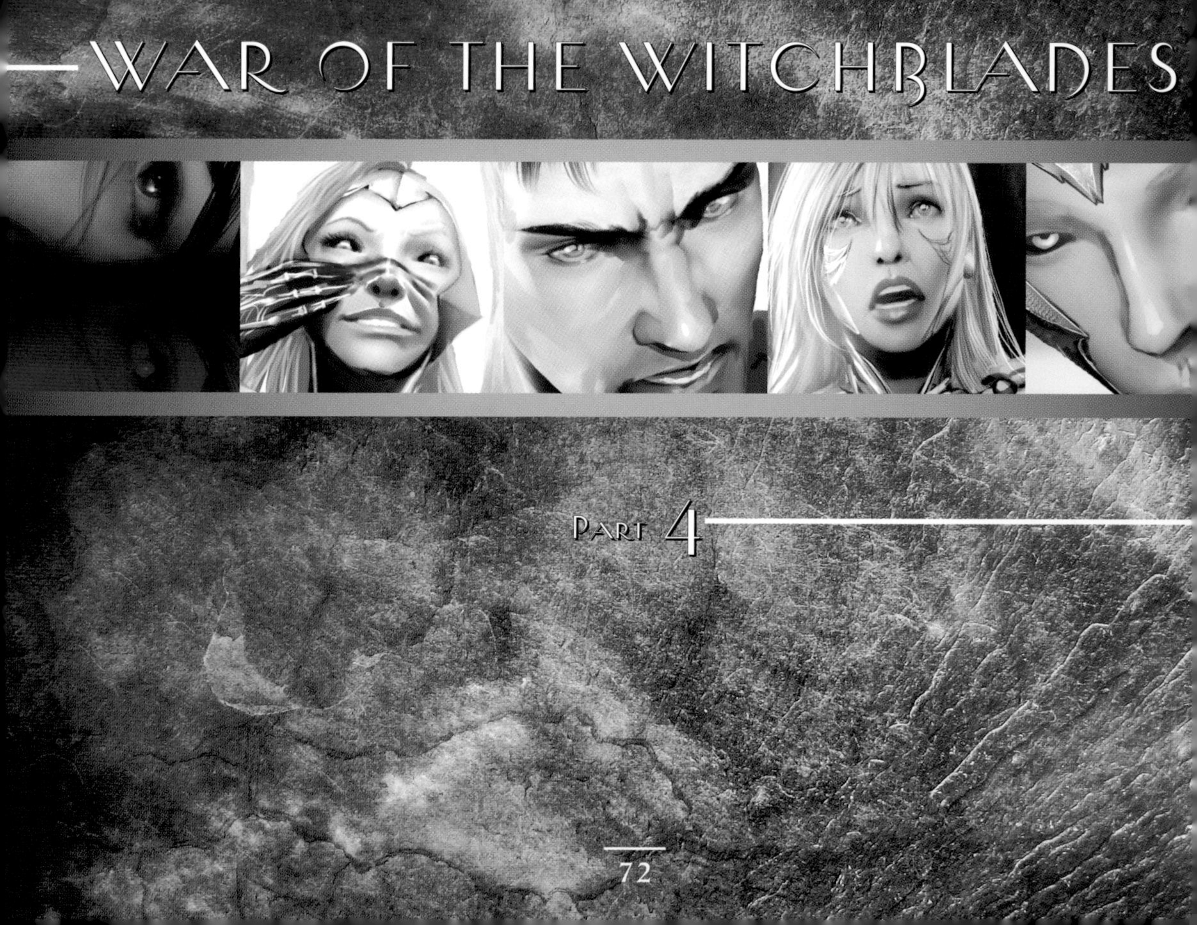

PART 4

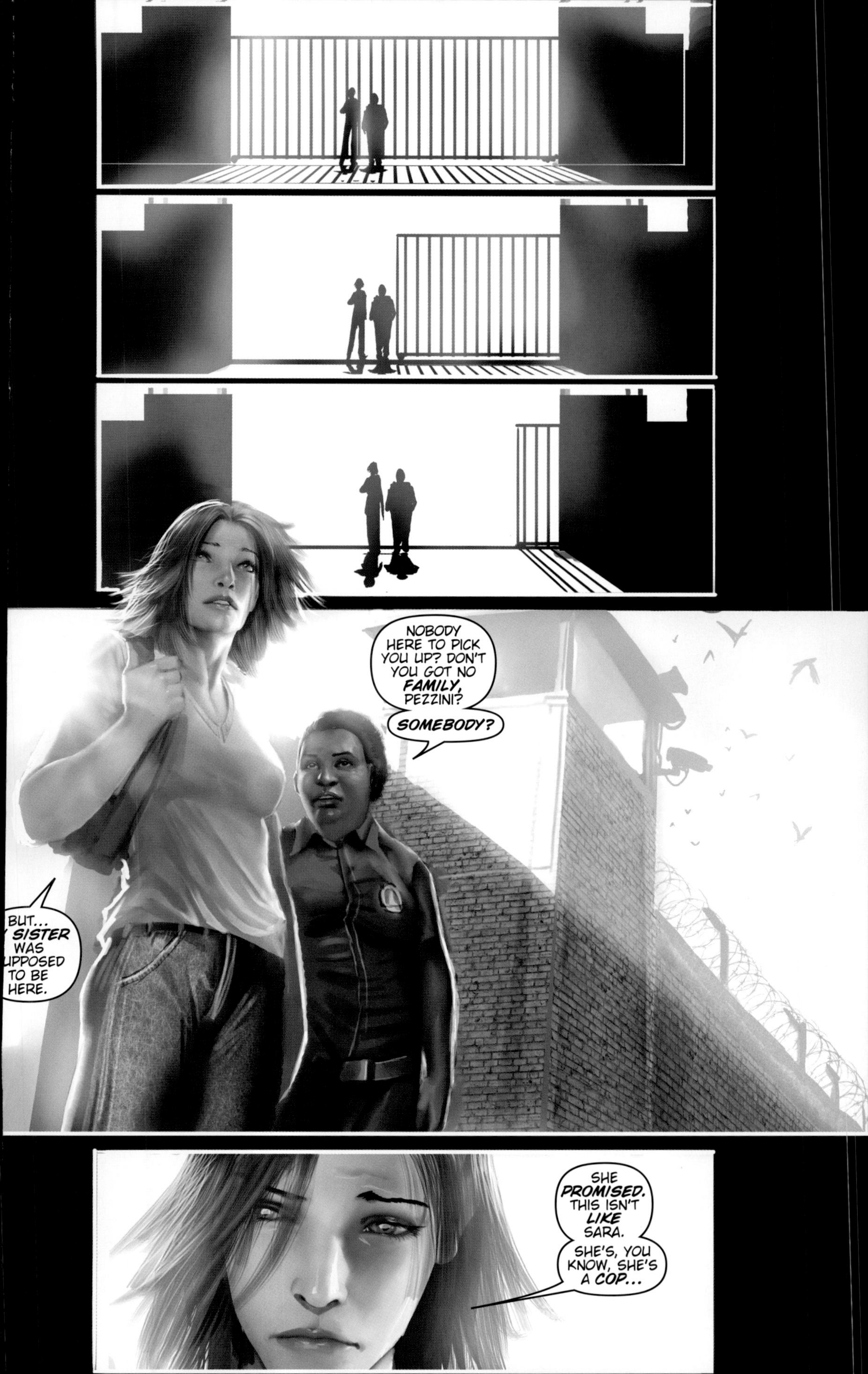

NOBODY HERE TO PICK YOU UP? DON'T YOU GOT NO **FAMILY,** PEZZINI?
SOMEBODY?
BUT... **SISTER** WAS UPPOSED TO BE HERE.
SHE ***PROMISED.*** THIS ISN'T ***LIKE*** SARA.
SHE'S, YOU KNOW, SHE'S A ***COP...***

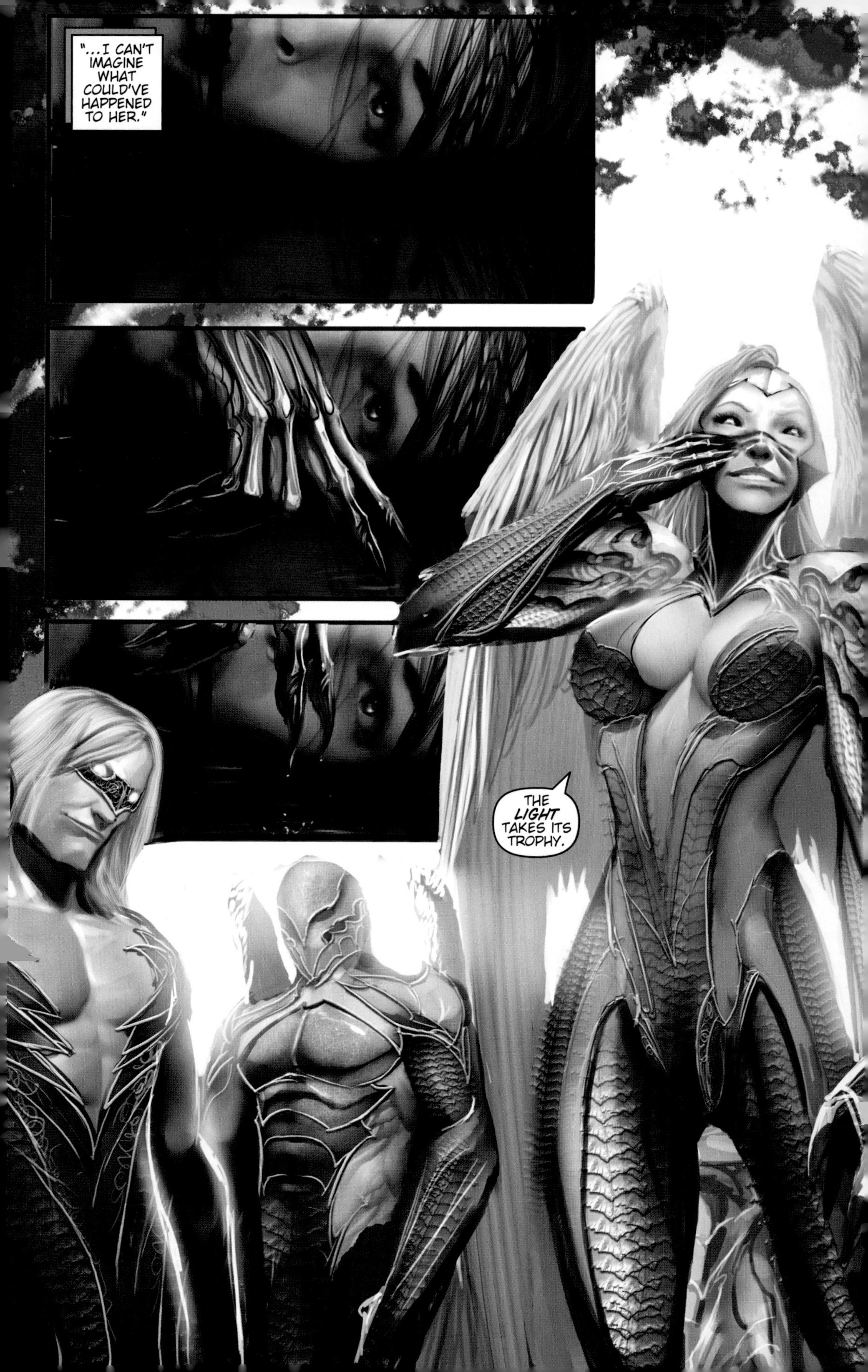
"...I CAN'T IMAGINE WHAT COULD'VE HAPPENED TO HER."
THE LIGHT TAKES ITS TROPHY.

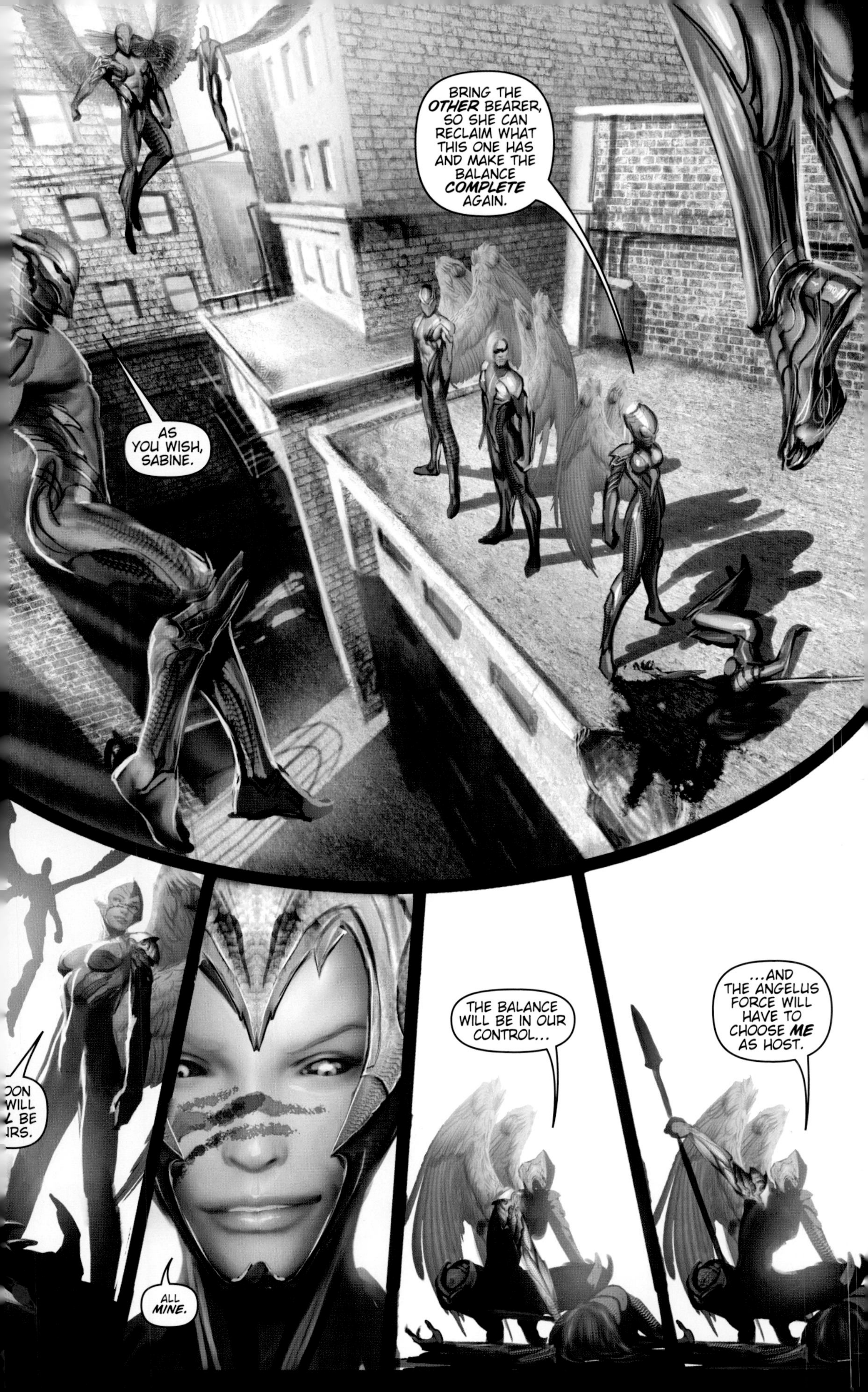
BRING THE OTHER BEARER, SO SHE CAN RECLAIM WHAT THIS ONE HAS AND MAKE THE BALANCE COMPLETE AGAIN.
AS YOU WISH, SABINE.
ALL MINE.
THE BALANCE WILL BE IN OUR CONTROL...
...AND THE ANGELUS FORCE WILL HAVE TO CHOOSE ME AS HOST.

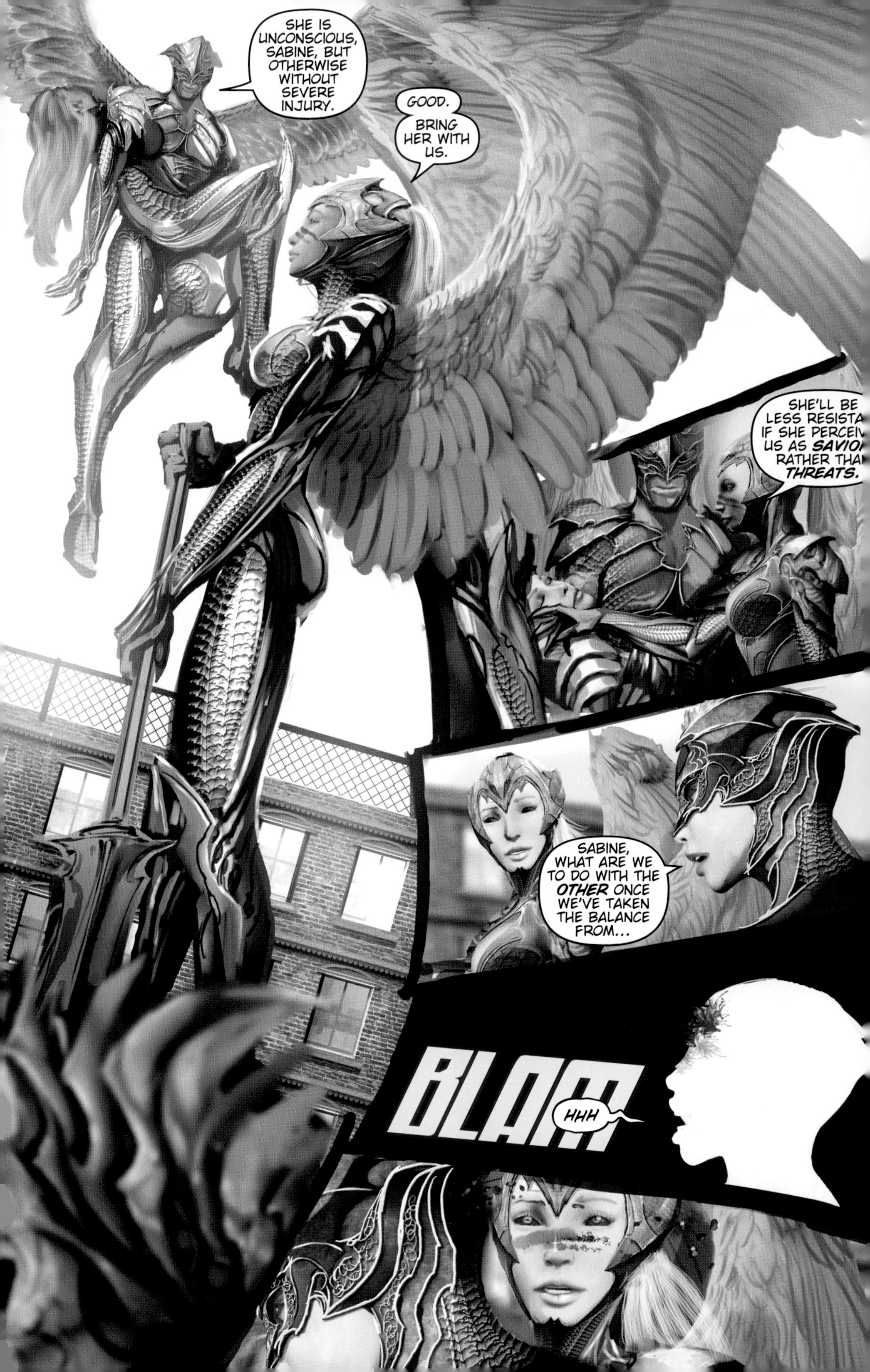
SHE IS UNCONSCIOUS, SABINE, BUT OTHERWISE WITHOUT SEVERE INJURY.
GOOD.
BRING HER WITH US.
SHE'LL BE LESS RESISTA IF SHE PERCEIV US AS SAVIO RATHER THA THREATS.
SABINE, WHAT ARE WE TO DO WITH THE OTHER ONCE WE'VE TAKEN THE BALANCE FROM...
BLAM
HHH

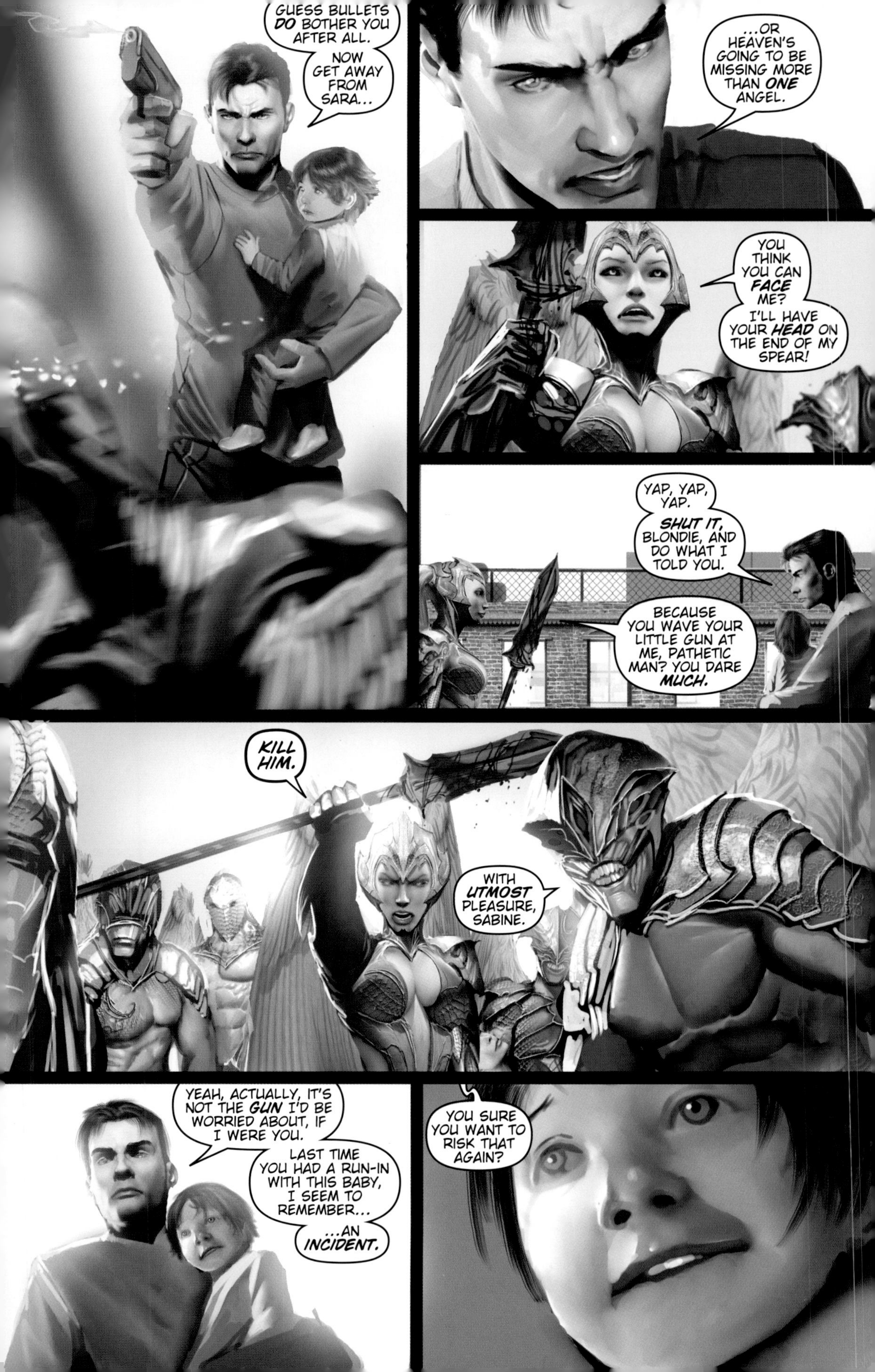

GUESS BULLETS DO BOTHER YOU AFTER ALL.
NOW GET AWAY FROM SARA...
...OR HEAVEN'S GOING TO BE MISSING MORE THAN ONE ANGEL.
YOU THINK YOU CAN FACE ME?
I'LL HAVE YOUR HEAD ON THE END OF MY SPEAR!
YAP, YAP, YAP.
SHUT IT, BLONDIE, AND DO WHAT I TOLD YOU.
BECAUSE YOU WAVE YOUR LITTLE GUN AT ME, PATHETIC MAN? YOU DARE MUCH.
KILL HIM.
WITH UTMOST PLEASURE, SABINE.
YEAH, ACTUALLY, IT'S NOT THE GUN I'D BE WORRIED ABOUT, IF I WERE YOU.
LAST TIME YOU HAD A RUN-IN WITH THIS BABY, I SEEM TO REMEMBER...
...AN INCIDENT.
YOU SURE YOU WANT TO RISK THAT AGAIN?

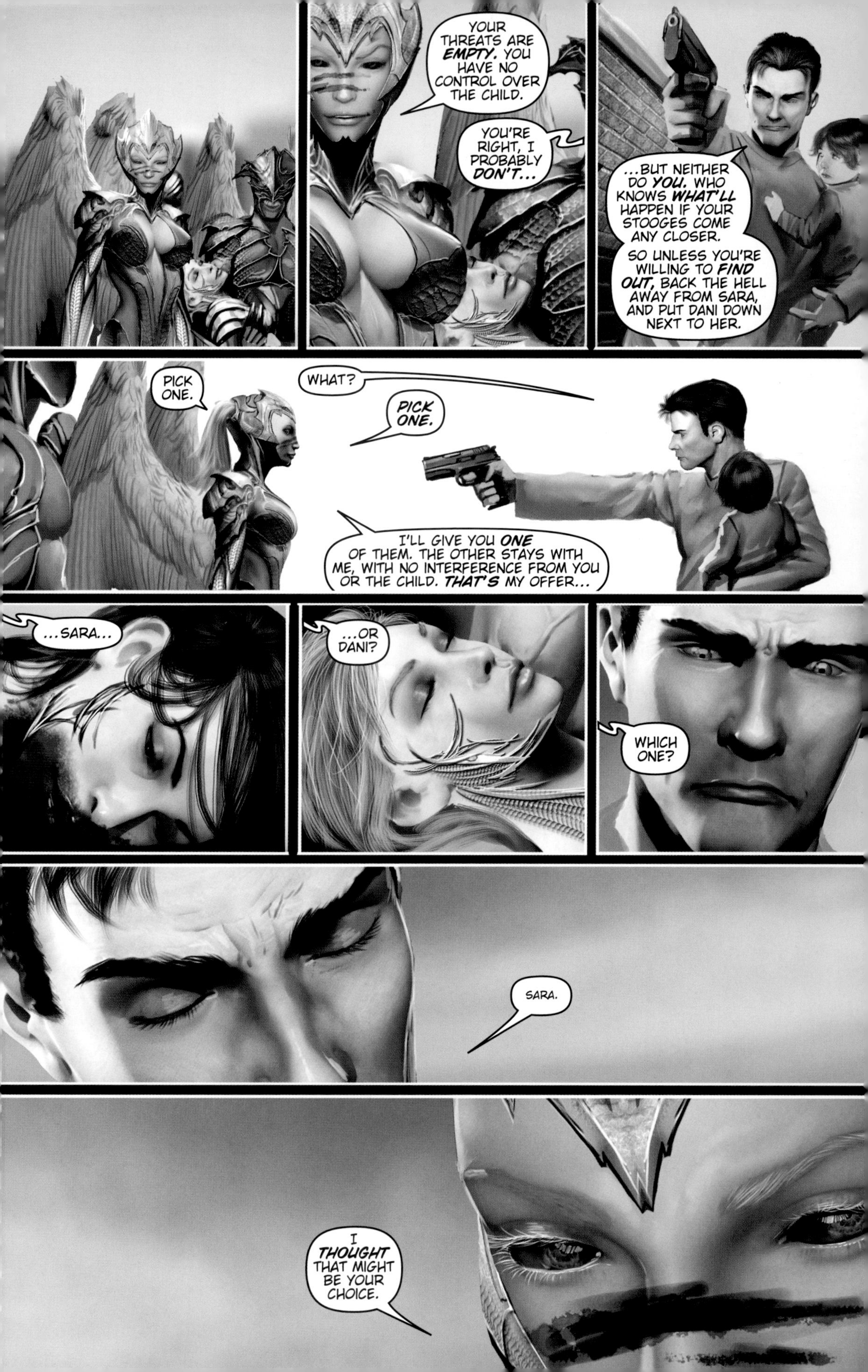
YOUR THREATS ARE **EMPTY.** YOU HAVE NO CONTROL OVER THE CHILD.
YOU'RE RIGHT, I PROBABLY **DON'T...**
...BUT NEITHER DO **YOU.** WHO KNOWS **WHAT'LL** HAPPEN IF YOUR STOOGES COME ANY CLOSER.
SO UNLESS YOU'RE WILLING TO **FIND OUT,** BACK THE HELL AWAY FROM SARA, AND PUT DANI DOWN NEXT TO HER.
PICK ONE.
WHAT?
PICK ONE.
I'LL GIVE YOU **ONE** OF THEM. THE OTHER STAYS WITH ME, WITH NO INTERFERENCE FROM YOU OR THE CHILD. **THAT'S** MY OFFER...
...SARA...
...OR DANI?
WHICH ONE?
SARA.
I **THOUGHT** THAT MIGHT BE YOUR CHOICE.

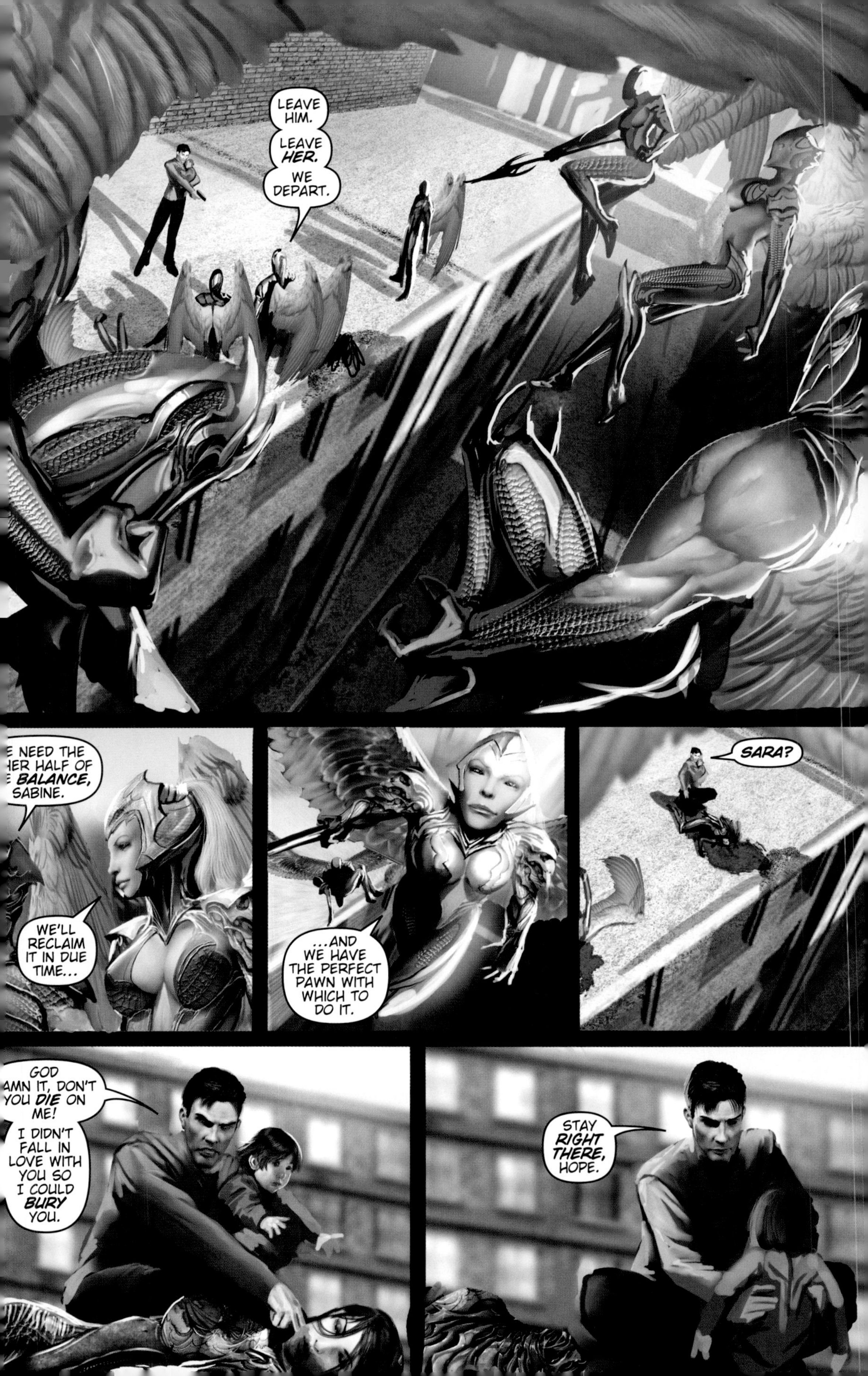
LEAVE HIM.
LEAVE *HER.*
WE DEPART.
E NEED THE HER HALF OF E *BALANCE,* SABINE.
WE'LL RECLAIM IT IN DUE TIME...
...AND WE HAVE THE PERFECT PAWN WITH WHICH TO DO IT.
SARA?
GOD AMN IT, DON'T YOU *DIE* ON ME!
I DIDN'T FALL IN LOVE WITH YOU SO I COULD *BURY* YOU.
STAY *RIGHT THERE,* HOPE.

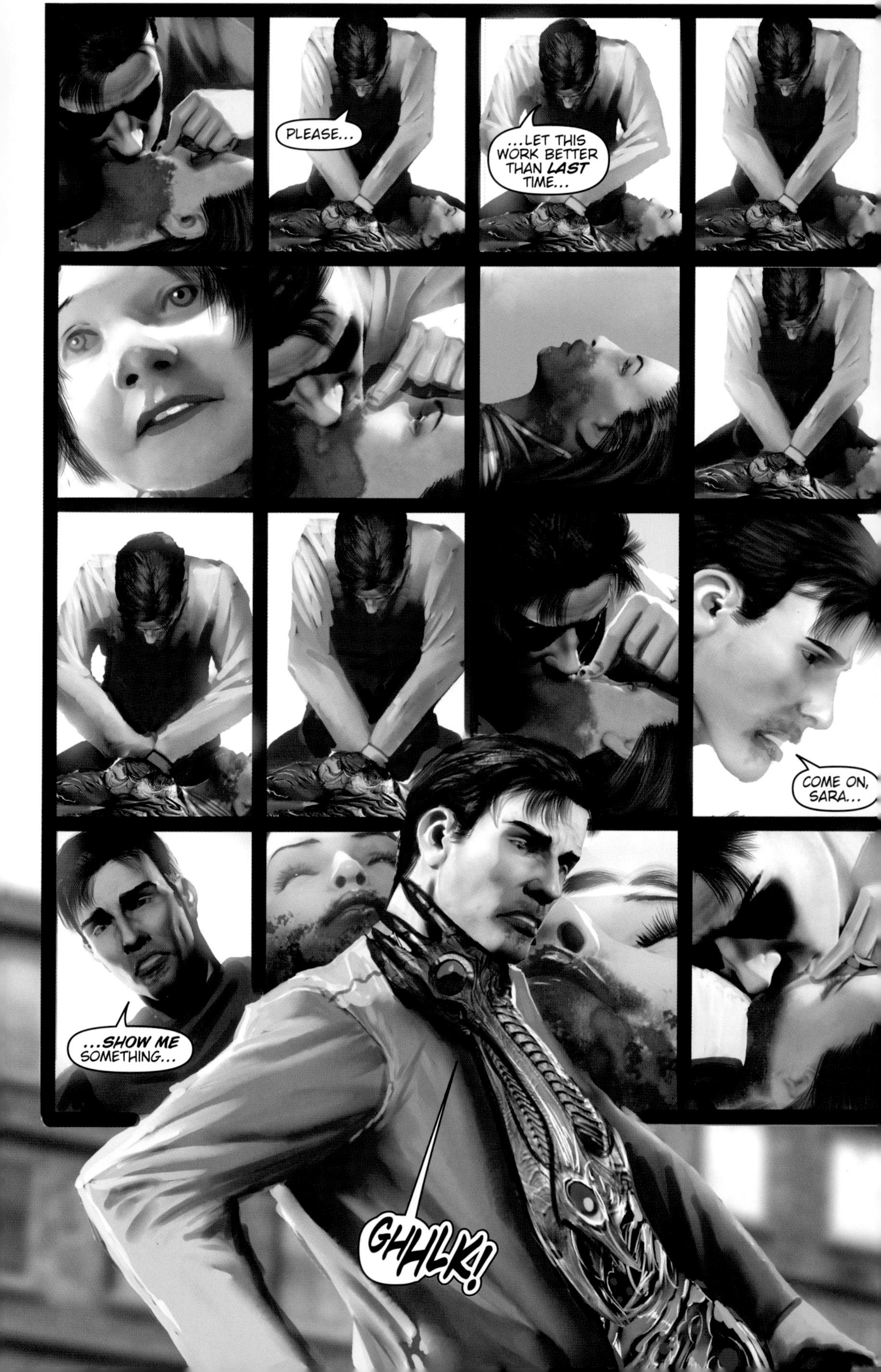
PLEASE...
...LET THIS WORK BETTER THAN LAST TIME...
COME ON, SARA...
...SHOW ME SOMETHING...
GHHLK!

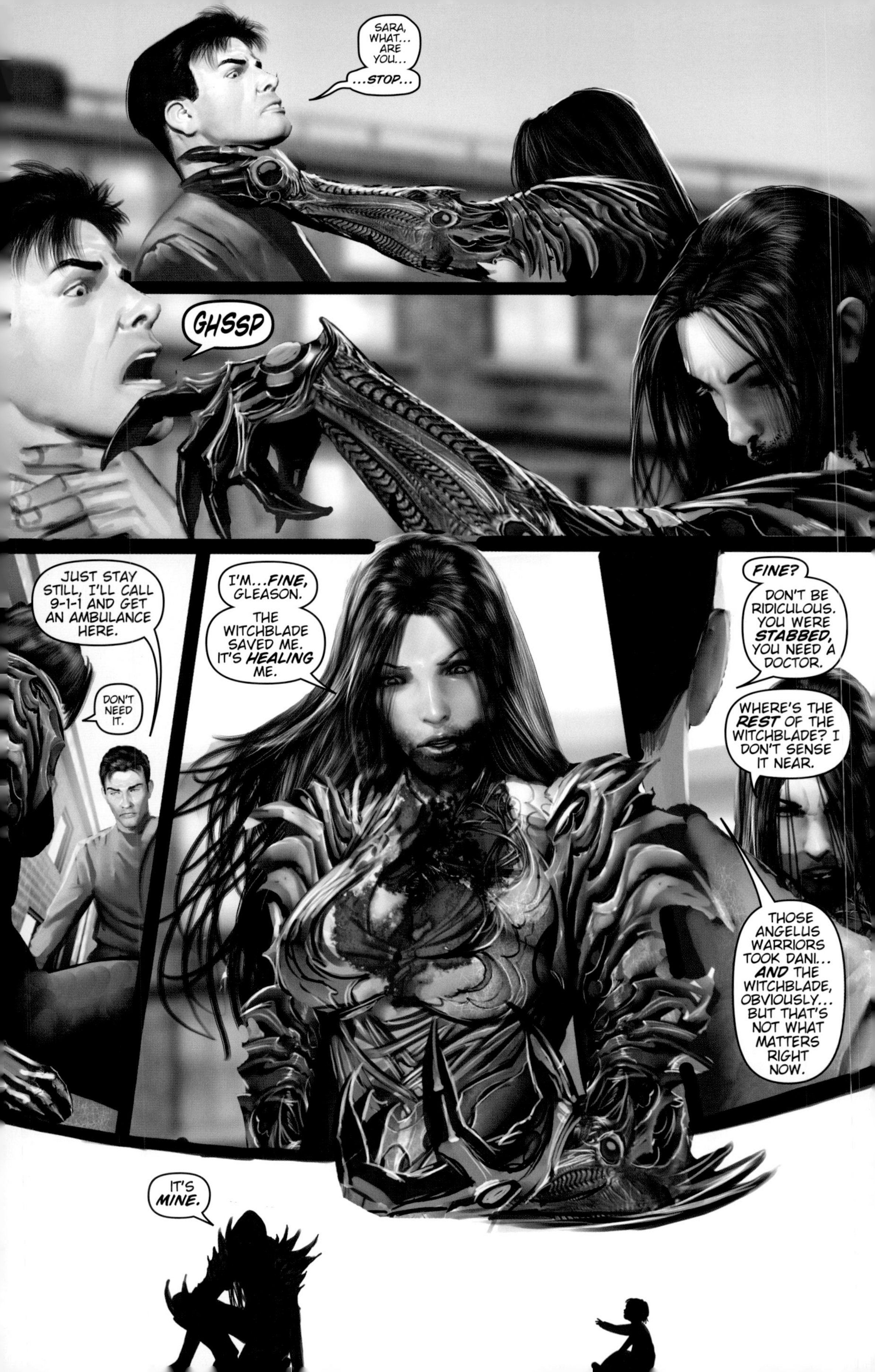
SARA, WHAT... ARE YOU... ...STOP...
GHSSP
JUST STAY STILL, I'LL CALL 9-1-1 AND GET AN AMBULANCE HERE.
DON'T NEED IT.
I'M...FINE, GLEASON.
THE WITCHBLADE SAVED ME. IT'S HEALING ME.
FINE?
DON'T BE RIDICULOUS. YOU WERE STABBED, YOU NEED A DOCTOR.
WHERE'S THE REST OF THE WITCHBLADE? I DON'T SENSE IT NEAR.
THOSE ANGELUS WARRIORS TOOK DANI... AND THE WITCHBLADE, OBVIOUSLY... BUT THAT'S NOT WHAT MATTERS RIGHT NOW.
IT'S MINE.

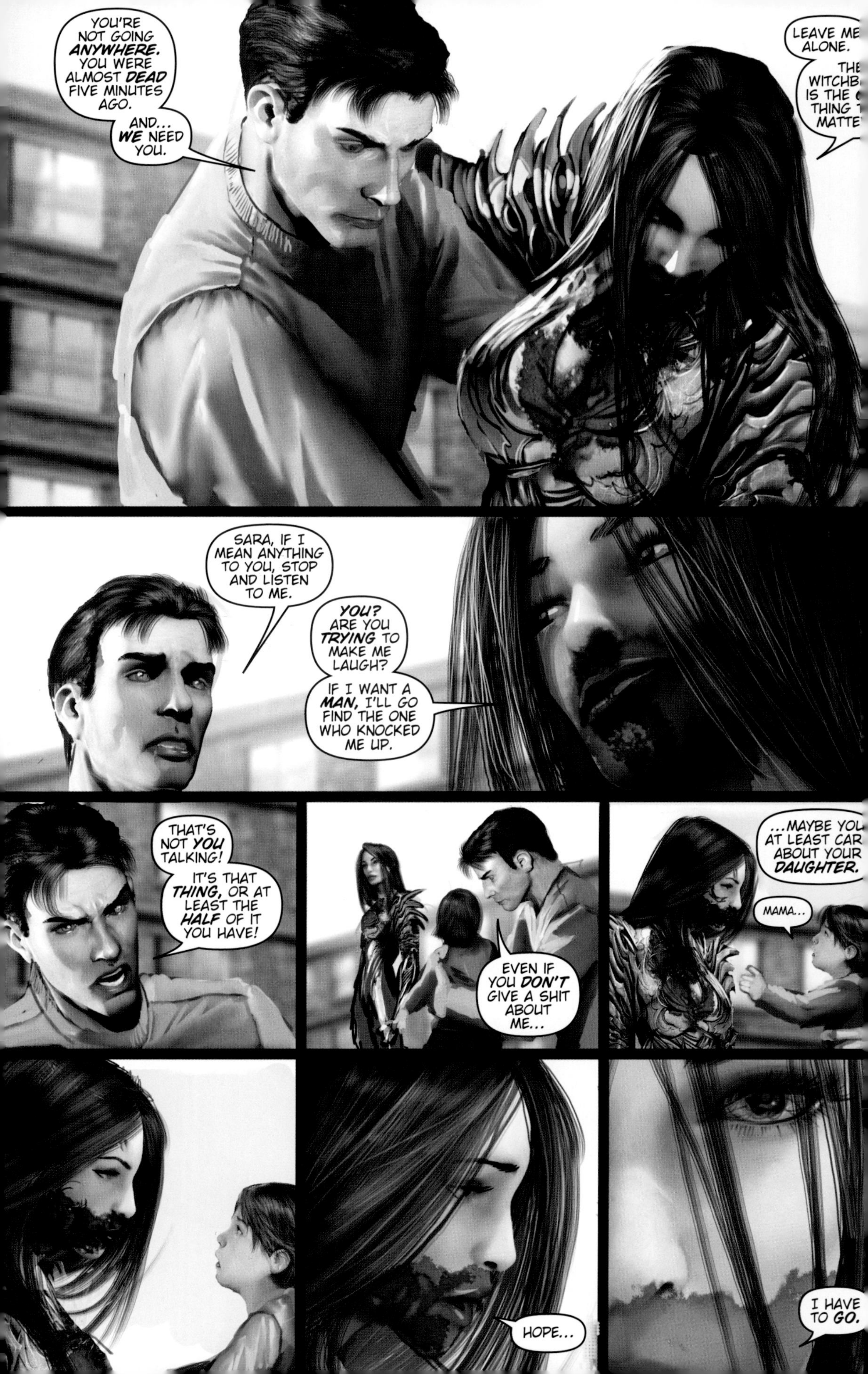

YOU'RE NOT GOING ANYWHERE. YOU WERE ALMOST DEAD FIVE MINUTES AGO.
AND... WE NEED YOU.
LEAVE ME ALONE.
SARA, IF I MEAN ANYTHING TO YOU, STOP AND LISTEN TO ME.
YOU? ARE YOU TRYING TO MAKE ME LAUGH?
IF I WANT A MAN, I'LL GO FIND THE ONE WHO KNOCKED ME UP.
THAT'S NOT YOU TALKING!
IT'S THAT THING, OR AT LEAST THE HALF OF IT YOU HAVE!
EVEN IF YOU DON'T GIVE A SHIT ABOUT ME...
MAMA...
HOPE...
I HAVE TO GO.

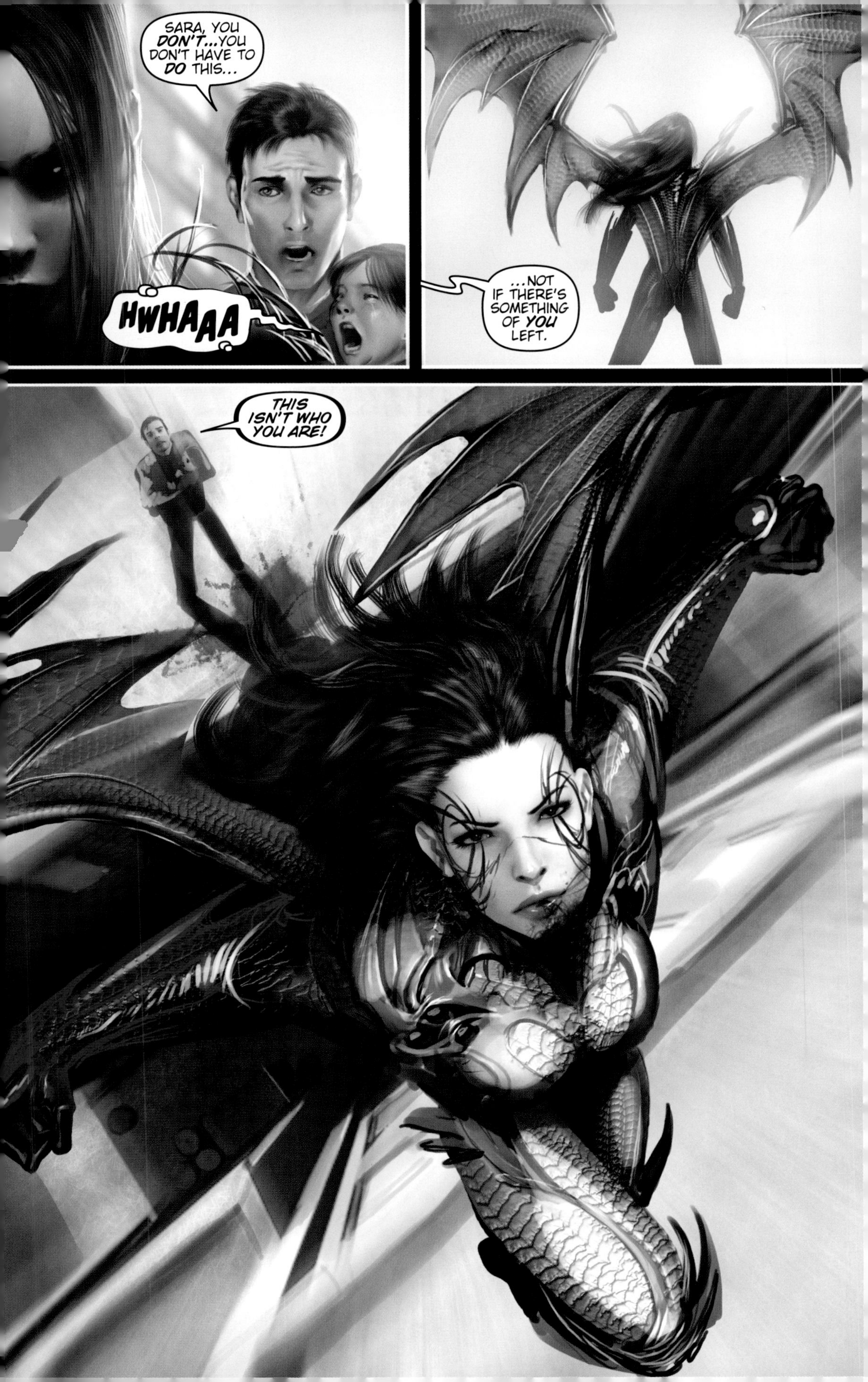
SARA, YOU DON'T...YOU DON'T HAVE TO DO THIS...
HWHAAA
...NOT IF THERE'S SOMETHING OF YOU LEFT.
THIS ISN'T WHO YOU ARE!

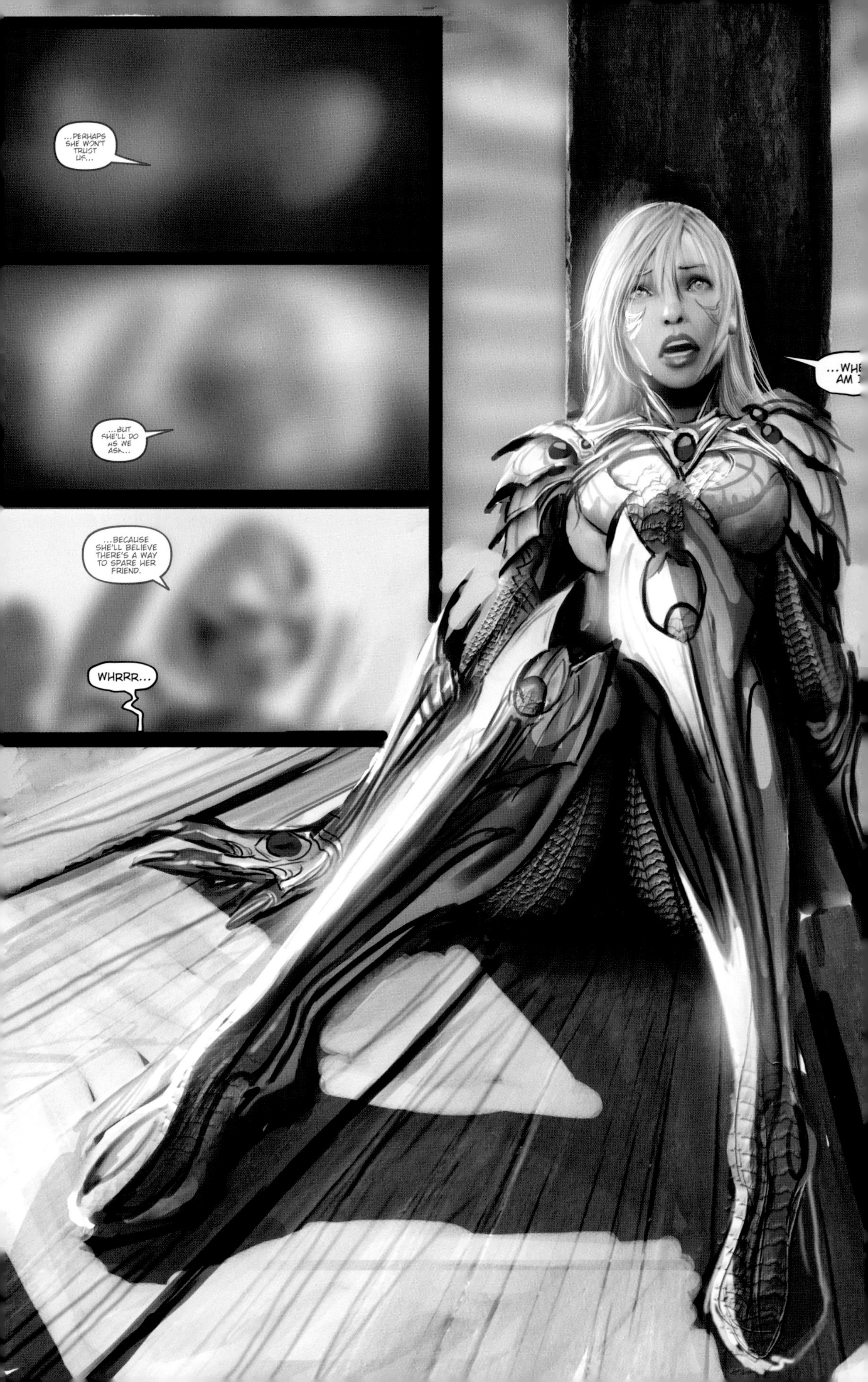

...PERHAPS SHE WON'T TRUST US...
...BUT SHE'LL DO AS WE ASK...
...BECAUSE SHE'LL BELIEVE THERE'S A WAY TO SPARE HER FRIEND.
WHRRR...
...WHE AM I

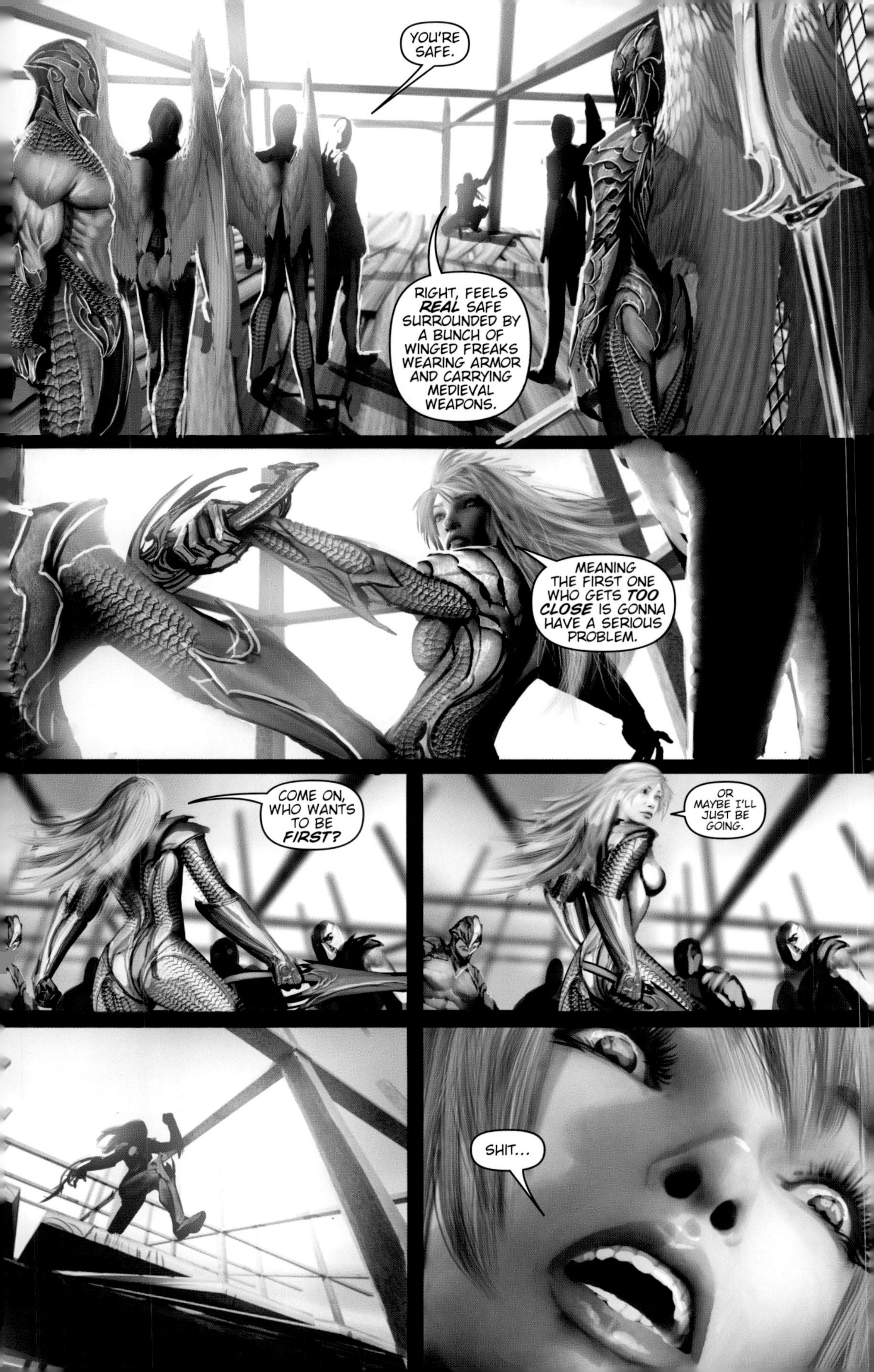
YOU'RE SAFE.
RIGHT, FEELS REAL SAFE SURROUNDED BY A BUNCH OF WINGED FREAKS WEARING ARMOR AND CARRYING MEDIEVAL WEAPONS.
MEANING THE FIRST ONE WHO GETS TOO CLOSE IS GONNA HAVE A SERIOUS PROBLEM.
COME ON, WHO WANTS TO BE FIRST?
OR MAYBE I'LL JUST BE GOING.
SHIT...

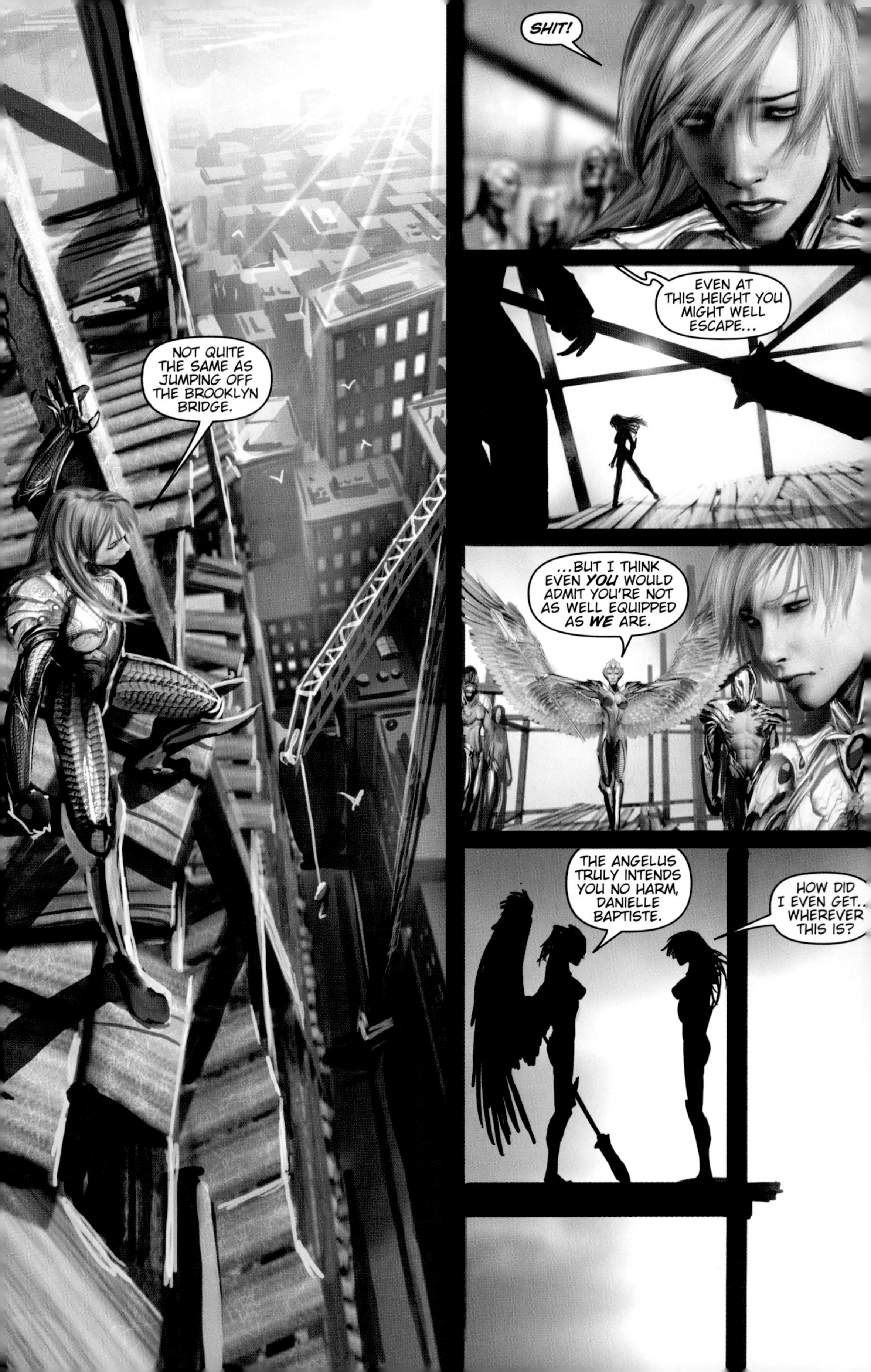
NOT QUITE THE SAME AS JUMPING OFF THE BROOKLYN BRIDGE.
SHIT!
EVEN AT THIS HEIGHT YOU MIGHT WELL ESCAPE...
...BUT I THINK EVEN YOU WOULD ADMIT YOU'RE NOT AS WELL EQUIPPED AS WE ARE.
THE ANGELUS TRULY INTENDS YOU NO HARM, DANIELLE BAPTISTE.
HOW DID I EVEN GET... WHEREVER THIS IS?

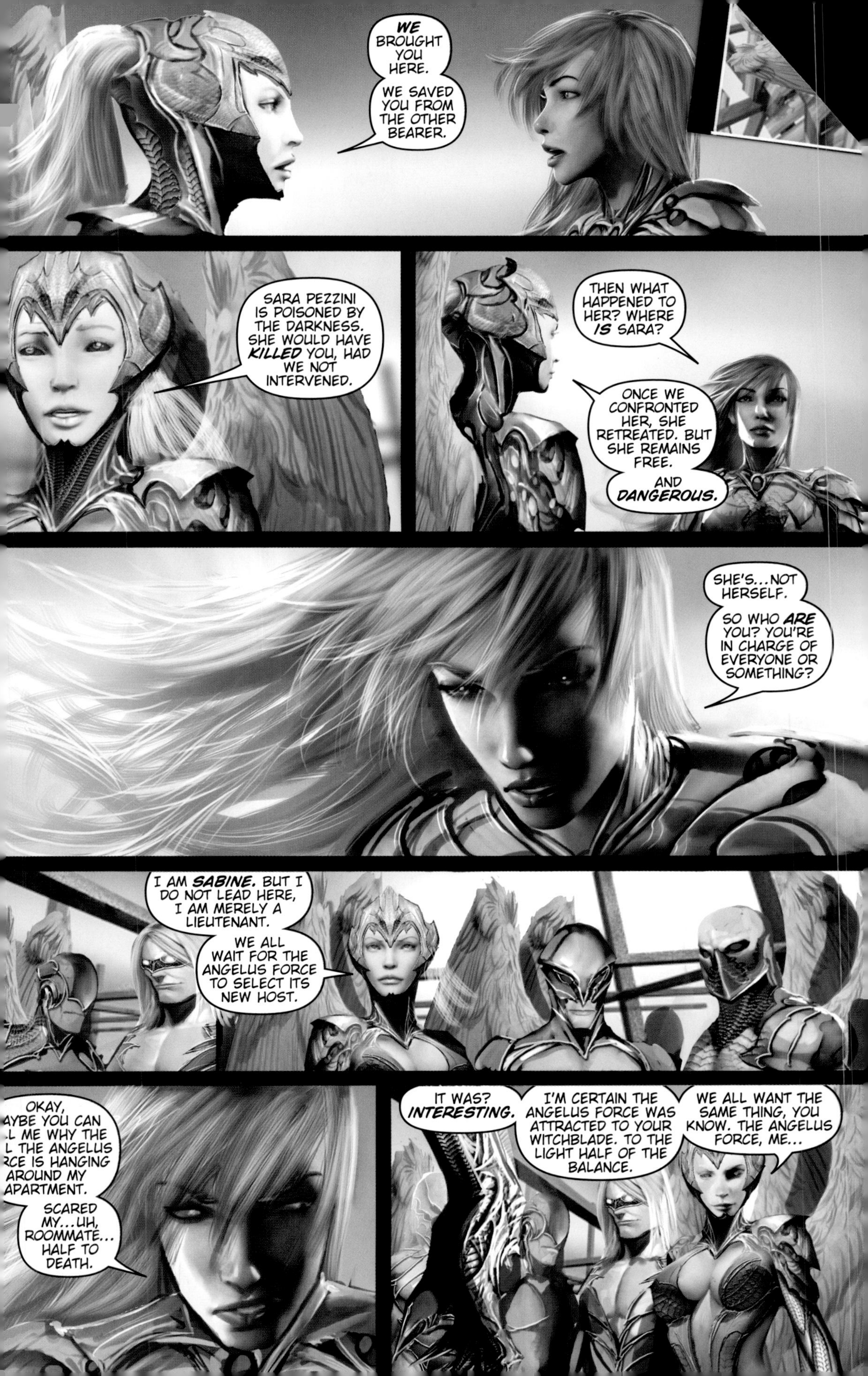
WE BROUGHT YOU HERE.
WE SAVED YOU FROM THE OTHER BEARER.
SARA PEZZINI IS POISONED BY THE DARKNESS. SHE WOULD HAVE KILLED YOU, HAD WE NOT INTERVENED.
THEN WHAT HAPPENED TO HER? WHERE IS SARA?
ONCE WE CONFRONTED HER, SHE RETREATED. BUT SHE REMAINS FREE.
AND DANGEROUS.
SHE'S...NOT HERSELF.
SO WHO ARE YOU? YOU'RE IN CHARGE OF EVERYONE OR SOMETHING?
I AM SABINE. BUT I DO NOT LEAD HERE, I AM MERELY A LIEUTENANT.
WE ALL WAIT FOR THE ANGELUS FORCE TO SELECT ITS NEW HOST.
OKAY,
AYBE YOU CAN
L ME WHY THE
L THE ANGELUS
RCE IS HANGING
AROUND MY
APARTMENT.
SCARED MY...UH, ROOMMATE... HALF TO DEATH.
IT WAS? INTERESTING.
I'M CERTAIN THE ANGELUS FORCE WAS ATTRACTED TO YOUR WITCHBLADE. TO THE LIGHT HALF OF THE BALANCE.
WE ALL WANT THE SAME THING, YOU KNOW. THE ANGELUS FORCE, ME...

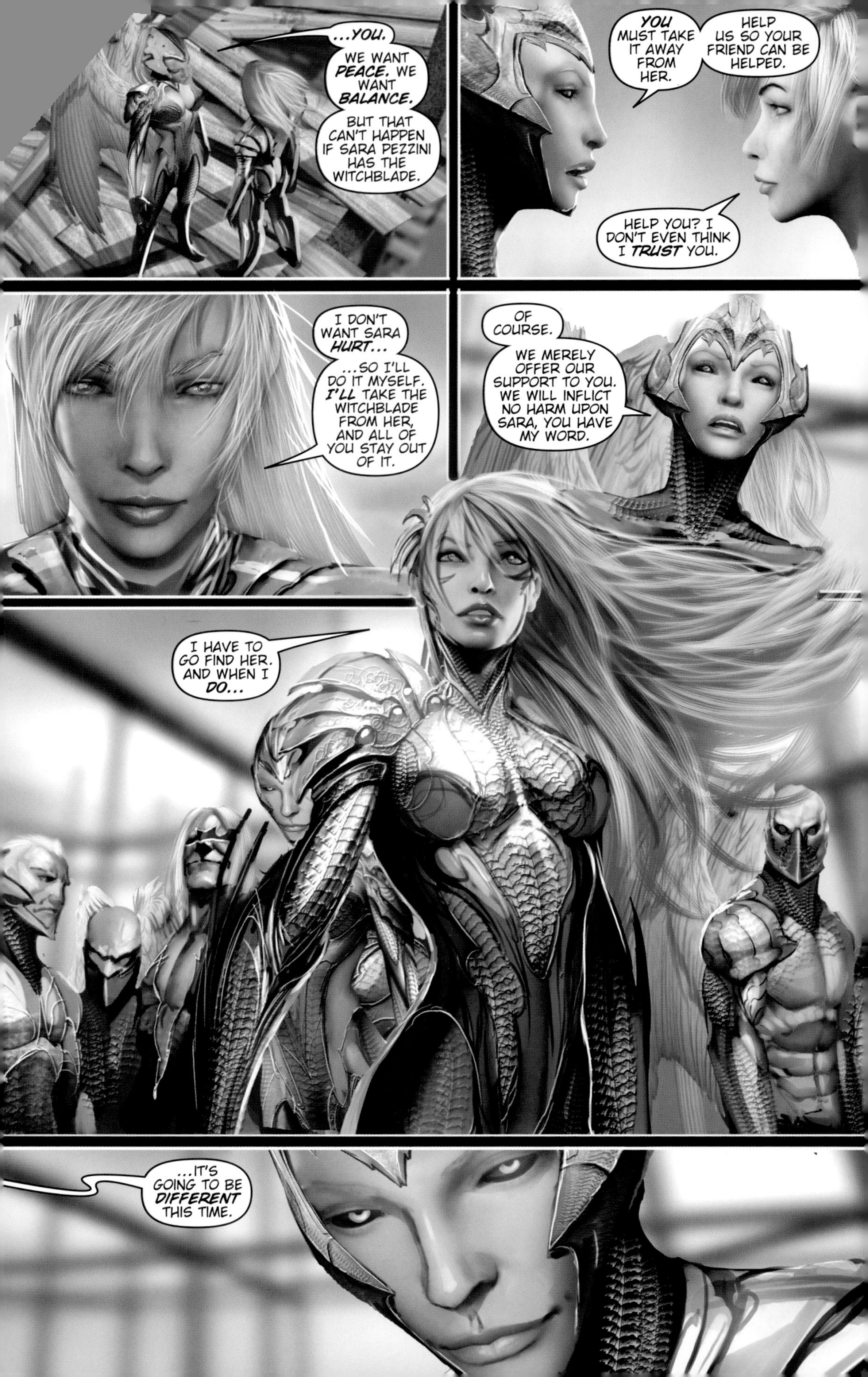
...YOU.
WE WANT PEACE. WE WANT BALANCE.
BUT THAT CAN'T HAPPEN IF SARA PEZZINI HAS THE WITCHBLADE.
YOU MUST TAKE IT AWAY FROM HER.
HELP US SO YOUR FRIEND CAN BE HELPED.
HELP YOU? I DON'T EVEN THINK I TRUST YOU.
I DON'T WANT SARA HURT...
...SO I'LL DO IT MYSELF. I'LL TAKE THE WITCHBLADE FROM HER, AND ALL OF YOU STAY OUT OF IT.
OF COURSE.
WE MERELY OFFER OUR SUPPORT TO YOU. WE WILL INFLICT NO HARM UPON SARA, YOU HAVE MY WORD.
I HAVE TO GO FIND HER. AND WHEN I DO...
...IT'S GOING TO BE DIFFERENT THIS TIME.

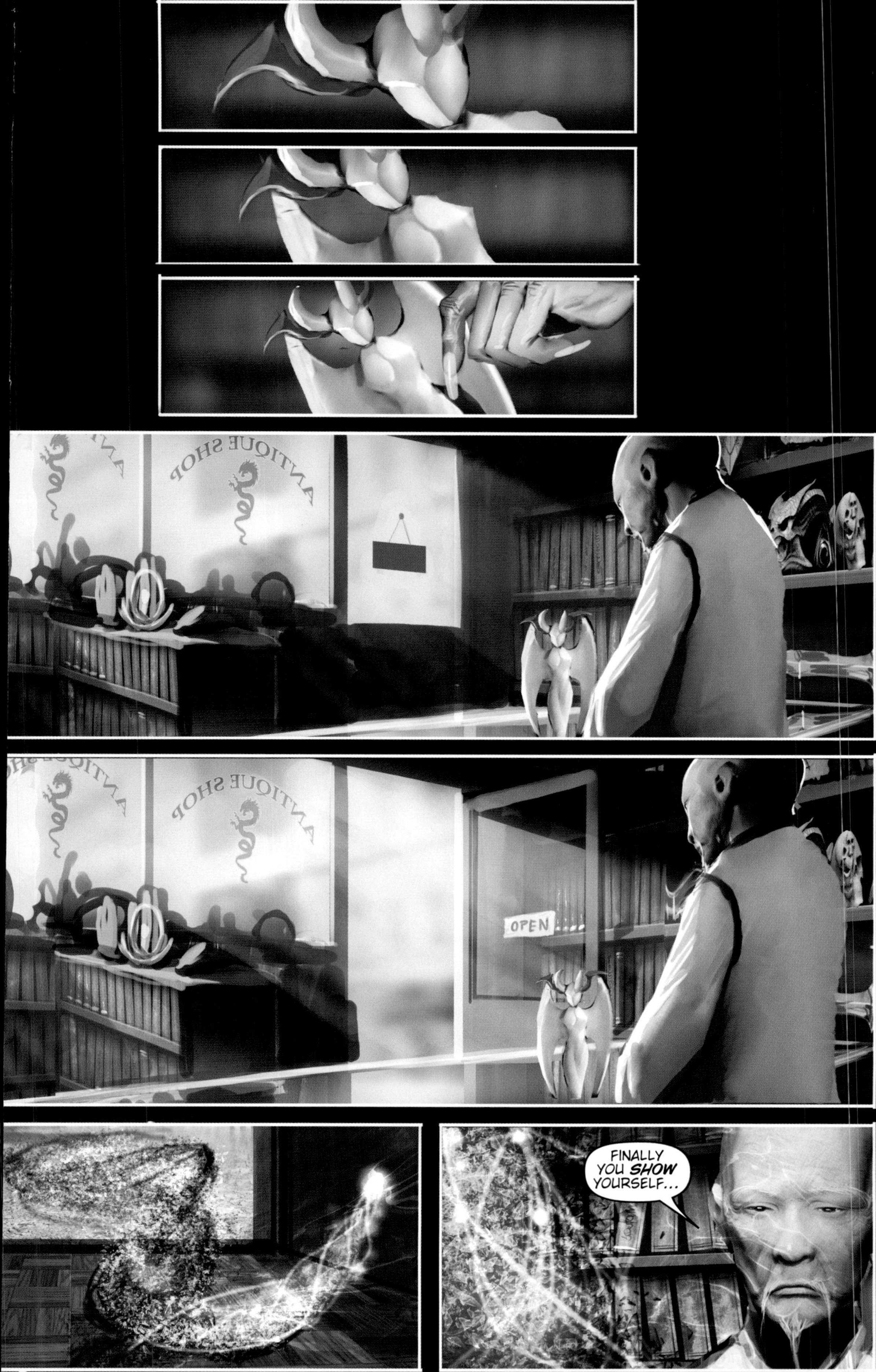

ANTIQUE SHOP
OPEN
FINALLY YOU SHOW YOURSELF...

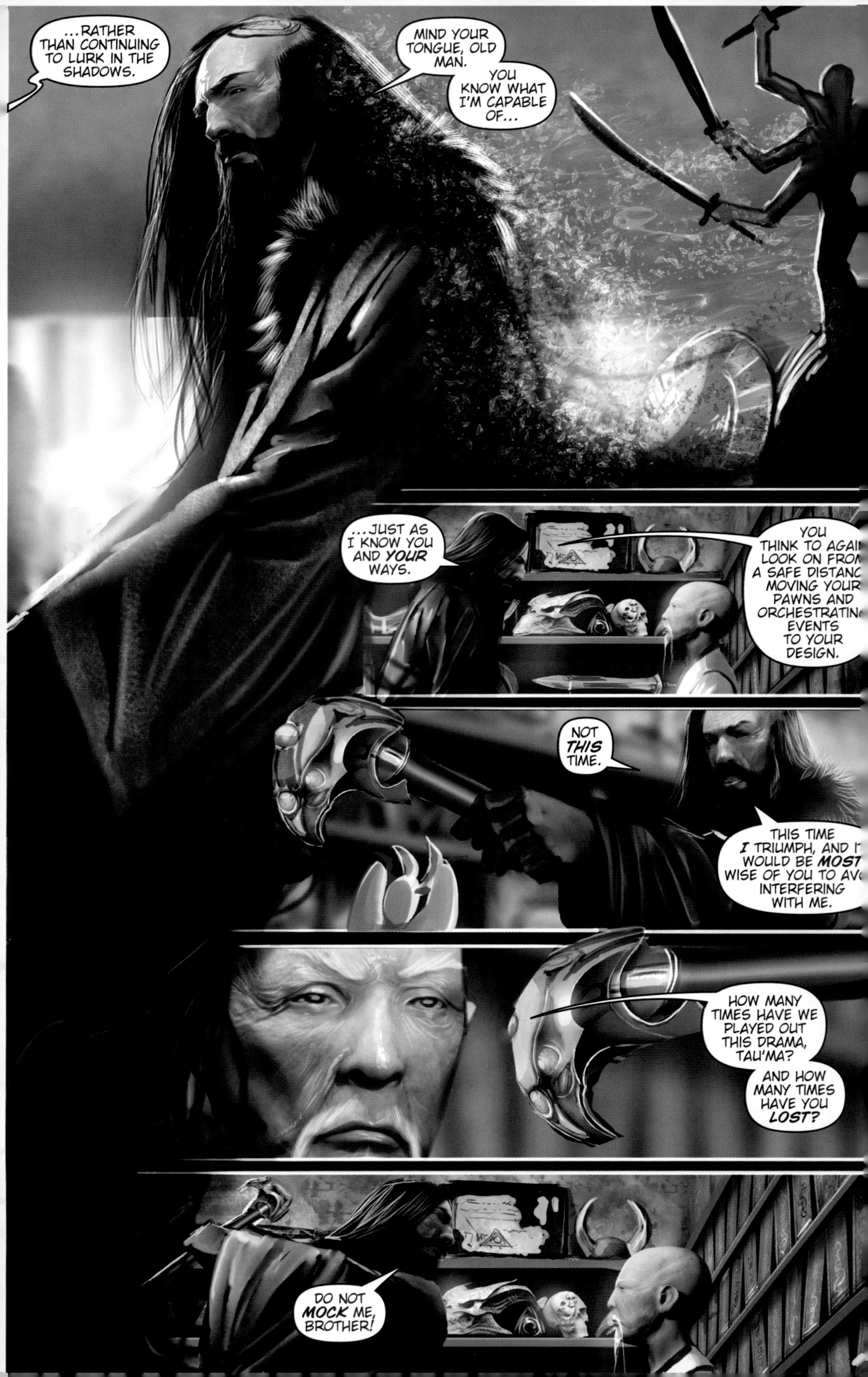
...RATHER THAN CONTINUING TO LURK IN THE SHADOWS.
MIND YOUR TONGUE, OLD MAN.
YOU KNOW WHAT I'M CAPABLE OF...
...JUST AS I KNOW YOU AND YOUR WAYS.
YOU THINK TO AGAI LOOK ON FROM A SAFE DISTANC MOVING YOUR PAWNS AND ORCHESTRATIN EVENTS TO YOUR DESIGN.
NOT THIS TIME.
THIS TIME I TRIUMPH, AND I WOULD BE MOST WISE OF YOU TO AV INTERFERING WITH ME.
HOW MANY TIMES HAVE WE PLAYED OUT THIS DRAMA, TAU'MA?
AND HOW MANY TIMES HAVE YOU LOST?
DO NOT MOCK ME, BROTHER!

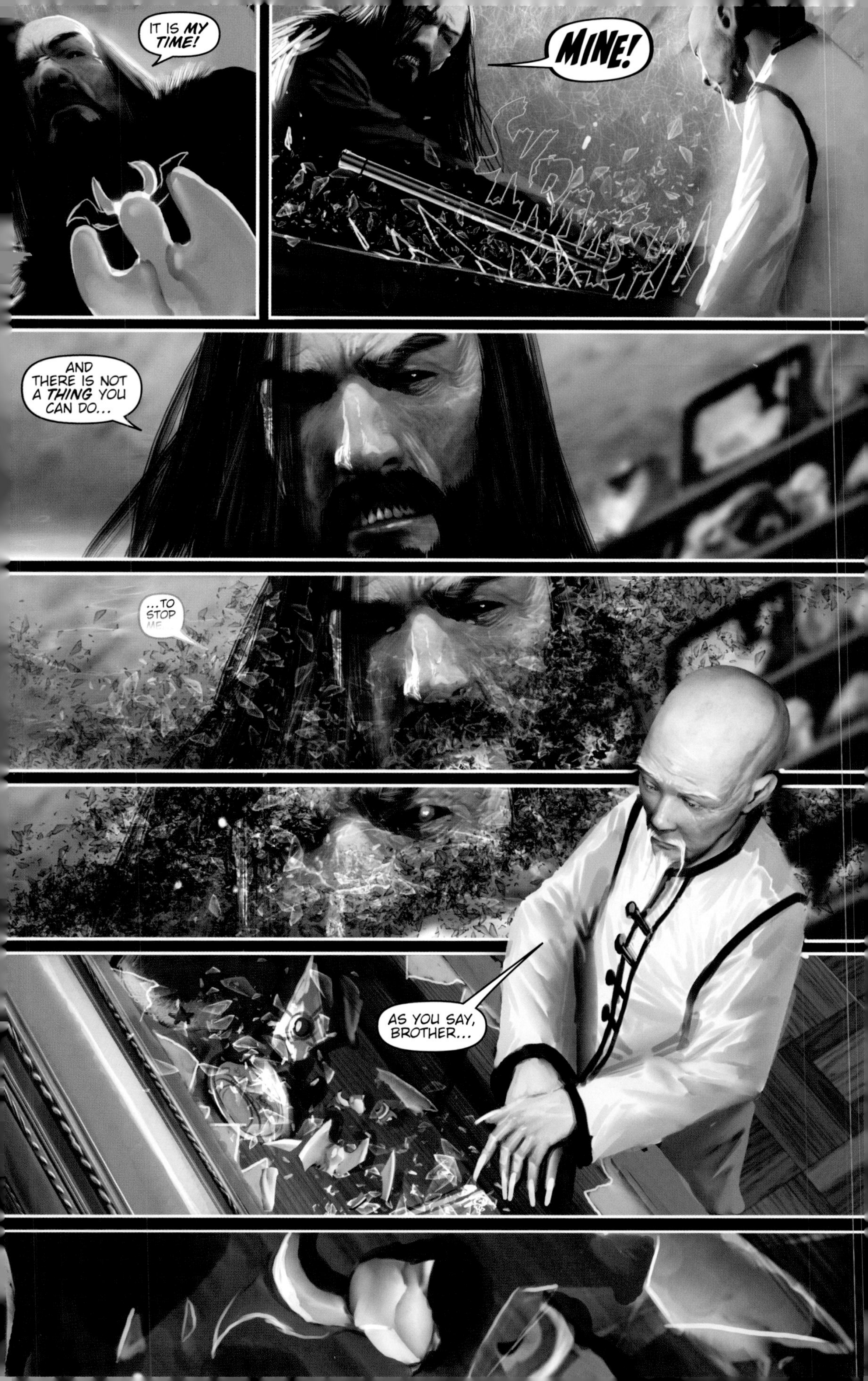
IT IS MY TIME!
MINE!
AND THERE IS NOT A THING YOU CAN DO...
...TO STOP ME.
AS YOU SAY, BROTHER...

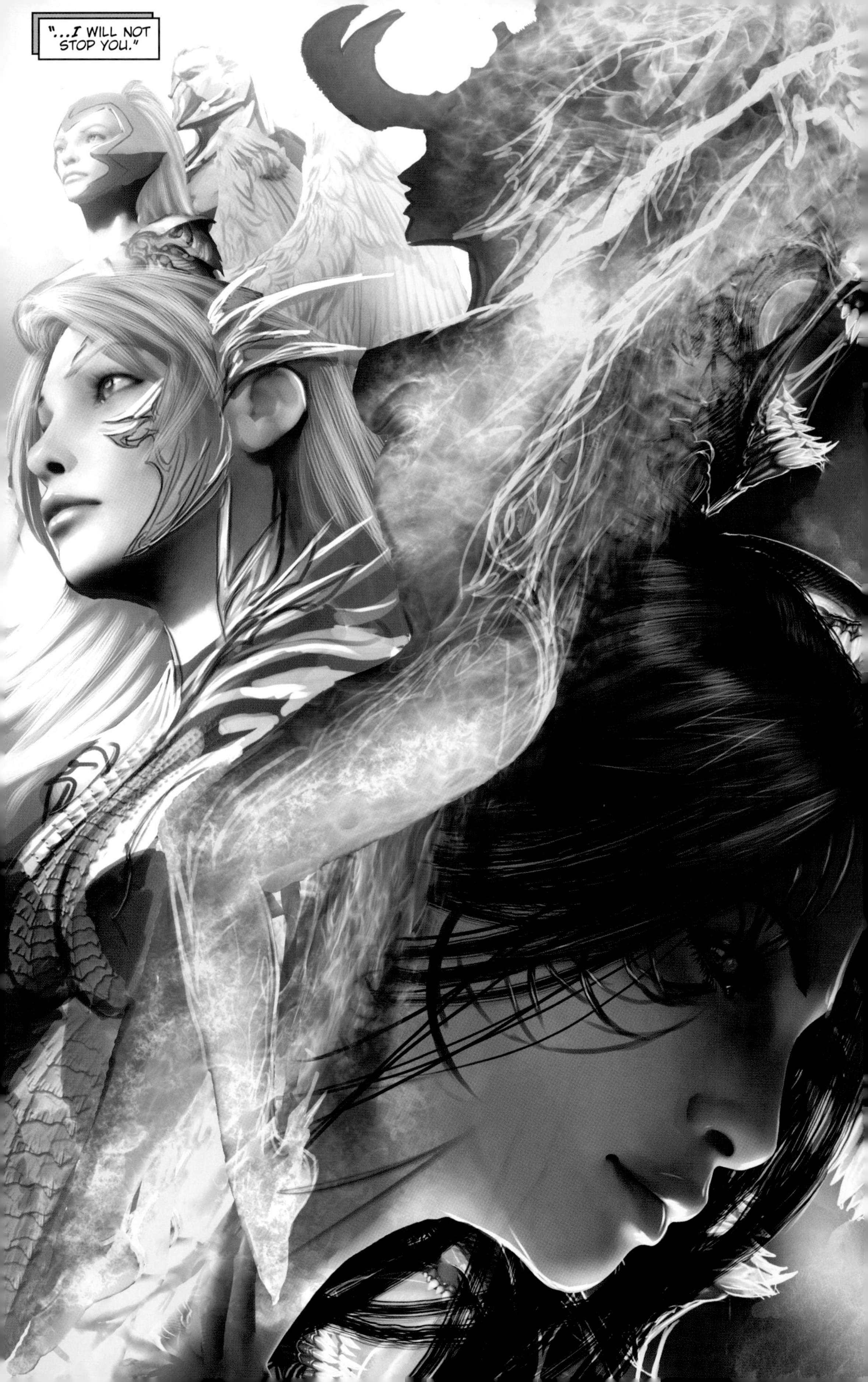
"...I WILL NOT STOP YOU."

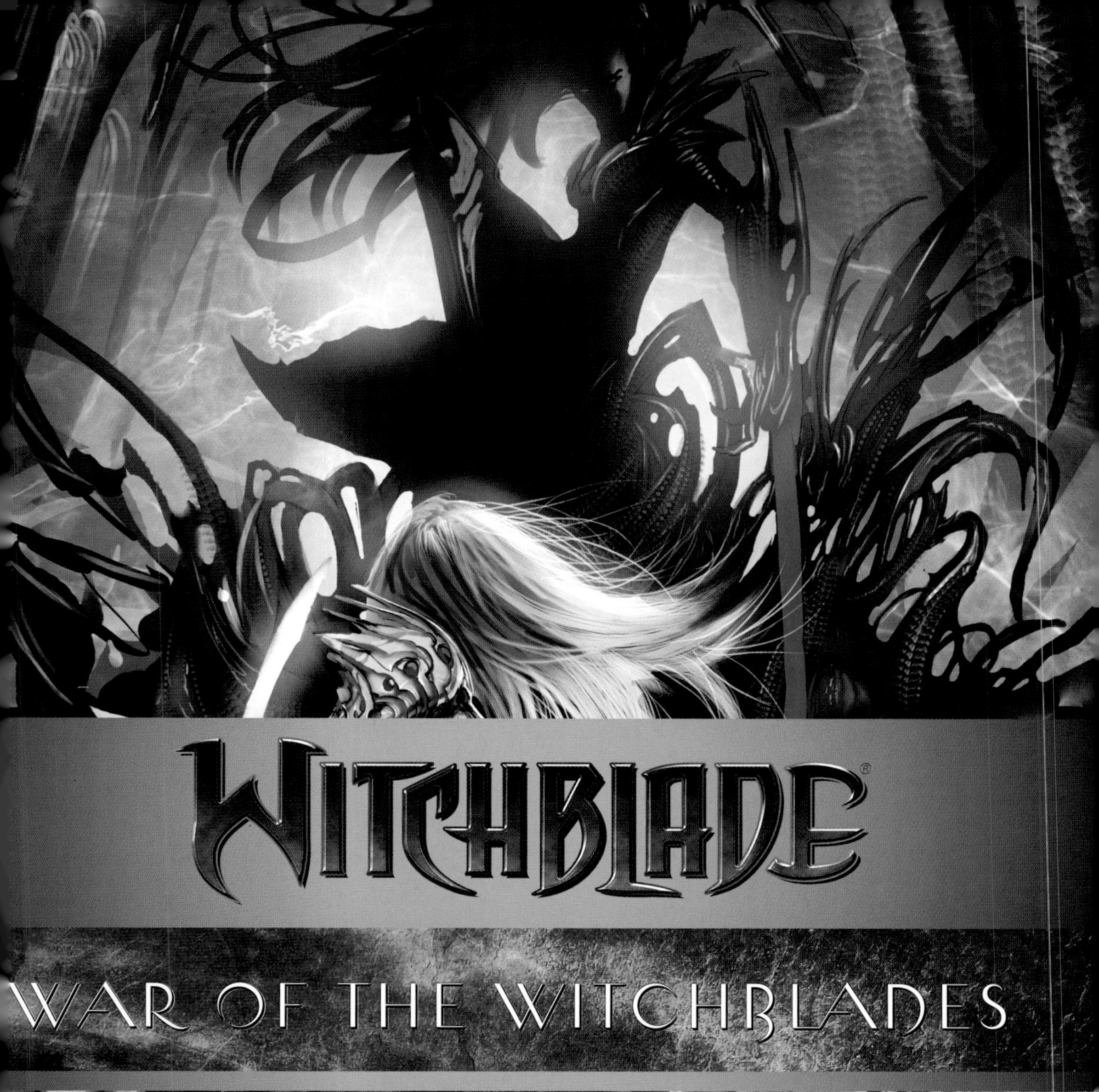

WITCHBLADE®

WAR OF THE WITCHBLADES

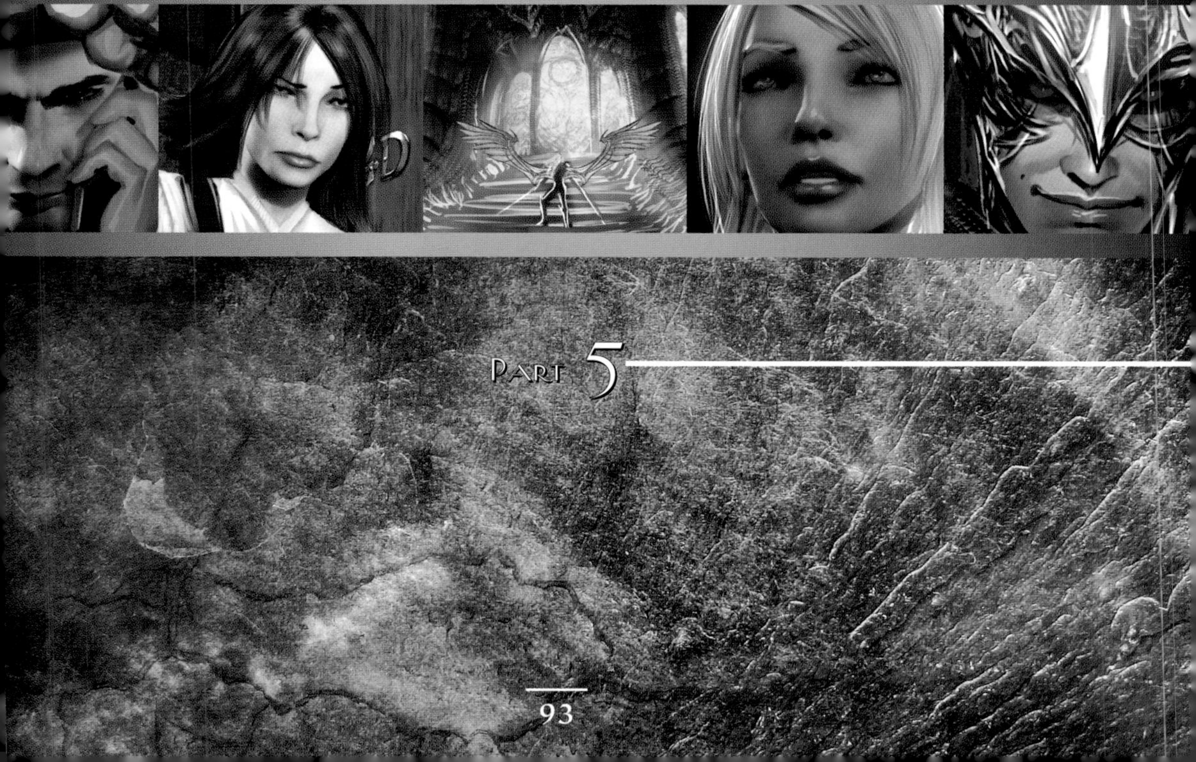

PART 5

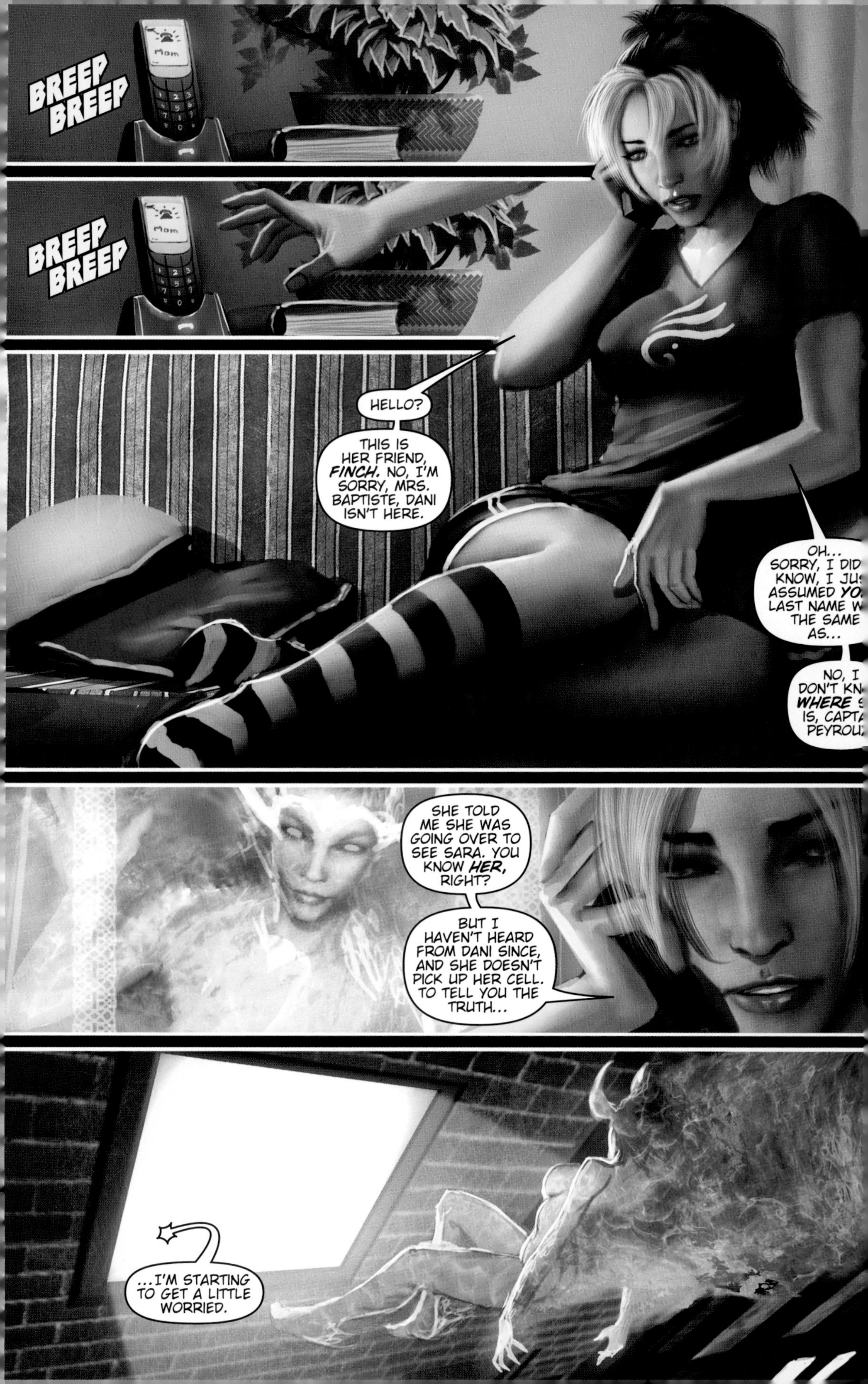

BREEP BREEP
BREEP BREEP
HELLO?
THIS IS HER FRIEND, FINCH. NO, I'M SORRY, MRS. BAPTISTE, DANI ISN'T HERE.
OH... SORRY, I DID KNOW, I JUS ASSUMED YO LAST NAME W THE SAME AS...
NO, I DON'T KN WHERE S IS, CAPTA PEYROU
SHE TOLD ME SHE WAS GOING OVER TO SEE SARA. YOU KNOW HER, RIGHT?
BUT I HAVEN'T HEARD FROM DANI SINCE, AND SHE DOESN'T PICK UP HER CELL. TO TELL YOU THE TRUTH...
...I'M STARTING TO GET A LITTLE WORRIED.

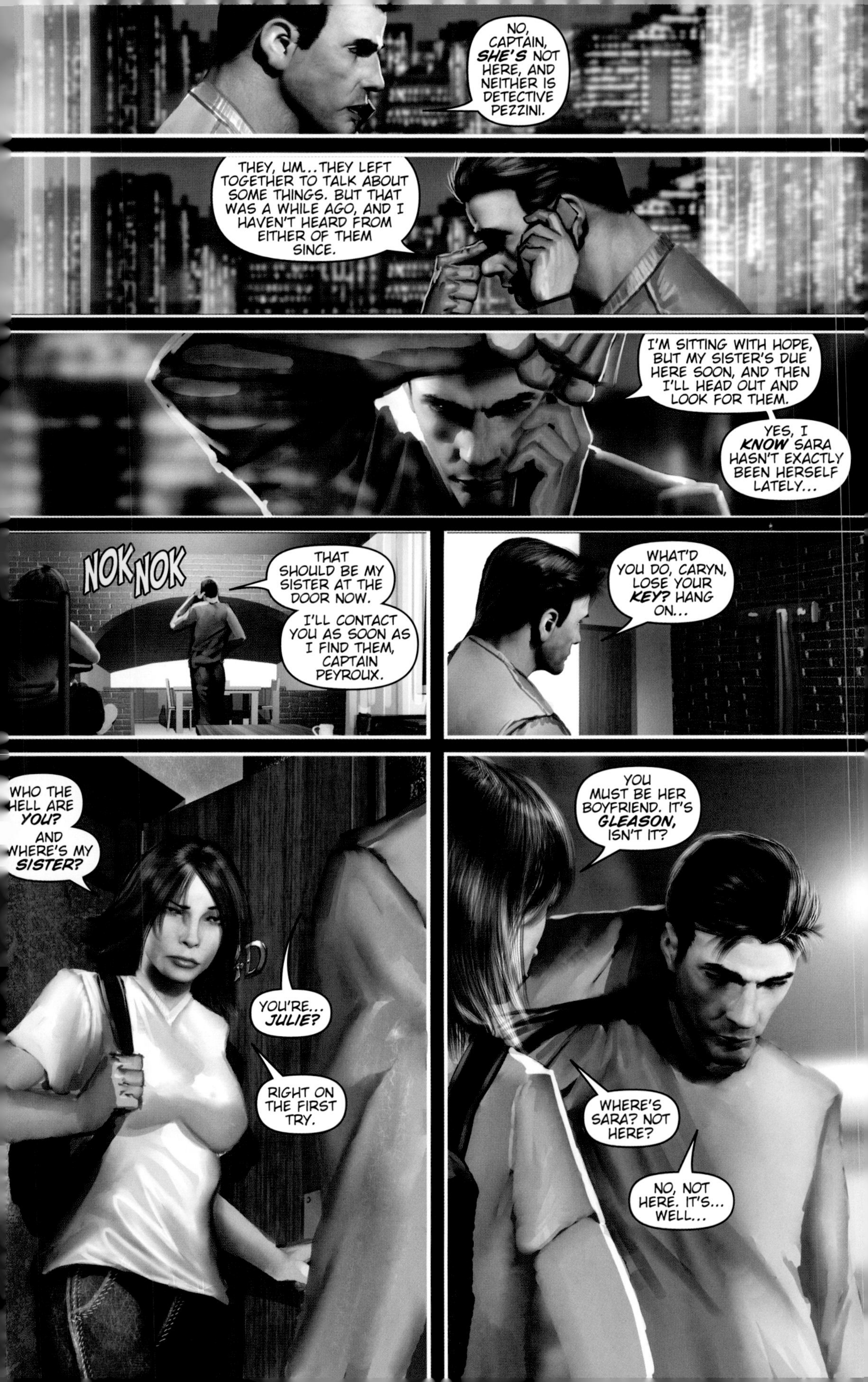
NO, CAPTAIN, SHE'S NOT HERE, AND NEITHER IS DETECTIVE PEZZINI.
THEY, UM...THEY LEFT TOGETHER TO TALK ABOUT SOME THINGS. BUT THAT WAS A WHILE AGO, AND I HAVEN'T HEARD FROM EITHER OF THEM SINCE.
I'M SITTING WITH HOPE, BUT MY SISTER'S DUE HERE SOON, AND THEN I'LL HEAD OUT AND LOOK FOR THEM.
YES, I KNOW SARA HASN'T EXACTLY BEEN HERSELF LATELY...
NOK NOK
THAT SHOULD BE MY SISTER AT THE DOOR NOW.
I'LL CONTACT YOU AS SOON AS I FIND THEM, CAPTAIN PEYROUX.
WHAT'D YOU DO, CARYN, LOSE YOUR KEY? HANG ON...
WHO THE HELL ARE YOU?
AND WHERE'S MY SISTER?
YOU'RE... JULIE?
RIGHT ON THE FIRST TRY.
YOU MUST BE HER BOYFRIEND. IT'S GLEASON, ISN'T IT?
WHERE'S SARA? NOT HERE?
NO, NOT HERE. IT'S... WELL...

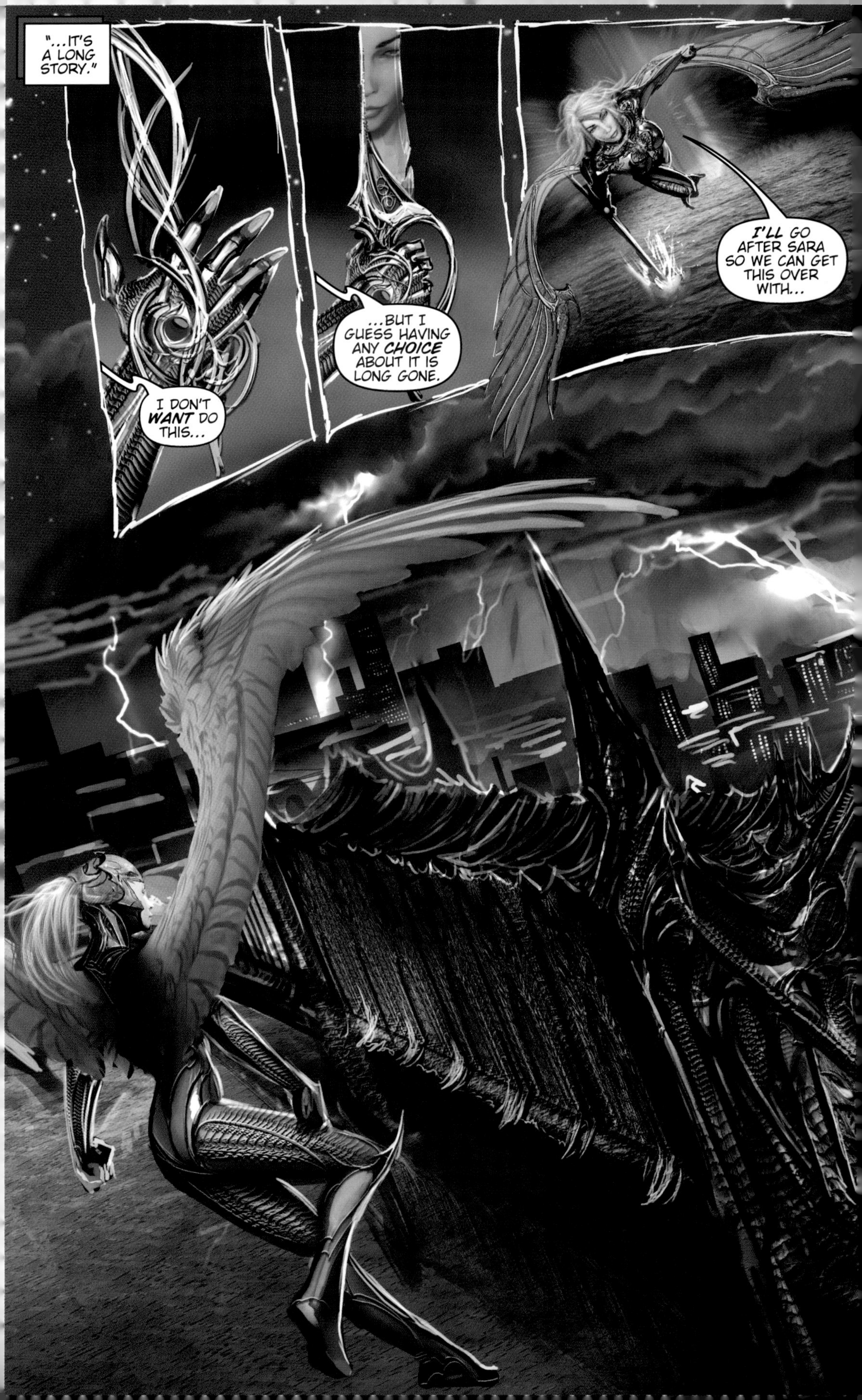
"...IT'S A LONG STORY."
I DON'T WANT DO THIS...
...BUT I GUESS HAVING ANY CHOICE ABOUT IT IS LONG GONE.
I'LL GO AFTER SARA SO WE CAN GET THIS OVER WITH...

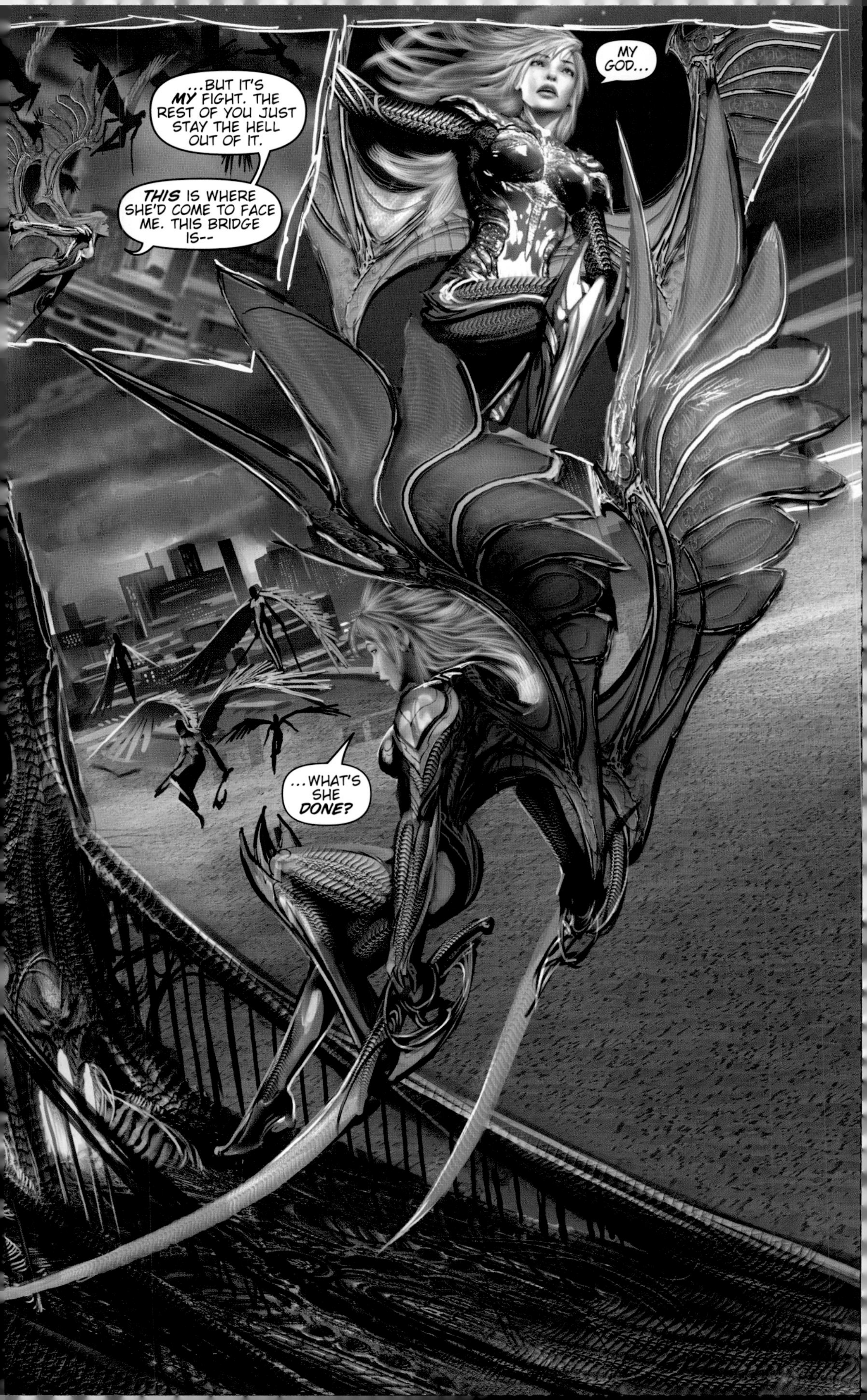
...BUT IT'S *MY* FIGHT. THE REST OF YOU JUST STAY THE HELL OUT OF IT.
THIS IS WHERE SHE'D COME TO FACE ME. THIS BRIDGE IS--
MY GOD...
...WHAT'S SHE *DONE?*

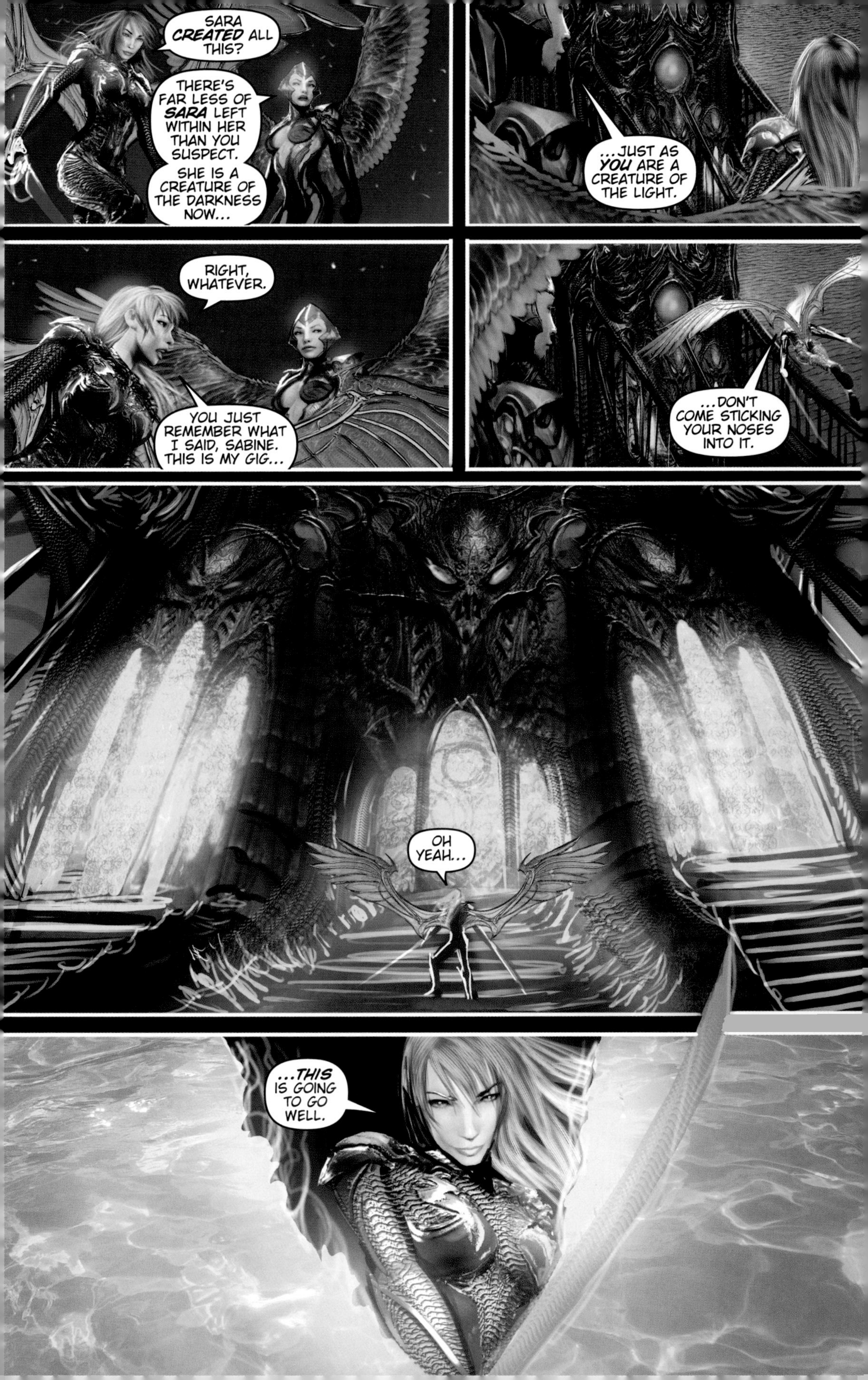
SARA CREATED ALL THIS?
THERE'S FAR LESS OF SARA LEFT WITHIN HER THAN YOU SUSPECT.
SHE IS A CREATURE OF THE DARKNESS NOW...
...JUST AS YOU ARE A CREATURE OF THE LIGHT.
RIGHT, WHATEVER.
YOU JUST REMEMBER WHAT I SAID, SABINE. THIS IS MY GIG...
...DON'T COME STICKING YOUR NOSES INTO IT.
OH YEAH...
...THIS IS GOING TO GO WELL.

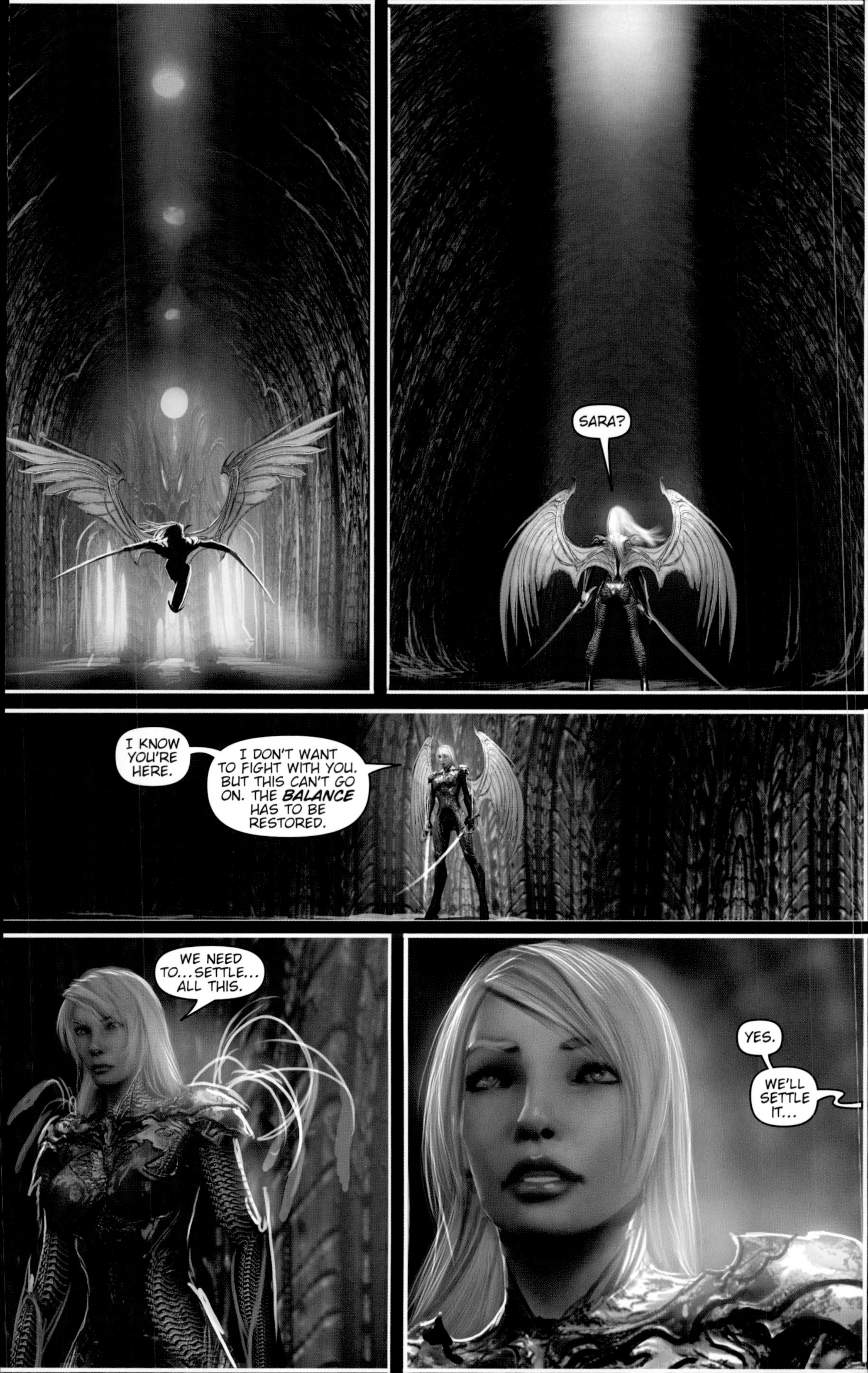
SARA?
I KNOW YOU'RE HERE.
I DON'T WANT TO FIGHT WITH YOU. BUT THIS CAN'T GO ON. THE **BALANCE** HAS TO BE RESTORED.
WE NEED TO...SETTLE... ALL THIS.
YES.
WE'LL SETTLE IT...

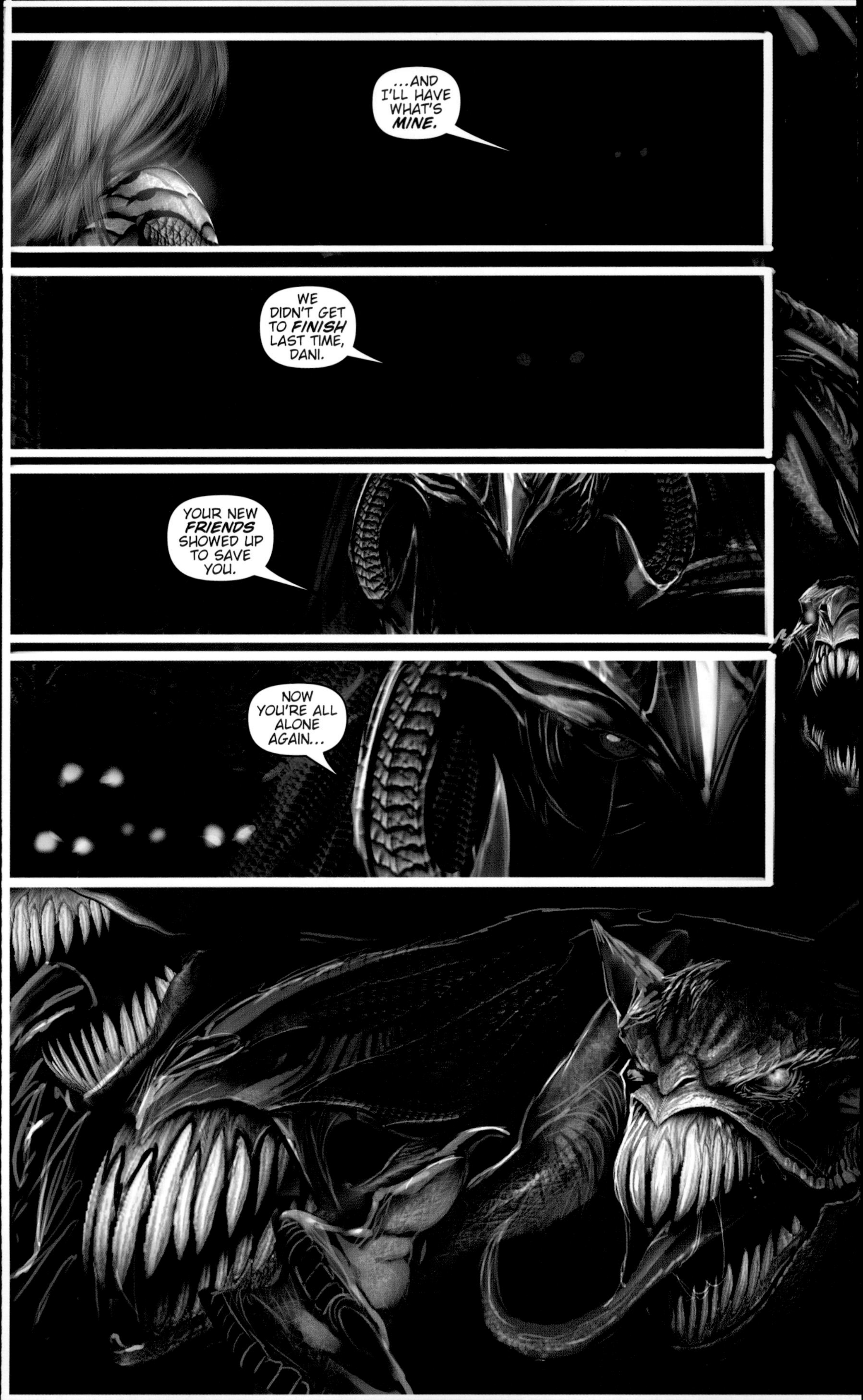
...AND I'LL HAVE WHAT'S MINE.
WE DIDN'T GET TO FINISH LAST TIME, DANI.
YOUR NEW FRIENDS SHOWED UP TO SAVE YOU.
NOW YOU'RE ALL ALONE AGAIN...

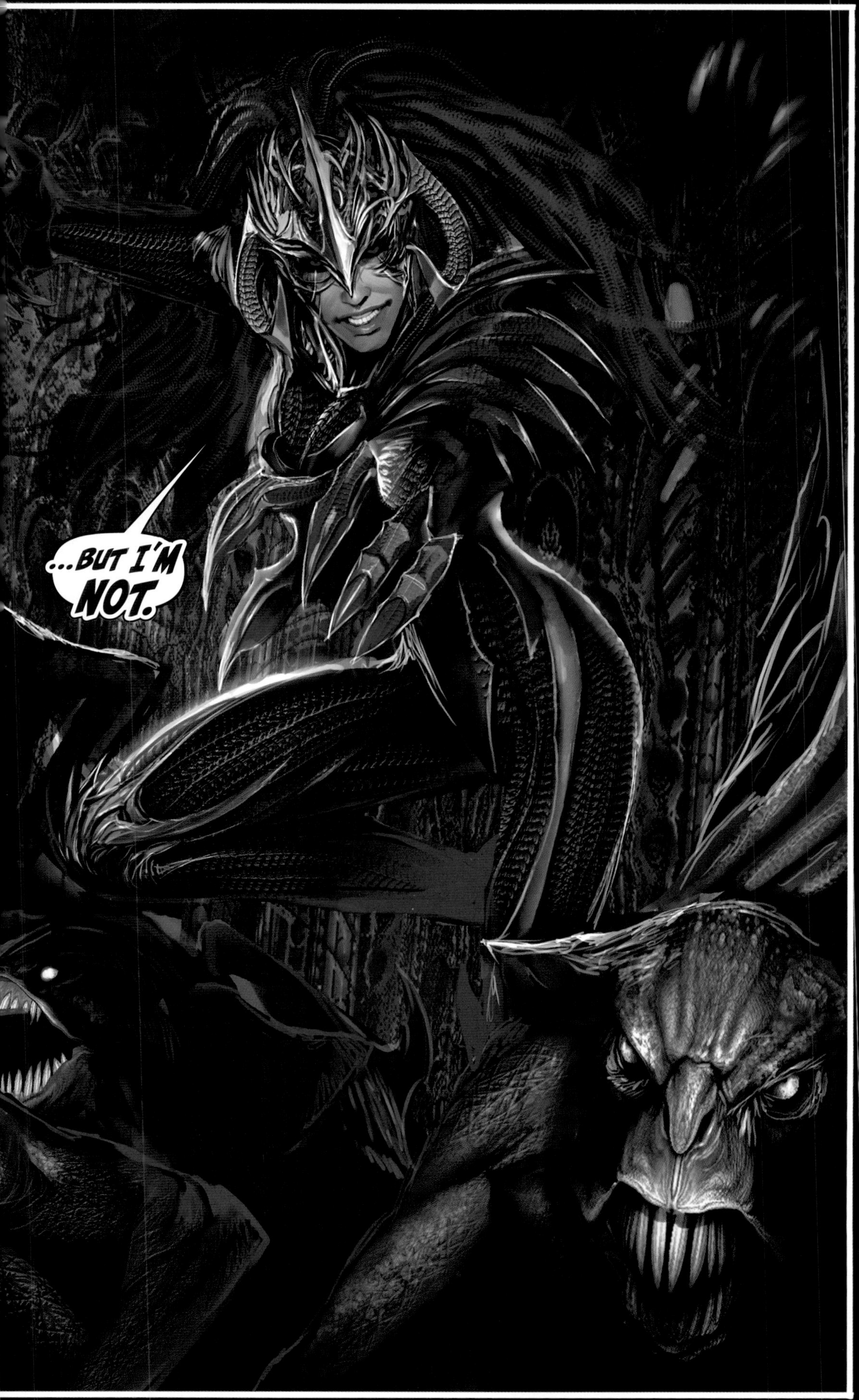
...BUT I'M NOT.

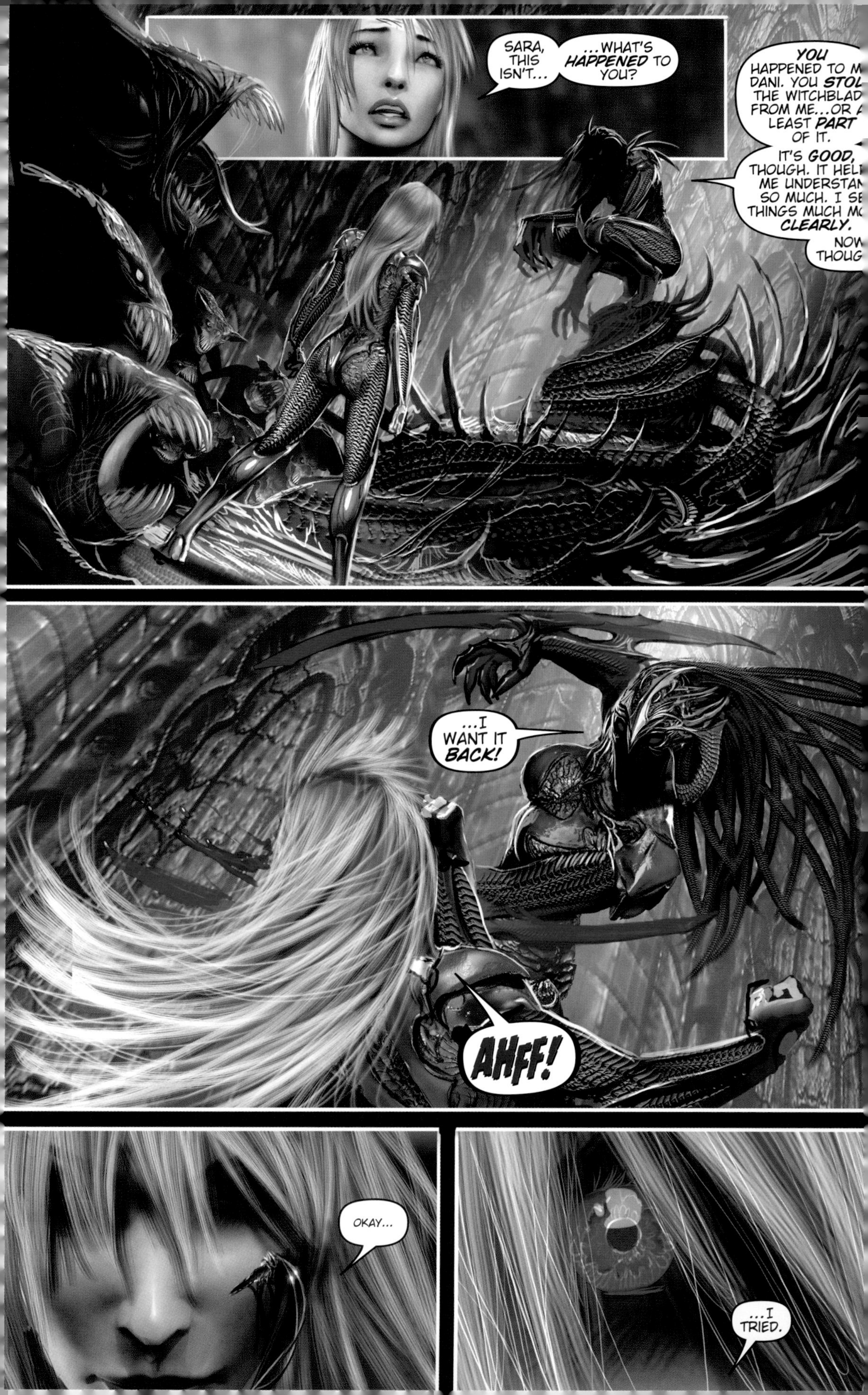
SARA, THIS ISN'T...
...WHAT'S **HAPPENED** TO YOU?
YOU HAPPENED TO M DANI. YOU **STOL** THE WITCHBLAD FROM ME...OR A LEAST **PART** OF IT.
IT'S **GOOD,** THOUGH. IT HEL ME UNDERSTAN SO MUCH. I SE THINGS MUCH MO **CLEARLY.**
NOW THOUG
...I WANT IT **BACK!**
AHFF!
OKAY...
...I TRIED.

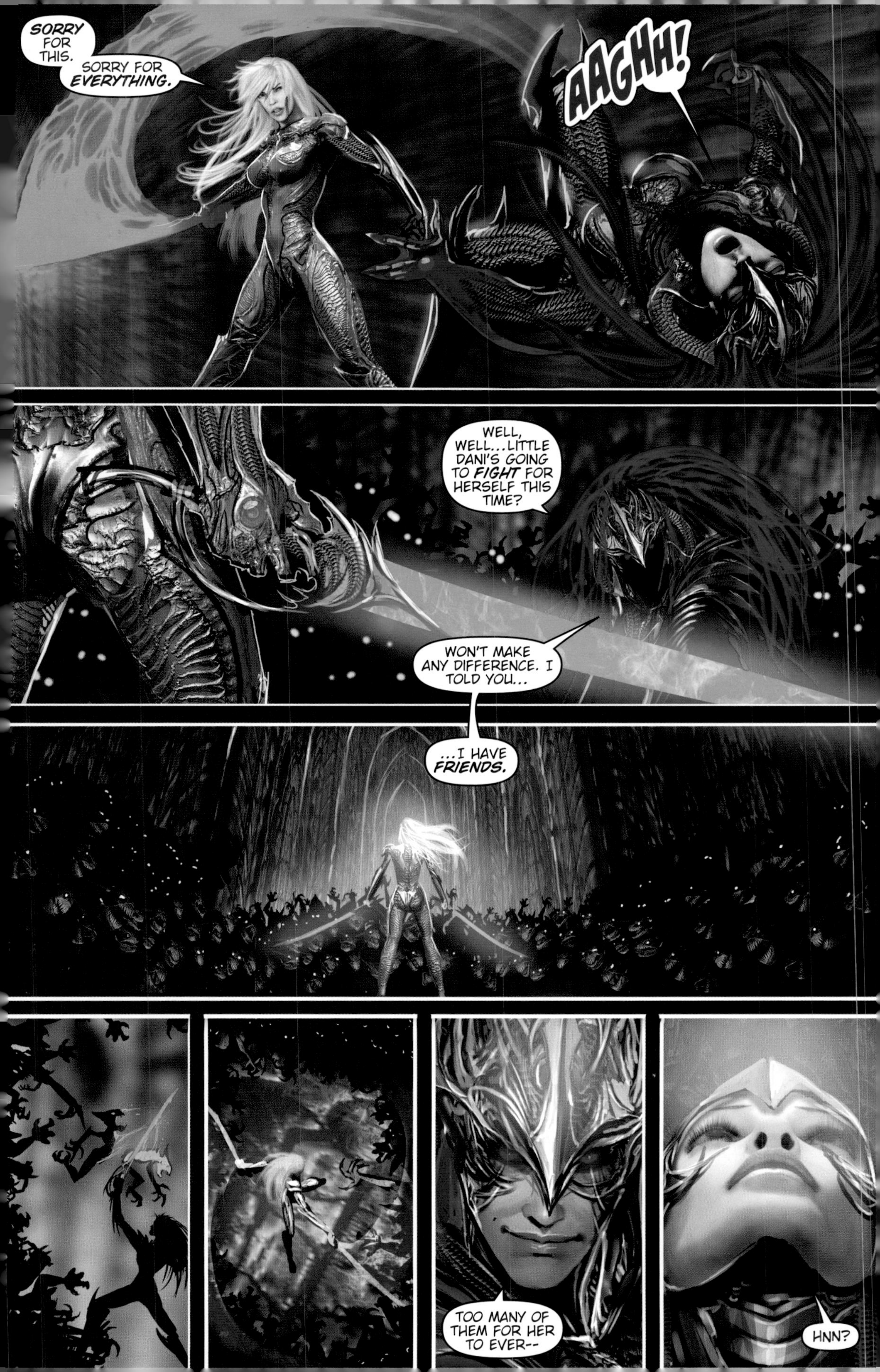
SORRY FOR THIS.
SORRY FOR EVERYTHING.
AAGHH!
WELL, WELL...LITTLE DANI'S GOING TO FIGHT FOR HERSELF THIS TIME?
WON'T MAKE ANY DIFFERENCE. I TOLD YOU...
...I HAVE FRIENDS.
TOO MANY OF THEM FOR HER TO EVER--
HNN?

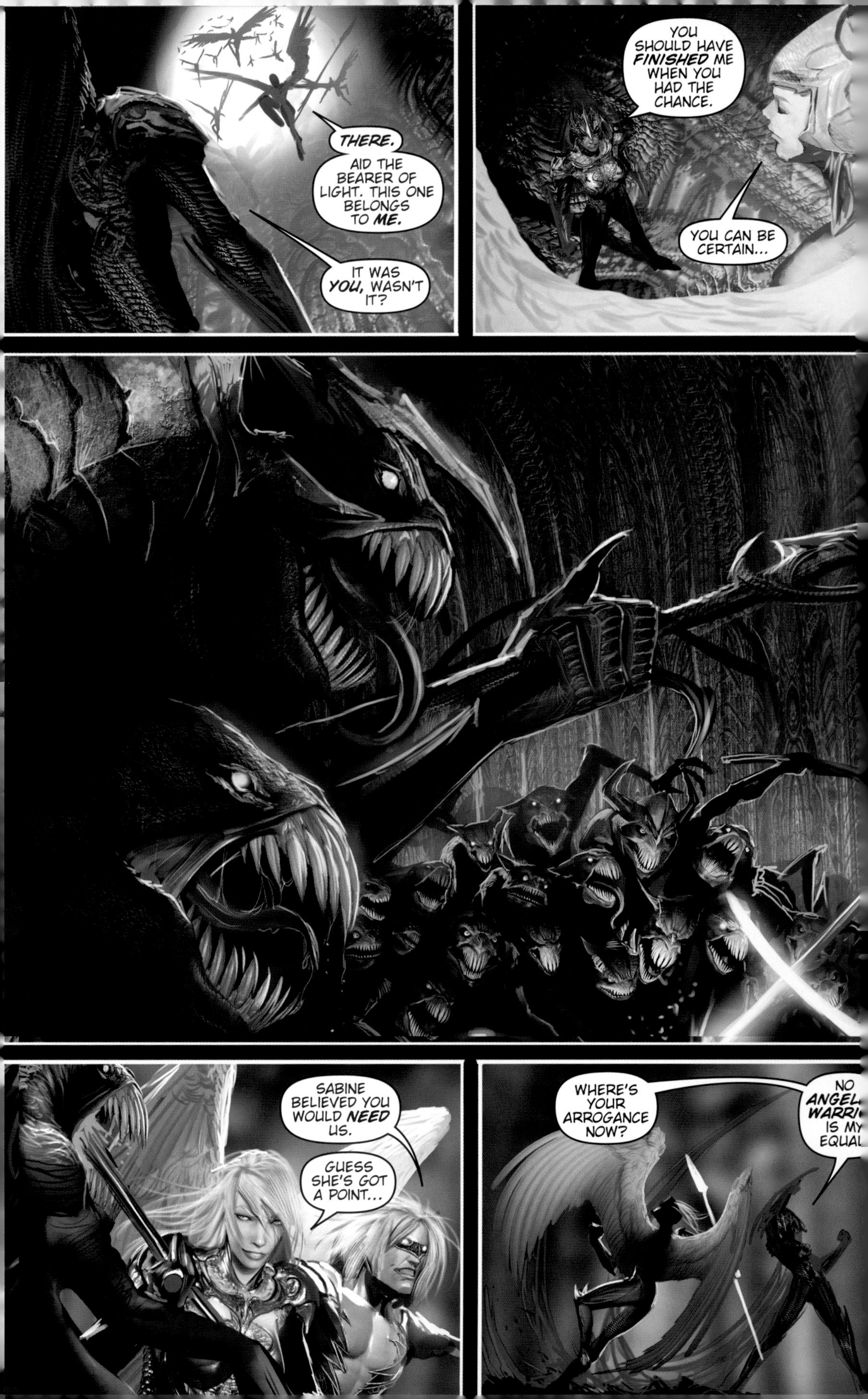
THERE.
AID THE BEARER OF LIGHT. THIS ONE BELONGS TO ME.
IT WAS YOU, WASN'T IT?
YOU SHOULD HAVE FINISHED ME WHEN YOU HAD THE CHANCE.
YOU CAN BE CERTAIN...
SABINE BELIEVED YOU WOULD NEED US.
GUESS SHE'S GOT A POINT...
WHERE'S YOUR ARROGANCE NOW?
NO ANGEL WARRI IS MY EQUAL

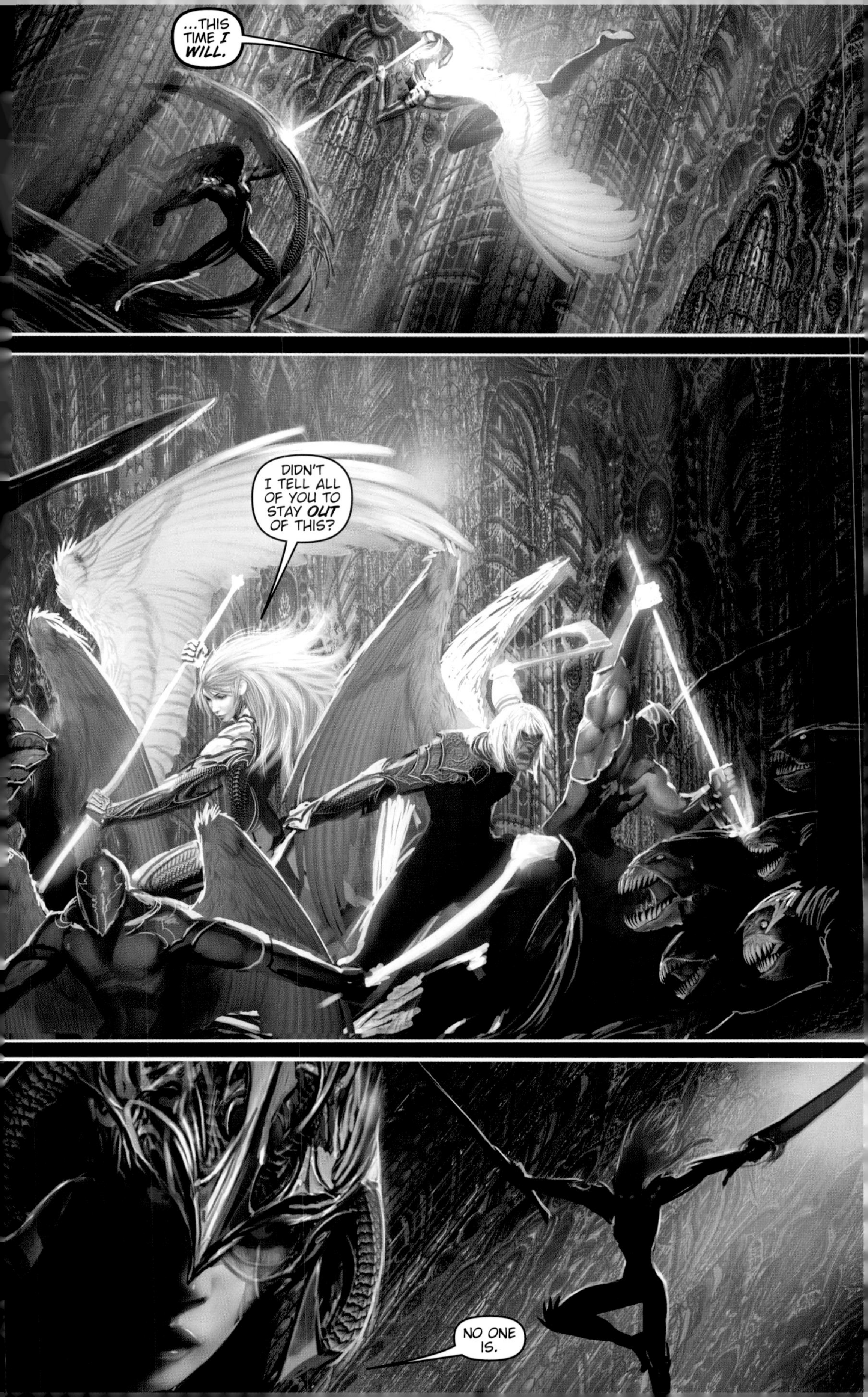
...THIS TIME *I* ***WILL.***
DIDN'T I TELL ALL OF YOU TO STAY ***OUT*** OF THIS?
NO ONE IS.

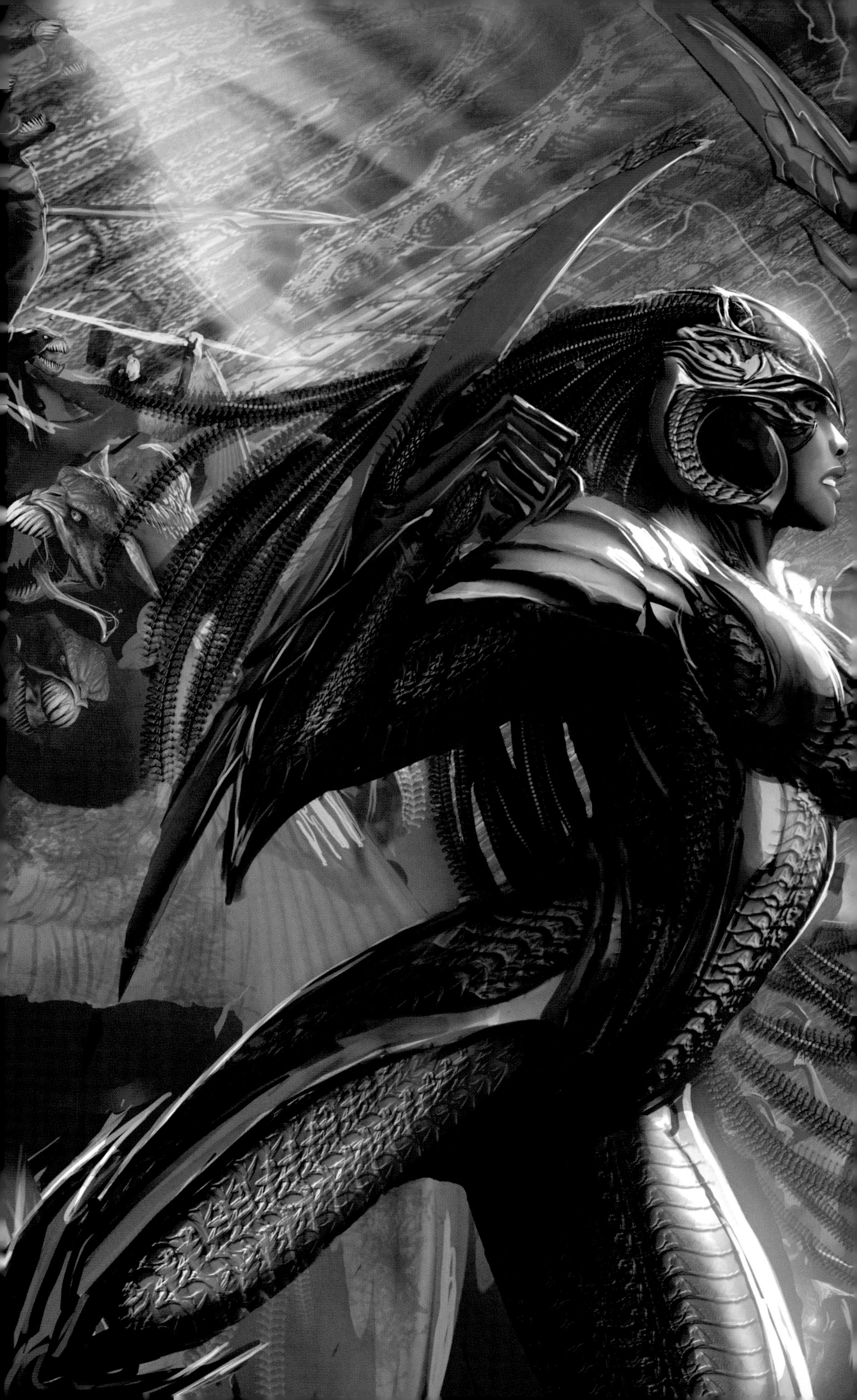

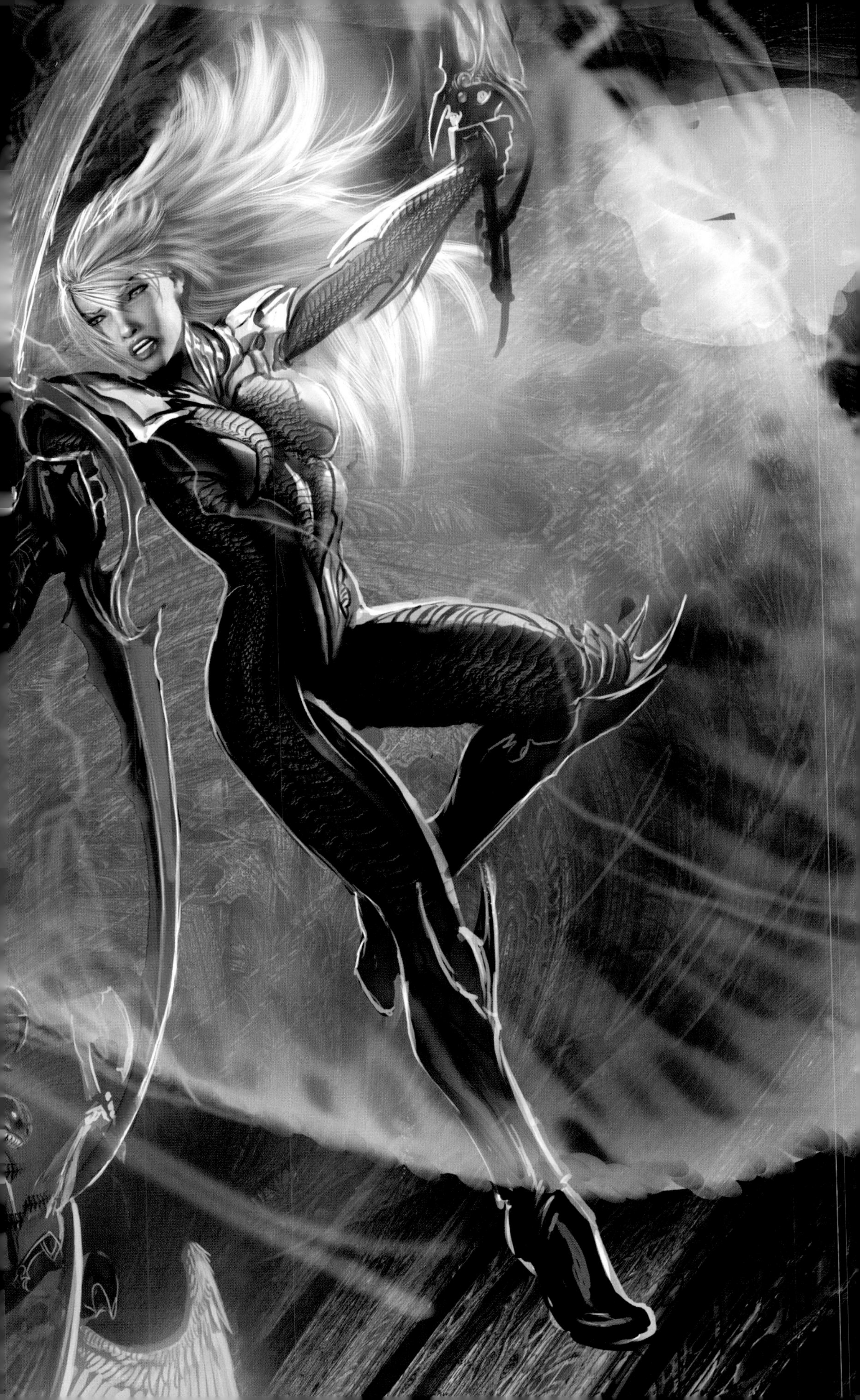

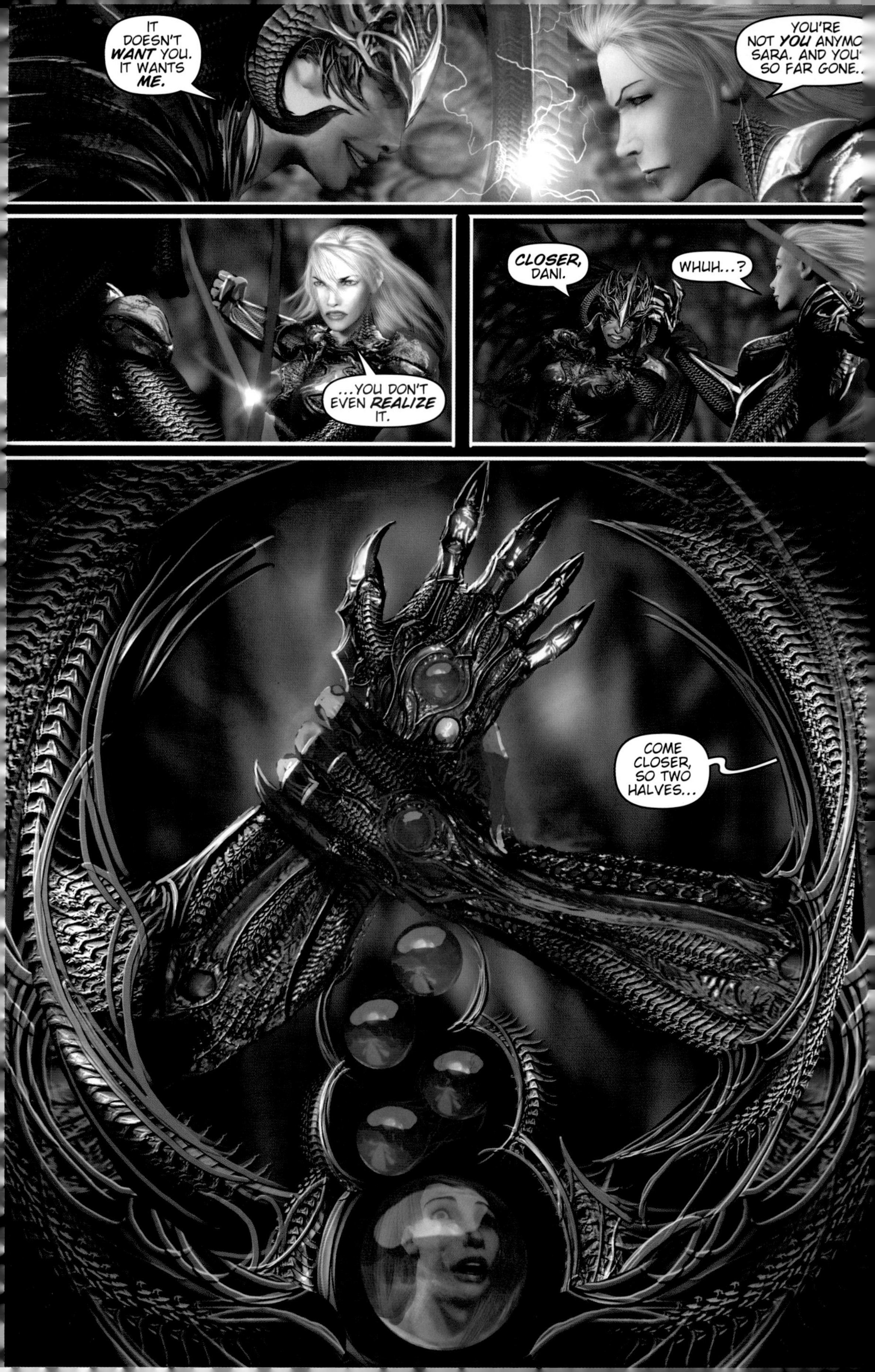
IT DOESN'T **WANT** YOU. IT WANTS **ME.**
YOU'RE NOT **YOU** ANYMO
SARA. AND YOU'
SO FAR GONE...
...YOU DON'T EVEN **REALIZE** IT.
CLOSER, DANI.
WHUH...?
COME CLOSER, SO TWO HALVES...

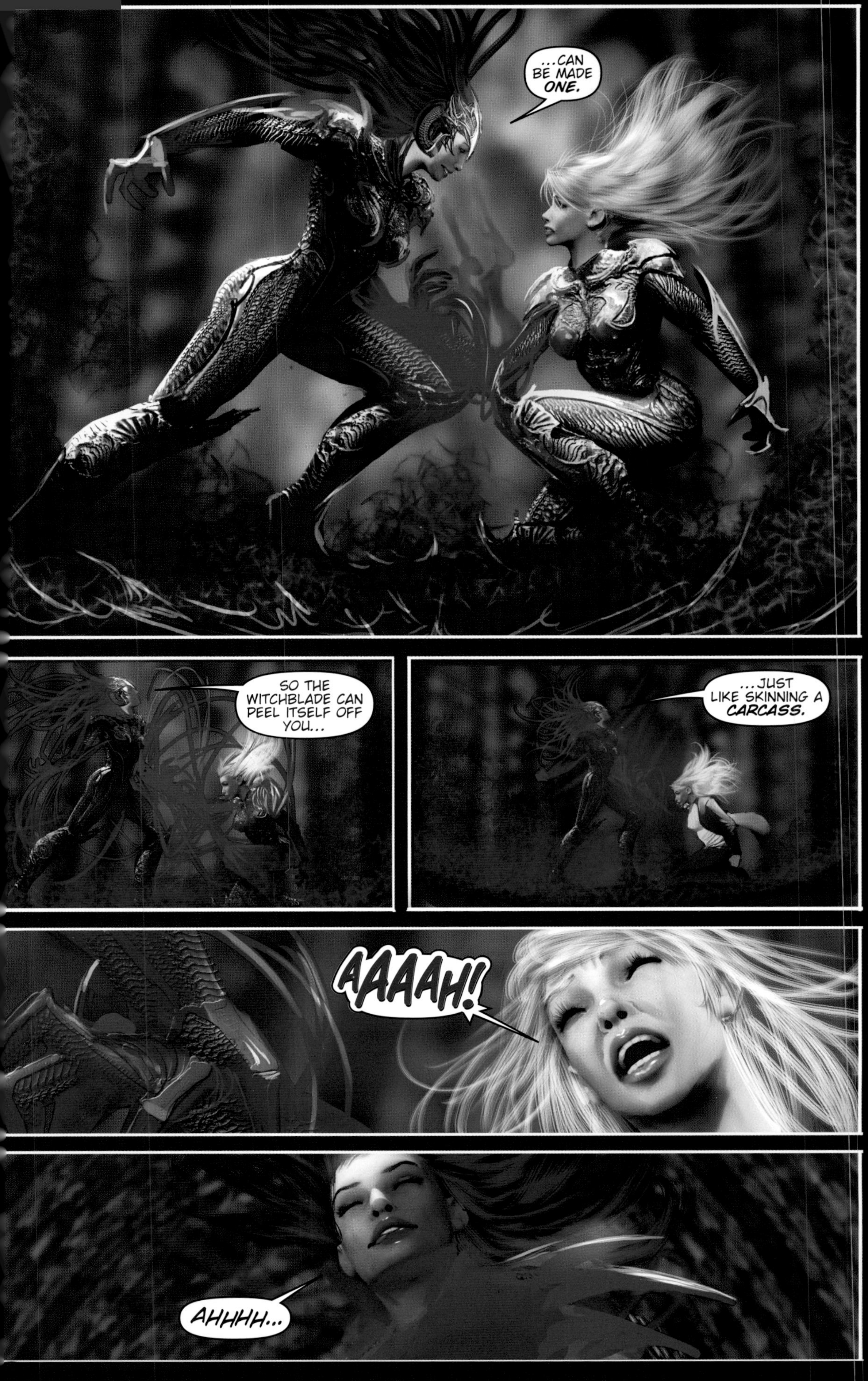
...CAN BE MADE ONE.
SO THE WITCHBLADE CAN PEEL ITSELF OFF YOU...
...JUST LIKE SKINNING A CARCASS.
AAAAH!
AHHHH...

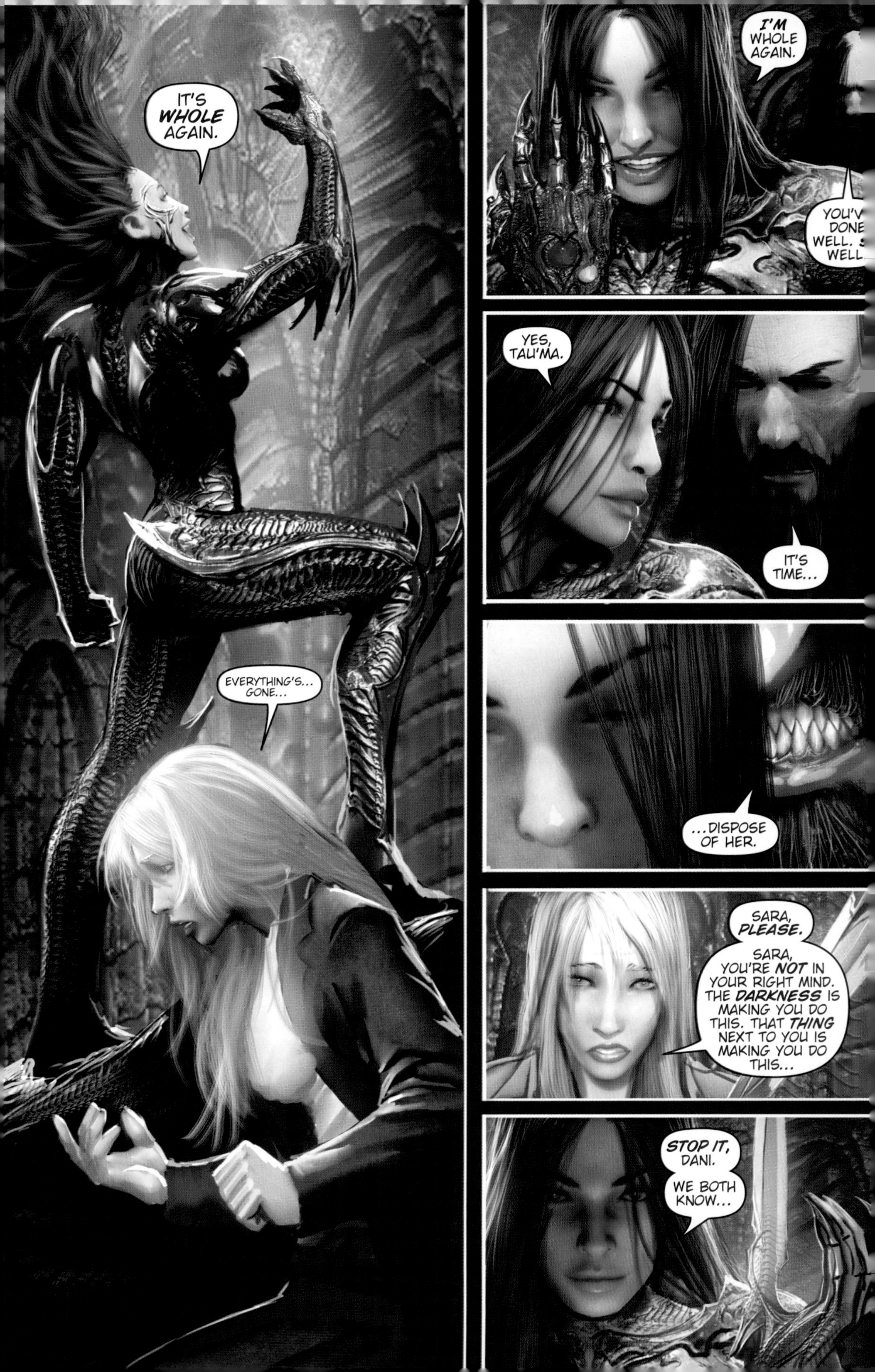
IT'S *WHOLE* AGAIN.
EVERYTHING'S... GONE...
I'M WHOLE AGAIN.
YES, TAU'MA.
IT'S TIME...
...DISPOSE OF HER.
SARA, *PLEASE.*
SARA, YOU'RE *NOT* IN YOUR RIGHT MIND. THE *DARKNESS* IS MAKING YOU DO THIS. THAT *THING* NEXT TO YOU IS MAKING YOU DO THIS...
STOP IT, DANI.
WE BOTH KNOW...

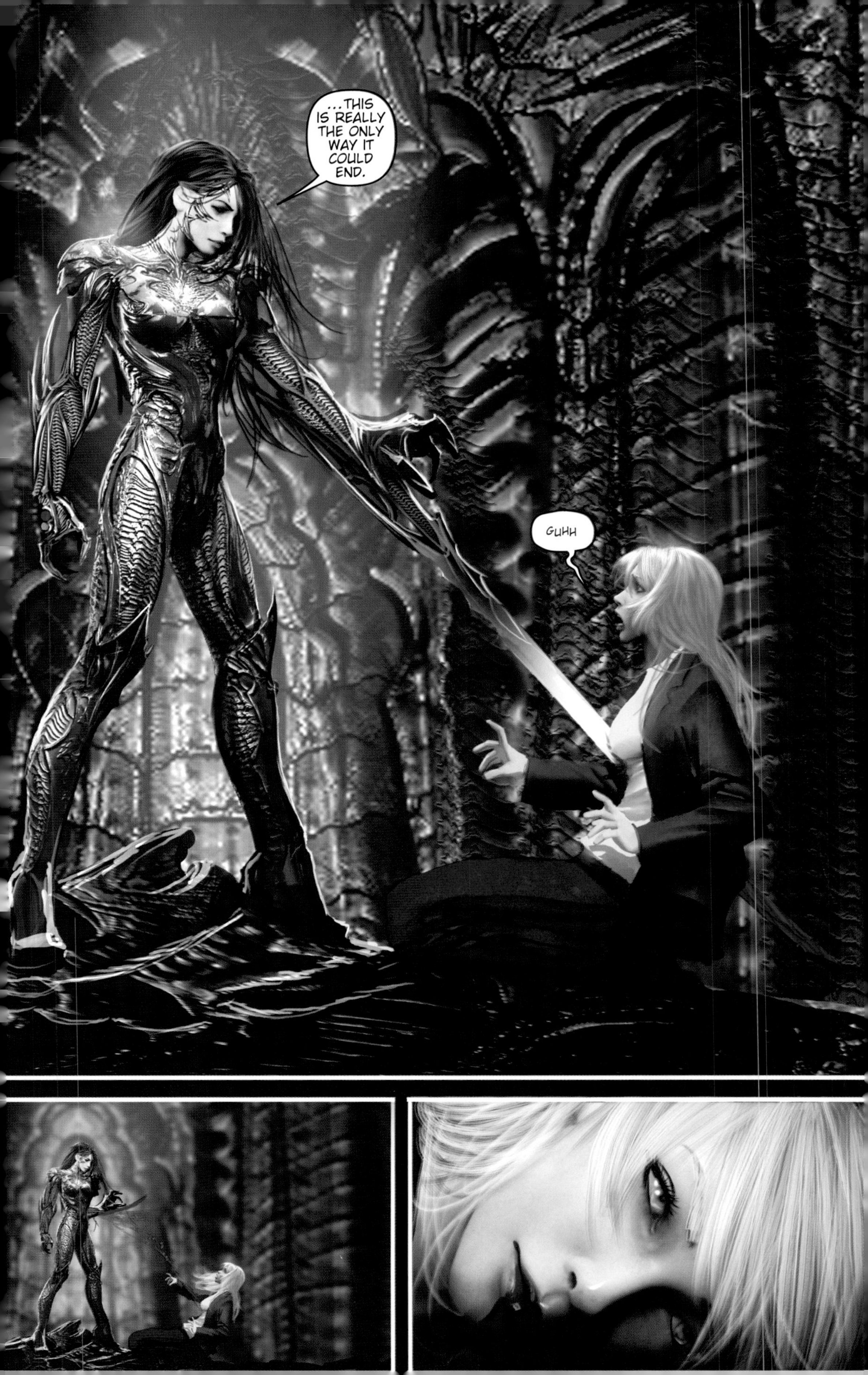
...THIS IS REALLY THE ONLY WAY IT COULD END.
GUHH

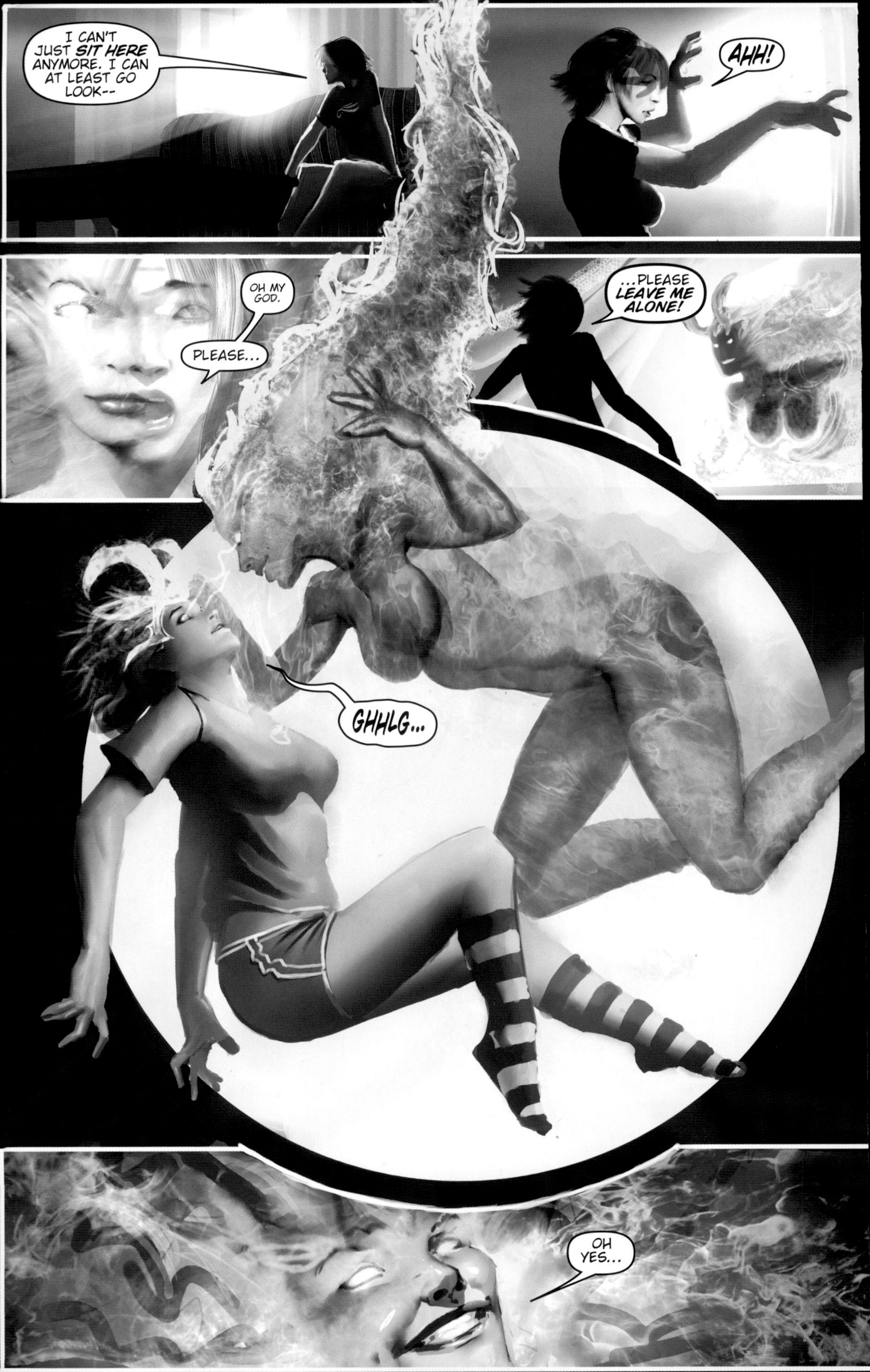
I CAN'T JUST SIT HERE ANYMORE. I CAN AT LEAST GO LOOK--
AHH!
OH MY GOD.
PLEASE...
...PLEASE LEAVE ME ALONE!
GHHLG...
OH YES...

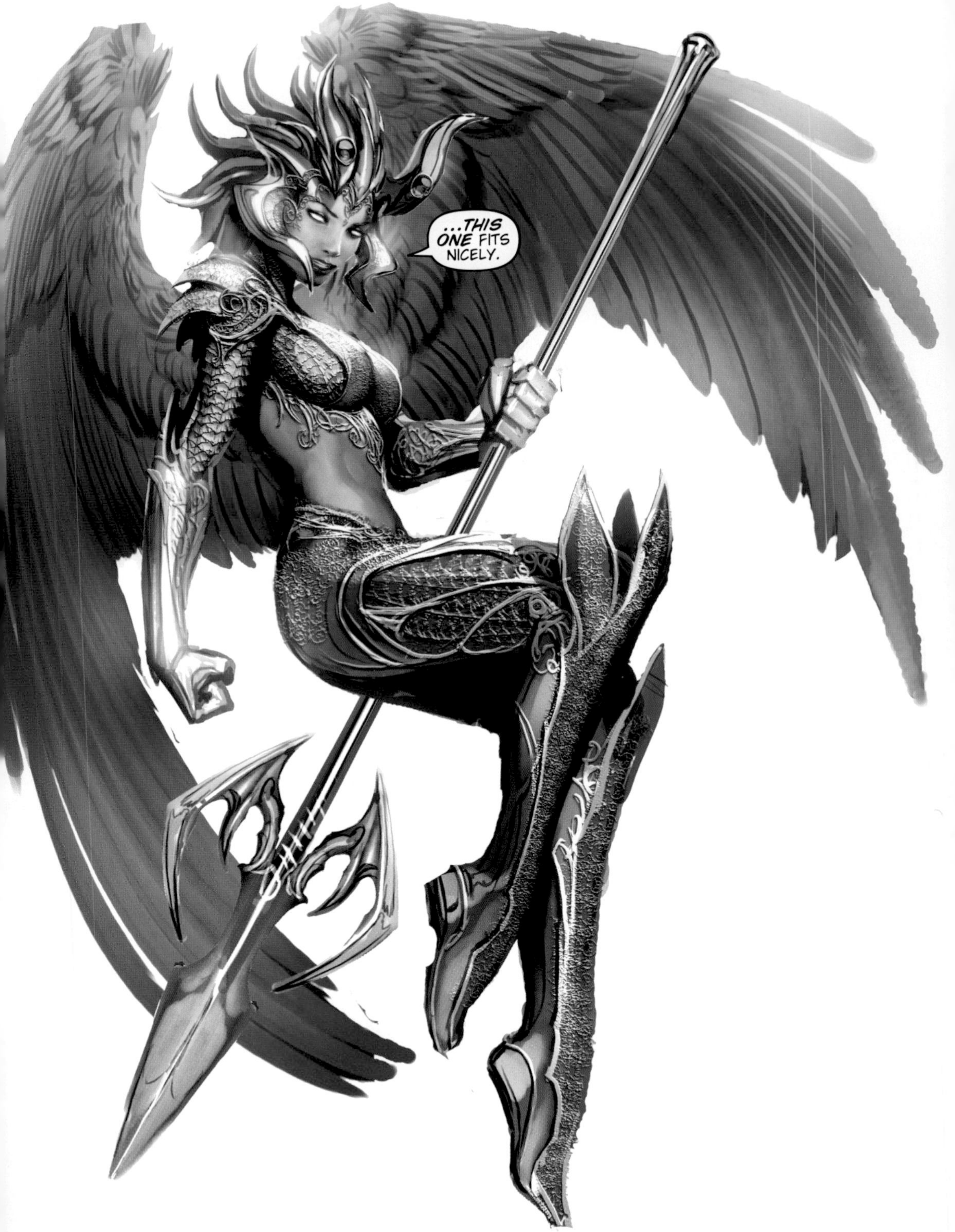
...THIS ONE FITS NICELY.

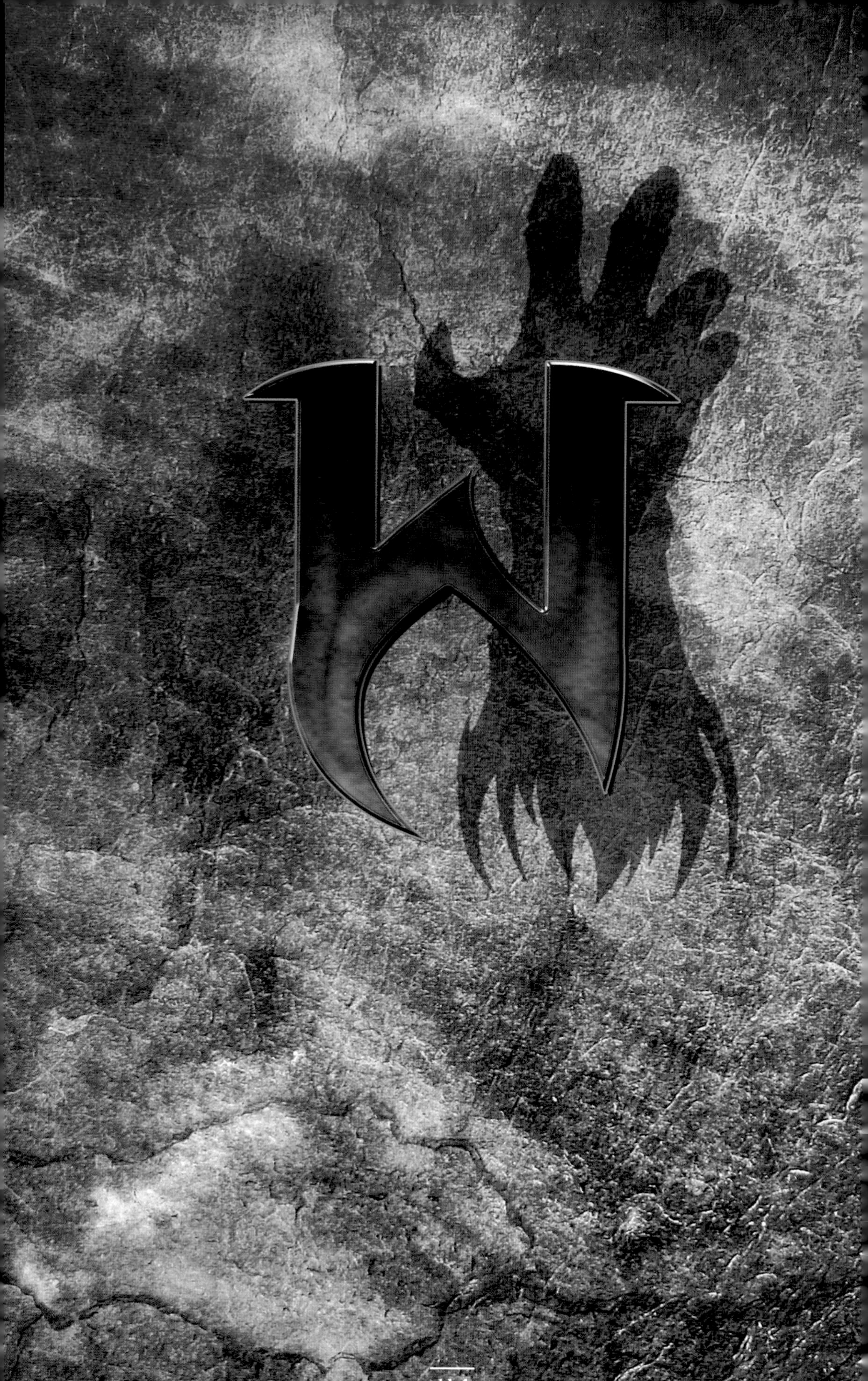

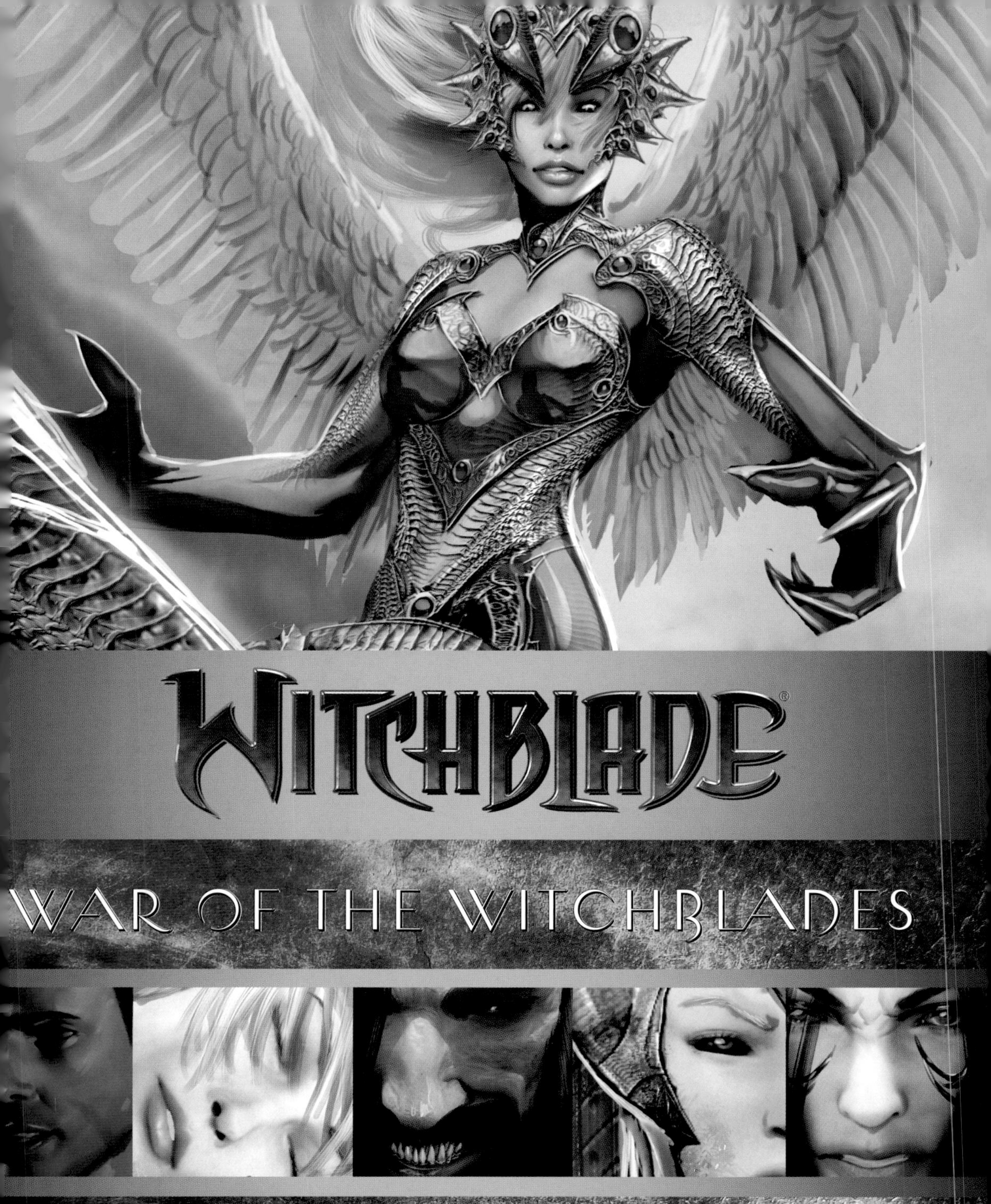

WITCHBLADE®

WAR OF THE WITCHBLADES

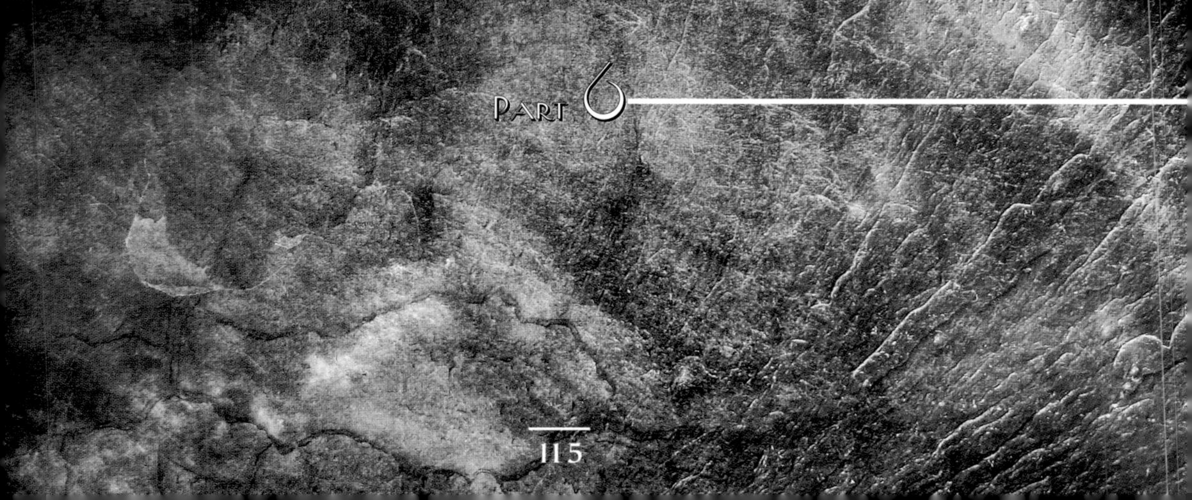

Part 6

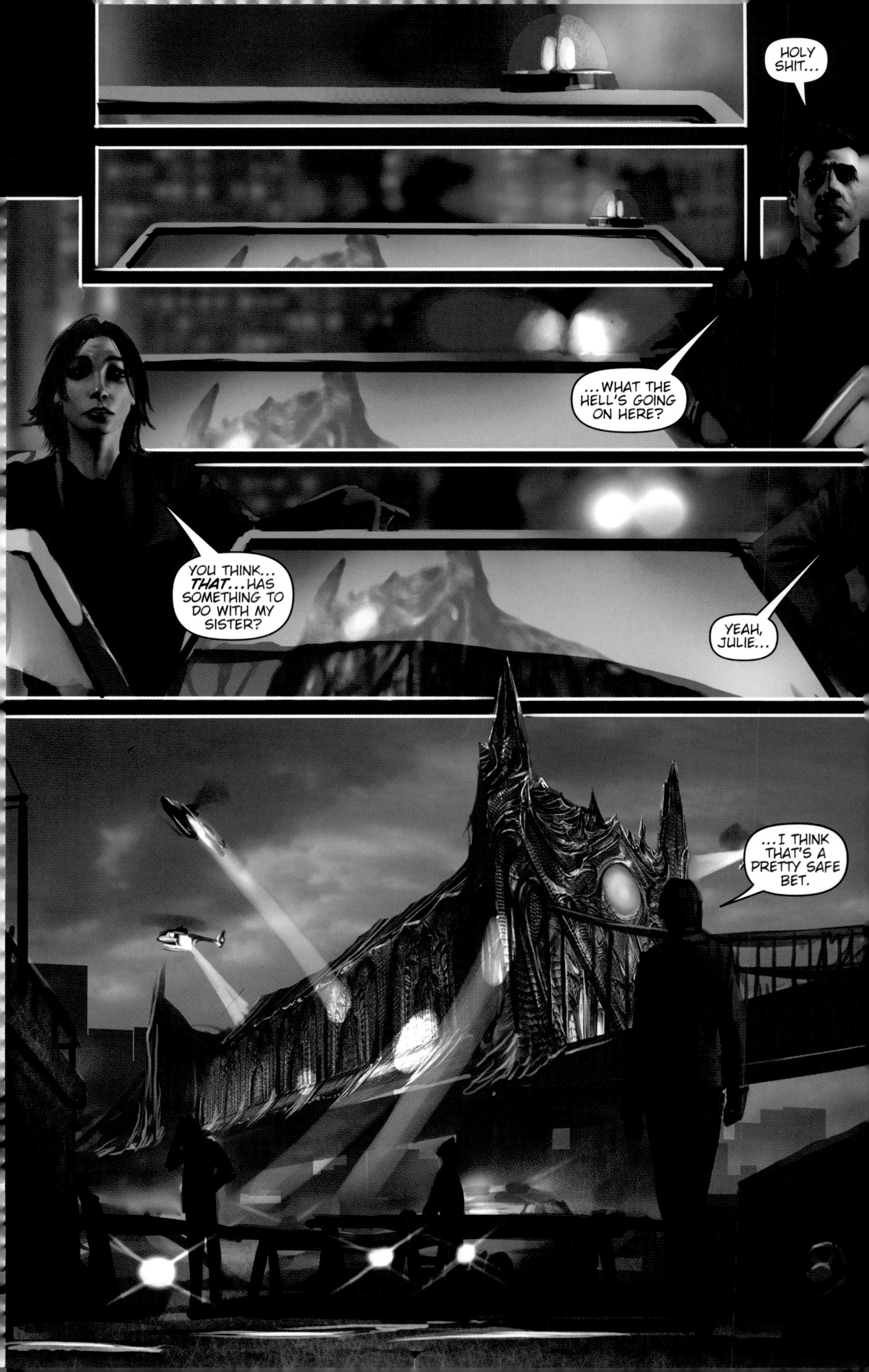
HOLY SHIT...
...WHAT THE HELL'S GOING ON HERE?
YOU THINK... ***THAT***...HAS SOMETHING TO DO WITH MY SISTER?
YEAH, JULIE...
...I THINK THAT'S A PRETTY SAFE BET.

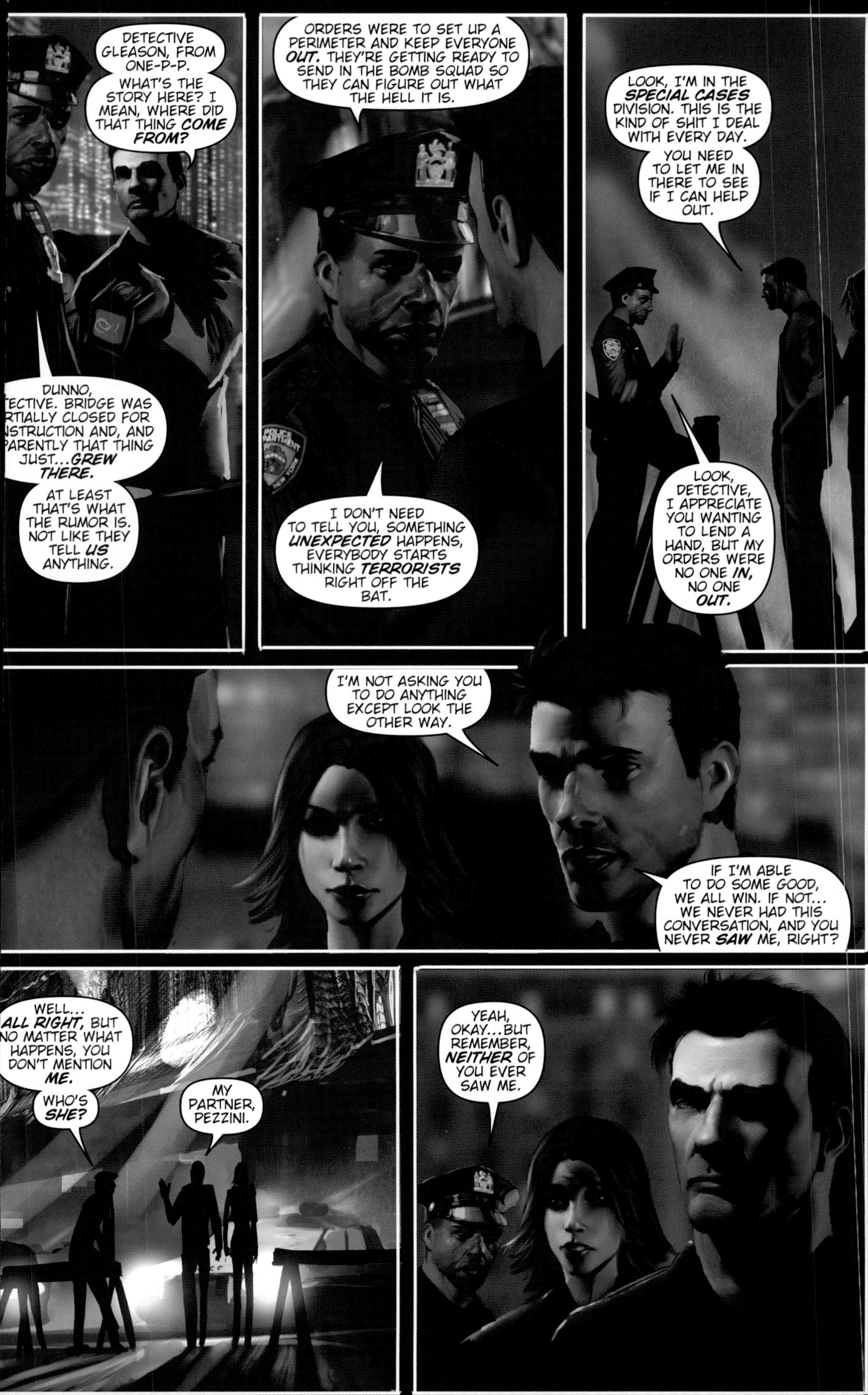
DETECTIVE GLEASON, FROM ONE-P-P.
WHAT'S THE STORY HERE? I MEAN, WHERE DID THAT THING COME FROM?
DUNNO, ...TECTIVE. BRIDGE WAS ...RTIALLY CLOSED FOR ...NSTRUCTION AND, AND ...PARENTLY THAT THING JUST...GREW THERE.
AT LEAST THAT'S WHAT THE RUMOR IS. NOT LIKE THEY TELL US ANYTHING.
ORDERS WERE TO SET UP A PERIMETER AND KEEP EVERYONE OUT. THEY'RE GETTING READY TO SEND IN THE BOMB SQUAD SO THEY CAN FIGURE OUT WHAT THE HELL IT IS.
I DON'T NEED TO TELL YOU, SOMETHING UNEXPECTED HAPPENS, EVERYBODY STARTS THINKING TERRORISTS RIGHT OFF THE BAT.
LOOK, I'M IN THE SPECIAL CASES DIVISION. THIS IS THE KIND OF SHIT I DEAL WITH EVERY DAY.
YOU NEED TO LET ME IN THERE TO SEE IF I CAN HELP OUT.
LOOK, DETECTIVE, I APPRECIATE YOU WANTING TO LEND A HAND, BUT MY ORDERS WERE NO ONE IN, NO ONE OUT.
I'M NOT ASKING YOU TO DO ANYTHING EXCEPT LOOK THE OTHER WAY.
IF I'M ABLE TO DO SOME GOOD, WE ALL WIN. IF NOT... WE NEVER HAD THIS CONVERSATION, AND YOU NEVER SAW ME, RIGHT?
WELL... ALL RIGHT, BUT NO MATTER WHAT HAPPENS, YOU DON'T MENTION ME.
WHO'S SHE?
MY PARTNER, PEZZINI.
YEAH, OKAY...BUT REMEMBER, NEITHER OF YOU EVER SAW ME.

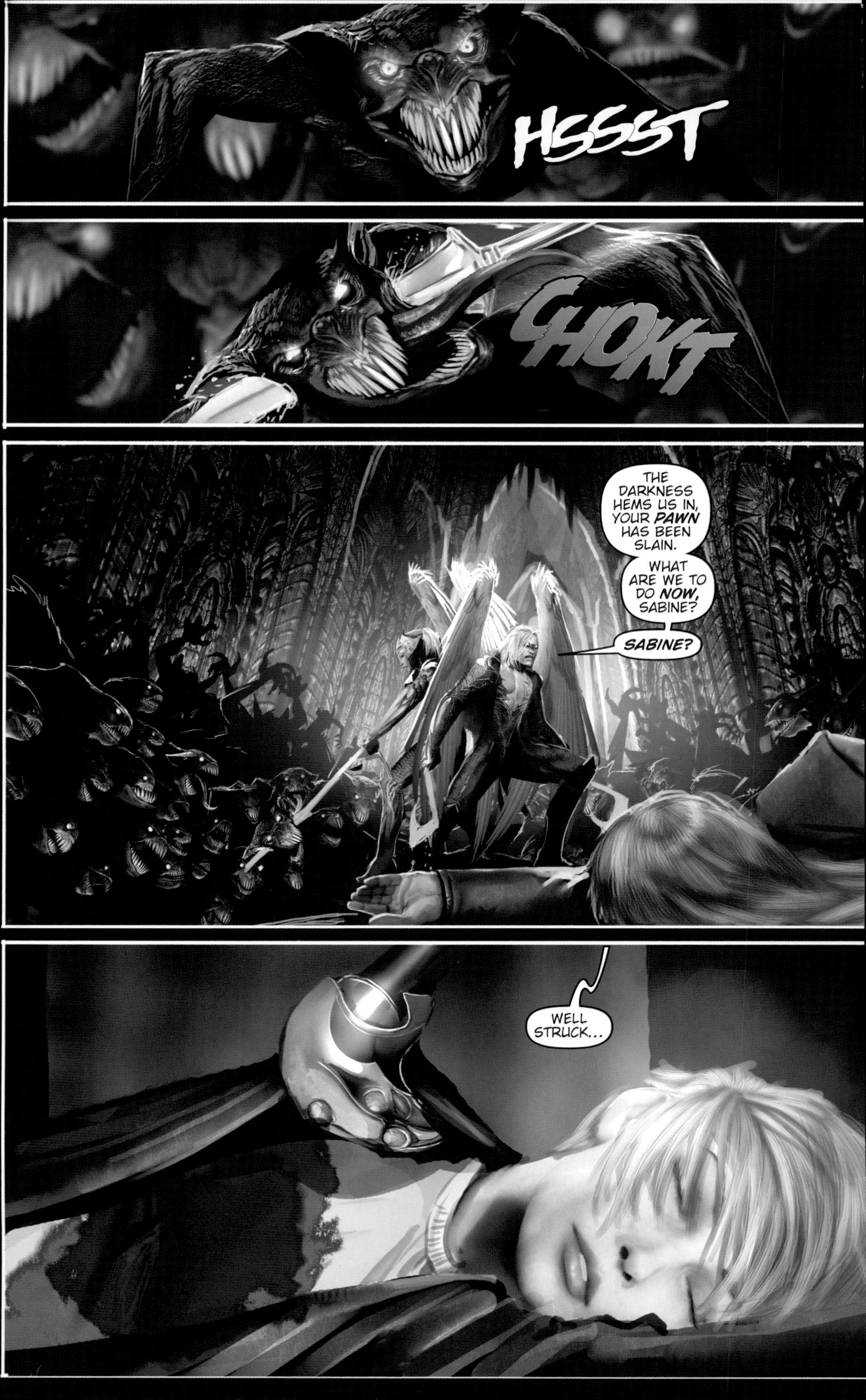
HSSST
CHOKT
THE DARKNESS HEMS US IN, YOUR PAWN HAS BEEN SLAIN.
WHAT ARE WE TO DO NOW, SABINE?
SABINE?
WELL STRUCK...

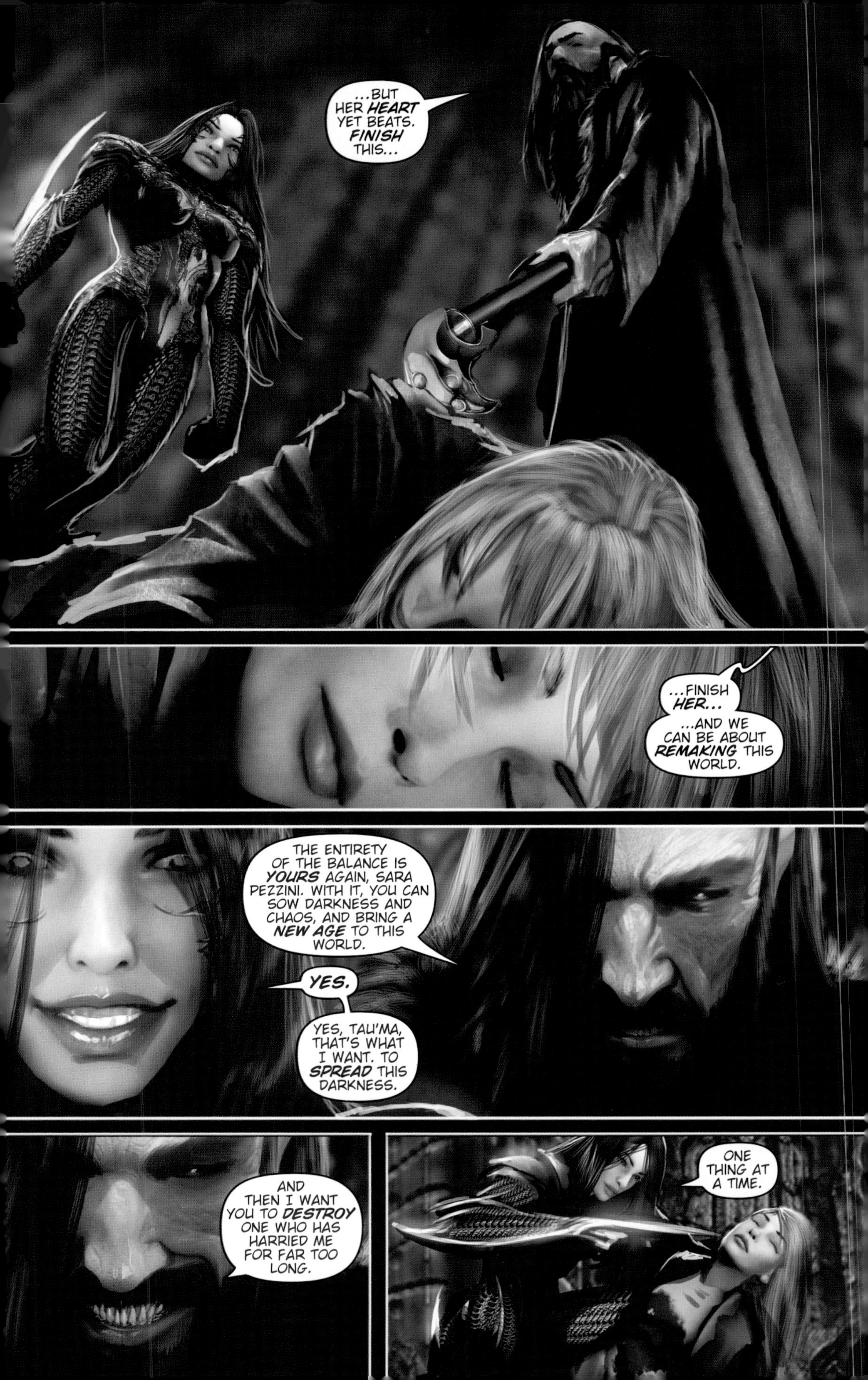
...BUT HER HEART YET BEATS. FINISH THIS...
...FINISH HER...
...AND WE CAN BE ABOUT REMAKING THIS WORLD.
THE ENTIRETY OF THE BALANCE IS YOURS AGAIN, SARA PEZZINI. WITH IT, YOU CAN SOW DARKNESS AND CHAOS, AND BRING A NEW AGE TO THIS WORLD.
YES.
YES, TAU'MA, THAT'S WHAT I WANT. TO SPREAD THIS DARKNESS.
AND THEN I WANT YOU TO DESTROY ONE WHO HAS HARRIED ME FOR FAR TOO LONG.
ONE THING AT A TIME.

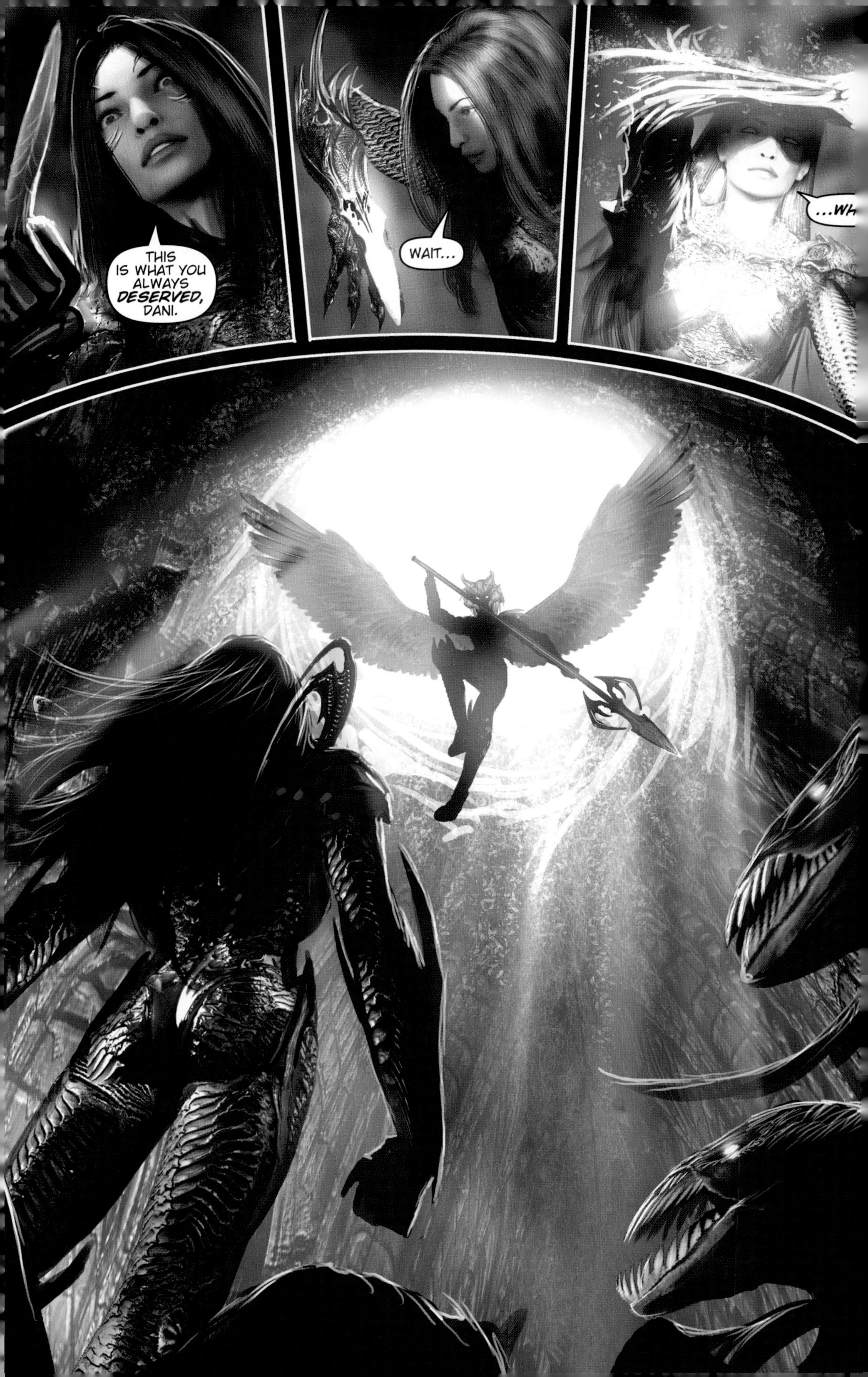
THIS IS WHAT YOU ALWAYS DESERVED, DANI.
WAIT...
...WH

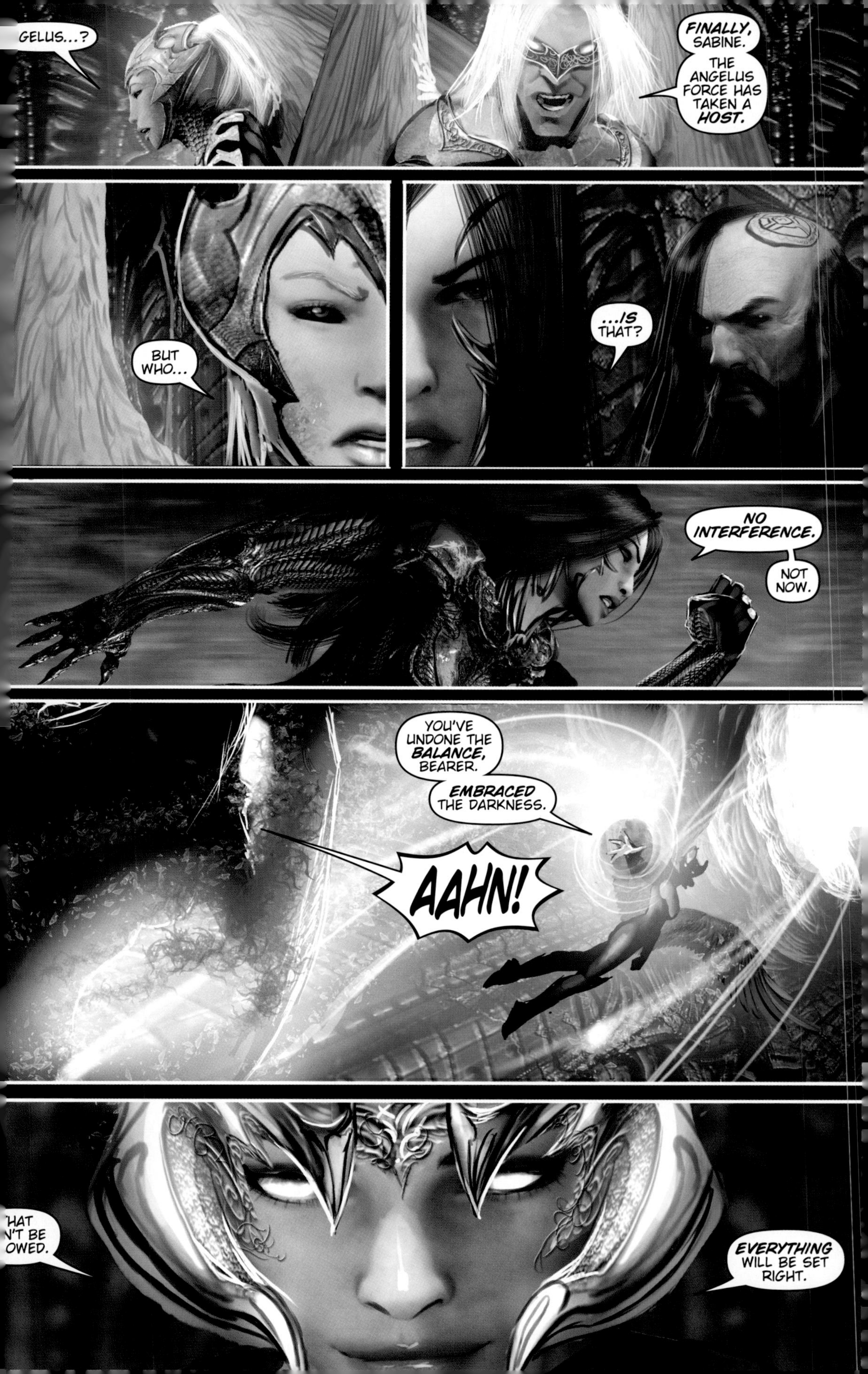
FINALLY, SABINE.
THE ANGELUS FORCE HAS TAKEN A HOST.
BUT WHO...
...IS THAT?
NO INTERFERENCE.
NOT NOW.
YOU'VE UNDONE THE BALANCE, BEARER.
EMBRACED THE DARKNESS.
AAHN!
EVERYTHING WILL BE SET RIGHT.

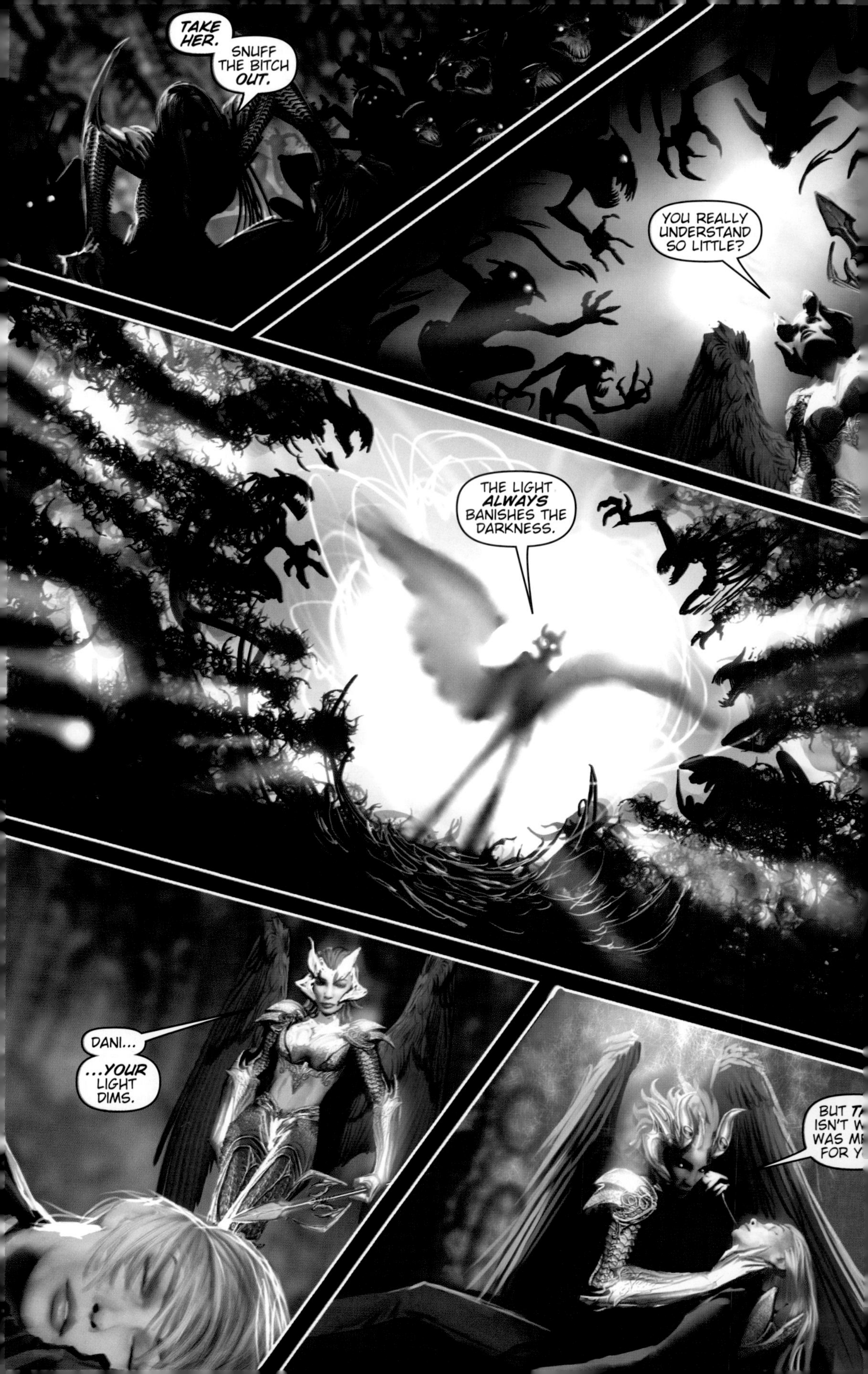
TAKE HER.
SNUFF THE BITCH OUT.
YOU REALLY UNDERSTAND SO LITTLE?
THE LIGHT ALWAYS BANISHES THE DARKNESS.
DANI...
...YOUR LIGHT DIMS.

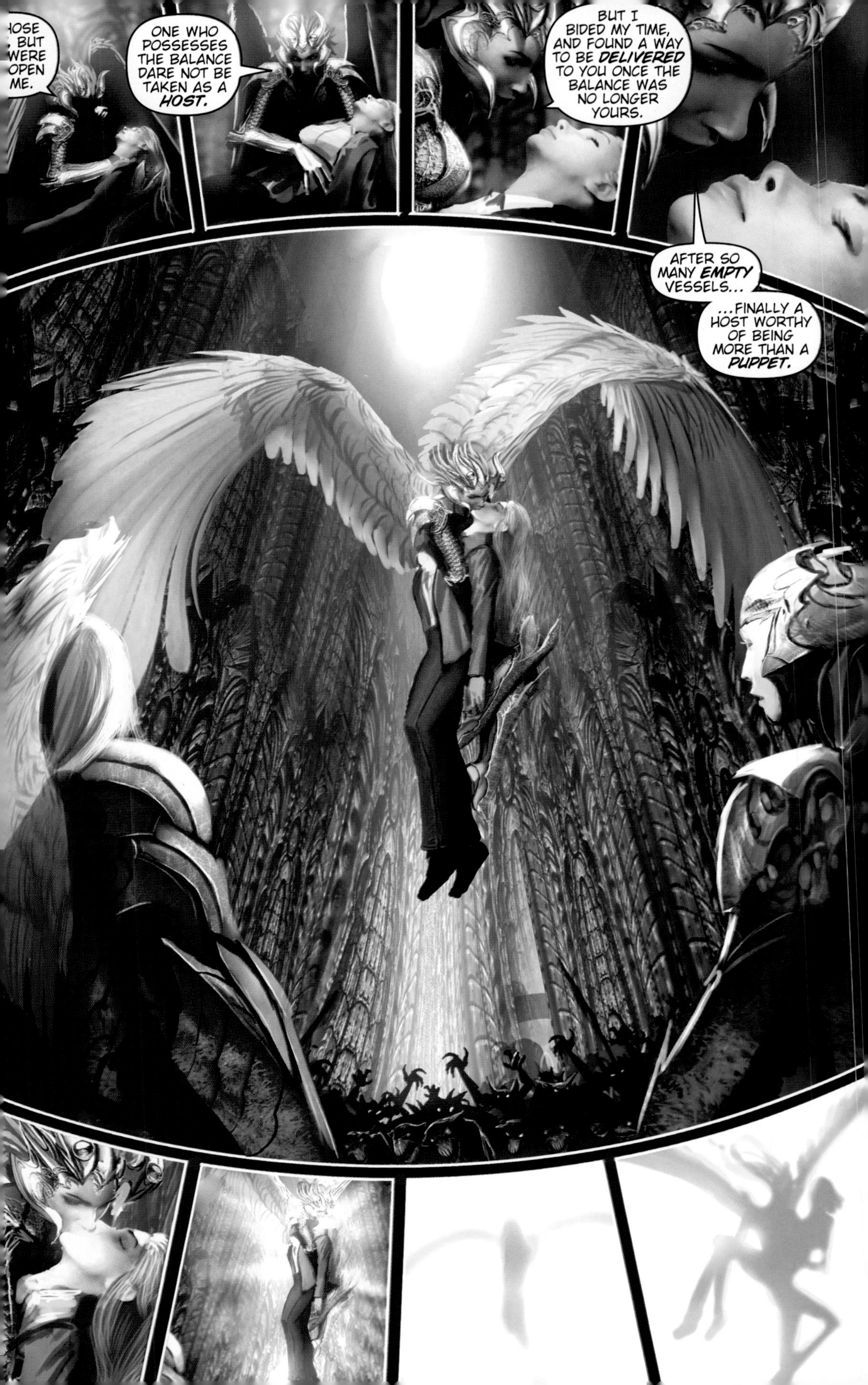
HOSE , BUT WERE OPEN ME.
ONE WHO POSSESSES THE BALANCE DARE NOT BE TAKEN AS A ***HOST.***
BUT I BIDED MY TIME, AND FOUND A WAY TO BE ***DELIVERED*** TO YOU ONCE THE BALANCE WAS NO LONGER YOURS.
AFTER SO MANY ***EMPTY*** VESSELS...
...FINALLY A HOST WORTHY OF BEING MORE THAN A ***PUPPET.***

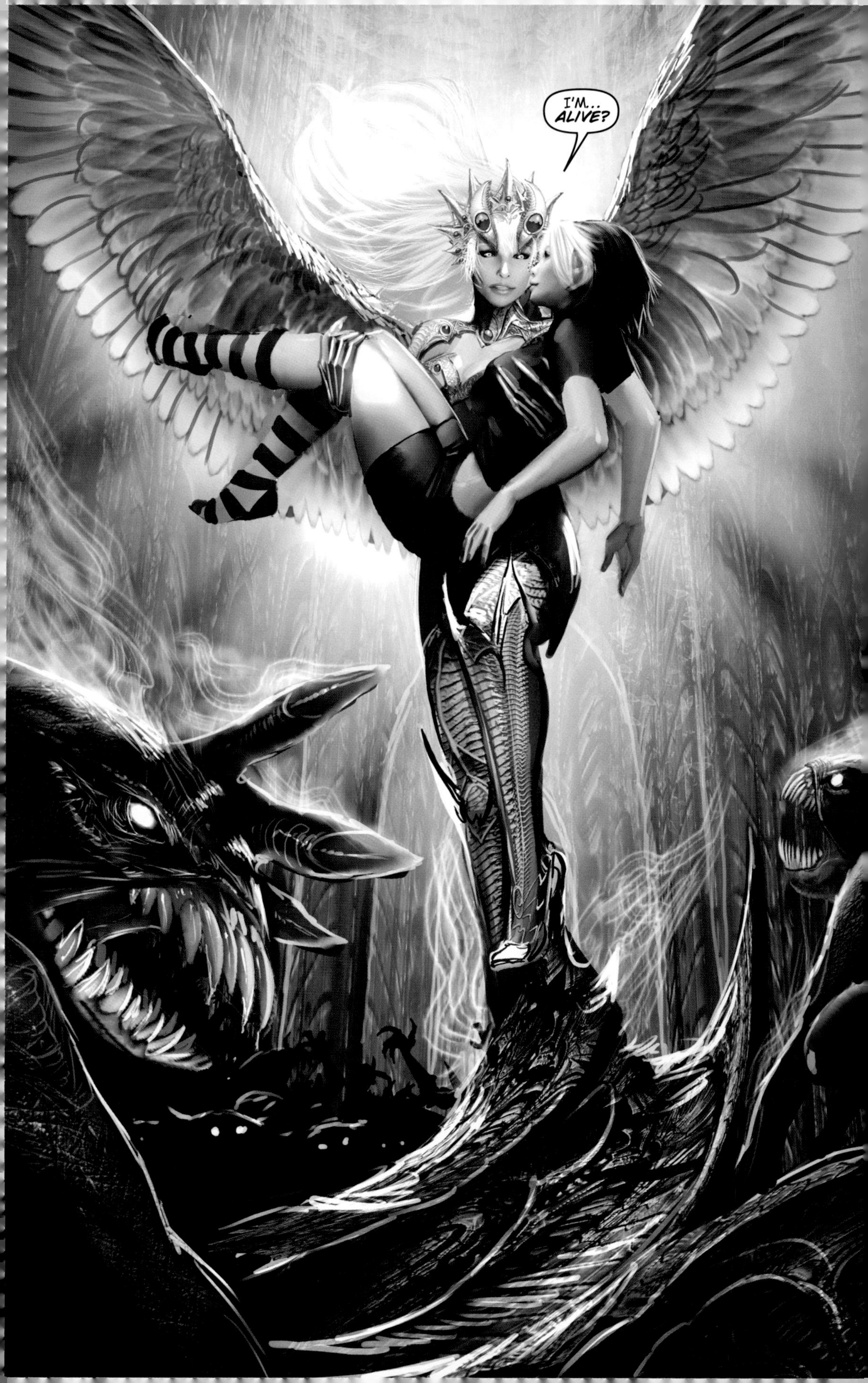
I'M... ALIVE?

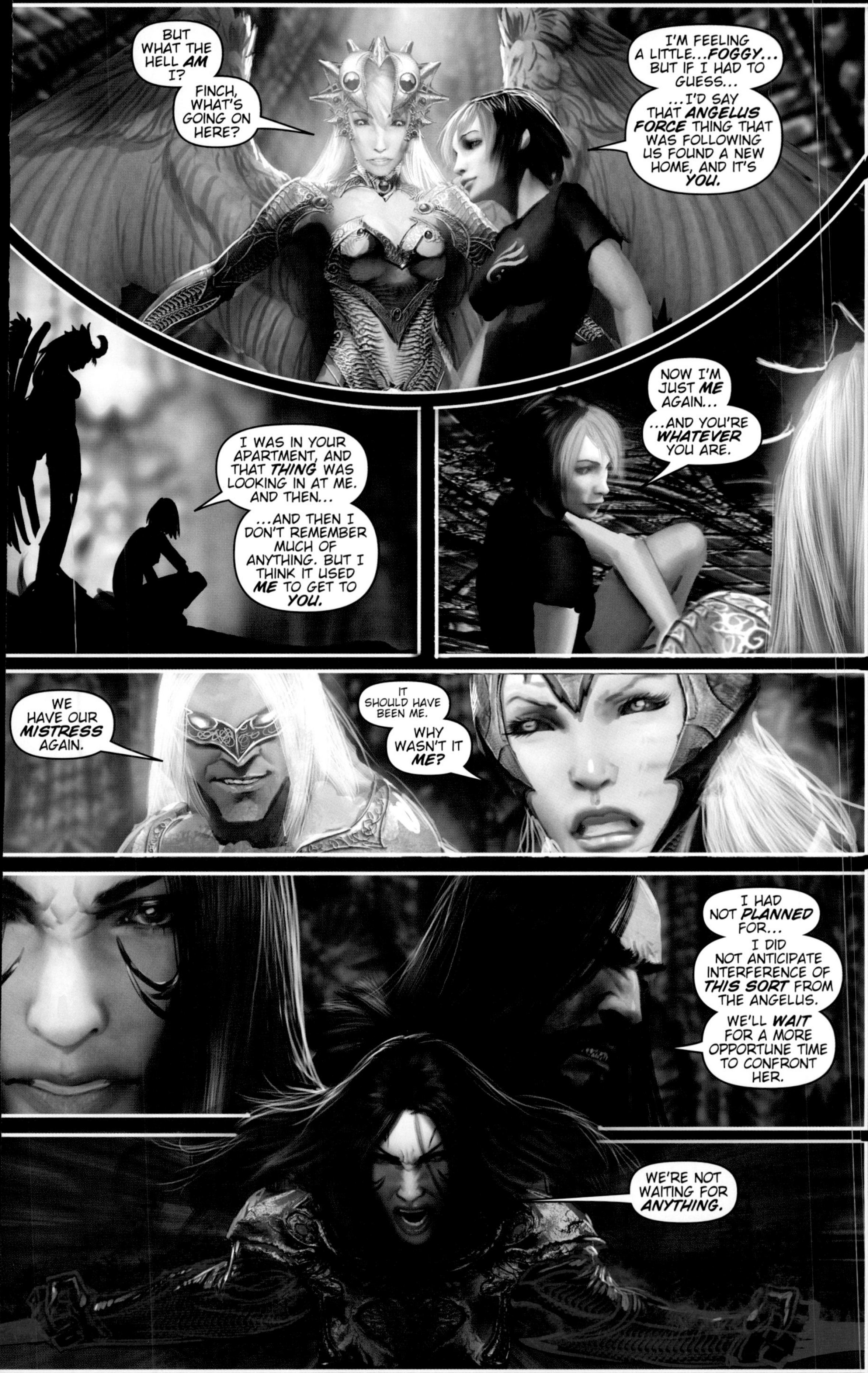
BUT WHAT THE HELL AM I?
FINCH, WHAT'S GOING ON HERE?
I'M FEELING A LITTLE...FOGGY... BUT IF I HAD TO GUESS...
...I'D SAY THAT ANGELUS FORCE THING THAT WAS FOLLOWING US FOUND A NEW HOME, AND IT'S YOU.
I WAS IN YOUR APARTMENT, AND THAT THING WAS LOOKING IN AT ME. AND THEN...
...AND THEN I DON'T REMEMBER MUCH OF ANYTHING. BUT I THINK IT USED ME TO GET TO YOU.
NOW I'M JUST ME AGAIN...
...AND YOU'RE WHATEVER YOU ARE.
WE HAVE OUR MISTRESS AGAIN.
IT SHOULD HAVE BEEN ME.
WHY WASN'T IT ME?
I HAD NOT PLANNED FOR...
I DID NOT ANTICIPATE INTERFERENCE OF THIS SORT FROM THE ANGELUS.
WE'LL WAIT FOR A MORE OPPORTUNE TIME TO CONFRONT HER.
WE'RE NOT WAITING FOR ANYTHING.

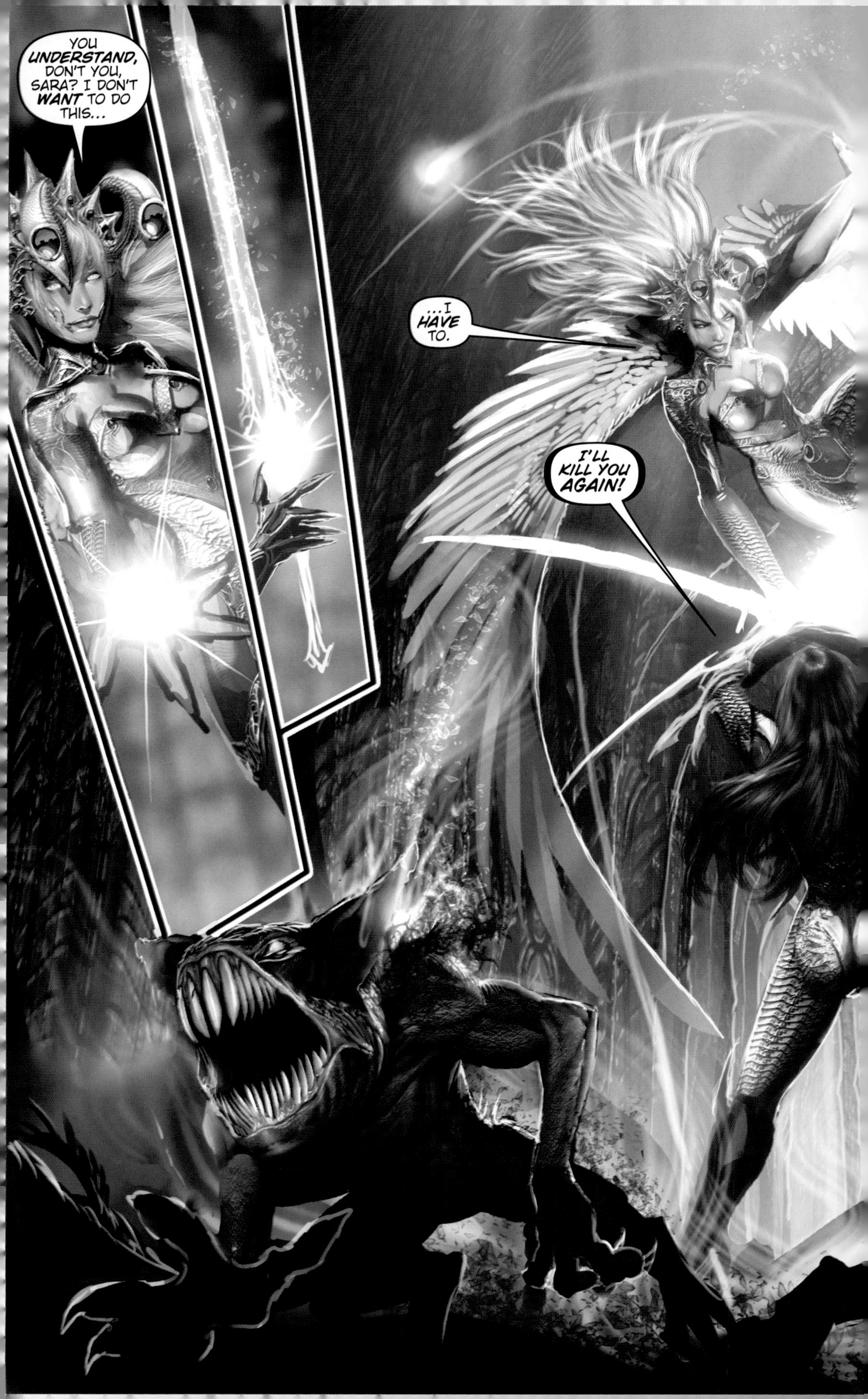
YOU UNDERSTAND, DON'T YOU, SARA? I DON'T WANT TO DO THIS...
...I HAVE TO.
I'LL KILL YOU AGAIN!

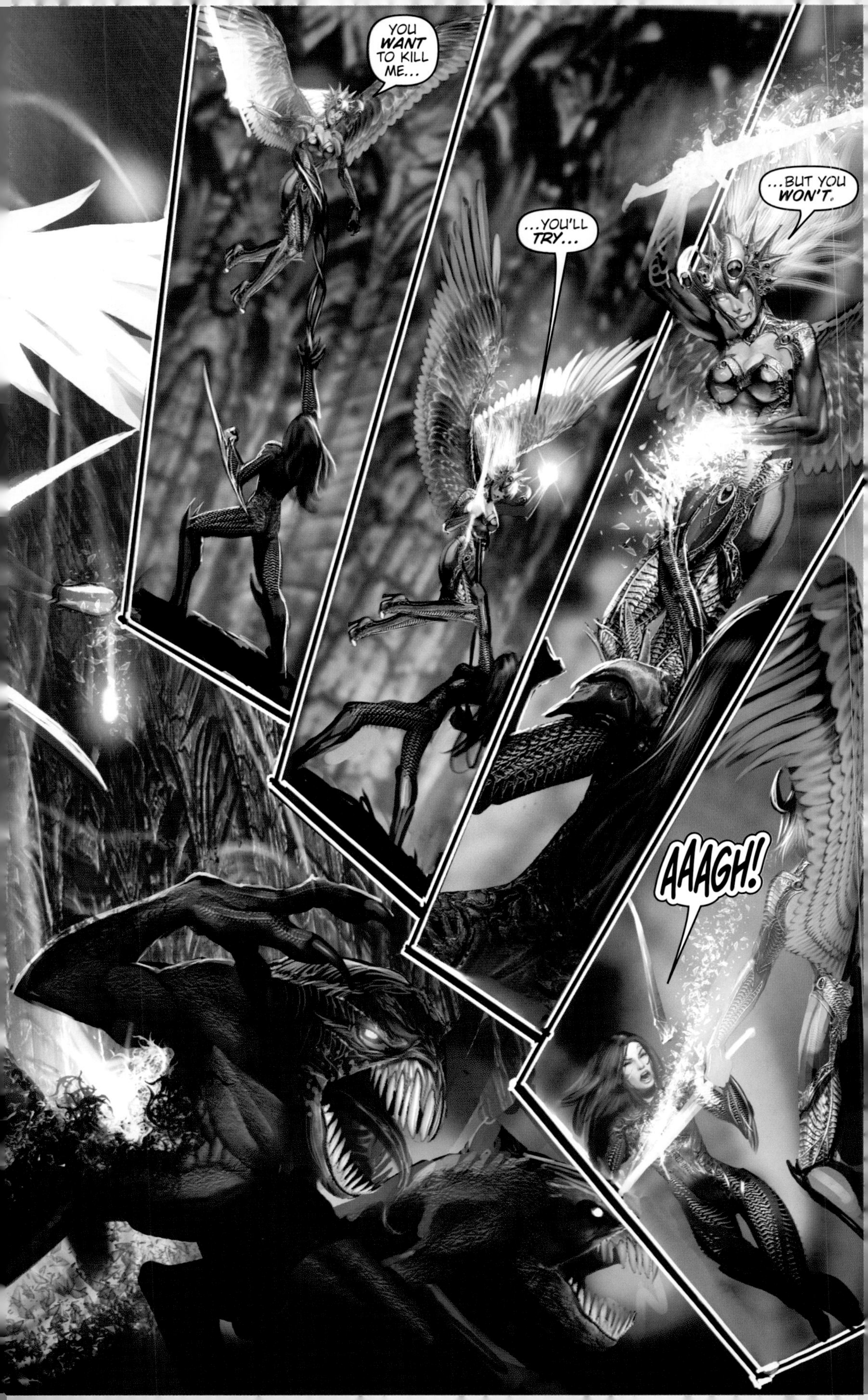

YOU **WANT** TO KILL ME...
...YOU'LL **TRY**...
...BUT YOU **WON'T**.
AAAGH!

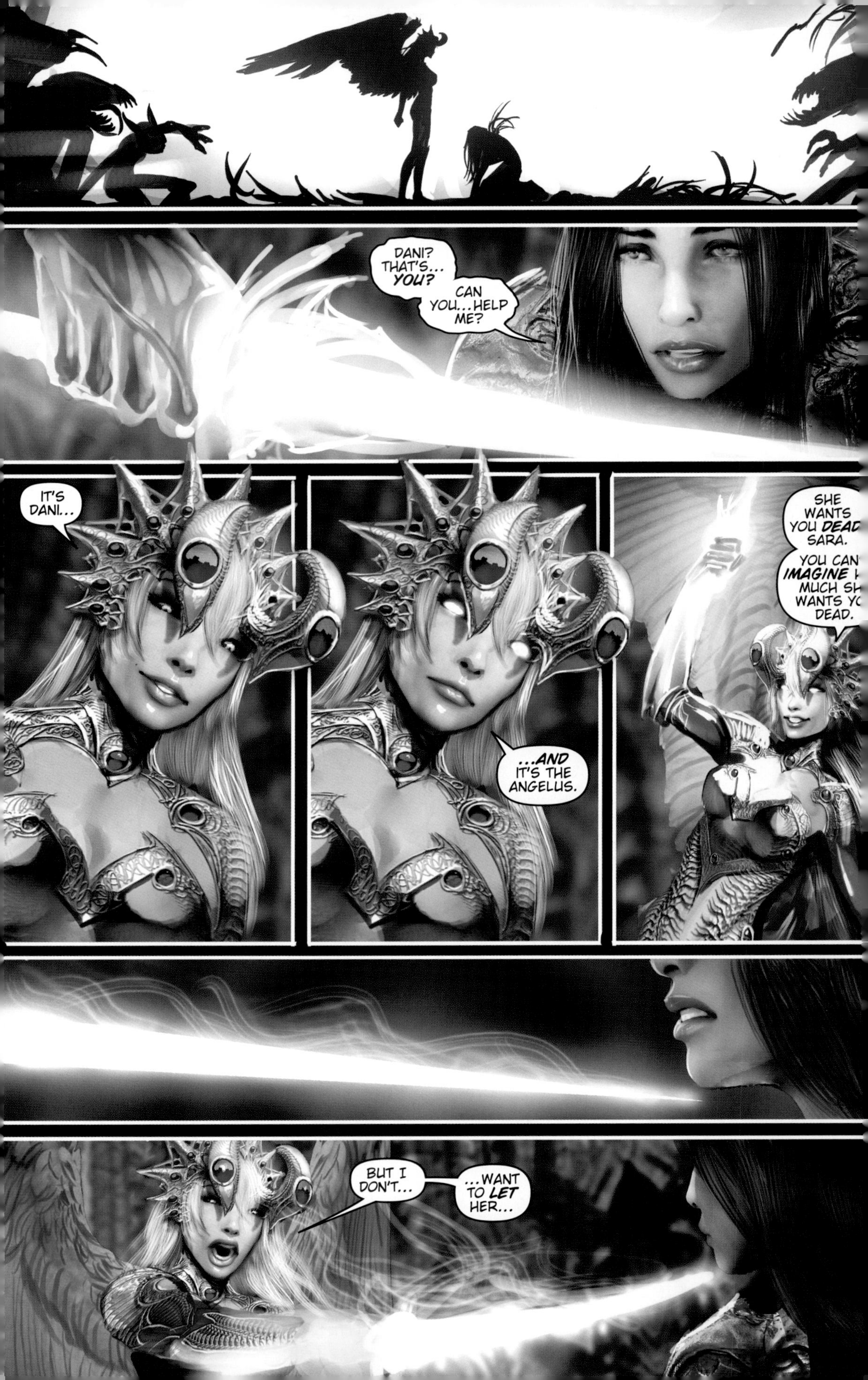

DANI? THAT'S... YOU?
CAN YOU...HELP ME?
IT'S DANI...
...AND IT'S THE ANGELUS.
SHE WANTS YOU DEAD SARA.
YOU CAN IMAGINE MUCH SH WANTS YO DEAD.
BUT I DON'T...
...WANT TO LET HER...

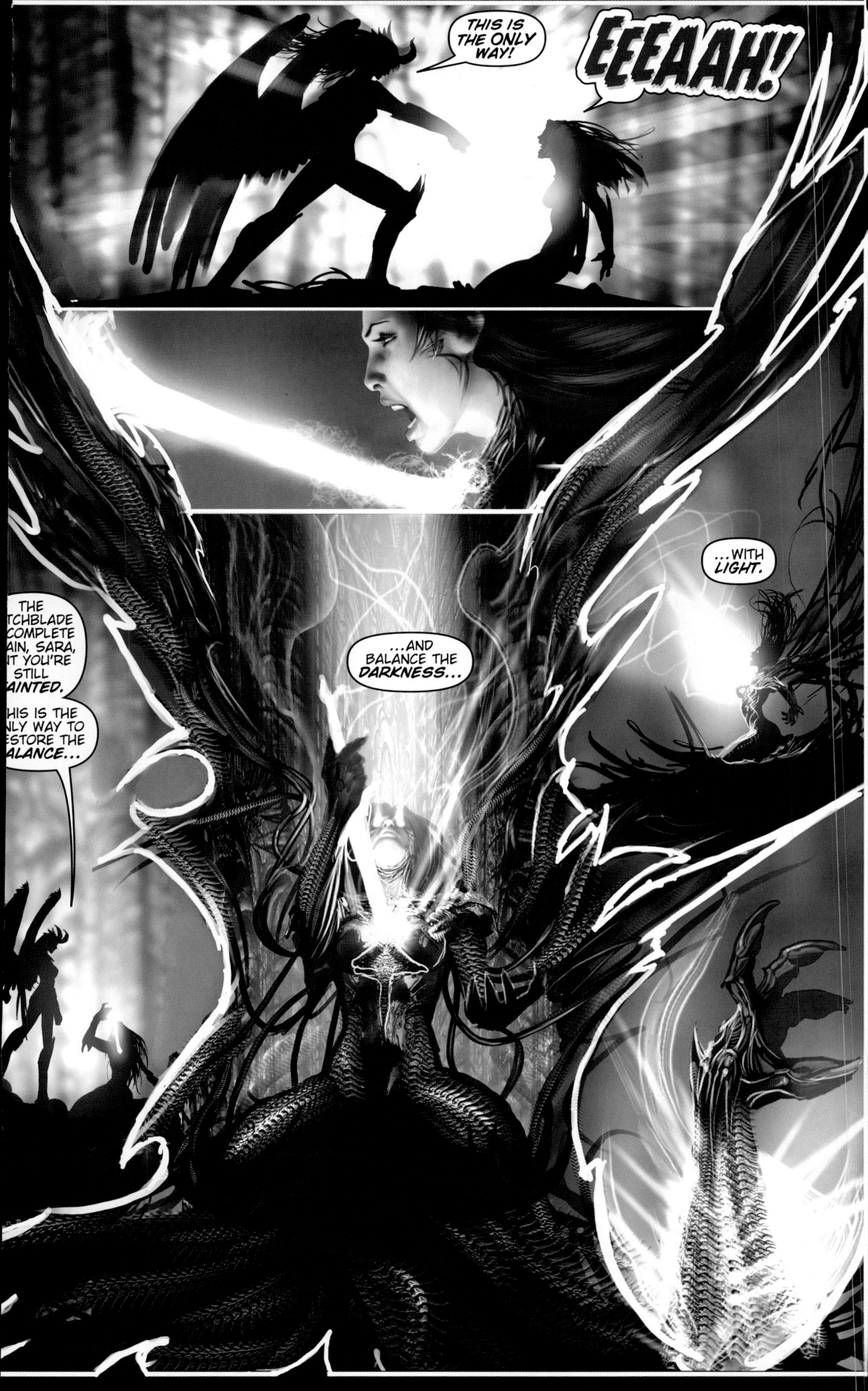

THIS IS THE ONLY WAY!
EEEAAH!
THE TCHBLADE COMPLETE AIN, SARA, T YOU'RE STILL AINTED.
HIS IS THE NLY WAY TO ESTORE THE ALANCE...
...AND BALANCE THE DARKNESS...
...WITH LIGHT.

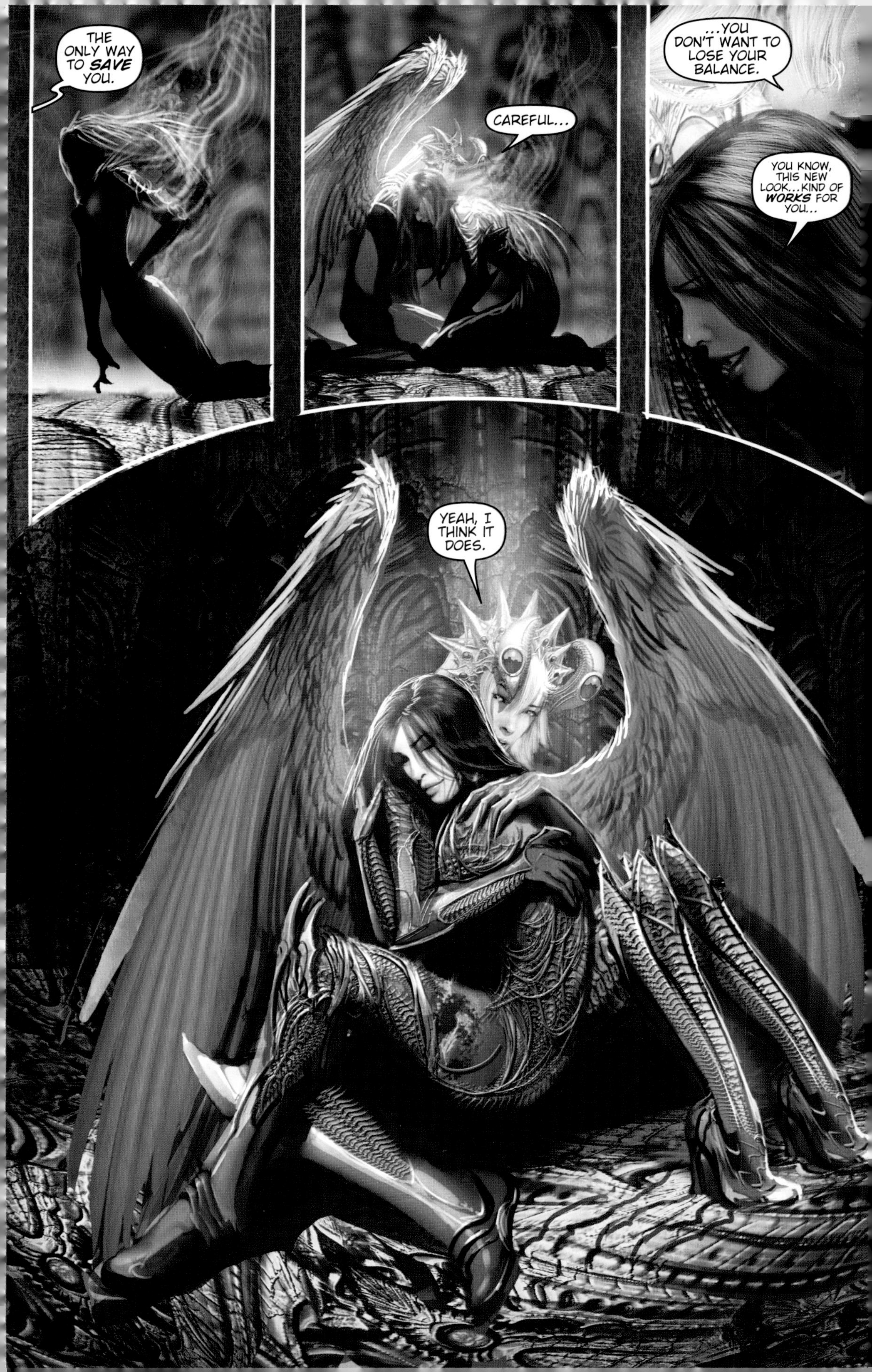
THE ONLY WAY TO SAVE YOU.
CAREFUL...
...YOU DON'T WANT TO LOSE YOUR BALANCE.
YOU KNOW, THIS NEW LOOK...KIND OF WORKS FOR YOU...
YEAH, I THINK IT DOES.

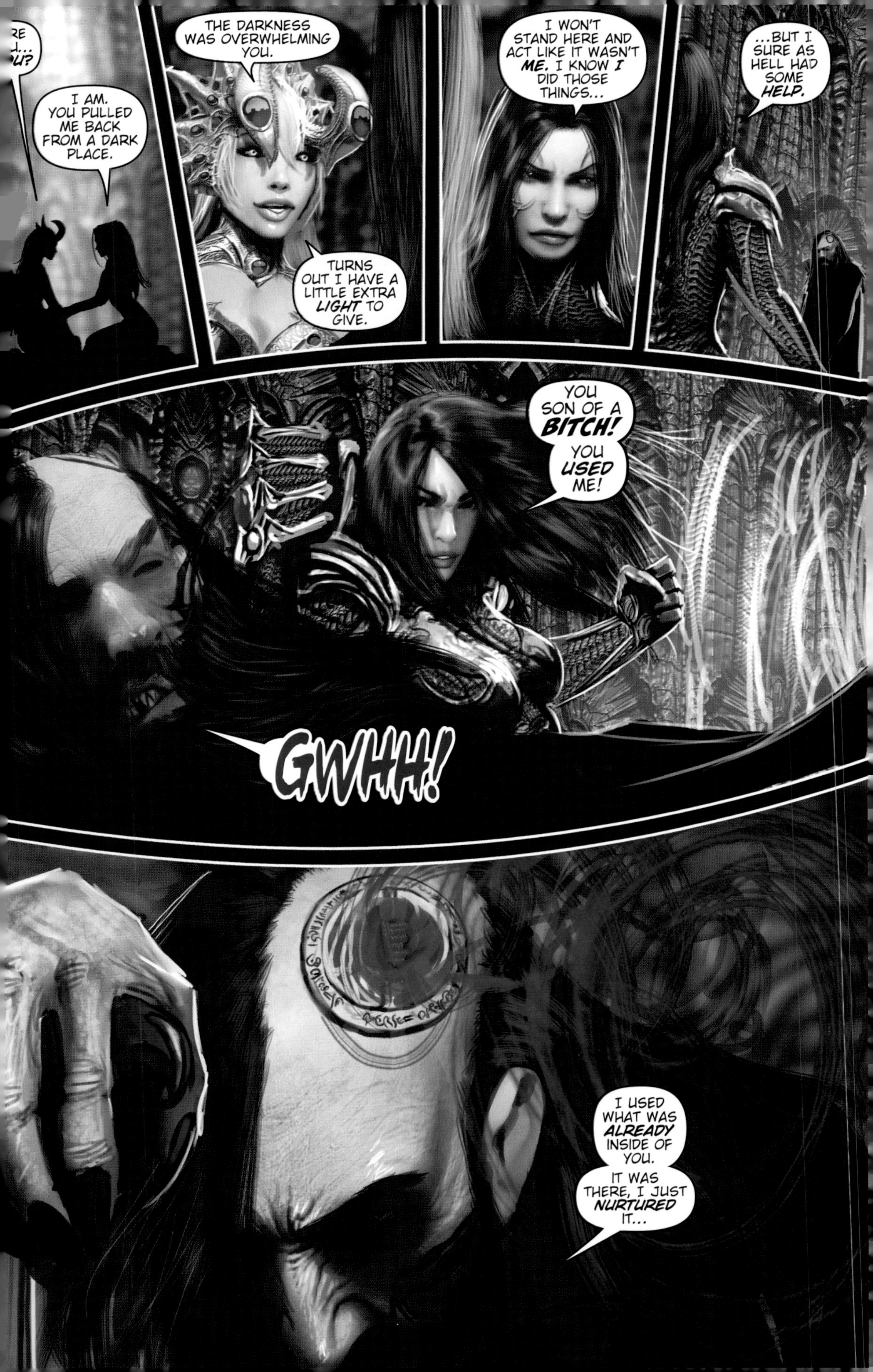
I AM. YOU PULLED ME BACK FROM A DARK PLACE.
THE DARKNESS WAS OVERWHELMING YOU.
TURNS OUT I HAVE A LITTLE EXTRA LIGHT TO GIVE.
I WON'T STAND HERE AND ACT LIKE IT WASN'T ME. I KNOW I DID THOSE THINGS...
...BUT I SURE AS HELL HAD SOME HELP.
YOU SON OF A BITCH! YOU USED ME!
GWHH!
I USED WHAT WAS ALREADY INSIDE OF YOU.
IT WAS THERE, I JUST NURTURED IT...

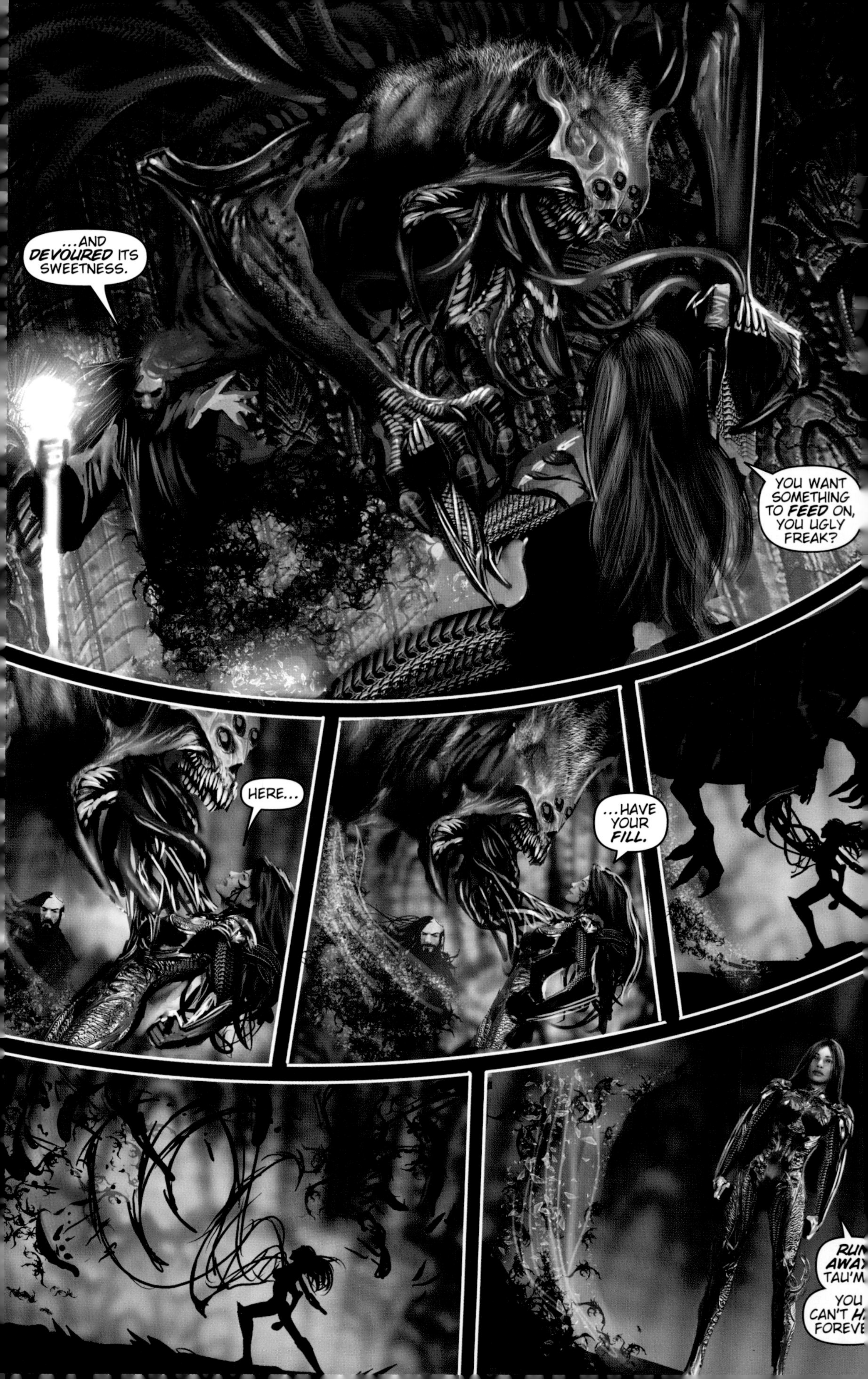
...AND *DEVOURED* ITS SWEETNESS.
YOU WANT SOMETHING TO *FEED* ON, YOU UGLY FREAK?
HERE...
...HAVE YOUR *FILL.*
RU
AWA
TAU'M
YOU
CAN'T *H*
FOREVE

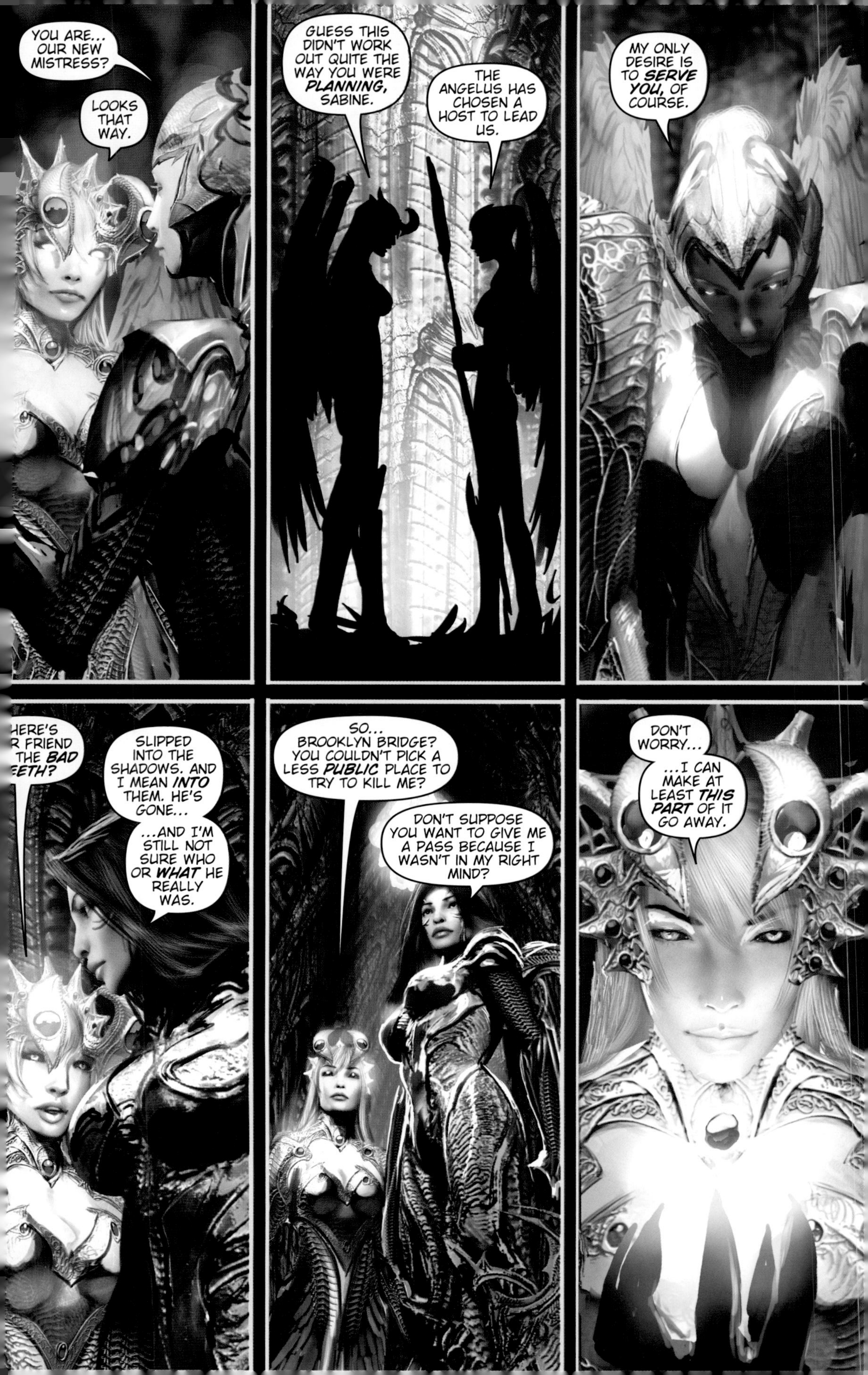
YOU ARE... OUR NEW MISTRESS?
LOOKS THAT WAY.
GUESS THIS DIDN'T WORK OUT QUITE THE WAY YOU WERE PLANNING, SABINE.
THE ANGELUS HAS CHOSEN A HOST TO LEAD US.
MY ONLY DESIRE IS TO SERVE YOU, OF COURSE.
HERE'S R FRIEND THE BAD EETH?
SLIPPED INTO THE SHADOWS. AND I MEAN INTO THEM. HE'S GONE...
...AND I'M STILL NOT SURE WHO OR WHAT HE REALLY WAS.
SO... BROOKLYN BRIDGE? YOU COULDN'T PICK A LESS PUBLIC PLACE TO TRY TO KILL ME?
DON'T SUPPOSE YOU WANT TO GIVE ME A PASS BECAUSE I WASN'T IN MY RIGHT MIND?
DON'T WORRY...
...I CAN MAKE AT LEAST THIS PART OF IT GO AWAY.

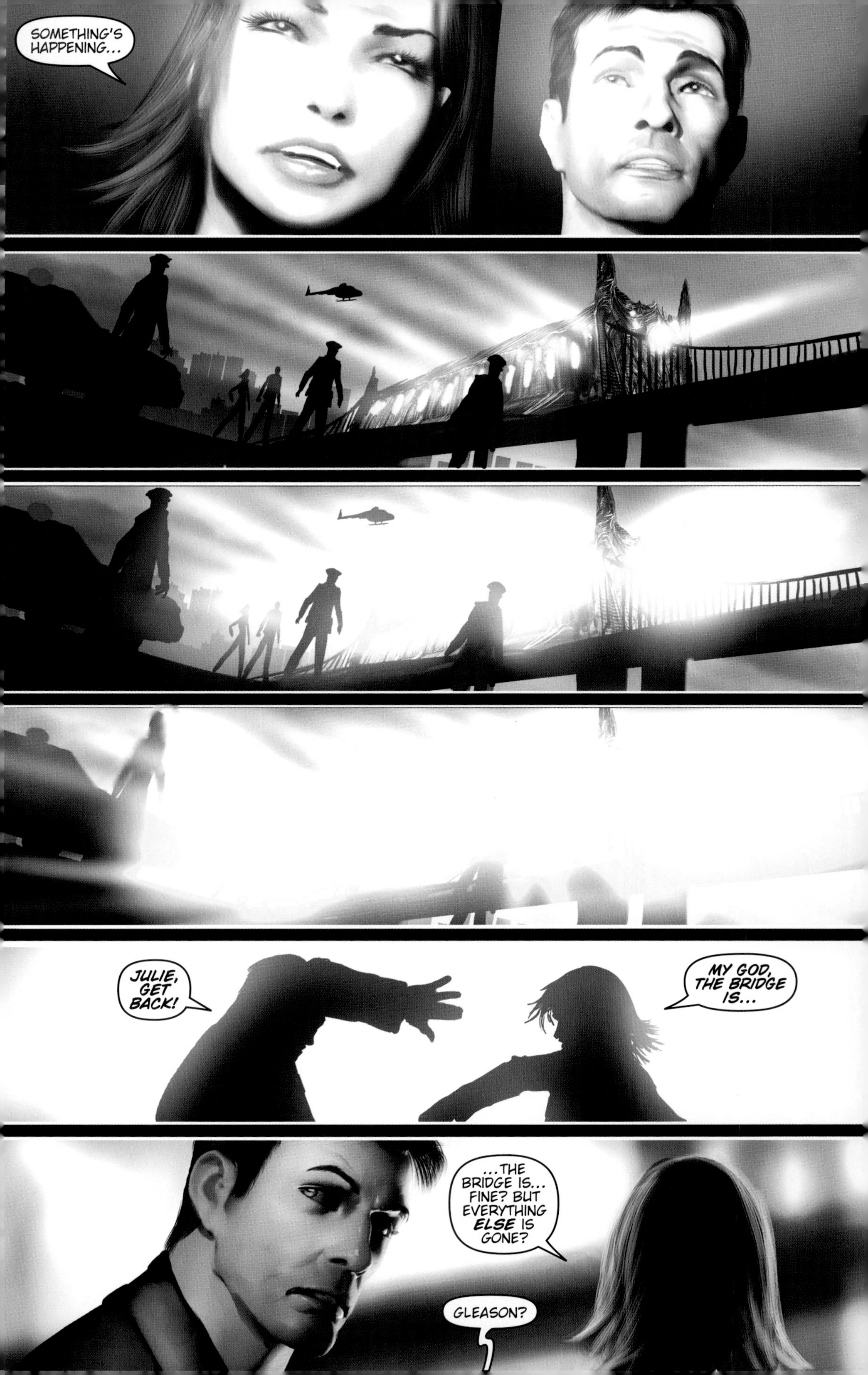
SOMETHING'S HAPPENING...
JULIE, GET BACK!
MY GOD, THE BRIDGE IS...
...THE BRIDGE IS... FINE? BUT EVERYTHING ELSE IS GONE?
GLEASON?

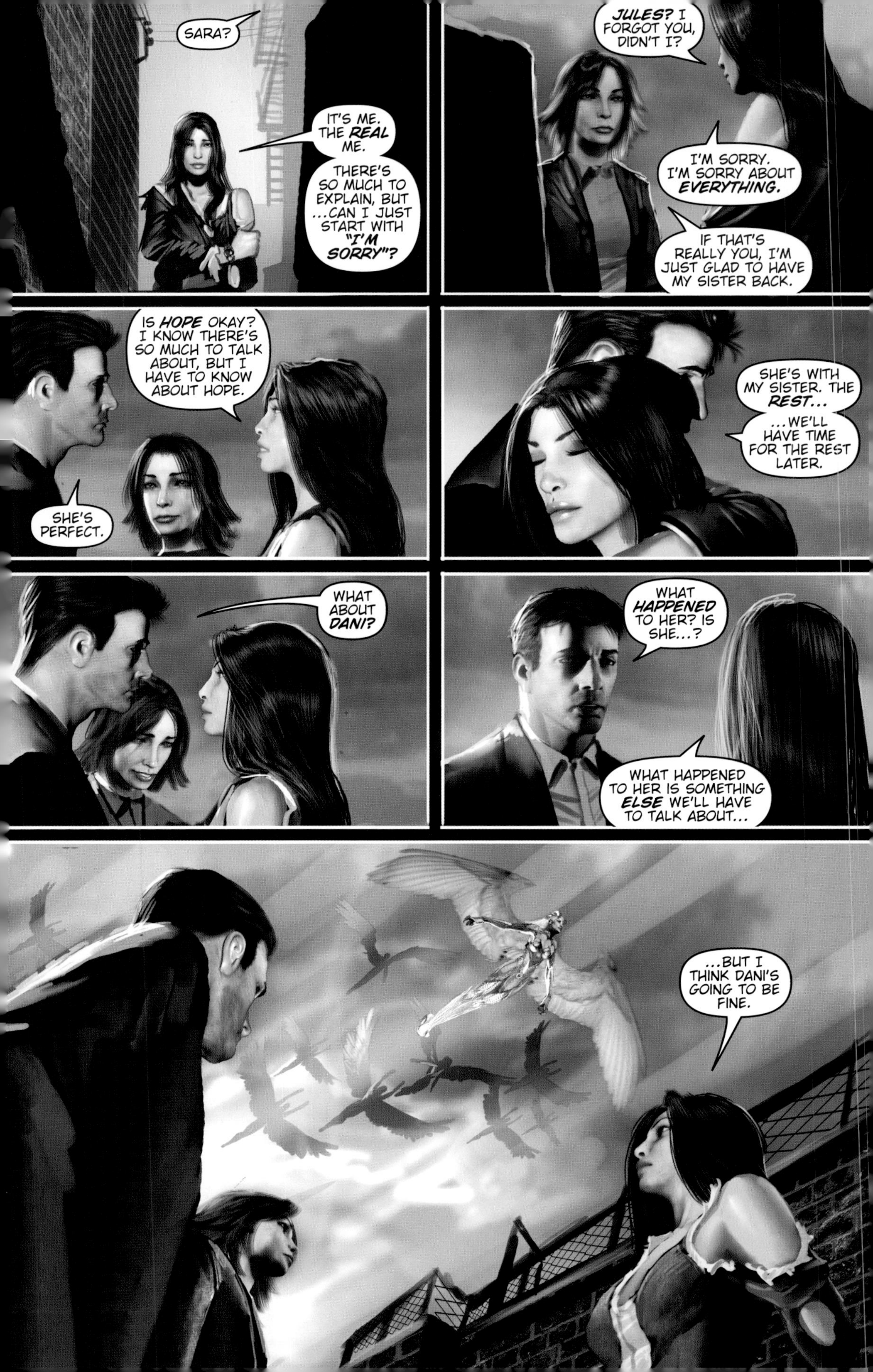
SARA?
IT'S ME. THE REAL ME.
THERE'S SO MUCH TO EXPLAIN, BUT ...CAN I JUST START WITH "I'M SORRY"?
JULES? I FORGOT YOU, DIDN'T I?
I'M SORRY. I'M SORRY ABOUT EVERYTHING.
IF THAT'S REALLY YOU, I'M JUST GLAD TO HAVE MY SISTER BACK.
IS HOPE OKAY? I KNOW THERE'S SO MUCH TO TALK ABOUT, BUT I HAVE TO KNOW ABOUT HOPE.
SHE'S PERFECT.
SHE'S WITH MY SISTER. THE REST...
...WE'LL HAVE TIME FOR THE REST LATER.
WHAT ABOUT DANI?
WHAT HAPPENED TO HER? IS SHE...?
WHAT HAPPENED TO HER IS SOMETHING ELSE WE'LL HAVE TO TALK ABOUT...
...BUT I THINK DANI'S GOING TO BE FINE.

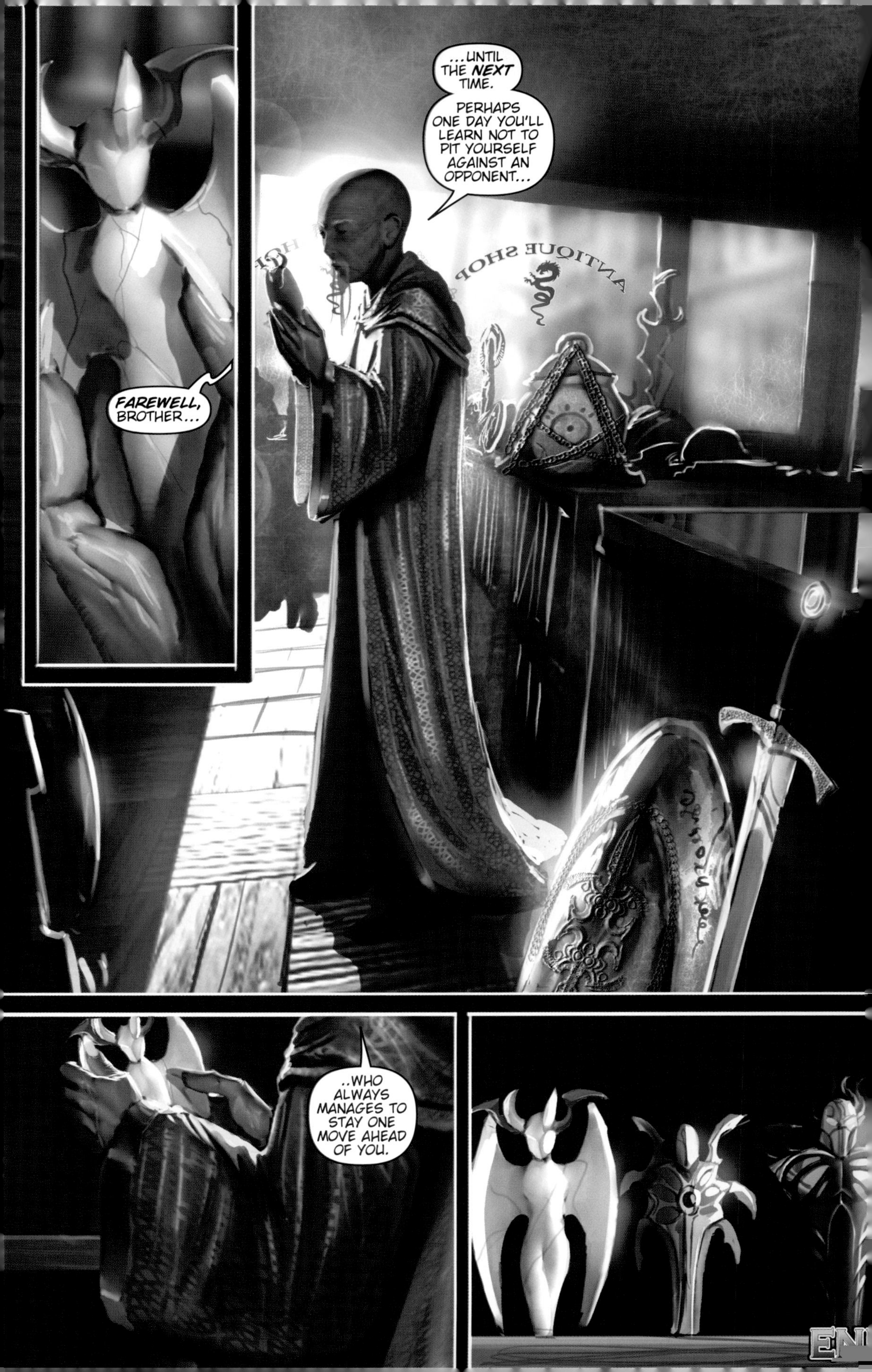

FAREWELL, BROTHER...
...UNTIL THE ***NEXT*** TIME.
PERHAPS ONE DAY YOU'LL LEARN NOT TO PIT YOURSELF AGAINST AN OPPONENT...
..WHO ALWAYS MANAGES TO STAY ONE MOVE AHEAD OF YOU.

Sara's story continues in the forthcoming
Witchblade: Redemption Volume 1 trade paperback (ISBN 978-1-60706-200-4)
which collects *Witchblade* issues #131-136

•••••

Dani's story continues in forthcoming
Angelus Volume 1 trade paperback (ISBN 1-978-160706-198-4)
which collects *Angelus* issues #1-6

WITCHBLADE

·VOLUME 8·

COVER GALLERY

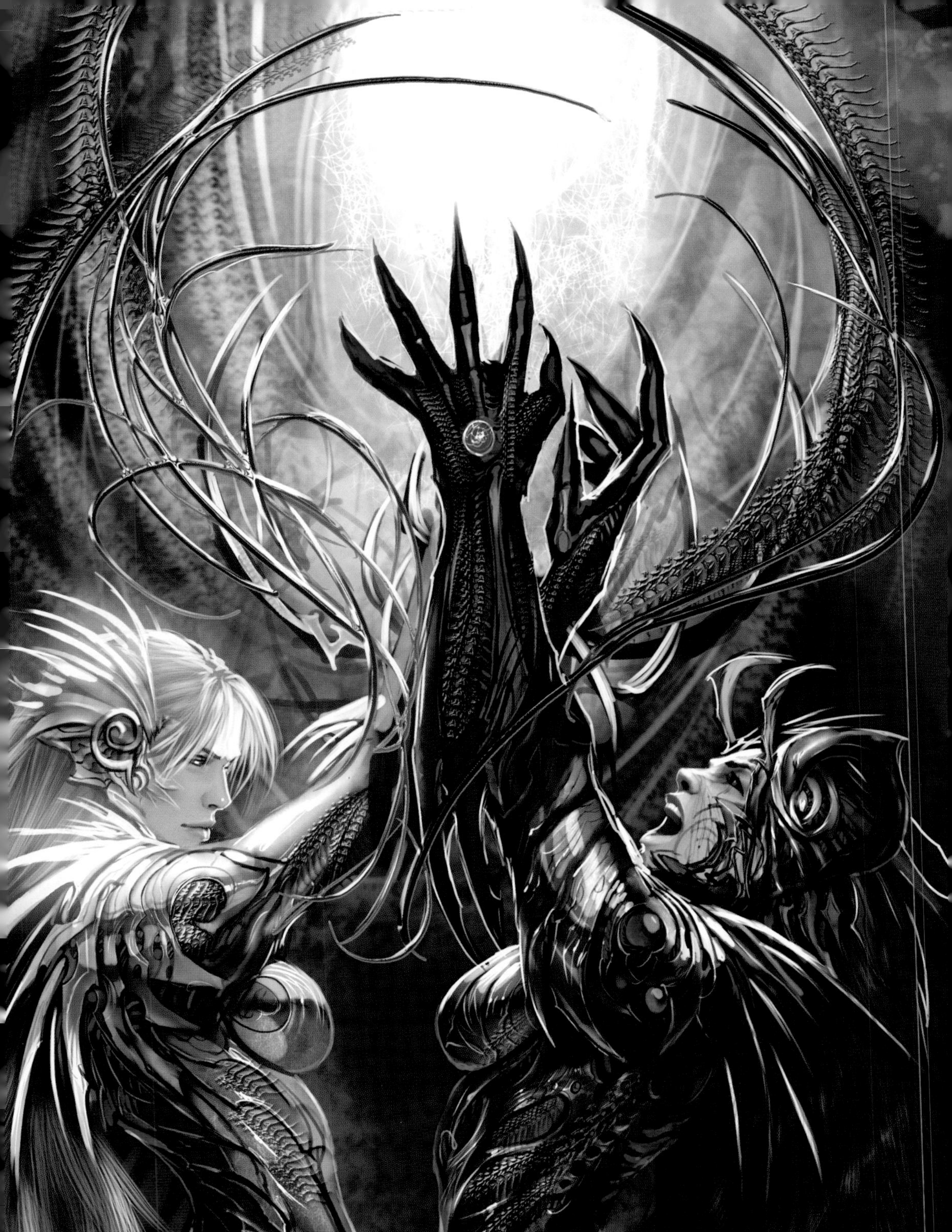

Witchblade issue #125 cover C
art by: **Stjepan Sejic**

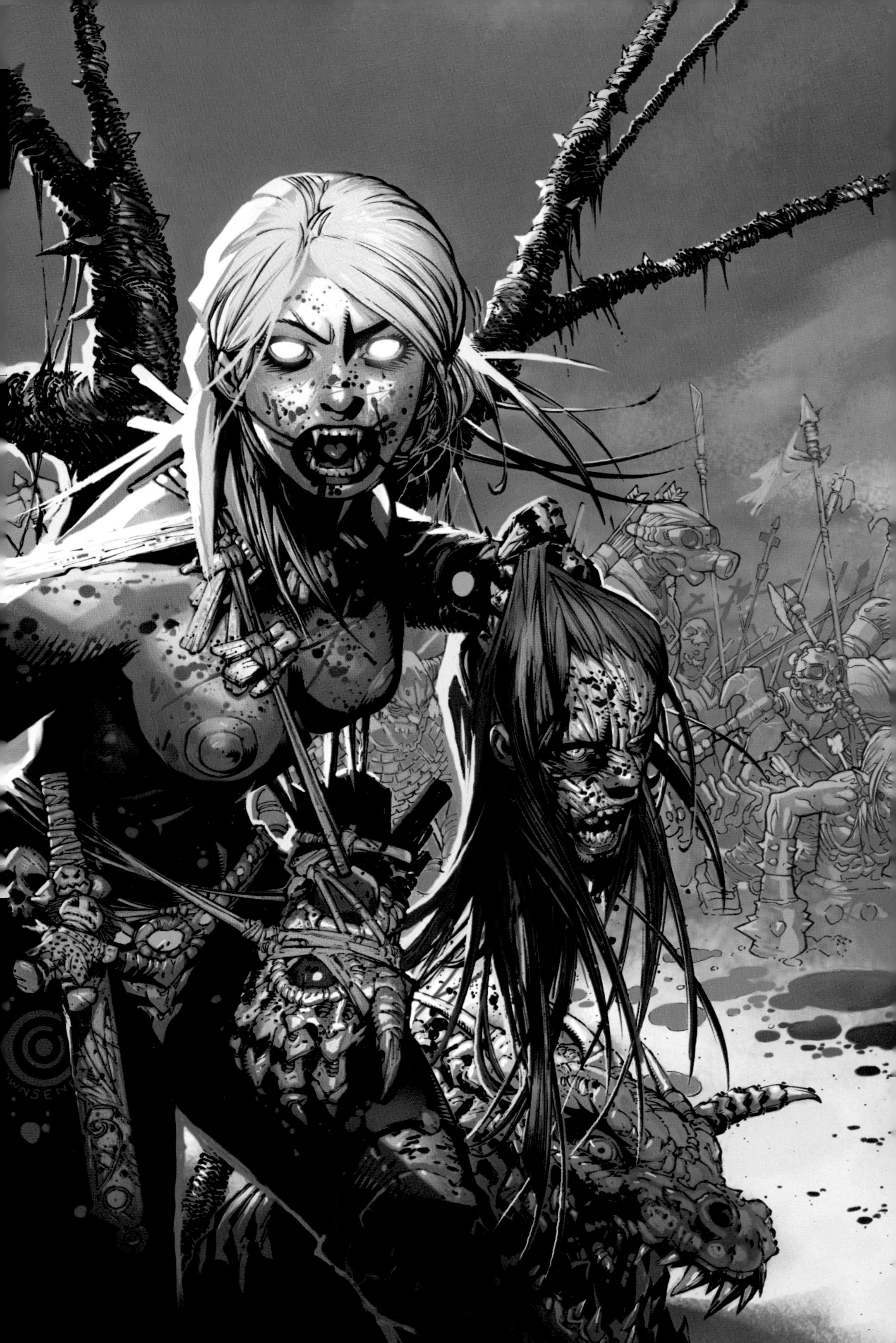

Witchblade issue #125 cover B
art by: **Chris Bachalo** and **Tim Townsend**

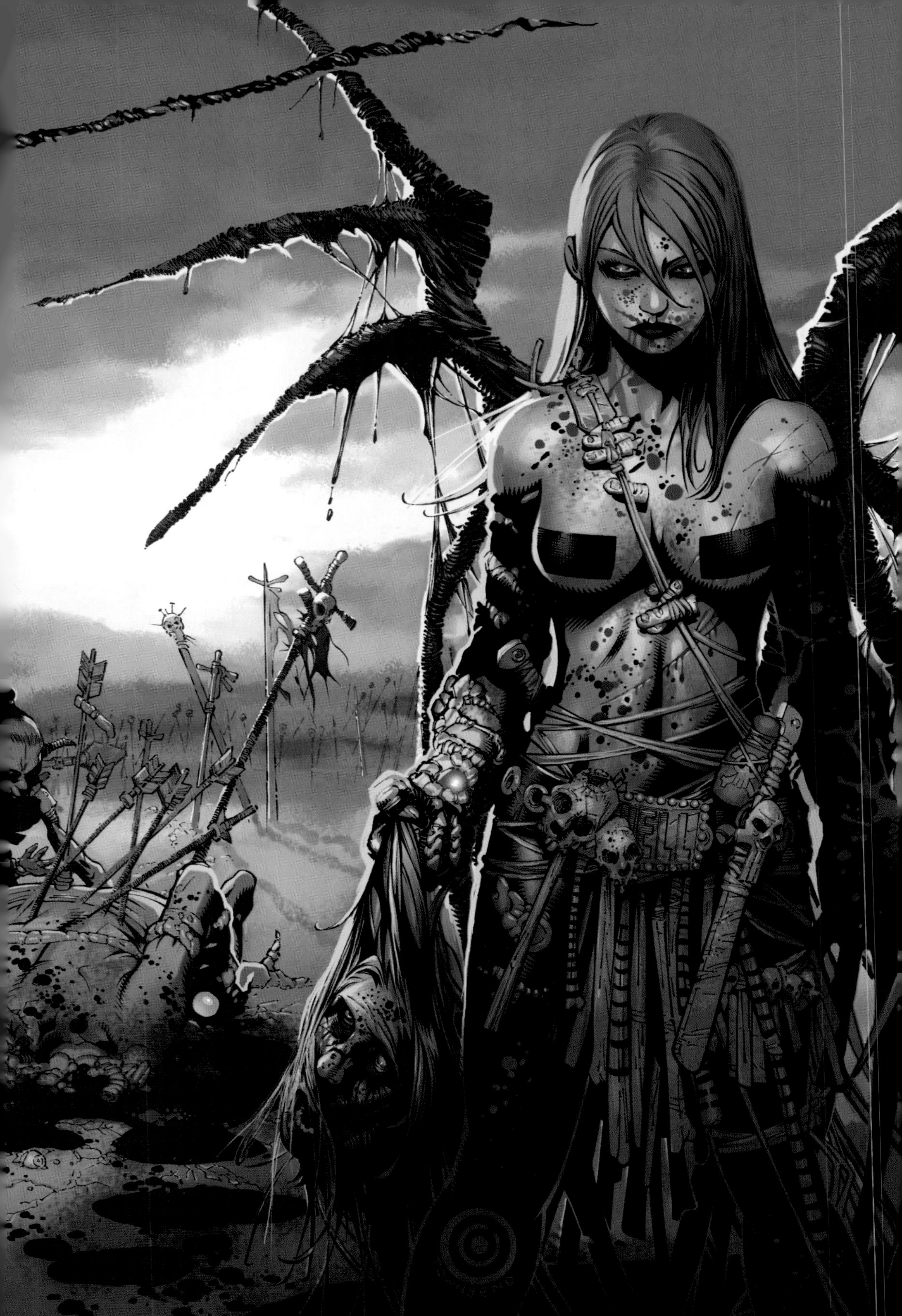

Witchblade issue #125 cover A
art by: **Chris Bachalo** and **Tim Townsend**

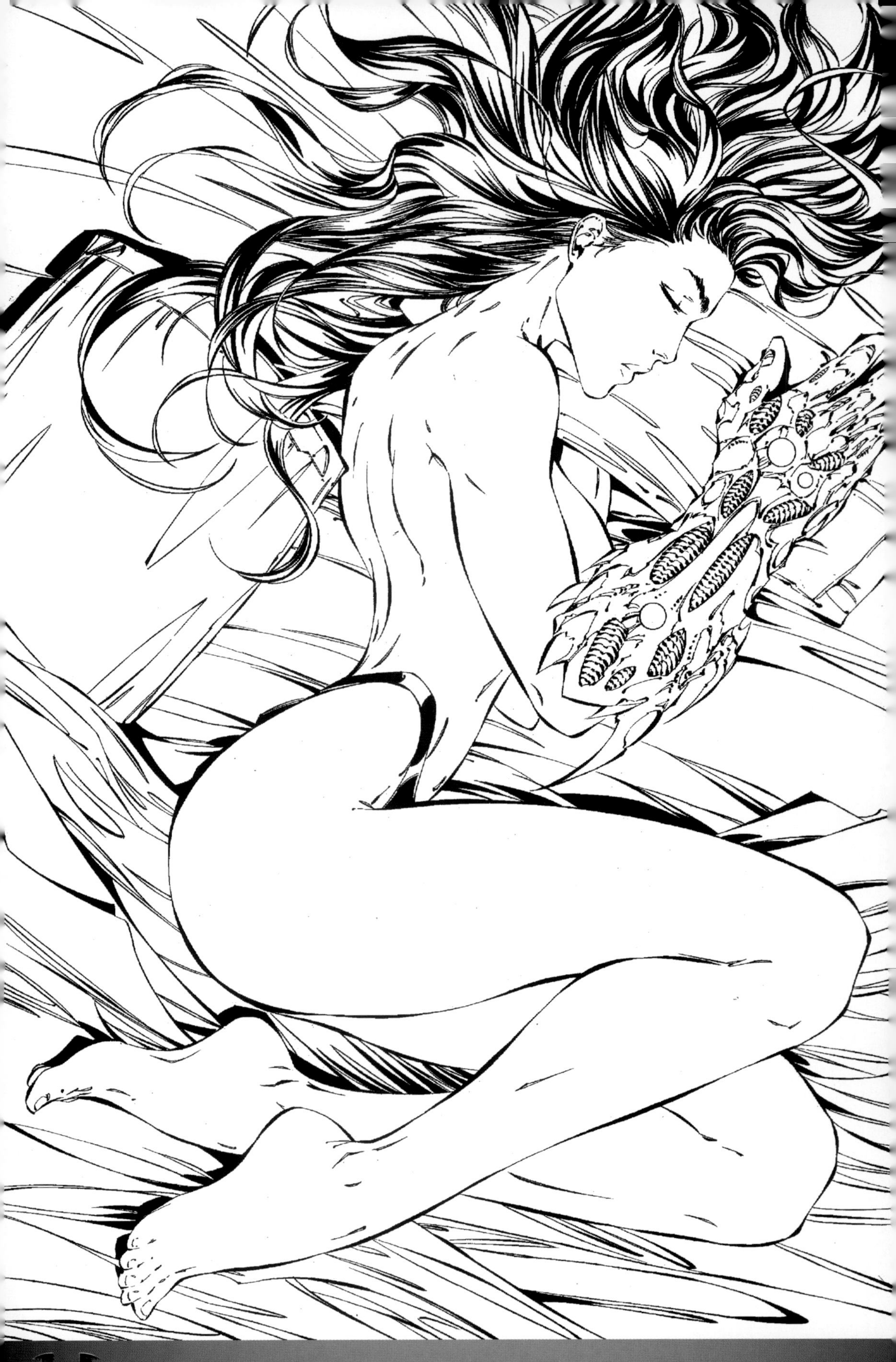

Witchblade issue #125 cover E, Fantastic Realm variant
art by: **Michael Turner** and **D-Tron**

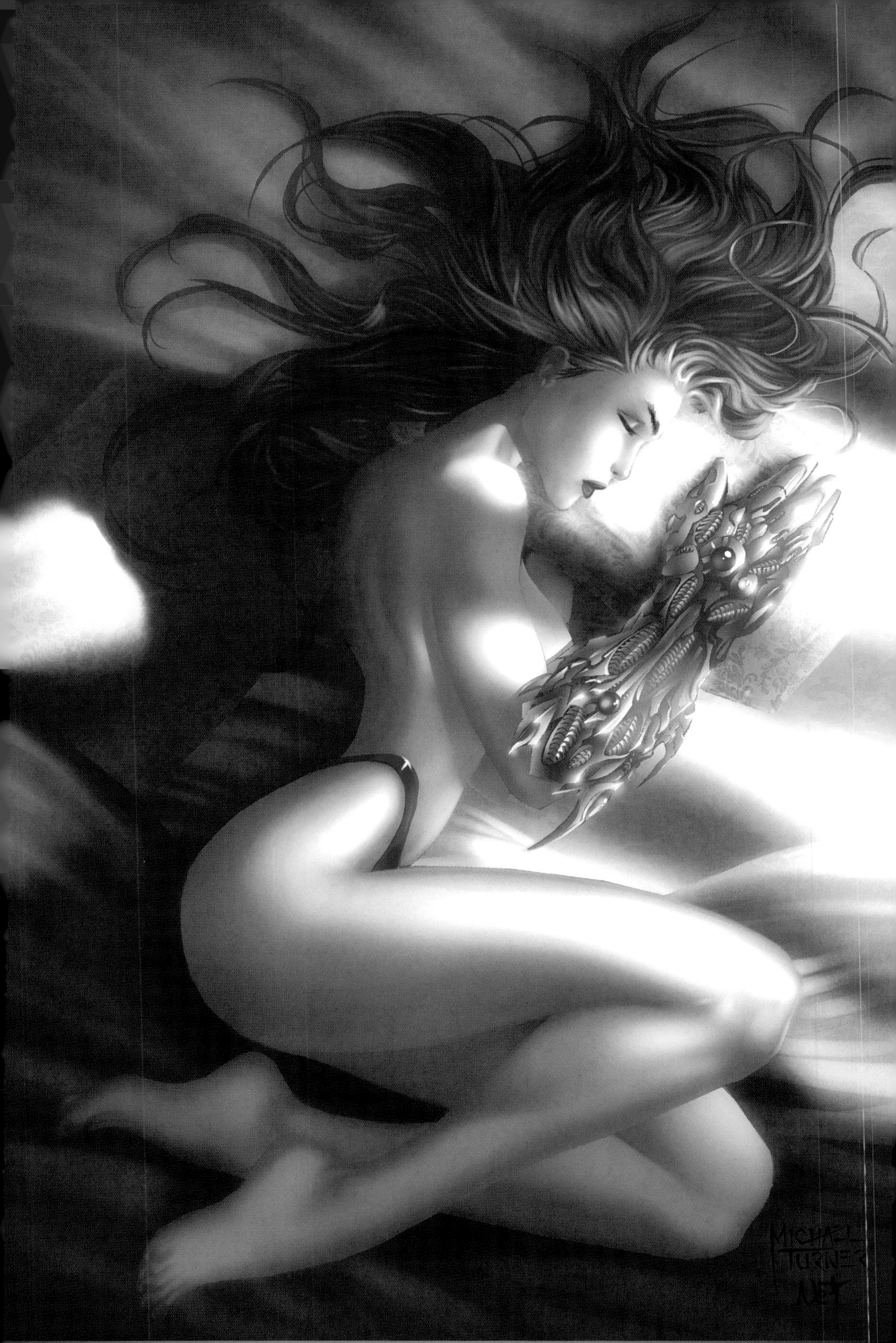

Witchblade issue #125 cover F, Fantastic Realm variant
art by: **Michael Turner, D-Tron** and **Nei Ruffino**

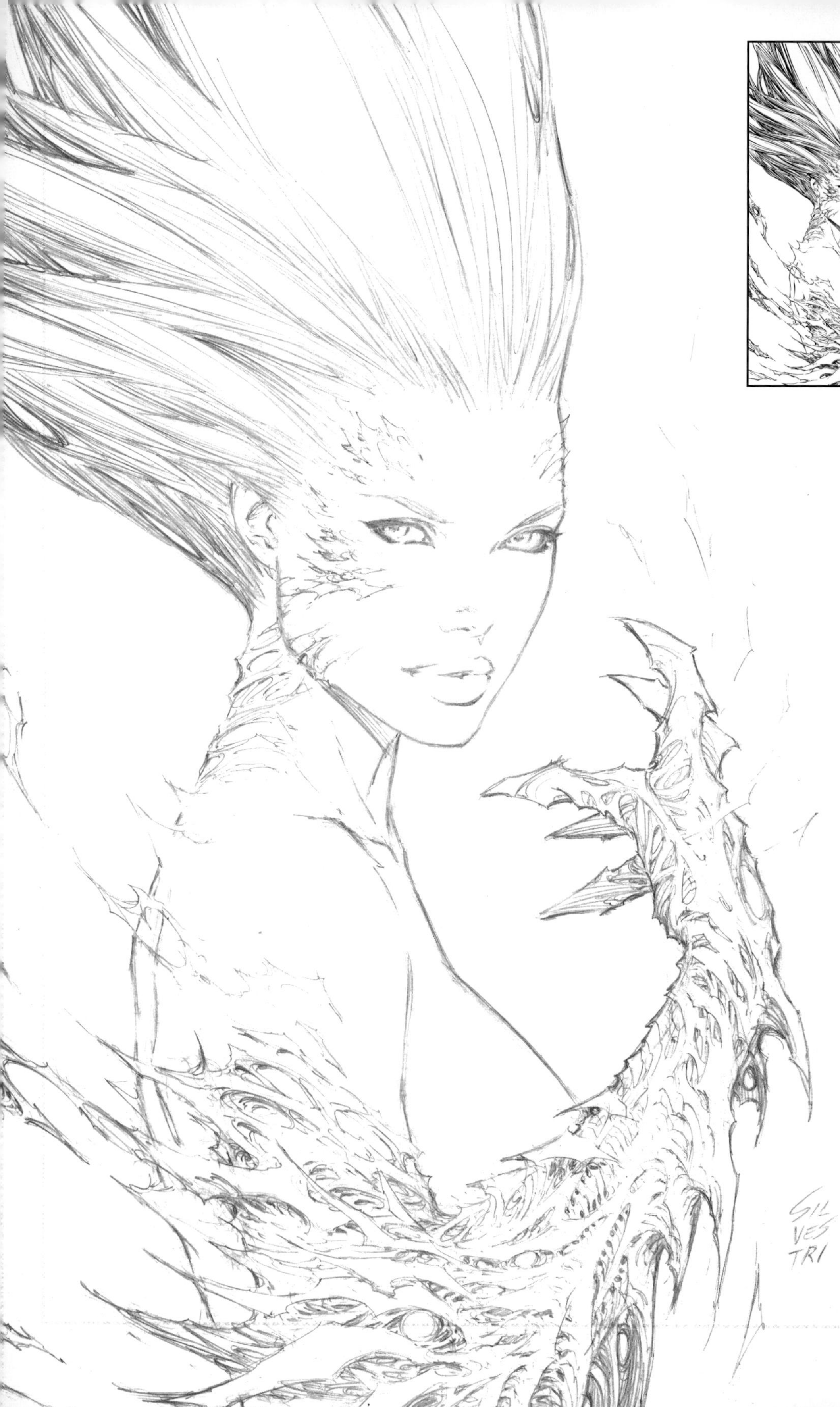
SIL
VES
TRI

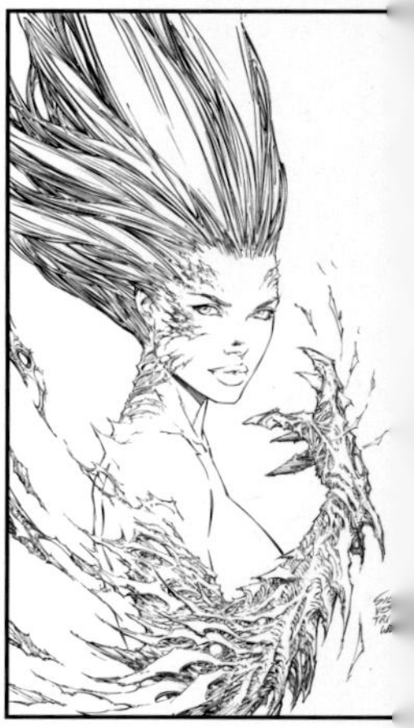

Witchblade issue #125 cover E inks inset, Emerald City Comic-Con variant pencils abo
art by: **Marc Silvestri** and **Joe Weems V**

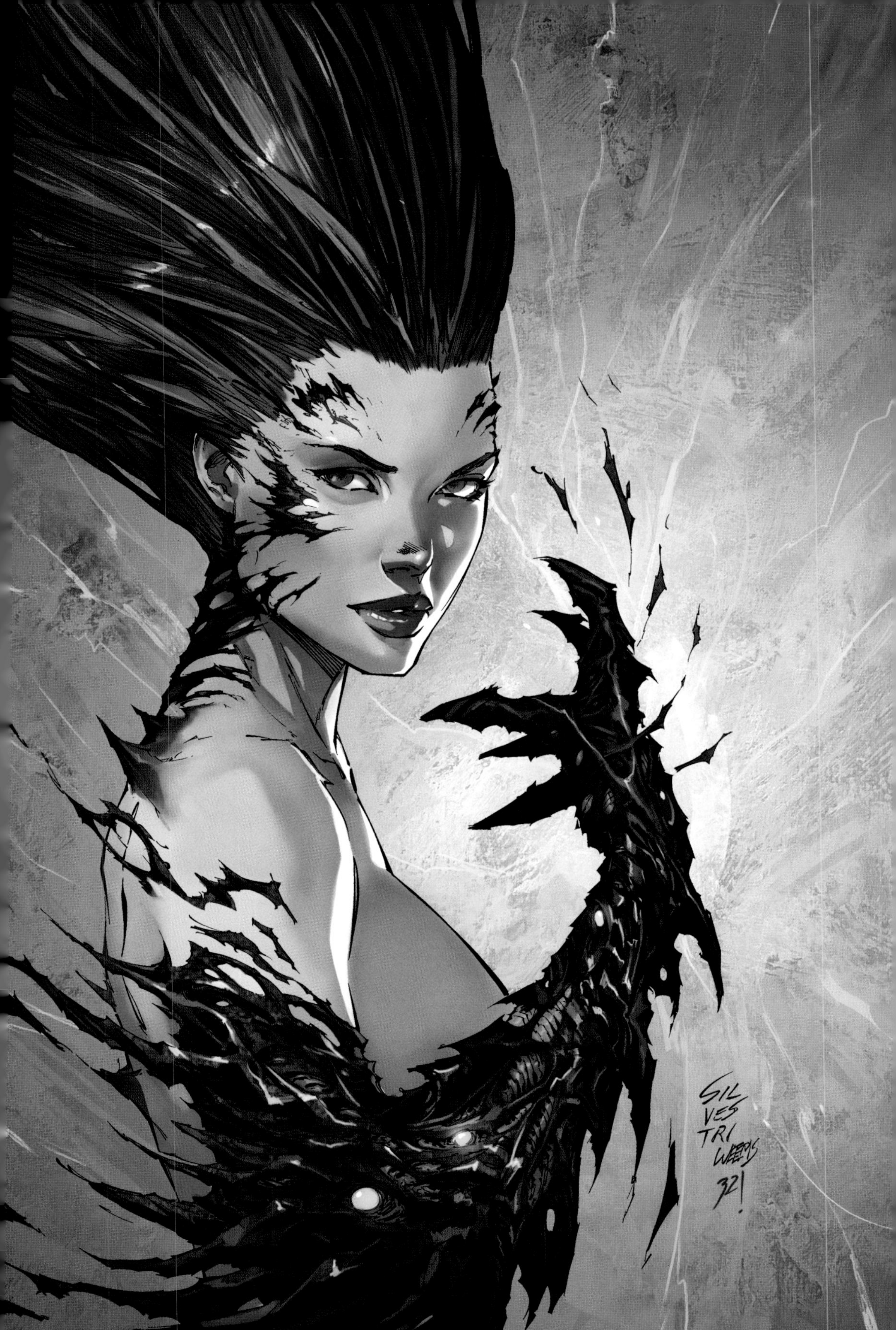

Witchblade issue #125 cover E, Emerald City Comic-Con variant
art by: **Marc Silvestri, Joe Weems V** and **Sunny Gho of IFS**

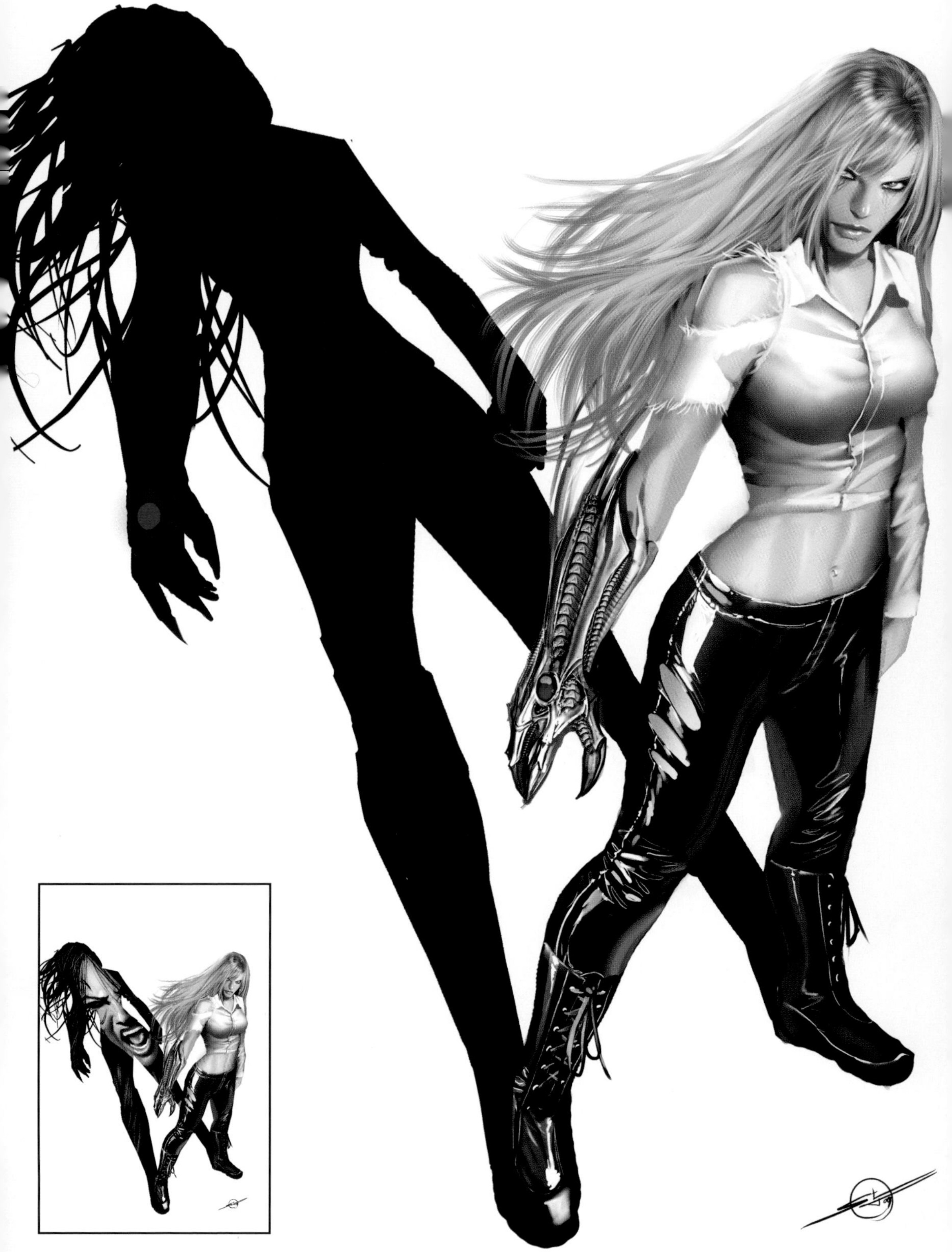

Witchblade issue #126 cover A above, inset cover C, “All Beef Edition”
art by: **Stjepan Sejic**

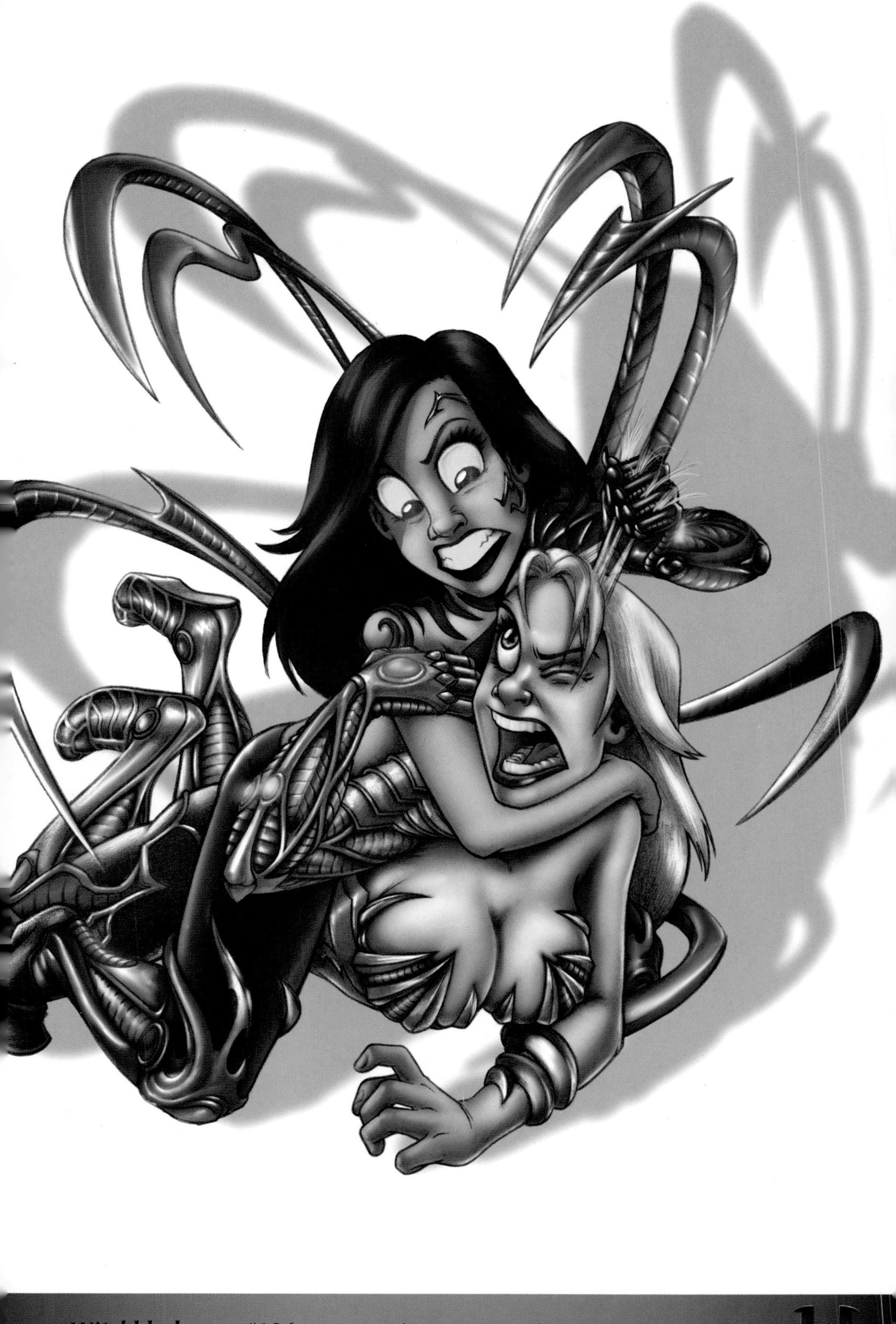

Witchblade issue #126 cover D, Calgary Comic and Entertainment Expo variant
art by: **Laurie B.** and **Felix Serrano**

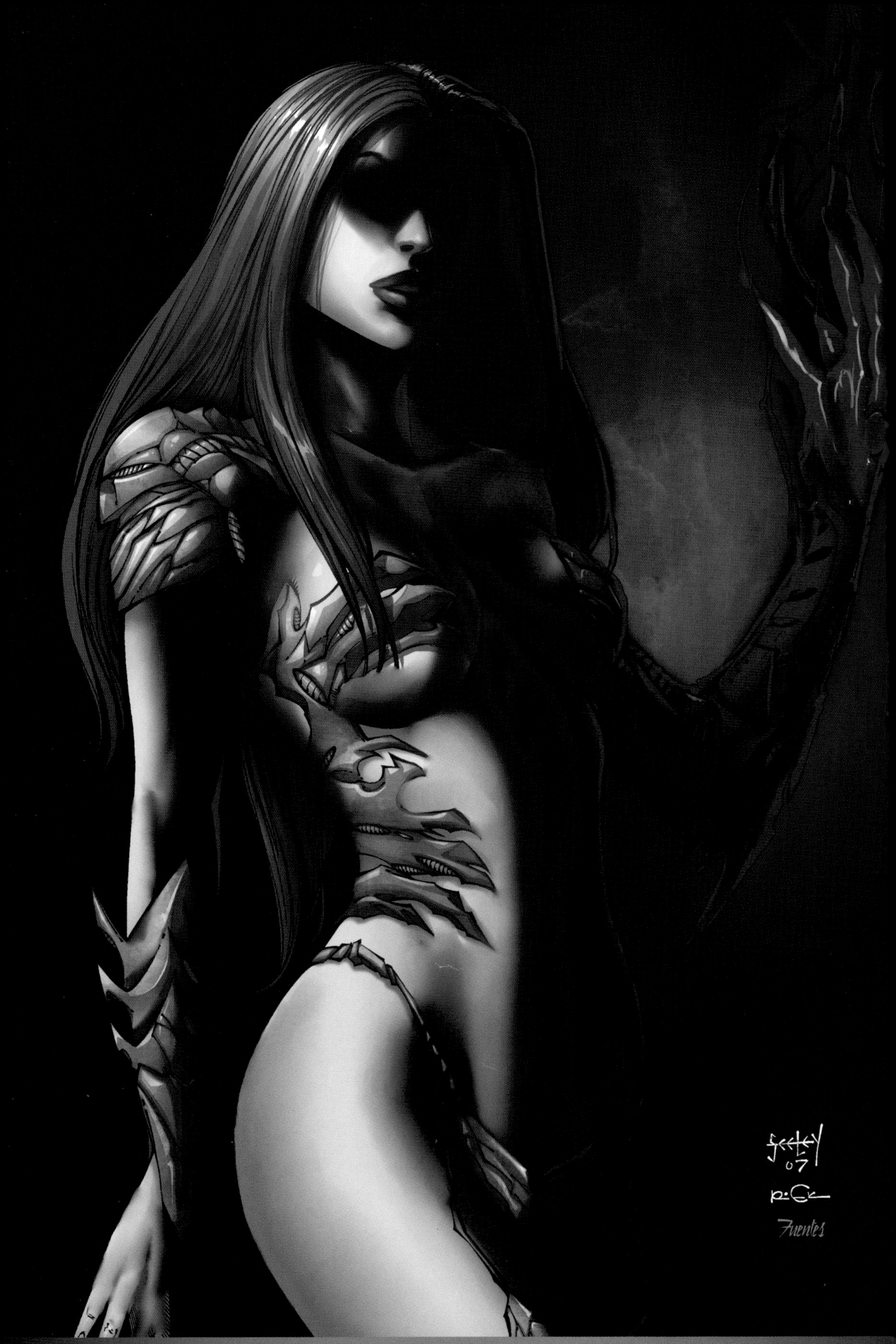
Seeley
07
Fuentes

Witchblade issue #126 cover B
art by: **Tim Seeley, Rick Basaldua** and **Stjepan Sejic**

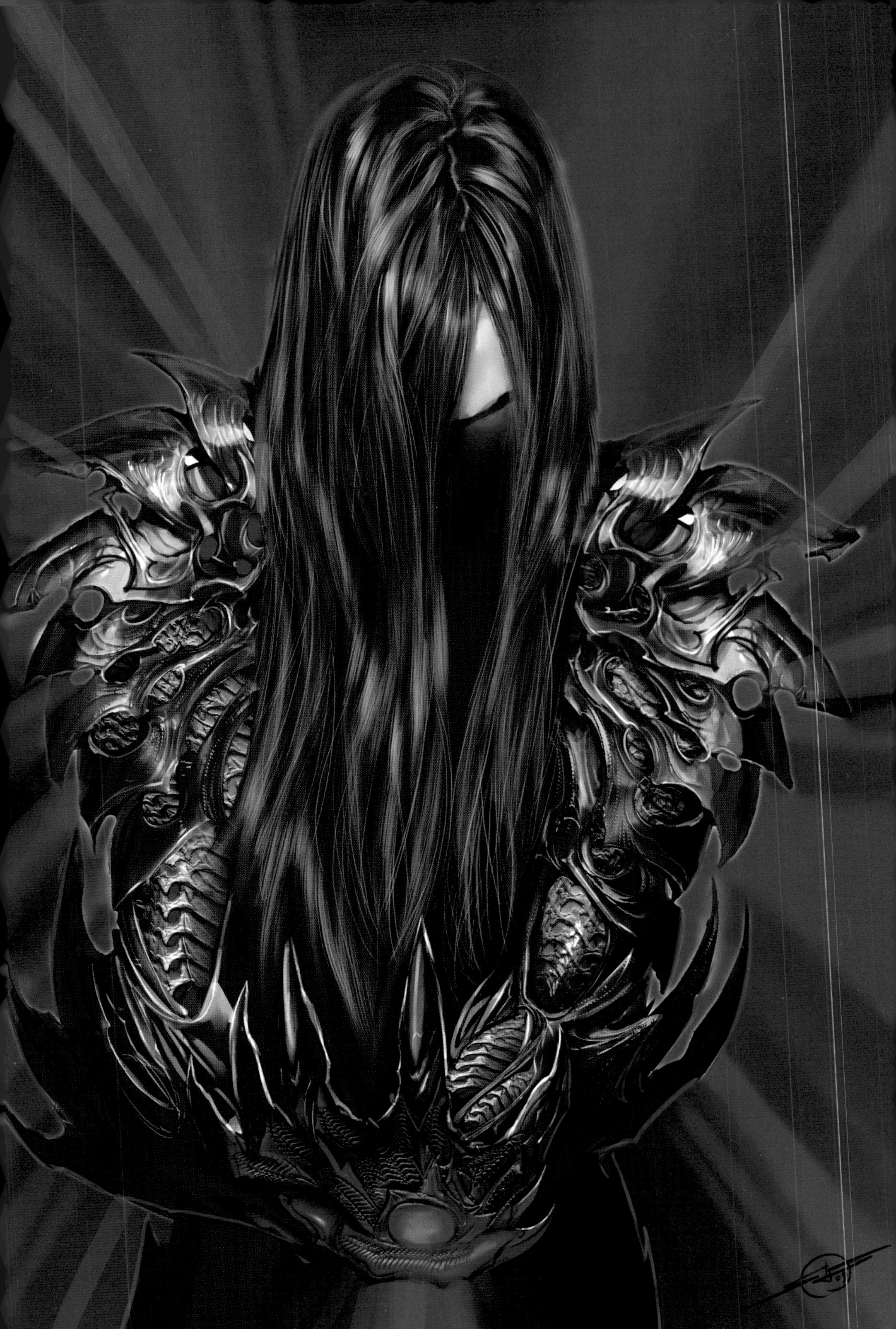

Witchblade issue #127 cover A
art by: **Stjepan Sejic**

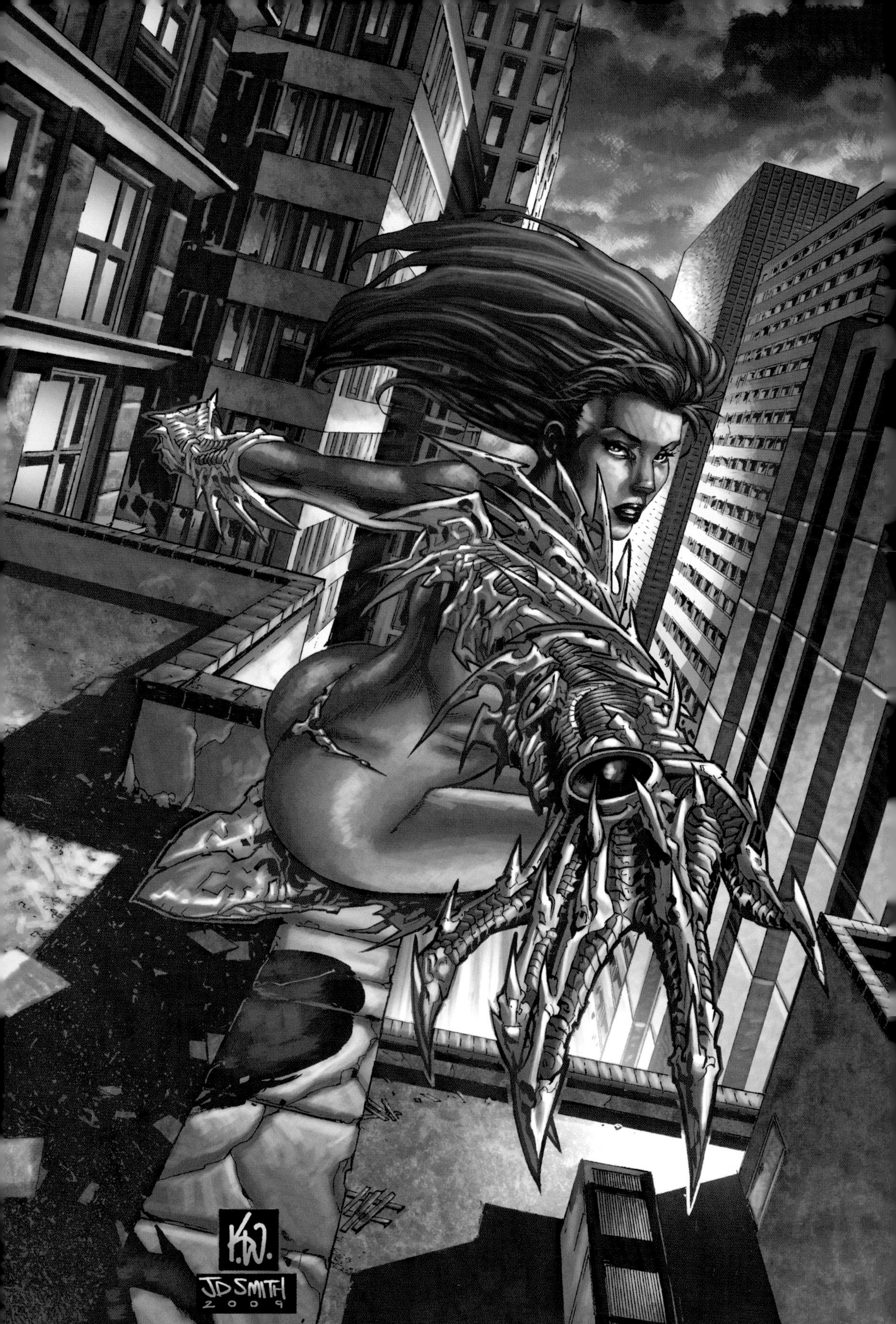
K.W.
JD SMITH
2009

Witchblade issue #127 cover C, Wizard World Philadelphia variant
art by: **Karl Waller** and **JD Smith**

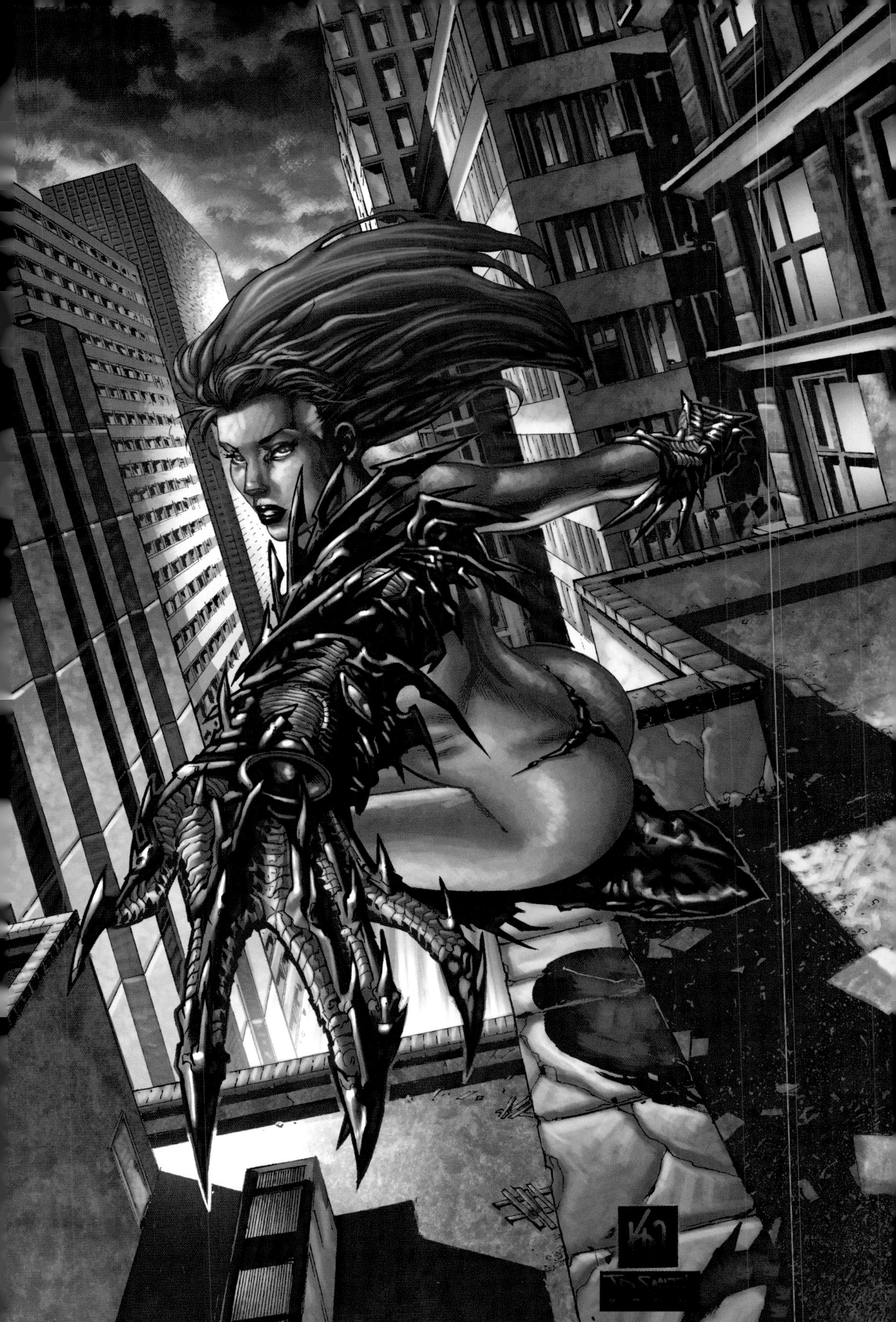

Witchblade issue #127 cover B
art by: **Karl Waller** and **JD Smith**

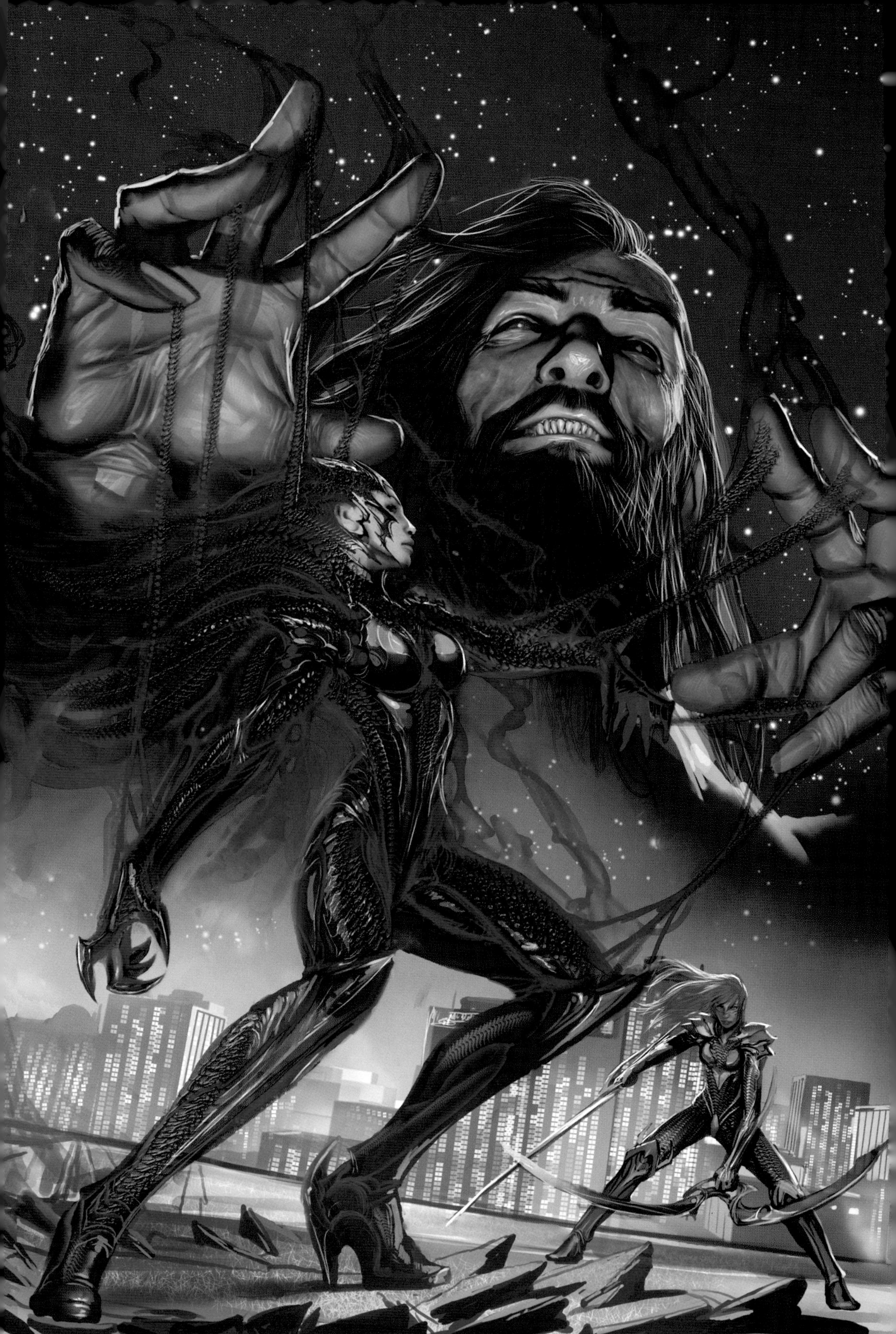

Witchblade issue #128 cover A
art by: **Stjepan Sejic**

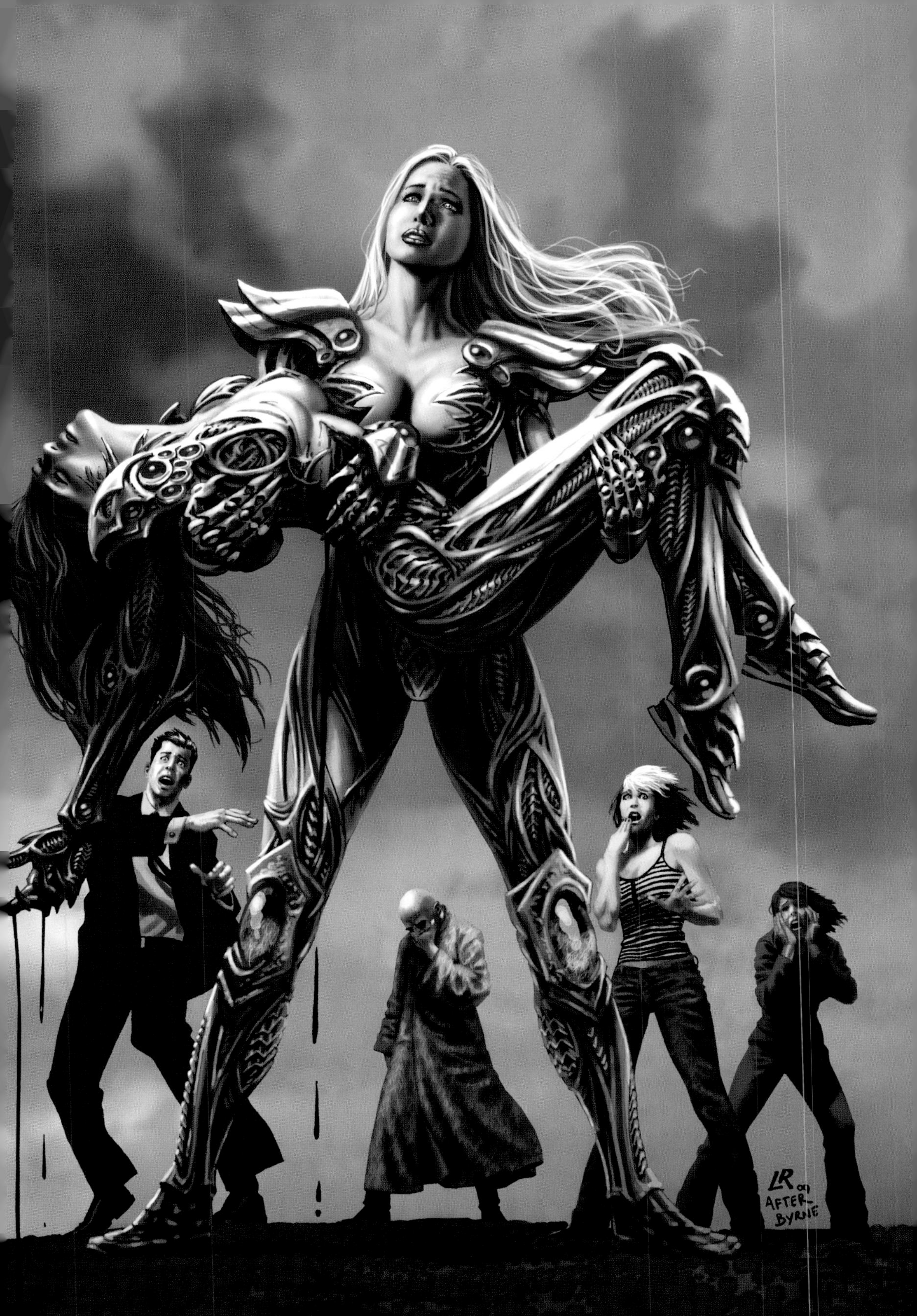
LR on
AFTER BYRNE

Witchblade issue #128 cover B
art by: **Luke Ross**

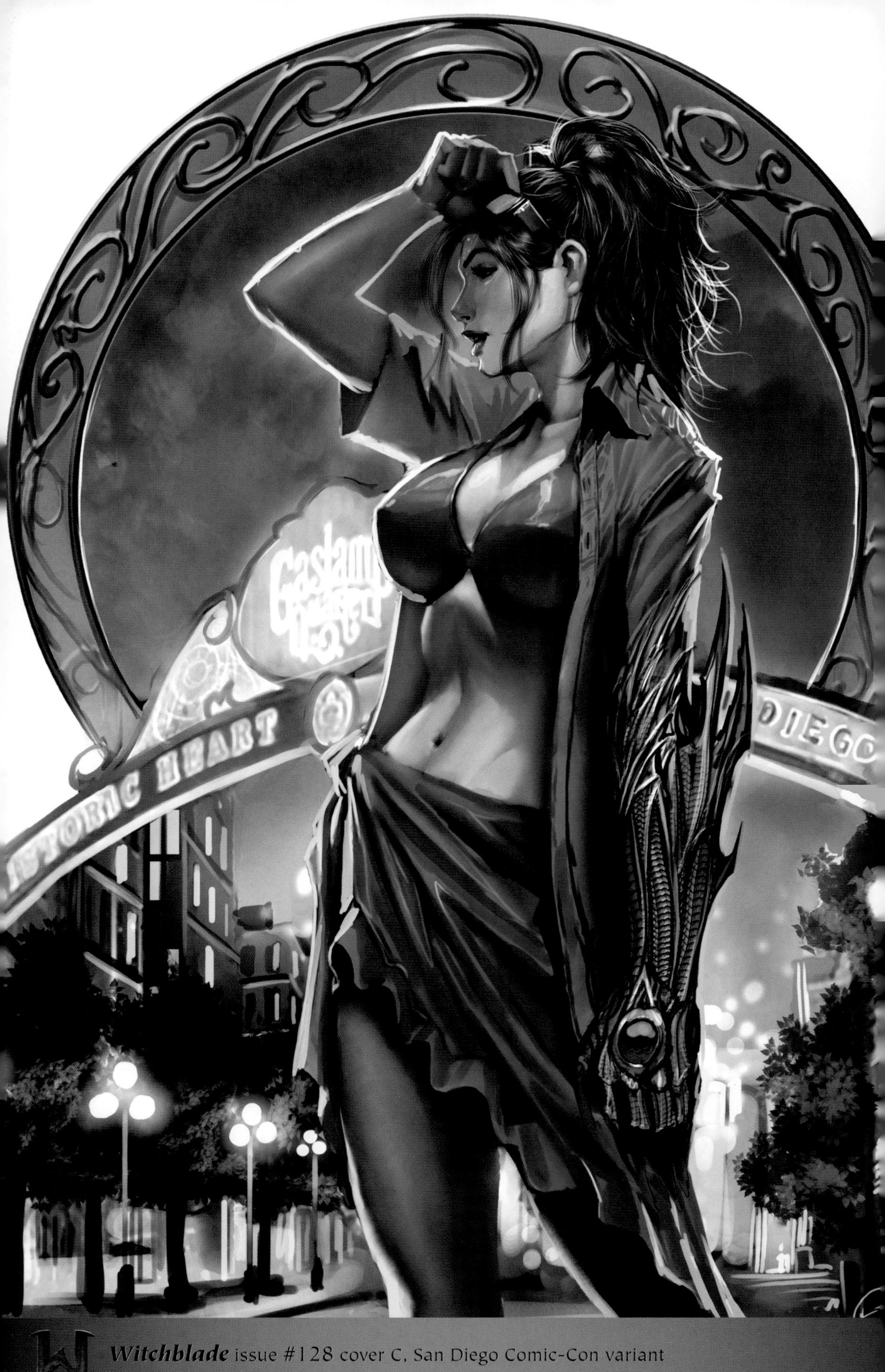
DIEGO

Witchblade issue #128 cover C, San Diego Comic-Con variant
art by: **Stjepan Sejic**

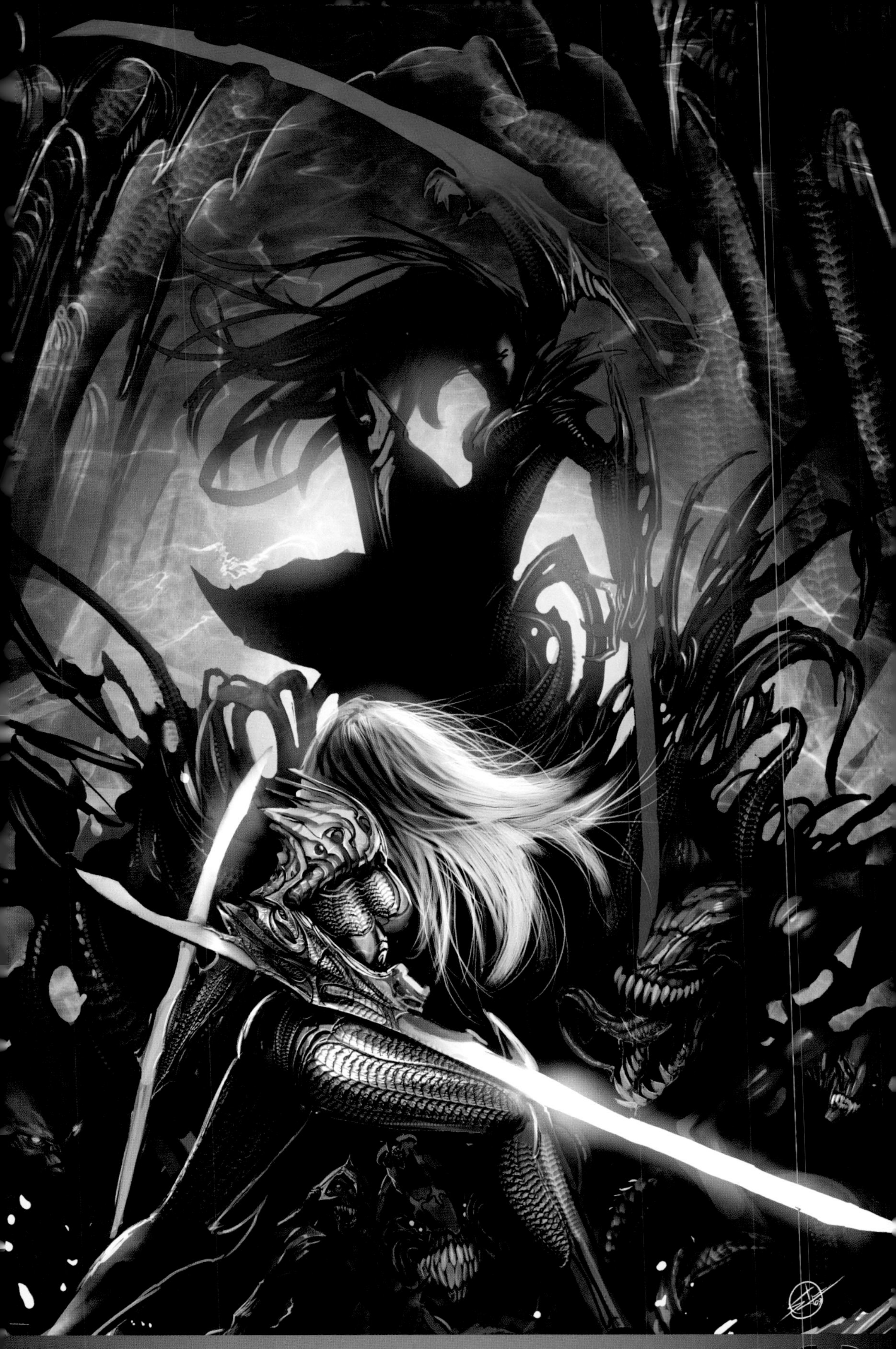

Witchblade issue #129 cover A
art by: **Stjepan Sejic**

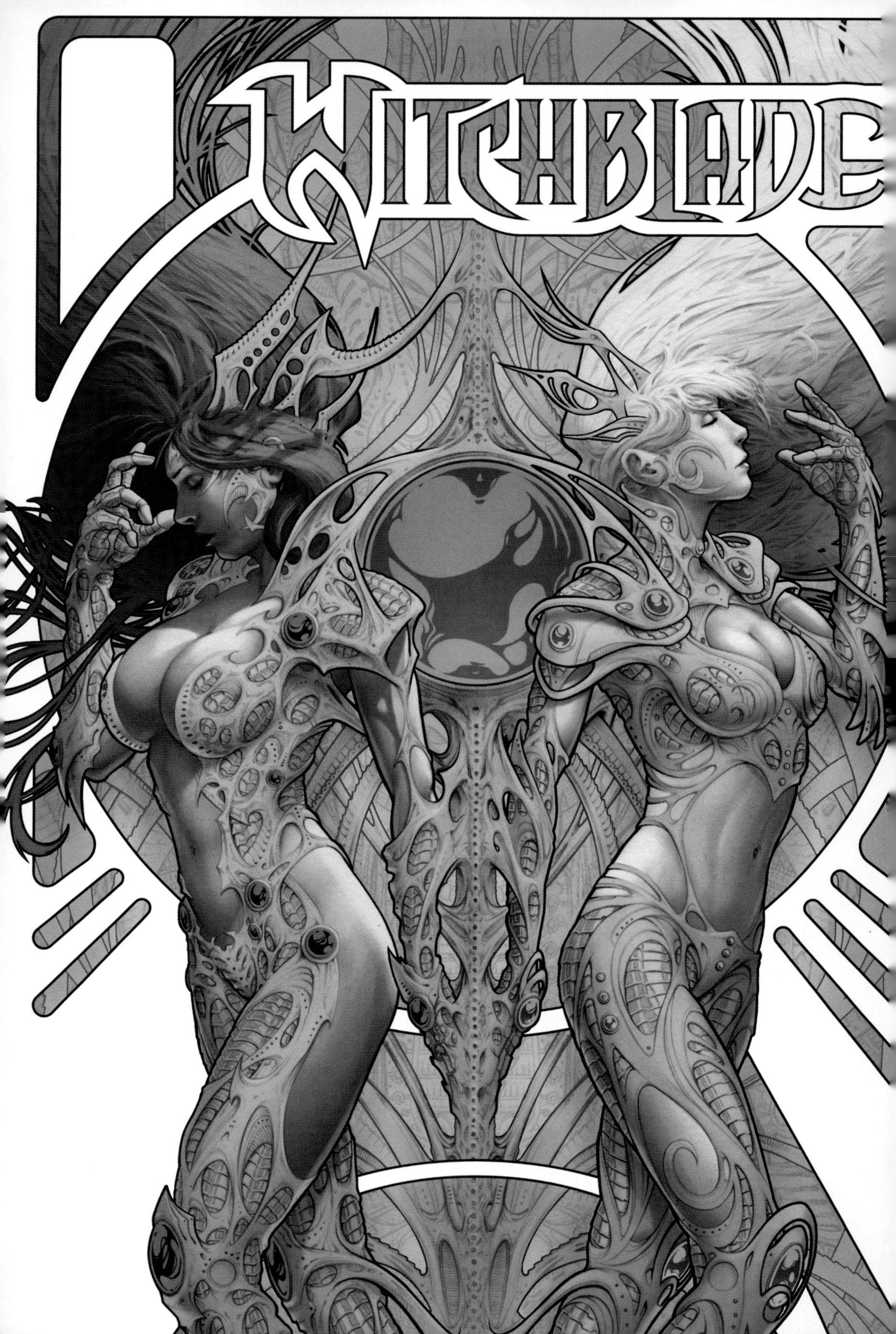
WITCHBLADE

Witchblade issue #129 cover C, Wizard World Chicago variant cover
art by: **John Tyler Christopher**

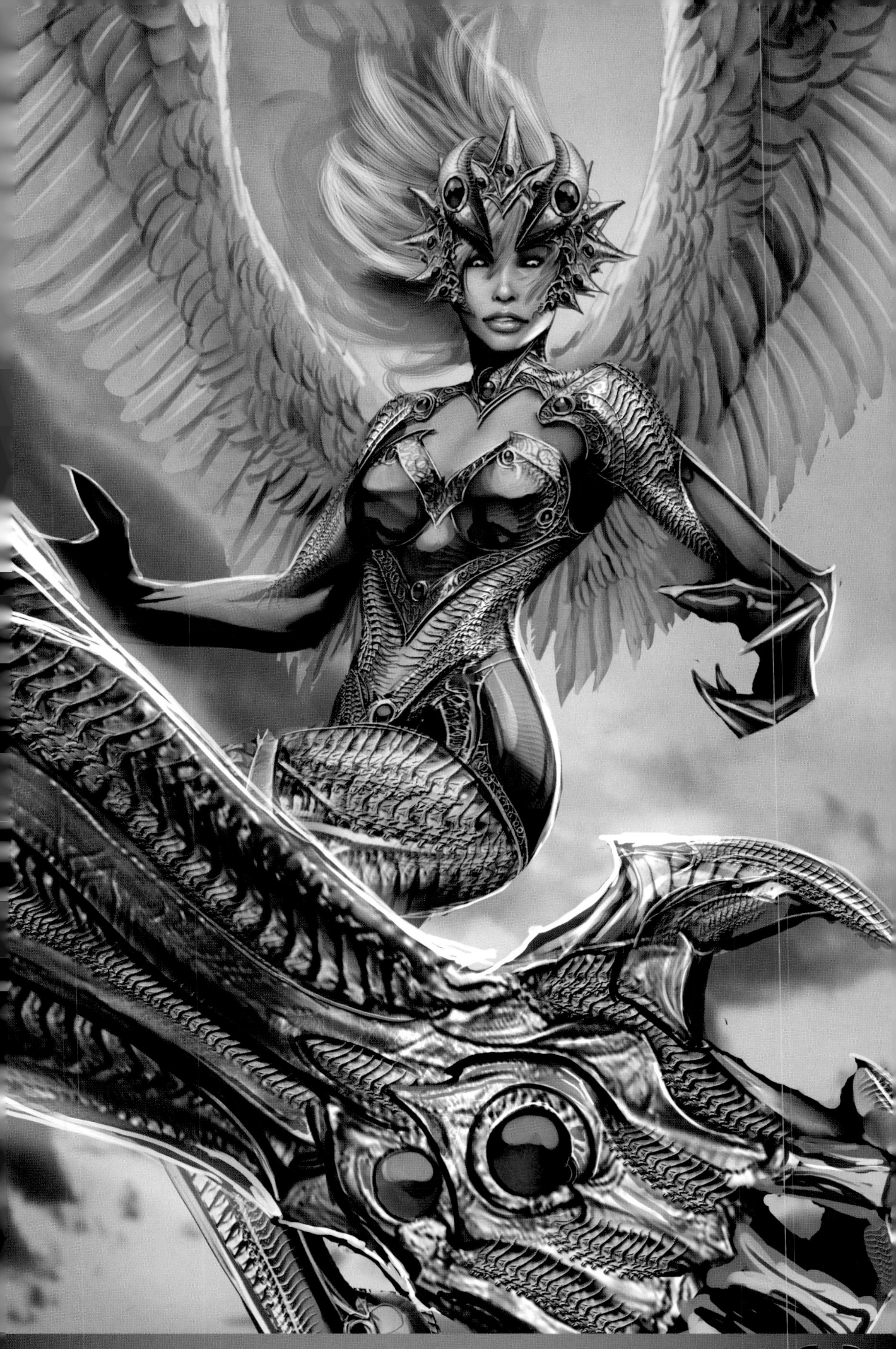

Witchblade issue #130 cover A
art by: **Stjepan Sejic**

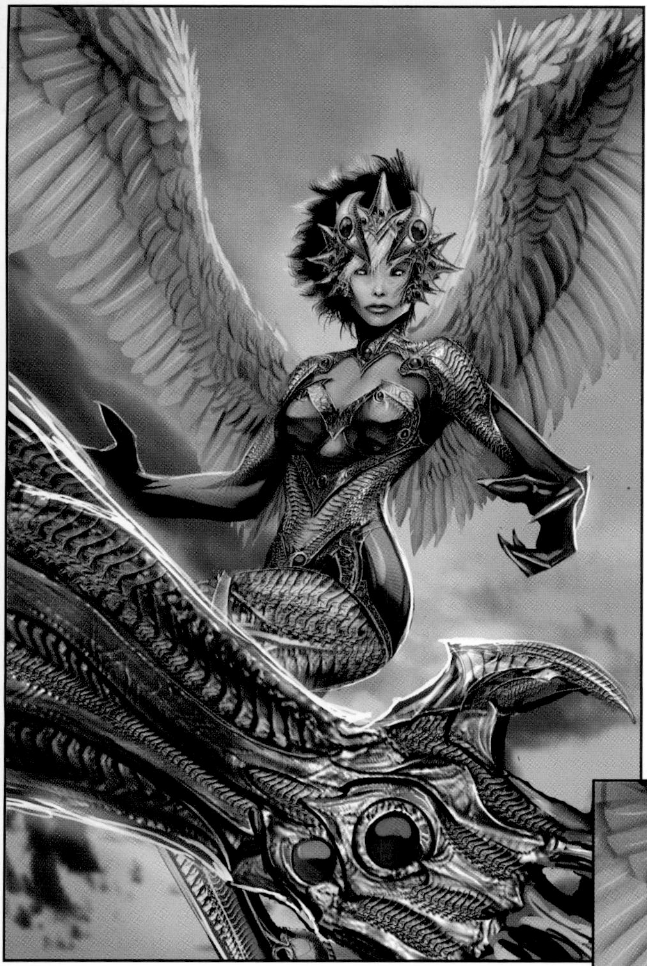

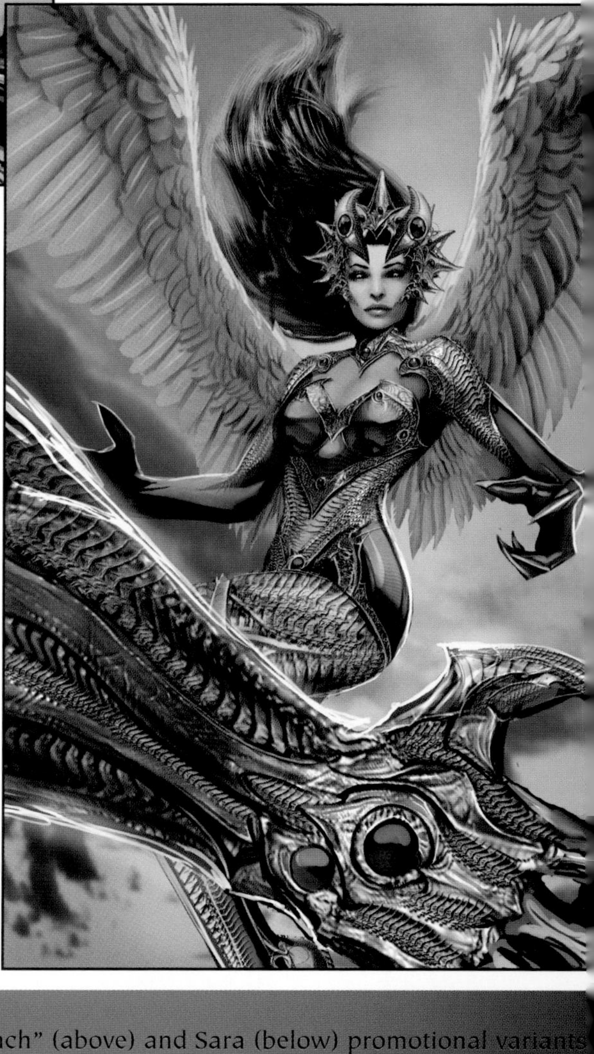

Witchblade issue #130 cover A, "Finch" (above) and Sara (below) promotional variants
art by: **Stjepan Sejic**

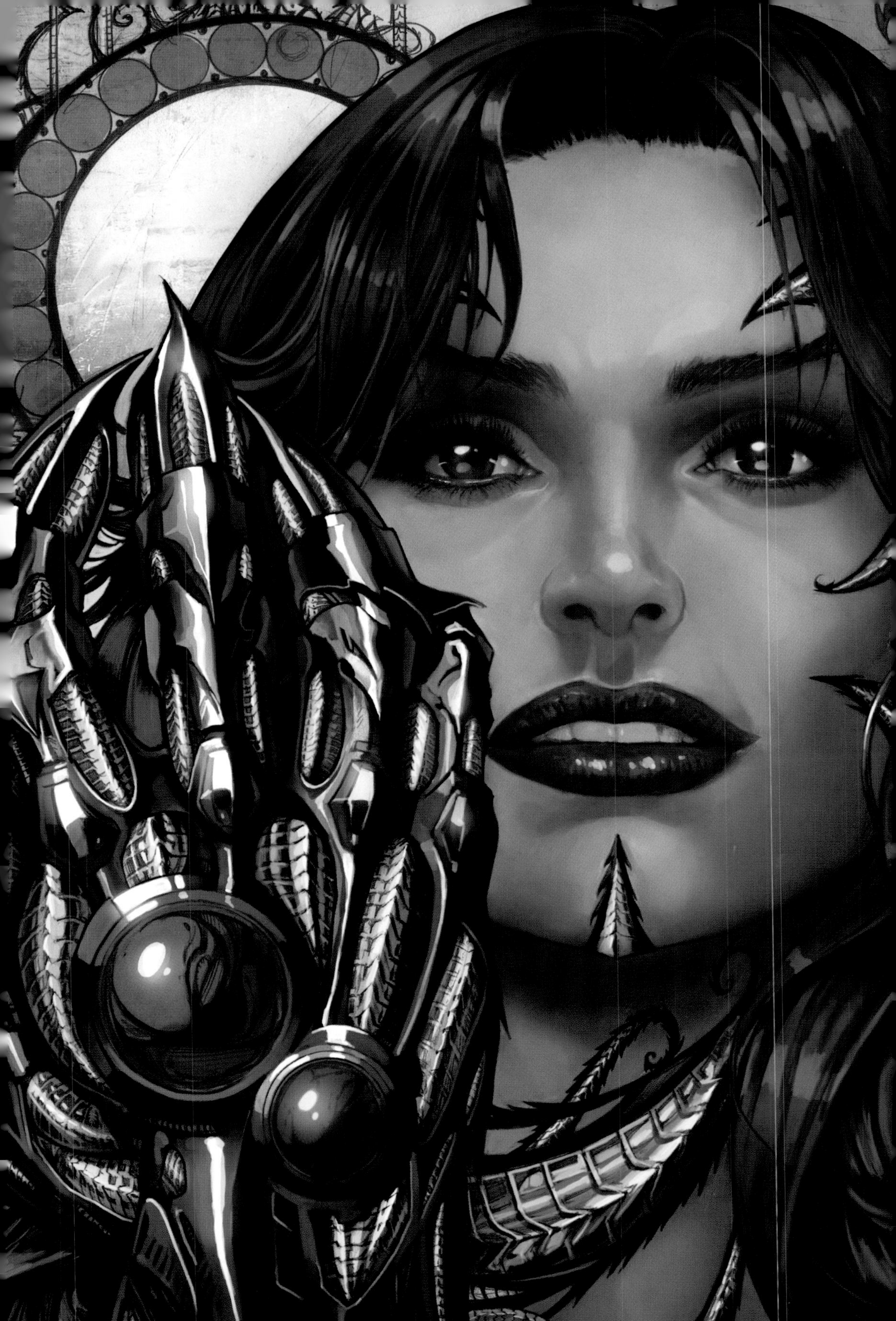

Witchblade issue #130 cover B
art by: **Adriana Melo** and **Sunny Gho of IFS**

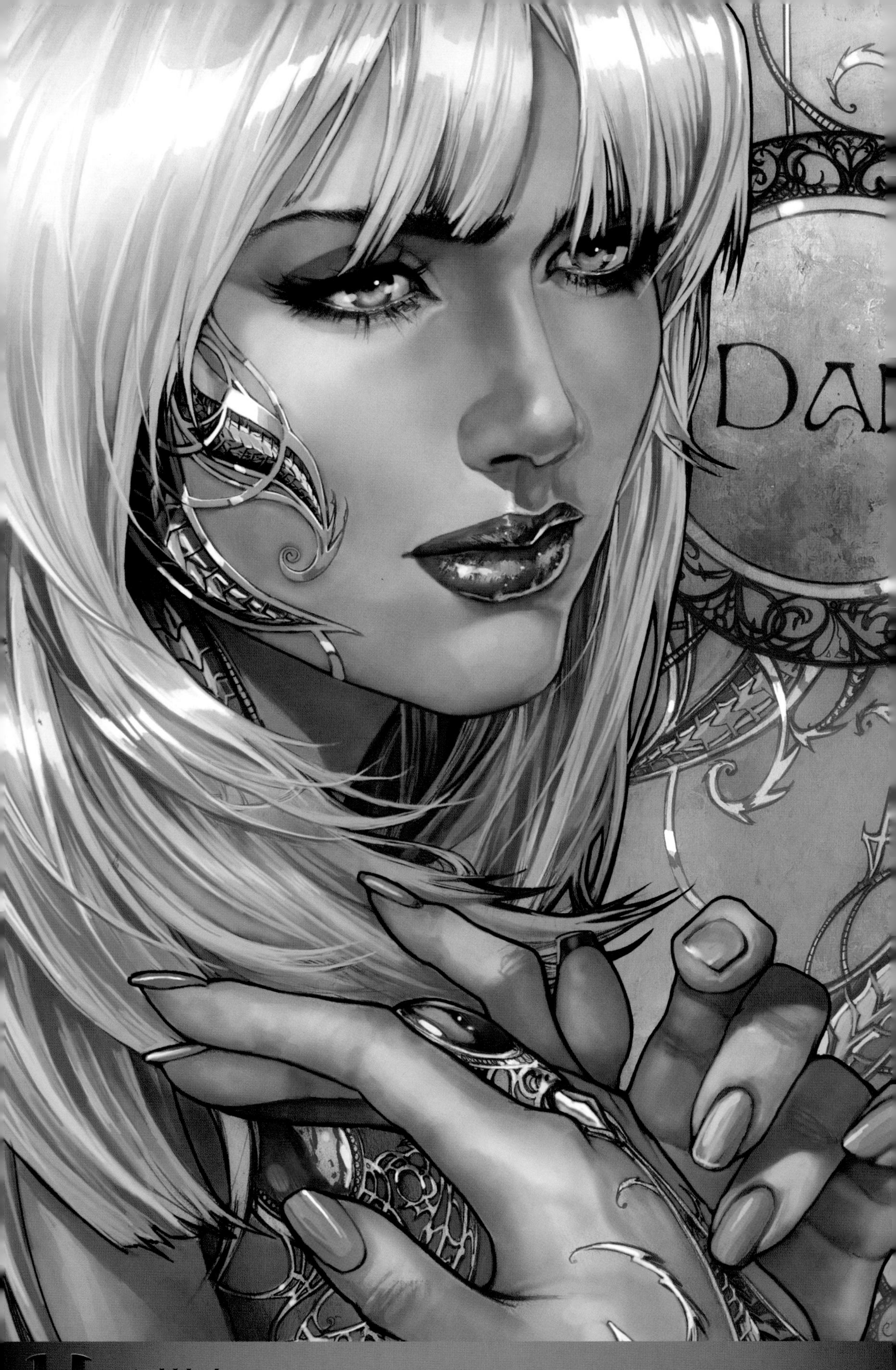

Witchblade issue #130 cover C
art by: **Adriana Melo** and **Sunny Gho of IFS**

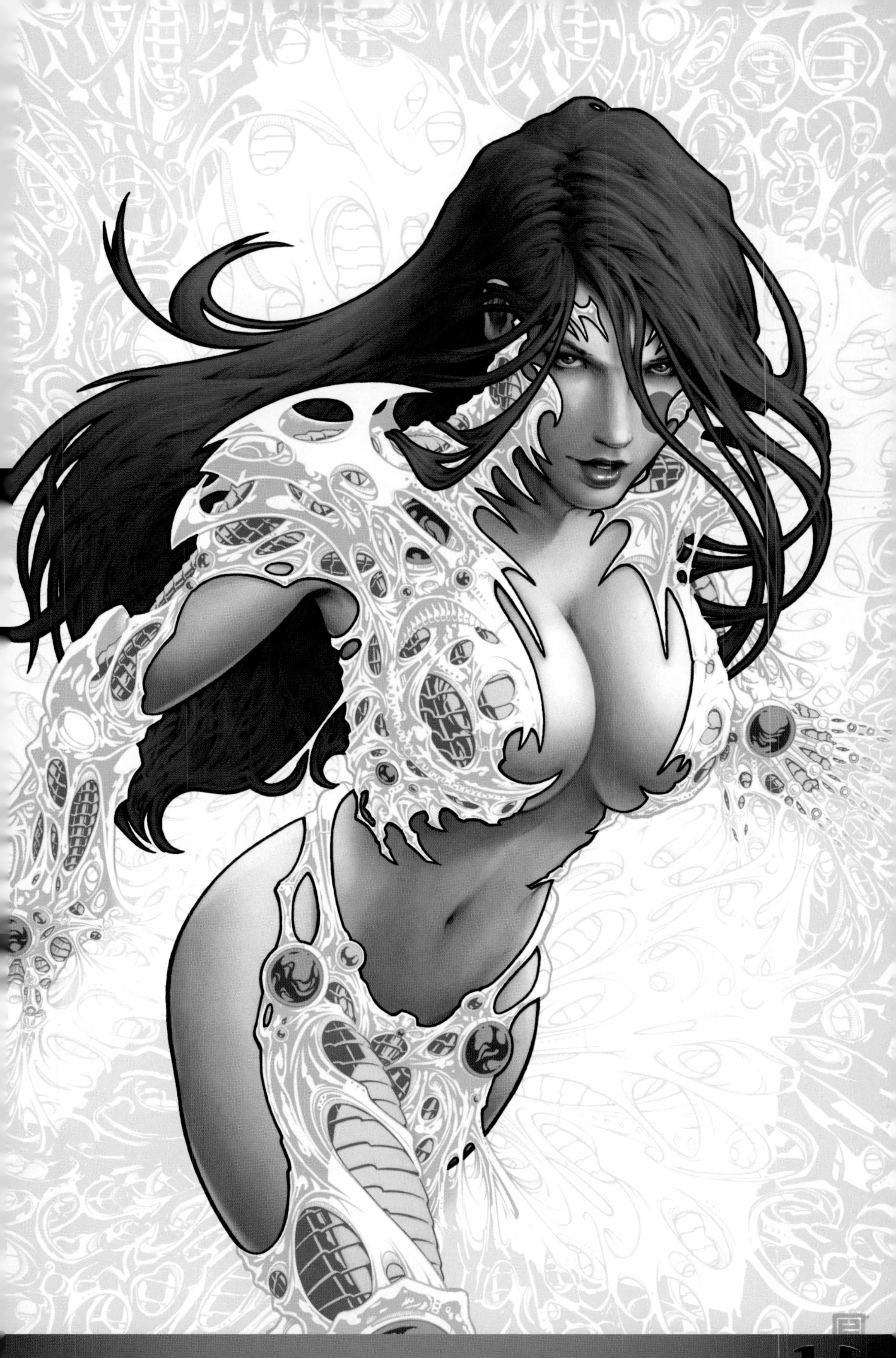

Witchblade issue #130 cover D
art by: **John Tyler Christopher**

WITCHBLADE®

·ISSUE #125·

SCRIPTBOOK

-RON MARZ-

Editor's note: sequential numbers seen immediately

balloons and captions are for lettering reference. -- Filip

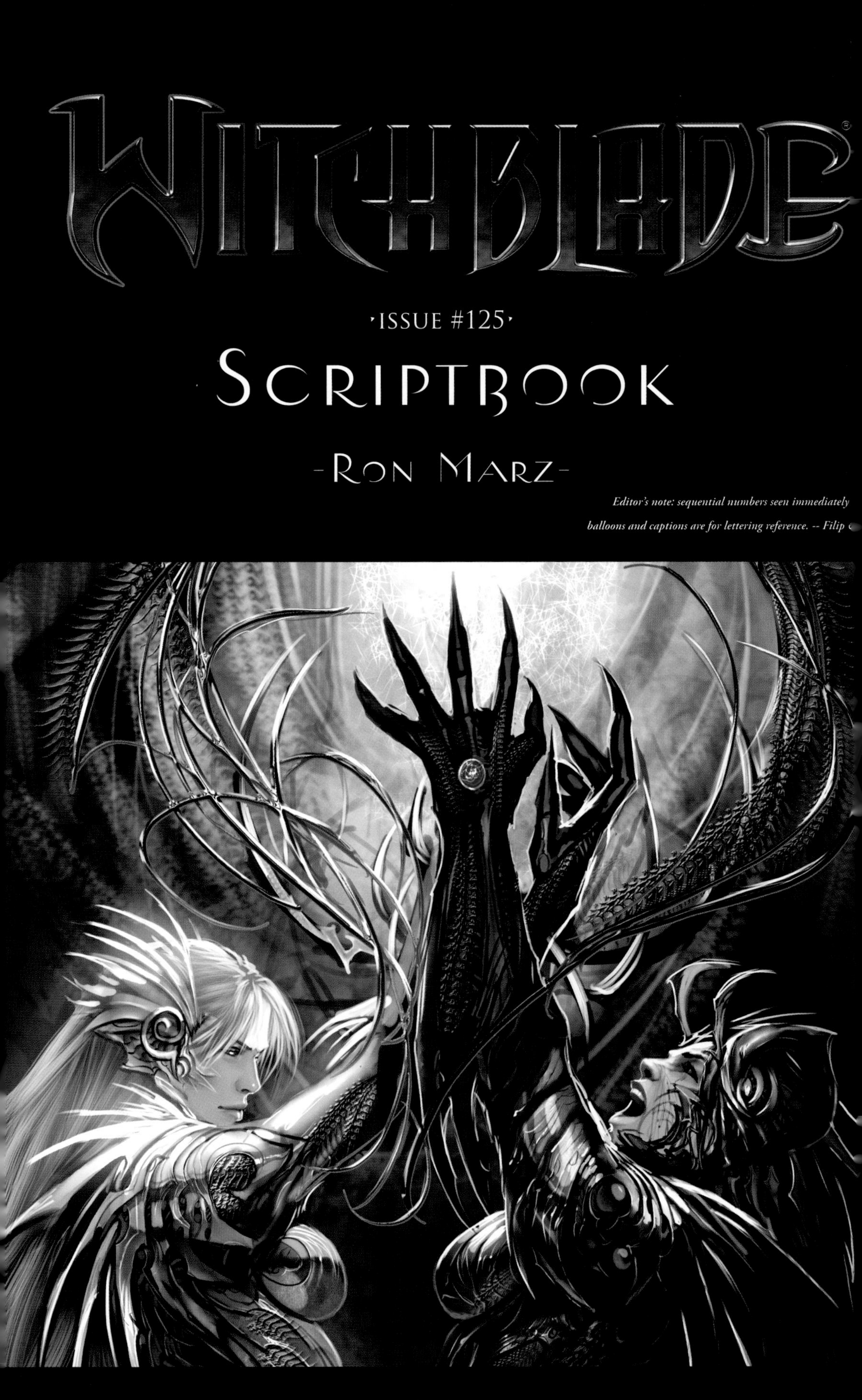

PAGE 1

a recap page.

Title: **War of the Witchblades**
Part 1 of 6

PAGE 2

L 1: We start off with a standard 9-panel grid. Each panel of this sequence is going
 tight shot of the WB material expanding, each shot a closely-cropped close-up of
body. This first panel is a tight shot of the red gem/bracelet as it starts to expand,
g out tendrils. Each panel of this page will be silent.
nels silent

L 2: The tendrils of WB material curl up and around Sara's elbow.

L 3: The WB material covers Sara's shoulder, tendrils branching off in a number of
nt directions.

L 4: We're in tight on the side of Sara's face here as some tendrils spread there. We
see her eye – we don't want too much of an indication of her identity.

L 5: We subtly hint at Sara's breast (or breasts) are the WB material continues to
. Sara is wearing a cut-off wife-beater type shirt, the kind of shirt she'd wear to bed.

EL 6: Tendrils spread down past Sara's belly button.

L 7: The WB spread down Sara's hip and onto her leg. We glimpse a bit of the bikini
s she's wearing (same style as the BT: Witchblade issue).

EL 8: The WB continues to spread down Sara's leg, swirling around her knee.

L 9: Finally, the tendrils start to cover one of Sara's feet.

above, page layout thumbnail

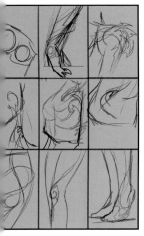

above, panel 6, final detail

PAGE 3

SPLASH: We pull back and reveal Sara in a full-figure shot. The setting is Sara's bedroom
in the middle of the night. We see enough of the bed, with the covers thrown back, that
we realize Sara was sleeping alone (Gleason is not sleeping over tonight). Toward the
foreground, we glimpse the crib, and see a bit of the peaceful. sleeping Hope; she is turned
away from the reader, so we can't see her face. Sara herself is clad in the WB armor. She
stands in front of the open bedroom window, looking out, almost in a trance-like state.
This is more of three-quarters view, rather than a side view. Her eyes glow red, but softly,
not with bright intensity. We definitely want a BIG figure of Sara here – eye candy. The
sheer curtains blow inward gently, stirred by a soft breeze. The room is lit with moonlight.
We want the reader to wonder why Sara is out of bed, and whether she's in complete
control of herself.
1 Baby talk: Mmmaa…
2 Baby talk: …mmmaa?

Troy, use the same type of balloons that we do for the nonsense baby talk.

Title: War of the Witchblades
	Part 1

Credits: (Same as usual, though swap Filip for Rob)

above, page layout thumbnail

above, splash, final detail

PAGE 4

PANEL 1: We cut to the same meeting area in the prison that we saw in issue #116. This is a shot from Julie's side of the partition, a close-up of Hope as she playfully puts her hands on the plastic divider, maybe even her face against it. Hope is smiling, amused by the divider. She has a teething ring/rattle sort of thing in one plump hand.
1 Baby: BUH-BWAAH!
2 Julie (from off): Oh, she's beautiful…

Troy: you can just have this balloon overlap into panel 1 on the right border, if that's easier.

PANEL 2: Pull back for more of an overall shot, so we can see Sara and Hope on one side of the glass, and Julie on the other. Sara is dressed casually, rather than her "work clothes." Sara is holding Hope up to the glass divider. Just as in WB #116, you'll have to vary the angles in this sequence to keep things from getting too static.
2 Julie: …looks just like her mommy.
3 Sara: Well, let's hope she turns out prettier than that, Jules.
4 Sara: This teething she's going through sure hasn't helped her disposition. Or mine.

PANEL 3: We have another two-shot of Julie and Sara, Julie still looking at the baby.
5 Julie: Sara, what about the father? He's still not in the picture?
6 Sara: No … and that's probably a good thing. He's not the stable, bread-winner type.
7 Sara: I truthfully don't even know where he is, which is also probably a good thing.

Troy: Balloon #7 can move into panel 4 if that's a better fit.

PANEL 4: Concentrate on Sara, maybe a something of the baby seen in the panel as well. Sara has a thoughtful expression on her face.
8 Sara: He was back in town for a little while a few months ago. It was … interesting.
9 Sara: But yeah, like I said, probably better that he's not around. Better for me, at least.

PANEL 5: We concentrate on Julie.
10 Julie: So what's the deal with your partner? Gleason, right?
11 Julie: He's still … your partner?

PANEL 6: We concentrate on the baby, who is suddenly excited and happy at the mention of Gleason's name.
12 Hope: GLEEEBL!

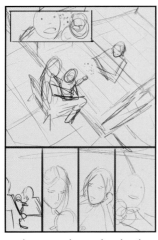

above, page layout thumbnail

above, panel 2, final detail

PAGE 5

PANEL 1: We see Sara and Hope on her lap, Hope still excited. She's now gumming teething ring, which is colorfully bright. Sara glances down at Hope and smiles, amu by Hope's reaction.
1 Sara: This one likes him a whole lot.
2 Sara: And Gleason's awesome with her. He babysits, and so does his sister Caryn.

PANEL 2: We have a shot that includes Sara (and Hope, obviously) and Julie.
3 Julie: But you're still working with him, right?
4 Sara: Yeah, the department – at least beyond our captain – hasn't caught on yet. Hopefully it stays that way.
5 Sara: If I had to choose between the job and Gleason…

PANEL 3: Concentrate on Sara, a thoughtful expression on her face as she sorts throu her feelings about Gleason.
6 Sara: …um, that not really a choice I'd want to make.
7 Sara: He's great, and I like being with him, but…

PANEL 4: Two-shot of Sara and Julie.
8 Julie: But he doesn't make you weak in the knees?
9 Sara: I guess that's a way to put it. I just … I thought I'd be sure when I met the one you know?
10 Sara: But maybe it doesn't work like that.
PANEL 5: Another two-shot of Sara and Julie.
11 Julie: The two of you are still in the same … division or whatever? Investigating th weird crimes?
12 Sara: Special Cases Division, which basically means all the stuff they don't know w to do with. Never a dull moment.

PANEL 6: We have a shot of Sara as she rolls her eyes a bit.
13 Sara: Right now we're getting reports of someone running around on rooftops in t Village. Red eyes looking in windows at night, shadowy figures on the fire escape, blah blah, blah.
14 Sara: I just want to grab whoever it is before the tabloids get hold of it and start screaming about vampires in New York City.

PANEL 6: Sara shrugs.
15 Sara: Still … pretty cool to go to work with your boyfriend, even if on any given d one of you could take a bullet.

PANEL 7: In the foreground of the panel we see Sara's left hand, and the WB bracelet it. Deeper in the panel we see Julie, who is nodding toward the WB.
16 Julie: I'd have to imagine that thing has to lessen the chances of getting shot on the

above, page layout thumbnail

above, panel 3, final detail

PAGE 6

L 1: Sara looks down at the WB. There's a small, self-deprecating grin curling one Sara's mouth.
Never have to worry about getting bored.

L 2: We have a two-shot of Sara and Julie. Sara is shooting Julie a sour glance – not angry, but it certainly shows this is not a subject she wants to talk about.
: How's that girl you said has the other half of it? That hasn't changed, right?
Dani.
: Right, you did tell me that. How's Dani?

L 3: Concentrate on Sara, still looking annoyed. A few tentative tendrils are starting w from the WB bracelet.
: She's … I truthfully don't see her much anymore.

L 4: Concentrate on Sara. She looks more annoyed. The tendrils are growing r up her arm, toward her elbow, though Sara does not seem aware of it. Hope seems py now, her brow furrowing.
(from off right): Really? It sounded like you two were close.
: No.
: Not close.

L 5: Closer on Sara. Her head is slightly down now, and we see just a hint of red

: She wasn't who I thought she was.

L 6: We're still in fairly tight on Sara, but now Hope is crying lustily. We probably bit of Hope as she's reaching for Sara. The bracelet tendrils are starting to recede, as state is broken by the crying. Sara starts to pick her head up again, and the red in her fading away.
pe: AWAAAH!
ra: Hope?

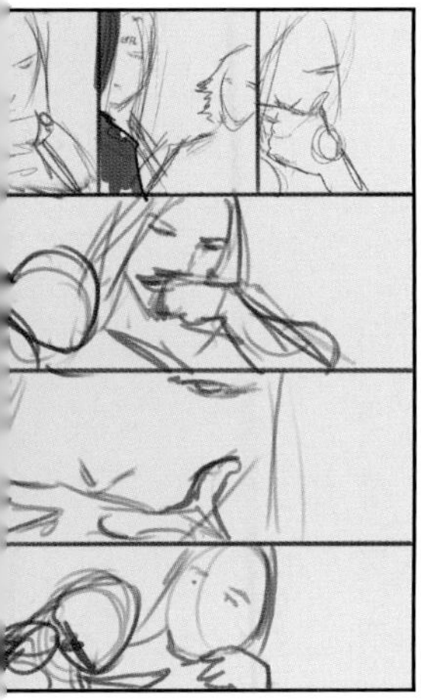

above, page layout thumbnail

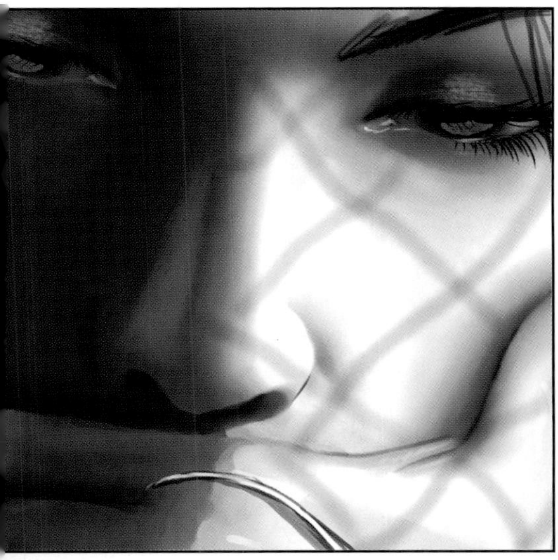

above, panel 3, final detail

PAGE 7

PANEL 1: Sara turns her attention to the crying Hope, trying to comfort her. The tendrils are almost completely pulled back into the bracelet, and Sara's eyes have returned almost to normal. Sara almost seems confused by why Hope is crying, an indication that's she's not aware of her "anger spells."
1 Hope: HWAAAA!
2 Sara: What is it, sweetie? What's wrong?

PANEL 2: Pull back so we include Julie in the shot. She's looking on at Sara, her expression a little surprised at what she's just witnessed. Sara is holding Hope, comforting her. Hope is calming down.
3 Sara (upper and lower "Shhh"): Shhh, don't cry.
4 Hope (getting smaller): HWUH … WUH…
5 Julie: Uh … everything okay there, sis?

PANEL 3: We have a Closer shot of Sara and Hope as they look at one another. Sara is smiling, back to normal, while Hope is not yet smiling. She's looking at her mother intently.
6 Sara: Sure, everything's just fine.
7 Hope: Isn't that right, Hope? We're just fine.

PANEL 4: Still holding Hope, Sara turns her attention back to Julie. Sara seems herself again, smiling and in a good mood.
8 Sara: So … getting short, huh, Jules?
9 Julie: Next week we won't have to talk to each other with a piece of plexiglass between us.

PANEL 5: We concentrate on Julie as she talks about her time in prison. She's gesturing in a general direction, referring to the prison as a whole.
10 Julie: Going away like this did me a lot of good. I cleaned up and I grew up. But I'm ready to walk out of here.
11 Julie: After being in here, seeing the kind of dead-end lives these people have, I'm sure as hell never coming back.

PANEL 6: We have a two-shot of Sara and Julie (with Hope seen as well, of course).
12 Sara: What are you going to do? You made any plans?
13 Julie: I'm not sure. It's not like the job market is especially kind to ex-cons, especially in this economy.

PANEL 7: We have a shot from behind Julie, and perhaps a little off to the side. We can see her reflection in the dividing glass. Her expression is pensive.
14 Julie: Maybe I can go back to modeling to get me through, though I don't think New York City is necessarily the best place for me right now.
15 Julie: I don't need the temptations.

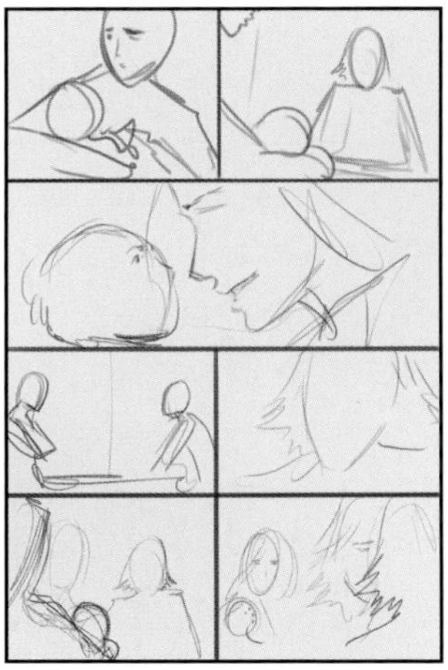

above, page layout thumbnail

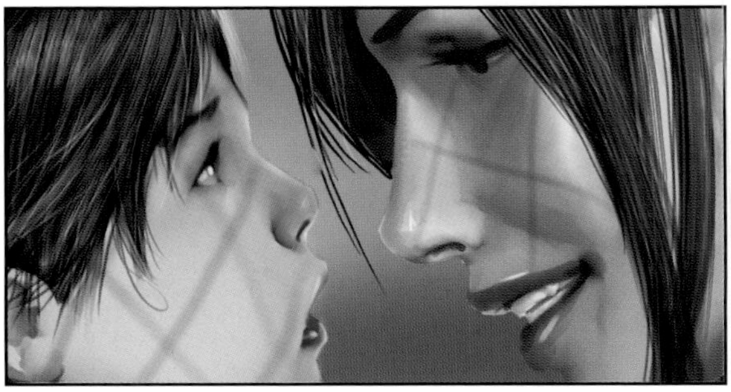

above, panel 3, final detail

PAGE 8

PANEL 1: We have a two-shot of Sara and Julie. Julie's expression brightens considerably.
1 Sara (from off left): Well, you come stay with me until you decide, all right?
2 Julie: Really? I mean … I know we've been through a lot, and maybe our relationship isn't what it used to be…

PANEL 2: Sara looks at Julie with a serious – but not stern – expression. Julie is still pleased.
3 Sara: Julie, you're my sister. No matter what, you're my sister, and nothing's even going to change that.
4 Sara: I'm always going to there for you.
5 Julie (from off right): Okay.
6 Julie (from off right): Thanks, staying with you would be great … if you're sure it's all right?

PANEL 3: We have a shot of Sara and Hope. Hope is very excited and happy, and Sara is grinning.
7 Hope: BWEE BWAH!
8 Hope: AHHYEEP!
9 Sara: See? The boss here says she wants to get to know her Auntie Julie.

PANEL 4: We have a shot that includes Sara and Julie.
10 Julie: I'd like that. I'd like that a lot.
11 Sara: I'll be here to pick you up on the day you get out.

PANEL 5: We're looking from Sara's perspective here. Julie is placing her right hand up against the glass divider.
12 Julie: Thanks, sis.
13 Julie: Love you.

PANEL 6: Move in tighter. Sara has placed her left hand on the glass, her hand/fingers in the same position as Julie's. Of course, we see the WB bracelet too. We see Sara's distorted reflection in the red gem.
14 Sara: Love you too.
15 Sara: See you soon.

above, page layout thumbnail

above, panel 1, final detail

PAGE 9

PANEL 1: We cut to a new scene. This should be set up so it looks similar to the last of the previous page, in that we're in tight on a hand. But this time it is Dani's right hand and it's covered in the gauntlet material. We see Dani's reflection in the blue gem.
1 Finch (from top border): It doesn't seem real, you know?

PANEL 2: This is the largest panel as we pull back to establish our location and character. We're in Dani's living room, which should be modest in décor and size. Danis is present and the WB is formed into the gauntlet. Much of her arm is covered, and some of it has reached her shoulder and chest. Dani is standing. Seated on the couch – or probably a futon – is Finch. Both women wear casual clothes, like warm-up pants, middie shirts. Finch's attention fixed on the WB, fascinated by it. Dani is showing it off to her. Dani's expression is serious as she explains how she got it, Sara having half, etc. Leave a little dialogue room near Dani.
2 Finch: I mean, I've seen it, and God knows I've seen what you can do with it, Dani, I like it's alive. But I still can't wrap my head around it.
3 Finch: How do you even have it?
4 Dani: A friend gave it to me. Or at least she used to be a friend. Her name's Sara, she's a cop who works under my mom.
5 Dani: The Witchblade – that's what it's called, that or The Balance – has been around pretty much forever, I guess. It gets handed down to a new bearer every generation.

6 Dani: I know all this sounds very New Age bullshitty, but the Witchblade's supposed to keep the peace between the dark and light…
7 Dani: …the Darkness and Angelus, both of which take human hosts. The Angelus doesn't have a host right now, though.
8 Dani: This is actually only half of the Witchblade.

PANEL 3: We move in for a two-shot of Dani and Finch, Dani still standing. The WB staring to recede. Both women are directing their attention toward the WB.
9 Finch: So this Sara still has the other half?
10 Dani: Yeah. Apparently she got the "bitch" half.

PANEL 4: Concentrate on Dani. The WB has receded a little more, but Dani's hand and wrist are still covered. Dani is sitting down on the couch.
11 Finch (from off left): Do you think she'll she try to take this half back someday?
12 Dani: Maybe.
13 Dani: It's hard for me to know what's going on in her head these days.

PANEL 5: Finch is reaching out and touching Dani's hand – the hand still covered by WB material. Finch's touch is tentative, almost skittish.
14 Finch: It's warm.

above, page layout thumbnail

above, panel 2, final detail

PAGE 10

L 1: Pull back for a longer two-shot of Dani and Finch, who is still touching Dani's They're looking at one another now, each kind of wondering what to do.
h: It's doesn't feel like metal. Not really.
h: I like it.

L 2: Move in closer. Finch leans in to kiss Dani again. Finch's eyes are closed. We're ite sure what Dani's going to do.
panel

L 3: This is much the same shot and angle as the previous panel. Now, however, s leaning back slightly, so that the kiss doesn't happen. Finch's eyes have opened, and oks a little confused. Maybe Dani has a gentle hand on Finch's upper chest, just to her pause.
i: Finch … don't.
i: I just don't think it's a good idea.

L 4: Pull back a little bit. Finch is no longer leaning in. She seems upset, unsure o do, on the verge of tears. She's a pretty confused kid. Finch is no longer touching s hand. The WB bracelet is back to normal.
h: But I thought … I mean, you helped me, you took care of me…
i: Because we're friends. But I'm not sure we should be more than friends.

L 5: We remain with a two-shot of Finch and Dani, though we pull back a little panel 5. 7 Finch: I feel safe with you, Dani. And I haven't felt that way in a long

h: Once I figured out I was bi, things made a lot more sense for me. Maybe that'll n for you too.
i: I do feel … different … about you. I do. But I have to figure myself out before I ink about whether this is right.

L 6: Finch is the focus of the panel, though we see a bit of Dani as well. Finch's head vn, and she's crying.
nch: I thought this could work, but now I don't know what's happening.
ch: It's like I don't have control over anything in my life.

above, page layout thumbnail

above, panel 2, final detail

PAGE 11

PANEL 1: Finch lifts her head and looks up at Dani. Tears are running down Finch's face, and she looks forlorn and lost.
1 Finch: If you want me to leave, just tell me.
2 Dani: You're not leaving, Finch. You don't have anyplace to go.

PANEL 2: Move in a little closer. We have the same basic shot as the previous panel. Here however, Dani is putting her arm around Finch's shoulders, letting Finch lean or cuddle against her. It's much more a gesture of comfort, rather than romance.
3 Finch: What are we going to do, Dani?
4 Dani: I don't know…

PANEL 3: Move in tighter, so Finch is in the foreground of the panel. We can look past Finch and see the apartment window in the background.
5 Dani: …I really don't.

PANEL 4: We push in further, so that we're looking out through the window. We hint at the Angelus force looming outside the window, as if watching Finch. We don't want to make it appear as if the Angelus force was looking directly in through the window, because logically that would be noticed by Dani and Finch inside. This can be a smaller panel. Stjepan, note that if you feel the storytelling needs another panel here, feel free to add one.
Silent panel

PANEL 5: We push through the window, so that we're getting a good look at the Angelus force as it hovers in the air. This is the largest panel on the page.
Silent panel

PANEL 6: We have a close-up of the Angelus force. There's a broad smile on her face. We want readers to think she's targeting Finch.
Silent panel

ZOOM ON GIRLS
ZOOM ON ANG
ZOOM ON ANG RISING

above, page layout thumbnail

above, panel 2, final detail

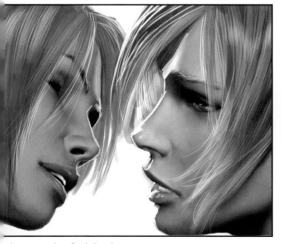

PAGE 12

PANEL 1: We cut to another scene. This is our "Sara as cop" sequence, so we can show off that aspect of the book to new readers. This is a close-up of Sara's badge – held in Sara's left hand – as she holds it up and shows it off.
1 Sara: POLICE!
2 Sara: Stop where you are and keep you hands where we can see them!

PANEL 2: We pull back to establish Sara and Gleason. Sara is closer to the foreground, maybe a medium shot of her. The badge is still in her hand, but she's not holding it up quite so forcefully. Both Sara and Gleason are dressed in their "work" clothes. Both Gleason and Sara have the guns drawn. Their attention directed ahead of them, at something we obviously can't see yet. The setting is a NYC rooftop – probably five stories tall or so, not a skyscraper. Deeper in the panel, we can see the lights on Manhattan. It's a night scene, maybe a moon in the sky. Sara looks annoyed.
3 Sara: Shit…

PANEL 3: Sara is a framing device in the foreground, so we look past her and across the rooftop. Sara is putting away her gun, slamming it back into her shoulder holster. In the distance, we see the object of their chase/investigation. After some thought, let's make the perp some nut who thinks he's a vampire. So black clothes, pale face, etc. Very goth. It will be revealed to be a regular guy, but for now we want the reader to think it's possibly real. The vampire is casting a glance back over his shoulder, looking in Sara's direction.
4 Sara: …he's rabbiting.
5 Gleason: This guy's supposed to be the real thing? So why doesn't he turn into a bat or a mist or something…

PANEL 4: A longer shot, showing Sara and Gleason starting to run across the rooftop, chasing their quarry. Both have but their guns away (cops don't usually run with their guns out). Include the vampire, if you feel like there's enough space. He's near the edge of the building.
6 Gleason: …and just fly away?

above, page layout thumbnail

above, panel 3, final detail

PAGE 13

PANEL 1: The vampire leaps across to the neighboring building. This is a fairly short just over an alley rather than street, so it's not a miraculous feat. Maybe angle this so vampire is leaping somewhat toward the reader, with Gleason and Sara still chasing h still on the other rooftop.
Silent panel

PANEL 2: We concentrate on close shots of Sara and Gleason as they run, chest-up even closer shots. Both are obviously serious and exerting effort. Gleason is glancing toward Sara, asking her why this dude doesn't turn into a bat or a mist and just fly aw Let's see the WB bracelet on Sara's left as she runs and pumps her arms.
1 Gleason: Guess he's serious about not getting caught.
2 Sara: Good for him…

PANEL 3: Sara and Gleason both leap over the gap separating the buildings. We shot them in mid-air here, having leapt from the building edge.
3 Sara: …but I'm serious about not spending another night in the East Village chasin this asshole.

PANEL 4: Sara and Gleason land on the neighboring building. We look past them to the vampire still running across the rooftop. Let's give this roof a water tower, like in e classic Romita Spider-man issue.
4 Gleason: How 'bout we just chase him until the sun comes up, then watch him expl or whatever's supposed to happen.
5 Sara: You watch too many movies.

PANEL 5: Sara and Gleason are running again, Gleason in the lead. His longer stride naturally allowing him to pull away from Sara. Gleason is gaining on the vampire, wh racing toward the opposite edge of the building. Gleason seems confident in catching
6 Gleason: End of the line. I don't care if he's Dracula on 'roids.

PANEL 6: We have a more expansive shot – maybe an overhead view – showing every relative position. The vampire is nearing the opposite edge, which is a large gap to the next building. The gap is really too far to jump, at least for any sane person. Gleason is pursuit, followed by Sara. We want to convey to the readers that this would be a suicic jump to make.
7 Gleason: …he's not jumping that gap.

above, page layout thumbnail

above, panel 2, final detail

PAGE 14

L 1: Gleason and Sara continue to race after the vampire, who is very close to
ge. The vampire is not slowing at all. Gleason's expression, what we can see of it,
tes he's taken aback that the guy's not slowing down.
ason: Hey, DON'T! You'll kill yourself…
ason (small): …unless you're already dead.

L 2: We concentrate on a wide-eyed Gleason as he realizes the vampire is going for
mp. Gleason says, "Holy shit…"
ason: Damn…

L 3: Vampire has leapt out into space, sailing toward the neighboring building
h is a story lower). The gap is pretty vast – not impossible to survive, but pretty
close.
: "…that asshole had better hope he really can fly."

L 4: The vampire slams into the edge of the building, his arms grasping the edge
aving himself from plunging downward.
pire: UFF!

L 5: Gleason is stopping at the edge of the building, his skidding feet maybe kicking
me pebbles from the gritty roofing texture. Gleason is staring across the gap, gaping
he guy actually survived. Gleason himself is not crazy enough to try it. The vampire
nging a leg up, starting to hoist himself up to the edge. Gleason is resigned to the
etting away.
ason: Son of a bitch…
ason: …he actually cleared it.

L 6: Gleason has stopped a few feet fro the edge of the building. Sara is running past
not even slowing. Gleason looks pretty surprised as Sara rushes past him. We can see
VB bracelet is starting to expand.
eason: Now how are we supposed to get--?
eason: Sara?

L 7: Sara leaps out into the gulf between the buildings. Sara is the focal point,
son looking on, slack-jawed. The WB starts to expand up her arm and onto her chest.
leason (from off left): SARA?

above, page layout thumbnail

above, panel 2, final detail

PAGE 15

Stjepan, my idea here is that this is a splash – one panoramic image, one continuous
background. However, it has a couple of insets so we can show multiple figures of Sara.

PANEL 1 (inset): This is a vertical panel showing Sara is mid-leap as she cross the
chasm between the buildings. The WB armor is spreading across more of her body. Her
expression is serious and confident.
1 Sara: Don't worry…

PANEL 2 (inset): This is a larger vertical panel. Sara is now closer to us, nearing the edge
of the building to which she's jumping. The WB armor is nearing completion.
Silent panel

PANEL 3 / SPLASH: Our angle here (meaning the angle for the overall background /
image) is from the building to which Sara is jumping. Sara lands her jump on the building
roof, looking cool and ready for action. Maybe her landing sends some little cracks
spider-webbing out from the impact point. She's fully armored up in the WB armor now.
In the background, we see Gleason at the edge of the other building, looking on at Sara,
impressed with her jump.
2 Sara: …he's not getting away.

above, page layout thumbnail

above, panel 3 splash, final detail

PAGE 16

PANEL 1: We look past Sara, who is in the foreground of the panel, and get a look at the vampire. He's starting to run away from Sara, casting a glance back over his shoulder and at Sara. The vampire is hissing, showing off his teeth.
1 Sara: Come on, Vlad, the longer I gotta chase you…

PANEL 2: Sara tackles the vampire in the largest panel on the page. At this point, Sara is getting pretty annoyed, maybe just a hint of red seen in her eyes.
2 Sara: …the more pissed off I'm gonna be when I catch you.
3 Vamp: NNGH!

PANEL 3: Move in closer. Sara and the vampire have gone down in a heap on the roof, Sara on top, in a more commanding position. The vampire is trying to bite Sara.
4 Sara: Enough dicking around.
5 Vamp (wavery, spooky balloon outline): HSSS!

PANEL 4: Sara rams her gauntleted fist into the vampire's face, delivering a pretty stern punch. We hint at a bit of the vampire's white face makeup coming off on her fist – the first indication we've had that's he's not the real thing. If you can work it out, her punch actually snaps off one of the fangs, which is obviously a denture/cap. Sara's eyes have more of a red glow to them.
6 Sara: You deaf? ENOUGH.
7 Vamp: GWHH!

PANEL 5: We move in closer on Sara. She's looking at her hand – the same hand she used to punch the vampire. She can see some of the white makeup has come off on her hand. There's a look of annoyed revelation on Sara's face. The red glow is fading as she realizes she's dealing with a fake.
8 Sara: You're shitting me.
9 Sara: Makeup?

above, page layout thumbnail

above, panel 2, final detail

PAGE 17

PANEL 1: Sara has her other hand knotted on the vampire's shirt, starting to lift him to his feet. We can see where the makeup is smeared on the vampire's face. A trickle of blood comes from his mouth, and he looks pretty well scared of Sara.
1 Sara: What's the matter, you don't sparkle in the moonlight all on your own?
2 Sara: You're a fake.
3 Vamp: You're not. What … are you?

PANEL 2: Sara hauls the vampire to his feet pretty roughly. Her whole manner is threatening, and the vampire is pretty timid.
4 Sara: I'm your arresting officer. Other than that, you don't have anything to say. Understood?
5 Vamp (small): Absolutely.

PANEL 3: Move in closer on Sara and the vampire. She's looking him up and down n a derisive expression on her face. The vampire has a rather pitiful, pathetic demeanor almost shrinking away like he's afraid Sara is going to pound on him.
6 Sara: So you're just a basic peeping Tom who's read too many shitty vampire novels.
7 Vamp: I only want to be with Tamara. She's my true love, but her parents are keepin apart, so I can only gaze upon her from—

PANEL 4: We have Sara and the vampire toward the foreground. Sara is putting the palm of her hand against the vampire's face, over his mouth so she doesn't have to liste to any more of his whining. She's not being overly rough with him, but she's definitely being dismissive, giving him a little shove. Sara is turning her head to look toward the background, where we can see a smallish figure of Gleason on the neighboring buildin Gleason is calling out to Sara.
8 Sara: Save it, Sally. Nobody cares.
9 Gleason: Everything cool?

PANEL 5: Concentrate on Sara as she calls out to the off-panel Gleason. The WB arm is starting to retract.
10 Sara: Just another emo loser with minimal self-esteem and even less fashion sense.
11 Sara: Lot of help you were.

PANEL 6: Concentrate on Gleason. He's shrugging, acting like this doesn't really both him, but we're planting the seeds for his "inferiority complex" that we'll exploit.
12 Gleason: Yeah, well, I must've been at the back of the line when they were giving ou magic gauntlets.
13 Gleason: You need me over there?

PANEL 7: We have a two-shot of Sara and the vampire from above. She's turning him around so that his back is to her. She's pulling his hands behind him with one hand, an taking out her handcuffs with the other. The WB armor is retracting even more. We hi at the feathers of a bird in the foreground of the panel. This is the weird bird that is the Anti-Curator's companion.
14 Sara: No, I'm good all by myself.
15 Sara: Let's go, hands behind your back.

above, page layout thumbnail

above, panel 4, final detail

PAGE 18

L 1: Pull back. We're looking down on small figures of Sara and the vampire as she ... the handcuffs on him. This is still a high-angle shot as we start to pull out on the ... We reveal the bird in full here as it continues to fly. Neither Sara nor the vampire ... the bird, as it's fairly high above them.
... You have the right to remain silent...

L 2: The bird continues to fly. We see it flying through the NY cityscape. Panels 2-5 ... smaller panels.
... panel

L 3: The bird continues to fly. We're just pacing this out a bit here. The specific ... r of panels in which we show the bird flying is up to you.

L 4: The bird spreads its wings and starts to come in for a landing. The general area ... rooftop of a fairly tall building, but we're mostly concentrating on the bird.
... panel

L 5: We have a tight shot of the Anti-Curator's shoulder as the bird settles in for a ... g, its claws latching onto his shoulder. The birds is opening it mouth, giving vent ... y.
... Good boy.

L 6: We have a fairly large panel as we reveal the Anti-Curator (AC) and the ... nding area. Our location is a NYC rooftop. On the roof in a large glass structure, ... uite a greenhouse, but more like an open-air cupola or pavilion, the kind of place ... would be used for gatherings, parties, etc. The AC is the main figure, of course, with ... avilion close by in the background. He's giving a small treat – we can't see what ... y – to the bird. He has his cane in his other hand.
... Soon we'll have her.

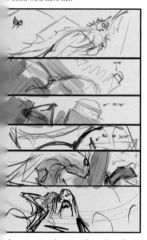

above, page layout thumbnail

above, panel 6, final detail

PAGE 19

PANEL 1: The AC has turned and is walking through the open pavilion, obviously taking his leave. The whole area is pretty shadowy. Maybe try this as an overhead shot?
Silent panel

PANEL 2: We see a bit of the AC is in the foreground, just to establish his proximity. We look past him to see a figure just starting to reveal itself in the shadows ahead. We can't make out much of the figure, but we can tell it's a woman. I'm still sorting out the specifics of the Angelus/Anti-Curator back story, so I'll plug in the dialogue later. For now, we know they're enemies.
1 Angelus chick: Still pulling demons out of your head, I see.

PANEL 3: We reveal the woman in full as she emerges from the shadows. It's the Angelus lieutenant we established in the BT: Angelus issue. She looks much the same here, seen again in her civilian guise. The clothes don't have to be exactly the same, but she should be easily recognizable as the same woman. She has the same confident, almost arrogant attitude.
2 Angelus chick: And putting them back in.
3 Angelus: I'd think that symbolism isn't lost even on you.

PANEL 4: We have a closer two-shot of the AC and the lieutenant. The AC is not afraid of her at all, and it's obvious these two already know each other, and don't necessarily like each other.
4 Angelus chick: This isn't your place.
5 AC: Shouldn't your attention be upon other matters, Sabine? Like tracking down your wayward mistress?

PANEL 5: We pull back for a more expansive shot. More figures are melting out of the shadows on three sides of the AC (not from behind him). The figures are men and women, probably about a dozen of them total, all dressed in normal clothes. These are Angelus warriors in their human guises. Let's see a bit of the Lieutentant here, so we can direct dialogue to her.
6 Angelus chick: I swore the Pezzini woman would be destroyed. I will see that come to pass.
7 Angelus chick: As for my mistress…

PANEL 6: We have a tight shot of the Lieutenant, concentrating on her face. Her eyes are glowing with bright energy now, flaring impressively. There's a grim smile on her face.
8 Angelus chick: …there are enough of us to attend to that matter.
9 Angelus chick: Or any other.
10 Angelus chick: Stay out of this.

Troy: Balloons 8 & 9 one one side of her, balloon 10 on the other.

Panel 7
11 AC: Oh, I'm already involved…
12 AC: …and you are not capable of dissuading me.

Panel 8
13 Angelus chick: Me alone?
14 Angelus chick: Perhaps not…

Troy: the art here should be changed so that there are 8 panels, the last panel being a shot of the Angelus chick. Let's see how that goes…

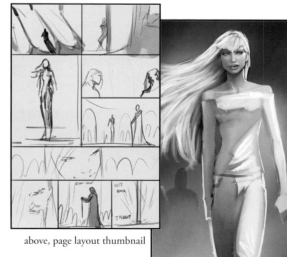

above, page layout thumbnail

above, panel 3, final detail

PAGE 20-21

(Double-page spread)

PANEL 1: This is a larger one. A huge and incredibly bright explosion is tearing apart the pavilion spectacularly, sending shards of glass everywhere. All the Angelus warriors – including the Lieutenant – are transforming to their Angelus state (though we do not reveal the specifics yet).
Silent panel

PANEL 2: This panel is the largest, our big-deal visual for the issue as we reveal the Angelus warriors in all their glory. They all carry weapons, some of them float in the air on extended wings. The Lieutenant is first and foremost among them, with the same look that she had in BT #3 and the BT: Angelus issue. Make this a stunning eye-candy visual.
1 Angelus chick: …but I am not alone.
2 AC: My, my.
3 AC: Aren't you all impressive?

PANEL 3: The Lieutenant seems regal as she commands the nearest warriors forward, telling them to destroy the AC. We see handful of warriors surging forward, weapons brandished.
4 Angelus: Take him.
5 Angelus: Take him apart.

PANEL 4: The AC does seem scared at all, and stands his ground. He's holding up his cane. In fact, the AC is almost defiant. The top of the AC's cane is flaring to brilliant life, almost like Gandalf using his staff to force back the Balrog in "Fellowship." The warriors do not stop to pause in their advance.
Silent panel

PANEL 5: The brilliant energy coming from the staff rolls over the charging Angelus warriors. The energy is burning them like an incredibly intense heat, turning them to charred skeletons.
Silent panel

PANEL 6: The Angelus warriors who had tried to attack have been turned to ash drifting lazily in the air. Obviously the AC is powerful indeed. The AC is standing his ground confidently, almost defiantly – let's see his hand and the cane in the foreground of the panel.
6 Angelus chick: You destroy a handful, yet an army remains.
7 Angelus: There are more Angelus warriors than you could ever hope to stand against.
8 AC: Very possible…

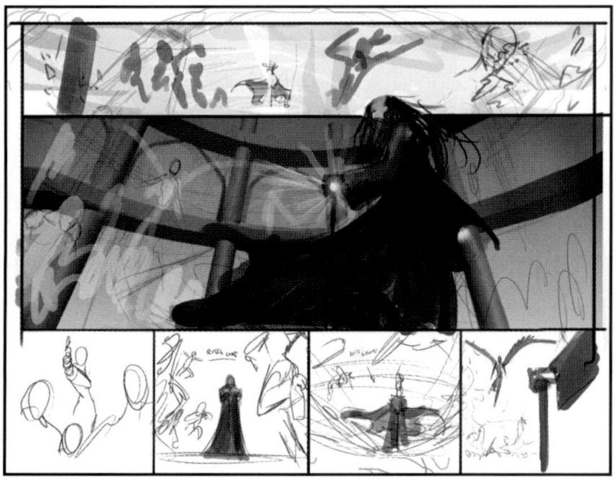

above, page layout thumbnail

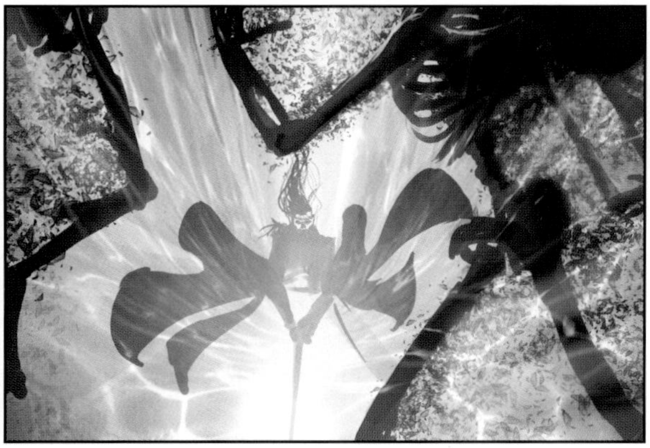

above, panel 5, final detail

PAGE 22

PANEL 1: We concentrate on the AC here, a medium shot, or perhaps closer. His ca still glows brightly as he warns the off-panel Lieutenant to mind her own business, ar stay out of his plans.
1 AC: …but how many of them are you prepared to lose?

PANEL 2: The glow coming from the AC's cane gets even brighter, so bright that it's almost blinding. We can hardly see the AC amidst the glow. The AC vows to triumpl
2 AC: Do not seek to interfere with me…

PANEL 3: The glow is dissipating, and we can see that the AC is gone. In the place w he was standing is a fading wisp of the energy. The Angelus Lieutenant looks on with grim expression. Other Angelus warriors surround the spot where the AC stood, all o them looking on, just as the Lieutenant is. We want the reader to get the sense that th only the first volley in the coming war.
3 AC (no tail, fading away): … or suffer the same fate.

PANEL 4: We end with a shot of the Lieutenant, maybe a head-and-shoulders or ches shot at the bottom of the page, with no panel borders. She's still grim, vowing to dest AC.
4 Angelus chick: We'll bury him right next to Pezzini.
5 Cap: CONTINUED!

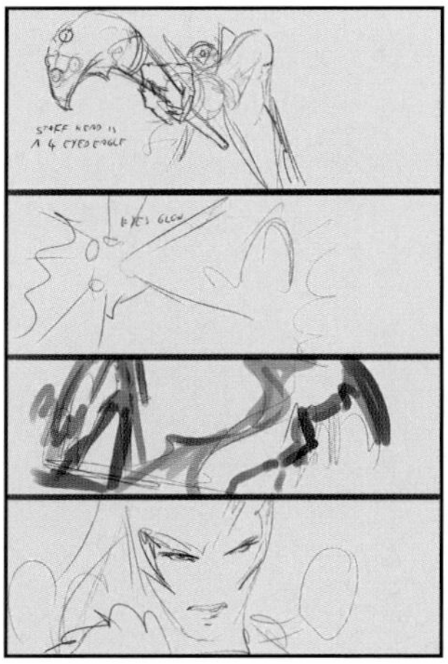

above, page layout thumbnail

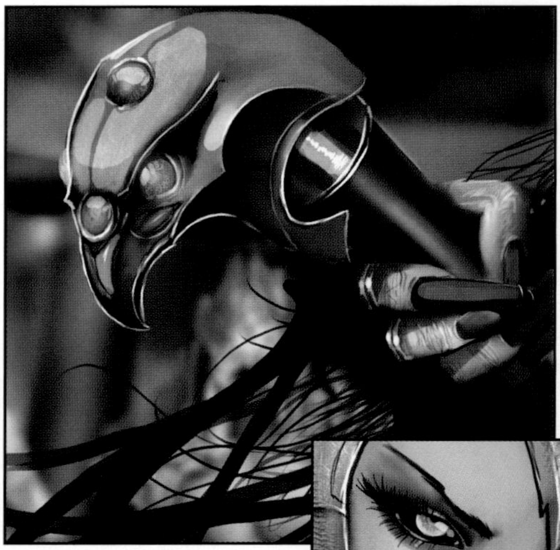

above, panel 1, final detail

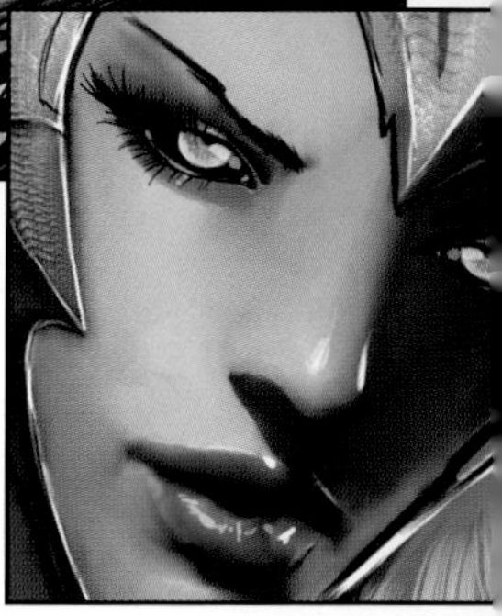

above, panel 4, final detail

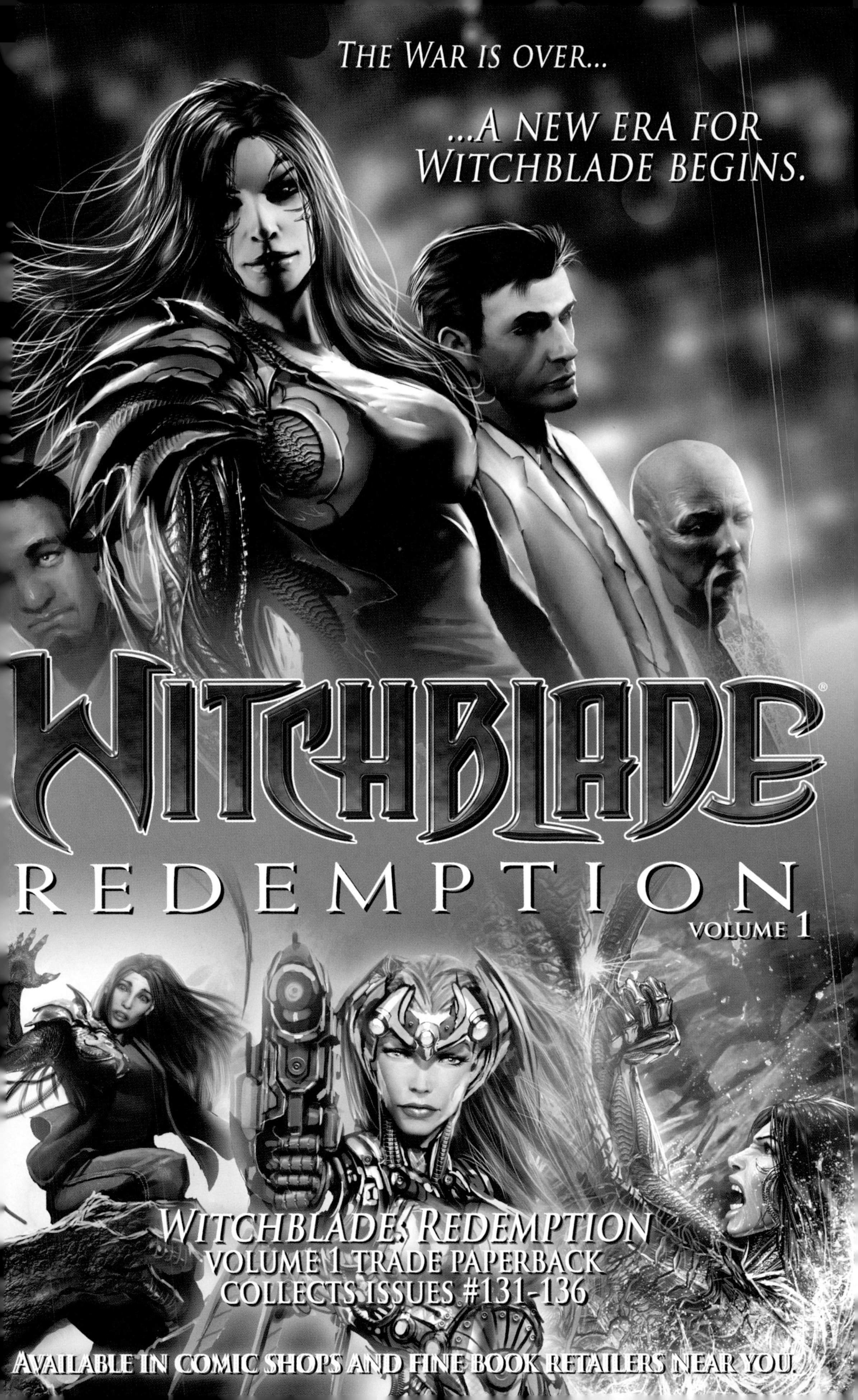
THE WAR IS OVER...
...A NEW ERA FOR WITCHBLADE BEGINS.
WITCHBLADE®
REDEMPTION
VOLUME 1
WITCHBLADE: REDEMPTION
VOLUME 1 TRADE PAPERBACK
COLLECTS ISSUES #131-136
AVAILABLE IN COMIC SHOPS AND FINE BOOK RETAILERS NEAR YOU.

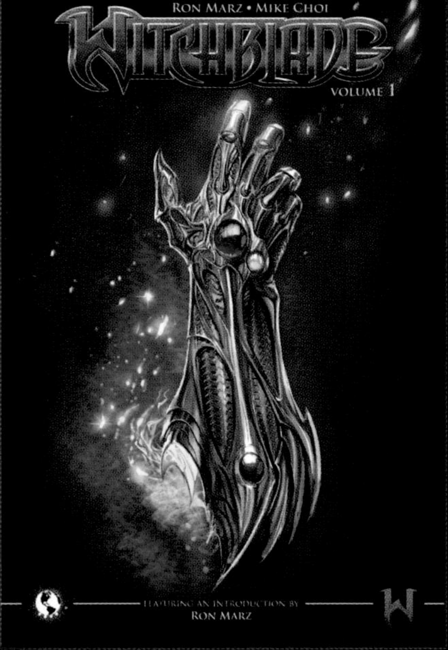
RON MARZ • MIKE CHOI
WITCHBLADE
VOLUME 1
FEATURING AN INTRODUCTION BY
RON MARZ

Witchblade

volume 1 - volume 7

written by:

Ron Marz

art by:

Mike Choi, Stephen Sadowski, Keu Cha, Chris Bachalo, Stjepan Sejic and more!

Get in on the ground floor of Top Cow's flagship title with these affordable trade paperback collections from Ron Marz's series-redefining run on Witchblade! Each volume collects a key story arc in the continuing adventures of Sara Pezzini and the Witchblade.

volume 1
collects issues #80-#85
(ISBN: 978-1-58240-906-1) $9.99

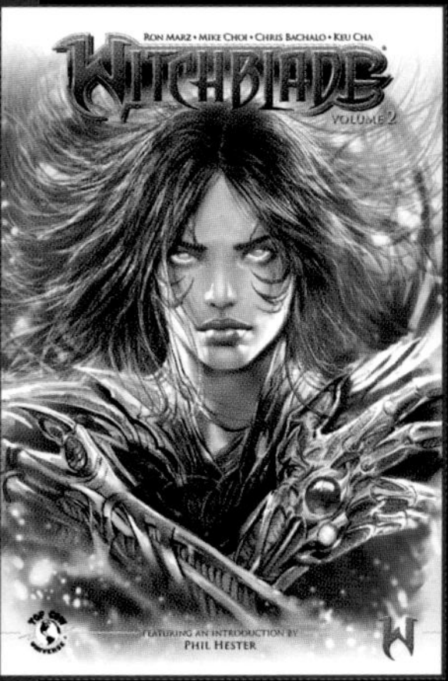
RON MARZ • MIKE CHOI • CHRIS BACHALO • KEU CHA
WITCHBLADE
VOLUME 2
FEATURING AN INTRODUCTION BY
PHIL HESTER

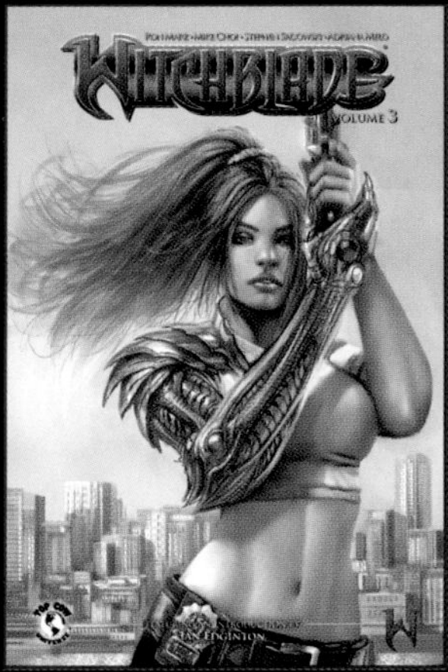
WITCHBLADE
VOLUME 3
IAN EDGINTON

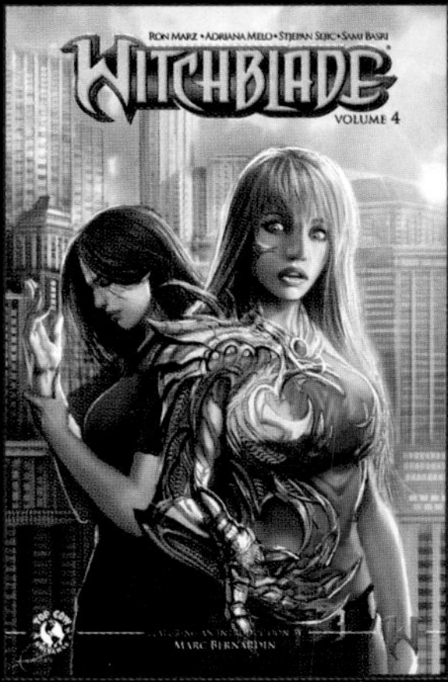
RON MARZ • ADRIANA MELO • STJEPAN SEJIC • SAMI BASRI
WITCHBLADE
VOLUME 4
MARC BERNARDIN

volume 2
collects issues #86-#92
(ISBN: 978-1-58240-886-6)
U.S.D. $14.99

volume 3
collects issues #93-#100
(ISBN: 978-1-58240-887-3)
U.S.D. $14.99

volume 4
collects issues #101-109
(ISBN: 978-1-58240-898-3)
U.S.D. $17.9

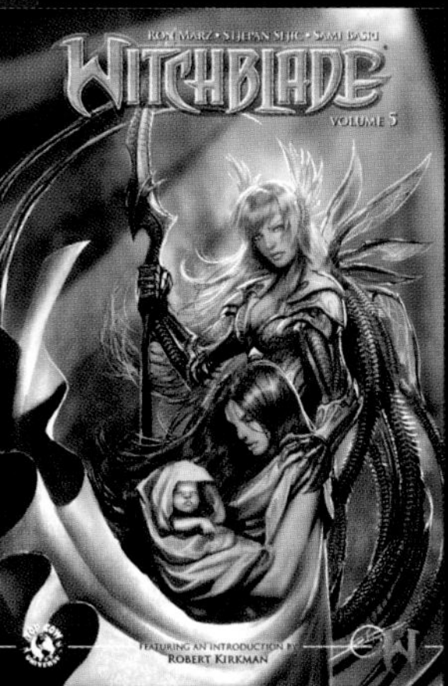
RON MARZ • STJEPAN SEJIC • SAMI BASRI
WITCHBLADE
VOLUME 5
FEATURING AN INTRODUCTION BY
ROBERT KIRKMAN

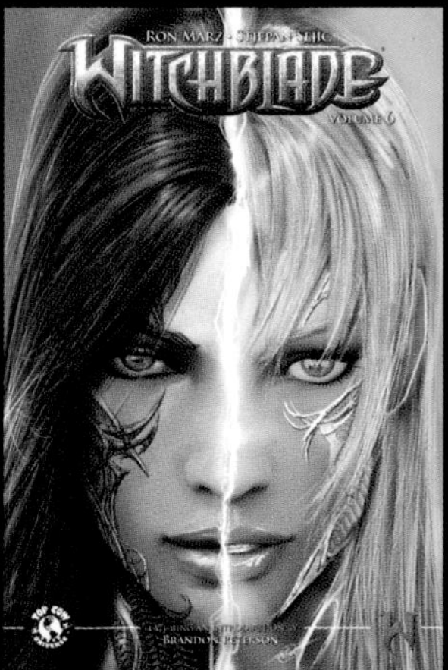
RON MARZ • STJEPAN SEJIC
WITCHBLADE
VOLUME 6

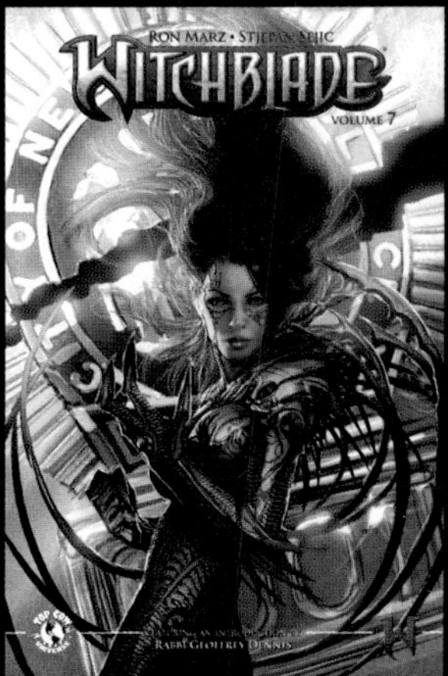
RON MARZ • STJEPAN SEJIC
WITCHBLADE
VOLUME 7

Premium collected editions

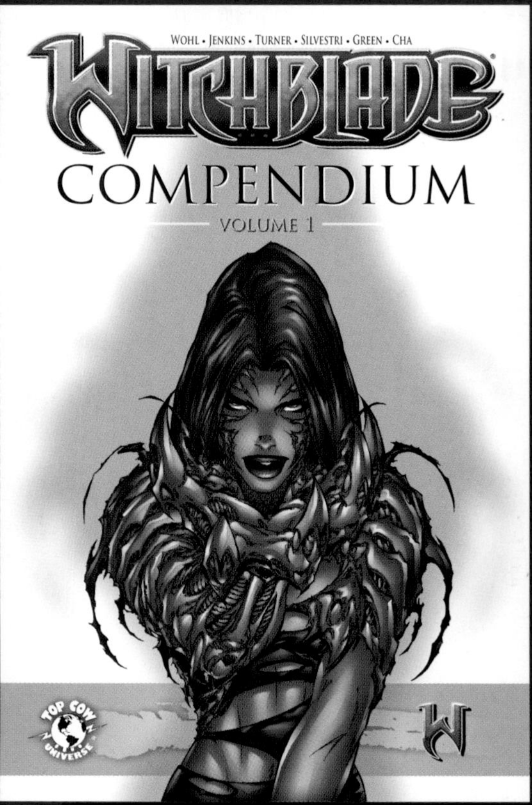

WOHL • JENKINS • TURNER • SILVESTRI • GREEN • CHA
WITCHBLADE
COMPENDIUM
VOLUME 1

Witchblade

Compendium vol.1

written by
David Wohl, Christina
Paul Jenkins
pencils by
Michael Turner, Randy
Keu Cha and more

From the hit live-action tv show to the current Japanese anime, [illegible] has been Top Cow's flagship title for a decade. There's nothing like [illegible] the beginning and reading [illegible] This massive collection houses [illegible] 50 in a single edition for the first [illegible] how the Witchblade chose Sara [illegible] her into the chaotic world of the [illegible] Get the first appearances of Sa[illegible] Ian Nottingham, Kenneth Irons [illegible] Estacado in one handy tome!

SC ISBN 13: 978-1-58240-634-[illegible]
HC ISBN 13: 978-1-58240-708-[illegible]

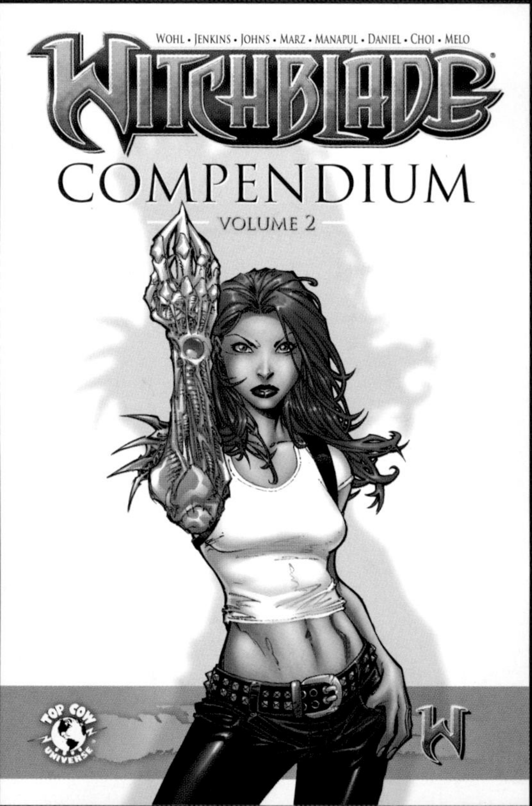

WOHL • JENKINS • JOHNS • MARZ • MANAPUL • DANIEL • CHOI • MELO
WITCHBLADE
COMPENDIUM
VOLUME 2

Witchblade

Compendium vol.2

written by
David Wohl, Christina
Paul Jenkins and Ron
pencils by
Michael Turner, Randy
Keu Cha, Mike Choi and

From the "Death Row" storyline [illegible] the death of a major Witchblade [illegible] heading up the NYPD's Special [illegible] Witchblade bearer Sara Pezzini a[illegible] partner Patrick Gleason find [illegible] with more questions than answe[illegible] investigations lead them from [illegible] museums, dark alleys and forgot[illegible] bensa[illegible] New York City. Mean[illegible] enigmatic Curator [illegible] Sara, ultimately leading her to the [illegible] origin of the Witchblade itself!

Collects Witchblade issues #[illegible]

SC ISBN 13: 978-1-58240-751-[illegible]
HC ISBN 13: 978-1-58240-920-[illegible]

Jump into the Top Cow Universe with The Darkness!

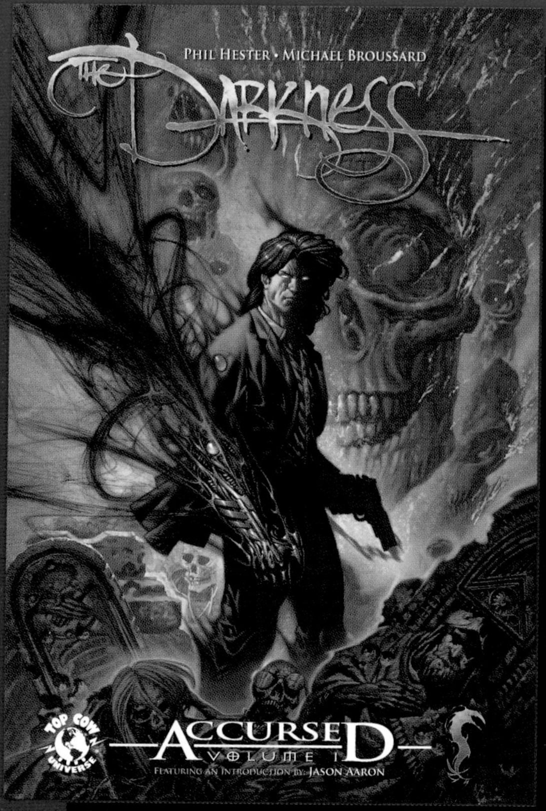
PHIL HESTER • MICHAEL BROUSSARD
THE DARKNESS
TOP COW UNIVERSE
ACCURSED VOLUME 1
FEATURING AN INTRODUCTION BY: JASON AARON

The Darkness

Accursed vol.1

written by:
Phil Hester

pencils by:
Michael Broussard

Mafia hitman Jackie Estacado was bc blessed and cursed on his 21st birthday wh he became the bearer of The Darkness, elemental force that allows those who wie it access to an otherwordly dimension a control over the demons who dwell the Forces for good in the world rise up to fa Jackie and the evil his gift represents; b there is one small problem. In this story...th are the bad guys.

Now's your chance to read "Empir the first storyline by the new creative tea of **Phil Hester** (*Firebreather, Green Arro* and **Michael Broussard** (*Unholy Union*) th marked the shocking return of *The Darkne* to the Top Cow Universe!

Book Market Edition
(ISBN 13: 978-1-58240-958-0) $9.99

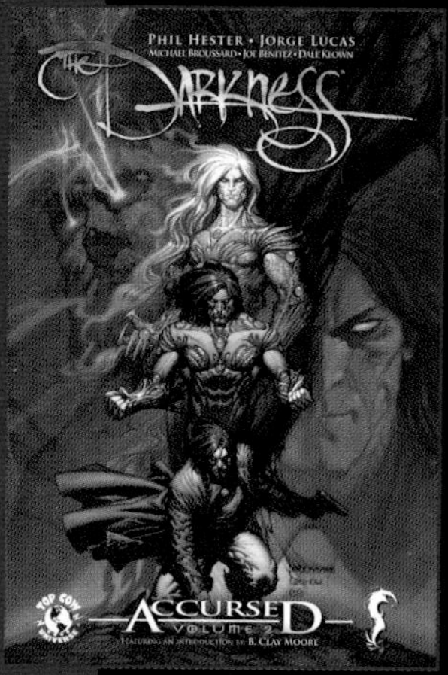
PHIL HESTER • JORGE LUCAS
MICHAEL BROUSSARD • JOE BENITEZ • DALE KEOWN
THE DARKNESS
ACCURSED VOLUME 2
FEATURING AN INTRODUCTION BY B. CLAY MOORE

The Darkness

Accursed vol.2

written by: Phil Hester

pencils by: Jorge Lucas, Michael Broussard, Joe Benitez
Dale Keown and more!

Collects *The Darkness* volume 3 #7-10 and the double-sized *Th Darkness* #75 (issue #11 before the Legacy Numbering took effec plus a cover gallery and behind-the-scenes extras!

(ISBN 13: 978-1-58240-044-4) $9.99

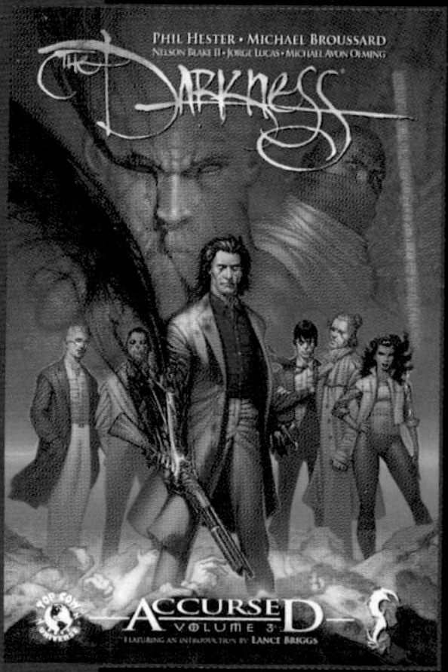
PHIL HESTER • MICHAEL BROUSSARD
NELSON BLAKE II • JORGE LUCAS • MICHAEL AVON OEMING
THE DARKNESS
ACCURSED VOLUME 3
FEATURING AN INTRODUCTION BY LANCE BRIGGS

The Darkness

Accursed vol.3

written by: Phil Hester

pencils by: Michael Broussard, Jorge Lucas,
Nelson Blake II and Michael Avon Oeming.

Collects issues #76-79 plus the stand alone Tales of The Darknes story entitled "Lodbrok's Hand." Features art by regular series artis Michael Broussard (*Unholy Union, Artifacts*), Nelson Blake II (*Magdalena Broken Trinity: Witchblade*), Jorge Lucas (*Broken Trinity: Aftermat Wolverine*), and Michael Avon Oeming (*Mice Templar, Powers*).

(ISBN 13: 978-1-58240-100-7) $12.99

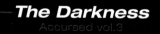